MODERN

KOREAN

LITERATURE

MODERN KOREAN LITERATURE

An Anthology

COMPILED AND EDITED

BY PETER H. LEE

UNIVERSITY OF HAWAII PRESS

HONOLULU

© 1990 University of Hawaii Press
English translation of "The Bronze Mirror" by O Chŏnghŭi
© 1986 Bruce and Ju-chan Fulton
All Rights Reserved
Printed in the United States of America
90 92 93 94 95 96   5 4 3 2 1

Library of Congress Cataloging-in-Publication Data
Modern Korean literature : an anthology / compiled
and edited by Peter H. Lee
p.   cm.
Includes bibliographical references and index.
ISBN 0-8248-1255-7. — ISBN 0-8248-1321-9 (pbk.)
1. Korean literature—20th century—Translations into English.
2. English literature—Translations from Korean. I. Lee, Peter H.,
1929–
PL984.E1M64   1990
895.7'090044—dc20   90–41824
                                                          CIP

University of Hawaii Press books are printed
on acid-free paper and meet the guidelines
for permanence and durability of the Council
on Library Resources

for Caroline and Joseph

CONTENTS

ACKNOWLEDGMENTS

I wish to express my gratitude to the contributors for permission to include their material, to University of Hawaii Press for material from *Flowers of Fire* and *The Silence of Love,* and to the Cornell University China-Japan Program for material from *Black Crane* 2 (1980). I also wish to thank Robert Huey, Stuart Kiang, and Don Yoder for offering valuable suggestions.

Thanks are also due the Korean National Commission for UNESCO, especially Cho Sǒngok, Hǒ Kwǒn, and Paek Sǔnggil, for support given the preparation of this book.

Headnotes, unless signed by a contributor, have been written by the editor.

INTRODUCTION

At the beginning of this century, a revolution in literature began in Korea as advocates of the so-called new literature attempted to break with the inherited conventions of the past. But liberation from literary tradition, itself a formidable goal, was impeded by the prevailing social and political conditions. For several decades Korea had faced a seemingly endless series of crises in its dealings with other, more powerful nations. Beginning in 1866, foreign warships had appeared in Korean waters demanding an opening of ports for trade as in China and Japan. The government vacillated, unable to choose between closing or opening the country, and improvised a futile, constantly shifting policy of relying on its neighbors China, Japan, and Russia for help and protection. The progressive cabinet of 1894, realizing the necessity of social and institutional change if Korea was to survive the threat of foreign aggression, decreed comprehensive reforms aimed at reorganizing the government and rectifying social ills associated with the traditional class system. It declared an end to slavery and childhood marriage, and it abolished the Confucian civil service examinations that had hitherto been the only path to officialdom, seeking instead to employ people of talent regardless of their social class or origin. But these reforms were insufficient and came too late. After stunning military successes in the Sino-Japanese and Russo-Japanese wars, Japan expanded its influence in the region and its claim to paramount political, military, and economic interests in Korea was sanctioned by England, the United States, and Russia. Without interference from its rivals, Japan set about to strip Korea of its national sovereignty by staffing the internal administration with its own advisers, dissolving the Korean army, and assuming all police powers. Finally, in August 1910, Korea was annexed by Japan.

Within this whirlwind of change, the advent of a literature that can be considered essentially modern was preceded by a transitional period—that of the new poetry and novel in the first decade of the century. Feeling the urgency of Korea's deepening crisis, a group of scholars and writers joined forces to denounce corruption in government and voice the need for national independence, public enlightenment, and patriotic fervor. Scholarly organizations, educational magazines, and songwriters using both traditional and improvised forms all strove to introduce the values of Western civilization, to enlighten the people, and to arouse a new national consciousness. In the belief that concrete examples work better than abstract precepts, some writers turned to the genre of exemplary lives in order to inspire future heroes who would steer the Korean state to the right course. In these works, historical figures such as Ŭlchi Mundŏk, Kang Kamch'an, Ch'oe Yŏng, and Yi Sunsin represented Korea, while Joan of Arc, Napoleon, Nelson, Peter the Great, Washington, and Bismarck represented the nations of the West.

In addition to the "song," or *ch'angga*, a new literary form appeared after the 1894 reforms. This was the "new novel," or *sinsosŏl*. Although burdened with a traditional moral stance and an overreliance on coincidence, the new novel was written in a prose that attempted to unify the spoken and written languages. Thematically, the writers of the new novel advocated modernization through contact with advanced countries, study abroad, diffusion of science and technology, and the abolition of superstition and outworn social conventions. The most significant of these writers, Yi Kwangsu (b. 1892), adopted a prose style that approximated the everyday speech of the common people and used it to fashion stories dealing with the enlightened pioneers who championed Western science and civilization. He made his reputation with The Heartless (*Mujŏng*, 1917), the first modern Korean novel, which advocated the values of free love and Western learning.

The "new poetry" movement began with the publication of "From the Sea to Children" (1908), by Ch'oe Namsŏn, in Children (*Sonyŏn*), the first literary journal devoted to producing cultural reform. Inspired by Byron's "Childe Harold's Pilgrimage," Ch'oe's poem celebrates the gathering strength of the young who will carry out the social and literary revolution. The poem's inventions include the copious use of punctuation marks (a convention borrowed from the West), stanzas of unequal length, a string of onomatopoeia in the first and seventh lines of each stanza, and the dominant images of the sea and children, which had been little mentioned in classical Korean poetry. Neither Ch'oe nor his contemporaries, however, could escape the bonds of traditional prosody or succeed in modernizing traditional forms of speech and allusion.

In 1919, shortly before the unsuccessful movement for independence from Japan, translations of Western poets such as Verlaine, Gourmont, and Fyodor Sologub began to appear, exerting a powerful influence on Korean poetry. The indirection and suggestiveness of French symbolism were introduced by Kim Ŏk (b. 1895), the principal translator, who opposed Mallarmé to the prevailing didacticism of the age and Verlaine to its hollow rhetoric and sentimentality. These translations also introduced to Korea the free-verse style which Kim regarded as the supreme creation of the symbolists. Kim's fascination with the symbolism culminated in the publication of *Dance of Anguish* (*Onoe ŭi mudo*) in March 1921, the first collection of translations from Western poetry in Korea. Kim's translations were done in a mellifluous, dreamy style, and their exotic and melancholy beauty coupled with expressions of ennui and spiritual anguish appealed to poets seeking models for their own sense of frustration and despair at the collapse of the independence movement of 1919.

Two years later, in June 1923, Kim published *Songs of a Jellyfish* (*Haep'ari ŭi norae*), the first volume of new verse by a single poet. As in *Dance of Anguish*, a mood of autumnal sorrow permeates its eighty-three poems. The volume depicts a homesick wanderer setting out on an endless journey in quest of a departed spring, a vanished home, a lost country. The image of a wandering youth blowing a sad old tune on his pipes was an apt metaphor for the state of mind of Korean poets during the 1920s, and Kim's strong sense of form, his frequent use of metaphor and personification, and his emphasis on musicality were all features of the symbolist heritage that stimulated the development of modern Korean poetry.

In the 1920s, a movement toward literary naturalism was launched by a group of young writers who rallied around a new definition of reality in the hope of rectifying defects of form and content in Korean fiction. Yŏm Sangsŏp (1897–1963), the first to introduce psychological analysis and scientific documentation into his stories, defined naturalism as an expression of awakened individuality. The purpose of naturalism, Yŏm argued, was to expose the barrenness of reality, especially the disillusionment and sorrow that follow when authority figures are debased and idols are shattered. Thus, many works of naturalist fiction were first-person narratives cast as case studies of the protagonist's attempts to cope with the pressures of reality. The dissonance between the individual and society induced some writers to turn to nature—the raw strength of the land and the virtues of simple folk were common themes of some of the better stories in the Zolaesque tradition. Other writers, such as Yi Sang (1910–1937), experimented with a stream-of-consciousness technique, while still others took to writing panoramic novels, lives of emancipated women, or historical novels.

The 1920s also produced the first two major poets of modern Korea: Han Yongun (1879–1944), the first authentic interpreter of the plight of his colonized people, and Kim Sowŏl (1902–1934), a folk and nature poet. Han used commonplace colloquial language and free verse to reveal how the individual can transcend such obstacles as enslavement, tyranny, and censorship. A poet of his time, Han reflected the crisis faced by his culture but also probed deeply into his own sense of self to find an awareness, beyond suffering, that was both ancient and timeless.

In *The Silence of Love* (*Nim ŭi ch'immuk*, 1926), Han draws on the epistemology of Buddhism, the religion most firmly rooted in the people, to conduct a spiritual exploration of the relationship between self and other, the one and the many. Like seventeenth-century English devotional poetry, Han's poems constitute a meditation on the origin and end of his *nim*—at once the beloved, the Buddha, and the nation. Creating a poetics of absence, Han addresses the departed lover as if he were present. Emptiness, he discovers, is not nothingness: it is in fact no different from the material that constitutes the world. The *nim* is boundless, and it is with him—the one who is truly nonexistent while at the same time mysteriously existent and permanent—that the poet seeks reunion.

Under the tutelage of Kim Ŏk, Kim Sowŏl used simplicity, directness, and terse phrasing to good effect. Many of his poems in *Azaleas* (1925) were originally set to music. But whether he assumed the anonymity of a folk-song writer or the individuality of a lyric persona in more personal pieces, Kim Sowŏl never forgot that the function of the poet in an enslaved society is to preserve his native language and expand its potential for expression.

The Manchurian incident of 1931 and the Japanese invasion of China in 1937 induced the military authorities in Korea to impose wartime restrictions on the people. The grinding poverty of the lower classes at home and abroad, especially in the Korean settlements in southern Manchuria, was the chief concern of the writers of the "new tendency" movement, which opposed the romantic and decadent writers of the day and later became openly proletarian in spirit. Writers of the class-conscious Korean Artist Proletariat Federation, first organized in 1925, insisted on the propagandistic function of literature, which was regarded solely as a means of achieving socialism in Korea.

Modern Korean literature attained its maturity in the 1930s through the efforts of a group of writers who drew freely upon European examples to enrich their art. Translation of Western literature continued, and works by I. A. Richards, T. S. Eliot, and T. E. Hulme were introduced. This artistic and critical activity was a broad-based protest against the reduction of literature to journalism and its use as propaganda by leftist writers.

The first truly successful poet of modern Korea was Chŏng Chiyong (b. 1903). Beginning as a student of Blake and Whitman, Chŏng went on to render details with imagistic precision. Chŏng's one hundred and twenty-three poems, written from 1925 to 1941, frequently employ imagery of the sea, the mountains, and the city in order to deal with national and religious themes. To invest his poetry with a classic strength and purity, Chŏng rendered detail exactly while also exploring the unlimited implication of words. Scorning belated romanticisms, Chŏng produced a body of work that is graceful, intensely phrased, and unrivaled in its technical elegance and controlled sense of form. *White Deer Lake* (1941), his second book of poetry, represents the progress of the spirit to a condition of lucidity, seen as a fusion of man and nature.

A defiant poetry of resistance, born out of sorrow for their ruined nation, is the legacy of Yi Yuksa (1904–1944) and Yun Tongju (1917–1945). In Yi's poem "The Summit," the self stands alone at a precipitous boundary but does not shrink from the terror and absurdity of the human condition. Yi posits a frightening discontinuity—the "I" of modern consciousness at the summit where "numb sky and plateau merge." Here there are no certainties, only the need for an authentic response. By recreating the sense of an existence in extremity, Yi forces us to contemplate our ultimate destiny. The poetry of Yun Tongju bears witness to Korea's national humiliation with unremitting sorrow for the victims of tyranny. For Yun, being a poet was "a sad mandate," but in accepting his fate he found new ways of identifying his spiritual anguish with that of his nation and culture. Arrested by the Japanese police in 1943 on suspicion of carrying out subversive activities for Korean independence while studying in Japan, he died two years later, at the age of twenty-seven, in Fukuoka prison.

Korean fiction of the 1930s took shape in the void created by the compulsory dissolution of the Korean Artist Proletariat Federation in 1935. Barred from involvement with social or political issues, prose writers became preoccupied with the search for technical perfection and the pleasures of pure art. Some returned to nature, exploring the mysteries of sexual energy; others retreated to the labyrinth of primitive religion and shamanism; still others sympathetically portrayed characters born out of their time, defeated and lonely figures bereft of true identity.

The early 1940s brought disaster to every branch of Korean literature as the Japanese colonial government moved to suppress all writings in Korean. In February 1940 Koreans were ordered to adopt Japanese names, and those who spoke the Korean language in public were seized and imprisoned. In 1941, when Japan's war with China widened into the Pacific War, a massive mobilization resulted in the conscription of more than three million Korean workers, who were sent as far as Sakhalin and Southeast Asia. While some Korean writers remained loyal to the spirit of the independence movement, others collaborated with the Japanese. Some joined the Korean Writers Patriotic Association or the Korean Press Patriotic Association and participated in meetings of the Greater East Asia Writers Congress. Some assisted in efforts to improve the morale of soldiers in northern China, and a few Korean writers even poured out unctuous rhetoric in Japanese extolling the military cause.

Korea was liberated on 14 August 1945, and the Republic of Korea (South Korea) was established on 15 August 1948. On the literary front, the controversy between left and right that had raged in the late 1920s and early 1930s revived in full force, and there were frantic groupings and regroupings. By 1948 most of the hardcore leftist writers, such as Yi Kiyŏng (b. 1896) and Han Sŏrya (b. 1900), had gone over to North Korea.

The liberation of 1945 produced a flowering of poetry of all kinds. Some poets were determined to record the terrible events of their time. Others sought to deepen their identification with traditional Korean values, while those of still another group drew variously on

Western traditions in the hope of elevating their art beyond local concerns and restrictions. What united Korean poets of all schools, however, was the desire to voice their own authentic testimony regarding the moments of crisis their culture had known.

In this connection, Sŏ Chŏngju (b. 1915) and Pak Tujin (b. 1916) deserve special mention for their lifelong dedication to modern Korean poetry. Often considered the most "Korean" of contemporary poets, Sŏ is credited with exploring the hidden resources of the language to express emotional states ranging from sensual ecstasy to spiritual quest, from haunting lyricism to colloquial earthiness. Pak Tujin is capable of a wide range of moods, and his language and style impart a distinctive tone to his Christian and nationalistic sentiments. Marked by sonorous lines and incantatory rhythms, Pak's poems are imbued with the strong historical and cultural awareness of one who has honestly confronted the contradictions of his time.

Throughout this century, the modern Korean poet has had the dual task of maintaining an awareness of national identity while at the same time forging a new poetry. The sense of selfhood evinced by the modern poet in East Asia varies from country to country, but it seems that the more unstable or oppressive the political setting, the stronger the sense of the poet's identity and function. Threatened with the extinction of their culture, modern Korean poets have devoted their energies to preserving their language and creating a poetry consonant with the appalling reality of modern Korean history. Despite the influx of Western literary influences, Korea's best poets have not succumbed to the temptation of colonialist or internationalist doctrine. Clinging tenaciously to the center of consciousness and history, they have shouldered the burden of the poet in his time.

As for Korean fiction, the single overwhelming reality since the Korean War has been the division of the country. As a symbol not only of Korea's trials but of the divided self, the Thirty-eighth Parallel torments the conscience of every protagonist seeking his destiny in modern Korean fiction. Some writers have attempted to record idealized images of the people in lyrical prose; others have resolutely explored the consciousness of the lost generation of the Korean War or exposed the self-deception and lassitude of the alienated generation of the 1960s. Other writers have profiled the defeat and disintegration of good, ordinary people, while still others have focused on the ways in which the individual's freedom and identity, let alone his need for transcendence and justice, are negated by modern society.

Whatever their concerns and techniques, postwar Korean novelists have refused to ignore the disagreeable facts of life or to simplify life's complexity. Literature cannot be divorced from history. Modern Korean writers cannot escape their fate, and so they must pay for the place they occupy in their society and culture. By affirming the connection between the texts they create and the world they inhabit, modern Korean writers have endeavored to conceive an identity that can encompass not only the terrible cost but also the genuine possibility of human freedom.

Today a host of talented writers in Korea are perfecting the art of being themselves. The poet Hwang Tonggyu (b. 1938), for example, draws his material not only from his own life but from the common predicament of his people. His is a voice that expresses what his fellow Koreans know but do not think of saying, or cannot say. Like every major poet, Hwang takes his place in society and assumes his responsibility to be heard. As Korea approaches the end of the century, the continued production of a literature of engagement and relevance attests to the resilience, strength, and tenacity of modern Korean writers.

MODERN FICTION

I

Yi Kwangsu

Originally serialized in the *Daily News (Maeil sinbo)* in 1917, Yi Kwangsu's first novel, *Mujŏng (The Heartless)*, depicts a young man and woman betrothed to each other in childhood but separated by a series of tragedies and reunited years later after the young woman, Yŏngch'ae, has become a professional entertainer *(kisaeng)*. The male protagonist, Hyŏngsik, abandons her to marry a woman named Sŏnhyŏng, the daughter of a wealthy former diplomat. Though the plot formally resembles a love triangle, all the relationships are devoid of love and thus manifest the "heartlessness" which forms the central theme of the novel. The characters denounce traditional values and beliefs, only to find themselves "lost children . . . cast out on their own without anyone to guide them, in a world in which no standards for life had been set, and in which there were no ideals for the Korean people to follow" (Chapter 115). In the didactic conclusion to the novel, the characters turn to nationalism in an attempt to escape what is perceived as the egoism of modern individualism.

The criticism of traditional marriage customs and norms of chastity in *The Heartless*, as well as the exaltation of emotion, reflect the influence of Japanese naturalist and romantic literature. Indeed, Yi had received his literary tutelage in early twentieth-century Meiji Japan, having attended Meiji Gakuin and Waseda University by the time he began writing *The Heartless*. While the political optimism of Yi's early period would eventually give way to a quietistic cynicism in later works such as *The Unenlightened (Mumyŏng*, 1939) and *Great Master Wŏnhyo (Wŏnhyo taesa*, 1942), the Japanese influence and moral

1

uncertainty evident in such works as *The Heartless* constituted conti-
nuities with his later works and were elements in his collaboration
with the Japanese colonial government toward the middle of his
career.

The five main characters in order of their importance in the novel
are as follows:

HYŎNGSIK: The central male character, a young middle-school English teacher in Seoul who is imbued with modern ideas and aspires to
become an enlightened educator.

PYŎNGUK: A strong young woman who embodies all the qualities of
an enlightened, modern woman. She boldly rejects the subservient
role traditionally assigned to Korean women.

YŎNGCH'AE: The daughter of Hyŏngsik's former patron as well as his
childhood love. In the wake of her family's misfortunes she becomes a
kisaeng. She is saved from her attempted suicide by Pyŏnguk and
transformed into a modern woman.

SŎNHYŎNG: The only daughter of Church Elder Kim of Seoul who,
recognizing in Hyŏngsik a young man of great promise, arranges an
engagement between Sŏnhyŏng and Hyŏngsik.

USŎN: Hyŏngsik's young journalist friend who envies Hyŏngsik's
good fortune and modern ideas because he feels trapped in a loveless
marriage.

KICHUNG KIM AND ANN SUNG-HI LEE

FROM *THE HEARTLESS*

[*Marriage on the basis of mutual affection is a novel idea even for Hyŏngsik
and Sŏnhyŏng, both educated in new-style schools, as it must have been for
most of Mujŏng's readers in 1917. As an enlightened young educator
aspiring to contribute to the modernization of Korea, Hyŏngsik believes that
his own marriage has to be based on mutual love. For this reason,
Hyŏngsik's joy in his forthcoming marriage to Sŏnhyŏng is seriously marred
by one unresolved question in his mind: whether Sŏnhyŏng really loves him*

or is merely complying with her father's wish as a dutiful Korean daughter.
While Hyŏngsik is reasonably certain that he loves Sŏnhyŏng, she has made
no clear declaration of love for him, either because of her modesty or lack of
love. Thus he is deeply troubled, even though their engagement has been
solemnized for some time. As difficult as it is for him to broach the subject,
Hyŏngsik resolves to put the question directly to Sŏnhyŏng.]

But Hyŏngsik went back to thinking about his own situation. Does
Sŏnhyŏng really love him, not only a small part but all of him? No
matter how hard he tried, he could not rid himself of the feeling that
Sŏnhyŏng's attitude toward him seemed rather cool. Was their
engagement really built on love?

It's true that Sŏnhyŏng did answer yes on the evening he proposed.
But what did her yes actually mean? Did it mean that she loved him,
or did it mean that she was prepared to submit to the will of her parents? Wasn't Sŏnhyŏng's attitude toward him similar to that of his
friend Pyŏnguk toward his wife?[1]

Such thoughts made Hyŏngsik unhappy. If Sŏnhyŏng felt no love
for him, and had said yes only because she could not go against her
parents' wishes, the engagement would be nothing more than a sacrifice of poor Sŏnhyŏng. In that case, Sŏnhyŏng would be wasting her
life with a husband she did not love, and for Hyŏngsik, too, it
couldn't possibly mean happiness. Was it not inhumane to knowingly
sacrifice another's life just to satisfy one's own selfish desires?
Hyŏngsik therefore resolved to find out how Sŏnhyŏng really felt.

Luckily, the following day, because Sunae[2] was sick with a headache, Hyŏngsik was able to be alone with Sŏnhyŏng. After complet-
ing the day's lessons, Hyŏngsik summoned up all his strength and
addressed Sŏnhyŏng:

"Miss Kim, I wish to ask you a question," he said, lowering his eyes.

Sŏnhyŏng gazed up into his face, looking intent as if debating a
question within herself.

"What is it, Mr. Yi?" she said, blushing slightly.

"Please answer my question honestly and directly. I'm doing the
right thing, I believe, for nothing should be held back between those
who love," Hyŏngsik said, his heart thumping loudly as if a life-and-
death question were to be decided in the next few seconds.

---

[1]Pyŏnguk felt no love for the wife chosen for him by his parents.
[2]Sunae: Sŏnhyŏng's friend who ordinarily took English lessons with her.

Because she had never had to respond to such a serious-sounding question, Sŏnhyŏng felt afraid at his words. So she merely said, "Yes," not knowing how else to respond.

This "yes" sounded exactly like her "yes" on the day of their engagement.

Hyŏngsik, too, found it difficult to say anything more. Besides, he was afraid of the answer she might give him. But he was even more afraid of going on in doubt without knowing her true feelings toward him.

Summoning up his courage, he looked straight into her eyes and asked in a tremulous voice: "Miss Kim, do you love me?"

Sŏnhyŏng's eyes grew large with surprise, for the question was utterly unexpected. She was afraid. The truth was that she had never asked herself whether or not she loved him. She did not even know she had a right to question such things. She already thought of herself as Hyŏngsik's wife, and to serve him was therefore her duty. She had strived to create as much affection as she could between them, but she had never even dreamt what she might do if there were little affection between them. Hyŏngsik's question came therefore as a complete surprise.

"Why do you ask such a question?" she said, staring at him.

"We must ask it. We ought to have done so before our engagement. This is the wrong way to go about it, but even if it's late, we ought to ask the question."

Sŏnhyŏng sat still without a word.

"Please, tell me clearly whether you do or do not," he asked again.

But to Sŏnhyŏng's thinking, the question seemed unnecessary and did not require a reply. For were they not already wife and husband?[3] Why then ask such a question? So she said, smiling, "Why do you ask?"

"Because it would be better for both of us to be certain before things are made definite."

"Why, what do you mean, made definite?"

"We are still only engaged, not yet married. So we can still right wrongs if there should be any."

Sŏnhyŏng grew still more afraid, shivers running through her. She could not understand the true meaning of Hyŏngsik's words.

---

[3] An engagement was tantamount to marriage at that time.

"Do you mean our engagement can be broken?" she asked, tears filling her eyes.

Seeing her tears, he regretted bringing up the question, but still he said, "Yes, that is what I mean."

"But why?"

"That is, if you do not love me . . ."

"Aren't we already engaged?"

"But it is not the engagement that matters."

"What matters, then?"

"Our love, of course."

"If there is no love?"

"The engagement has no meaning."

After a long pause she asked: "What about you, Mr. Yi?"

"I, of course, love you, Miss Kim. I love you more than my life."

"Well, there's no problem, then."

"But there is. You, too, must love me."

"How can a wife not love her husband?"

Hyŏngsik turned his eyes on Sŏnhyŏng, who dropped her gaze.

"Who spoke those words? Are they yours, Miss Kim?"

"Doesn't the Bible say so?"

"But what do *you* think? What's *your* true feeling?"

"I think as the Bible says."

"But is it because you have become a wife that you love or is it because you loved that you became a wife?"

This, too, was a question she had never heard before.

"Aren't they the same thing, Mr. Yi?" she said, since she didn't understand what the words meant.

Hyŏngsik was astonished by her words. How could they be the same thing? This girl has obviously never given any thought to such matters, he thought to himself.

"Please answer me in one word," he said boldly. "Do you love me, Miss Kim?" It sounded like a plea. If she should answer no, it would be his death, he thought. He realized that her tightly closed lips had the power of life and death over him.

Sŏnhyŏng, for her part, felt so confused that she could no longer think clearly. Looking at Hyŏngsik's ashen face, she became only more afraid. So she merely said, "Yes . . ."

He was about to ask once more, but fearing her yes might change to no, he swallowed hard and grasped her hands firmly. Her soft and warm hands felt as if they would melt away in his. She said nothing.

He gripped her hands once more, this time even more firmly, hoping she would grip his hands in return, but she remained still, with lowered eyes, saying nothing.

Quickly releasing her hands, Hyŏngsik hurried home. He himself didn't understand why he had left so abruptly. Sŏnhyŏng, too, without a word, watched him leave.

Leaning her head on the desk, Sŏnhyŏng closed her eyes, deep in thought. Hyŏngsik's words came back to her very clearly. What did he mean? How could he have uttered the words, "Do you love me?" Wasn't he embarrassed? Didn't the fact that he could say them without embarrassment mean that he might not be chaste? Wasn't it the kind of thing he was used to telling a *kisaeng* at a *kisaeng* house? She felt as though she had been violated. To love God, to love fellow Koreans, to love the person one is married to—all these sounded very fine, even sacred. But for a man and a woman to ask for love from the other or to say "I love you!"—this somehow seemed unclean and improper.

From what she had been taught so far at home and in church, all other loves were clean and sacred, but the love between a young man and woman seemed unclean and sinful. She did not understand that both the idea and the word for love had originated from the love between man and woman. For this reason Hyŏngsik's words concerning love had offended her. Because in her mind she believed her fiancé to be utterly pure and proper, that he could speak unashamedly of love made him seem like a sinner. "He did an unclean thing to me, the sort of thing he's probably used to doing to a *kisaeng*," Sŏnhyŏng thought to herself, frowning.

And now she looked at her hands, which Hyŏngsik had grasped. Remembering how they had been buried in his large hands and how he had gripped them so hard that they hurt, she shook them a few times and wiped them with her skirt as though trying to remove something dirty that had become embedded in them. But as she thought about it still more, she realized that she hadn't really disliked his grasping her hands and his telling her he loved her. In fact she had felt a thrill of delight pulsing throughout her whole body. So she held out her hands again, looked at them, and stealthily brought them to her lips, smiling.

Once again Sŏnhyŏng pondered. Did she indeed love Hyŏngsik? His words came back to her: did she love him because she had become his wife or did she become his wife because she loved him? And further: without love their engagement would be null and void.

If that were so, then what about the will of the parents? Suppose she felt no love for Hyŏngsik. Could she, for that reason, have refused the marriage arranged by her parents? Would it have been the right thing to do? Impossible. Marriage is a holy institution God has provided for us. We cannot simply do with it as we please. Therefore, Hyŏngsik's words are wrong; his words are not pure. But she is now his wife, and no man can undo that.

Sŏnhyŏng rose and walked about the room. Unable to quiet her agitated mind, she prayed, once again leaning her head on the desk: "Our Father in heaven, forgive thy daughter who is full of sin, teach her the right path to take, protect her from temptation. . . ." Then, after a brief pause, she added: "Make me love my husband with all my heart."

[*Once Hyŏngsik and Sŏnhyŏng are engaged, it is decided that they will leave for the United States before the summer is over so they can start their studies at an American university in the fall. In this episode Hyŏngsik explains to Usŏn, a journalist friend of his, why he plans to specialize in education.*]

"At the end of July?" said Usŏn, surprised. "Leaving so soon?"

"Yes. Because we'll lose a whole year unless we enroll in September."

"What will you be studying?"

"I won't know for sure till I get there, but I'll probably study education. My work so far has been in that discipline, and I believe it's what's most important to our country right now. So, as best as I can, I plan to put my energies into studying new educational theories and practices, and spend the rest of my life working in that field."

"Education . . . what do you mean by education?"

"By education I mean, of course, primary and secondary teaching. What our country needs right now is an educator like Johann Pestalozzi.[4] How else except through education can we remake our people? This is so in every age and every country, but it's especially true with us, I believe, for we must quickly slough off the old, worn-out Korea and build a new, enlightened one by every one of us contributing to

---

[4]Johann Heinrich Pestalozzi (1746–1827): a Swiss educator who tried to promote creative and self-motivated methods in child education.

education. You, too, I hope, through your writing, will promote a zeal for education, because our present system doesn't amount to much."

"Then you'll devote all four years to that pursuit?"

"Why, does four years seem too long to you? Even ten years wouldn't be long enough, I think, to make a thorough study of it."

"Yes, I understand that. What I meant was whether you'll be studying only education and nothing else."

"Of course, I'll be studying other subjects, too, other subjects related to education, but I mean to make education the core of my study. With a special emphasis on social systems and ethics," said Hyŏngsik, looking at Usŏn and thinking to himself, you probably don't quite follow my reasoning.

In fact, Usŏn didn't understand it all, though what he didn't quite grasp, he tried to guess.

"Well, what about your wife . . . what shall I call her . . . your sweetheart, I mean?" Usŏn said, smiling.

"I wouldn't know," Hyŏngsik said with a smile, blushing.

"If the husband doesn't, who does?"

"Why, she does . . . in today's world, even a husband cannot deny his wife's freedom to do as she wishes."

"So you mean to say that whatever she decides to study, you won't interfere with it?"

"Of course not. For we must not forget the 'I.' We must respect everyone's right to do as he or she wishes. No one else has any right to interfere with that right. Of course, we may counsel or suggest to another person that this or that might be a better course, but to tell another person to do this or that simply because we think it better is deplorable."

Usŏn was truly amazed. Hyŏngsik's words seemed true. Yet he wondered if that really were the way it was. Still, he did not mean to question Hyŏngsik's words. He only nodded to himself, for he now realized that Hyŏngsik's beliefs and ideas were quite different from his own.

[*On the train to P'yŏngyang, determined to drown herself in the Taedong River, Yŏngch'ae meets Pyŏnguk entirely by chance. Pyŏnguk quickly draws out of Yŏngch'ae the story of her planned suicide and the reasons for it. Pyŏnguk, a young woman studying in Tokyo, now on her way home for the summer, turns out to be a forceful, if somewhat boyish, enlightened "new" woman determined to take life into her own hands.*]

"Do you still love Hyŏngsik?" Pyŏnguk asked after she listened to Yŏngch'ae's account of her misfortunes.

Yŏnch'ae's heart thumped at the question. Had she ever really loved him? She couldn't tell. She had simply been thinking of him as the man she had to find, the man she had to dedicate herself to. During the past seven or eight years she had been looking for him, the question of whether or not she really loved him had never occurred to her. She only knew that she had yearned to find him, quickly, and once she found him all her wishes would come true and she would be happy. That had been all. . . .

"I'd never thought about the question. Because we parted from each other when we were children, we could hardly remember each other's face. . . ."

"Then you spent all this time looking for him just because your father had once said you should become his wife, even though you yourself did not feel much love for him?"

"Yes. And I remember we'd been fond of each other as children. When I think of those days, I still feel an intense yearning for him."

"That's only natural. None of us ever forget the things that happened to us in our childhood. But you also remember other childhood friends, don't you?"

Yŏngch'ae replied after a thoughtful pause: "Yes, I remember many besides him, although he's the one I remember with the greatest affection. But when I actually saw him the other day, he seemed a different person, different from what I'd imagined him to be in my mind. The love I had seemed to break apart. . . . I couldn't understand what happened. That evening when I returned home, I felt very sad, and I cried."

Pyŏnguk, nodding her head as if to say she understood, asked, although she seemed to find it difficult to say the words: "Then, you don't feel much love for him anymore?"

"Well, I don't know," Yŏngch'ae said after some time. She seemed unsure of her own mind. "Although I was happy when I saw him, somehow he didn't seem to be the man I'd pictured in my mind. I wondered what had happened. And he didn't seem particularly happy to see me. . . ."

"I see," Pyŏnguk said, closing her eyes.

Yŏngch'ae, too, closed her eyes, wondering what Pyŏnguk was thinking.

"Why then did you decide to die?"

"What else could I do? I'd been living all this time with only the thought of him, and suddenly I'm dirty." Yŏngch'ae continued with a pained expression on her face. "I could no longer serve him. What did I have to live for?" Yŏnch'ae said, her head cast down in utter despair.

"I do not think it is reason enough for you to die," Pyŏnguk said.

"What should I do, then?"

"Live! Why should you die?"

Yŏngch'ae, dumbfounded, stared at Pyŏnguk.

The latter spoke forcefully: "First of all, you've been living a lie. You've been keeping your chastity for a man named Yi Hyŏngsik without even loving him. Because of your father's single remark, probably in jest, you've wasted the last seven or eight years of your life in devotion to him. Isn't it an utter waste of your life to be devoted to someone you do not love, or with whom there's no mutual understanding? How is it different from devotion to someone dead, to someone who's not in this world? Your thought is beautiful, your unswerving fidelity praiseworthy, but that's all. Don't you think there ought to be another special person who really deserves your beautiful thought and firm, unswerving devotion? So if you really love Yi Hyŏngsik, then give your body and soul to him from now on. But if not, look for love in another man. . . ."

"But how can I change my mind now after thinking only of him all this time? And what about the teachings of the ancient sages?" Yŏngch'ae asked.

"No, you've only been living in a dream till today. How can you give yourself to someone when you hardly know his face or mind? This has been part of our bondage to the mistaken ideas of the past. One lives for one's own sake. A husband one doesn't love is unthinkable. Therefore, think of your past as only a dream. A new and truer life will open up for you from this moment."

Yŏngch'ae was astounded by these words. They didn't sound like the words of a virtuous woman. Yet they somehow sounded true, for in fact Yŏngch'ae had never loved Hyŏngsik. She had merely set up a pleasing phantom in her mind which she called Hyŏngsik, and because she had imagined this phantom to be Hyŏngsik she had sought him. But when she actually found him, she realized he was not the person she had been seeking, and she fell into despair because she now believed she could never find the Hyŏngsik of her dreams.

Looking at it this way, Yŏngch'ae thought she now saw not only her mistake but also a glimmer of light in the depth of her despair.

"Is a new and truer life really possible for me? Can I really start my life over again?" Yŏngch'ae said, looking at her companion.

"Yes. You've been deceiving yourself so far, but now a truer life can open up. Happiness awaits you. Why should you turn away from it by trying to cut short your precious life?" Pyŏnguk said, now confident that she had dissuaded Yŏngch'ae from suicide. "So stop your crying and smile! Yes, let's laugh!" she said, smiling.

Yŏngch'ae smiled, too, but still feeling uneasy, she asked: "Will there really be happiness for me? What about our moral duty? Can we seek happiness while disobeying our moral duty? Would that be right?"

"Moral duty? Do you believe it's your moral duty to die?"

"Yes, I think so."

"Why? Why is it your moral duty to die?" Pyŏnguk asked.

"I gave my heart to someone, yet soiled my body before I could give that to him too. How else but through death could I redeem myself?"

"Let me ask you a few questions," Pyŏnguk said confidently. "First, was it you who gave your heart to Mr. Yi? In other words, did you do it yourself because you wanted to? Or was it your father who decided it?"

"Of course it was my father who decided it."

"If so, it was your father who decided your whole life, wasn't it?"

"Yes, that's right. Isn't that the Way of Three Submissions?"

"Oh, yes. The so-called Way of Three Submissions. It has killed off many thousands of women throughout our history and it has also made as many men miserable. Yes, those fatal few words!"

"Are you saying The Way . . . is not right?" Yŏngch'ae said, shocked.

"To submit to the will of one's parents is, I suppose, as it should be for a child," Pyŏnguk said. "Similarly, to submit to the will of one's husband is as it should be for a wife. But doesn't the child's whole life matter more than the will of the parents and the wife's whole life more than the will of the husband? To allow your own life to be decided by another person is to kill yourself. It is surely a crime against your own humanity. In particular, the creed that if the husband dies, his wife must submit to her own son is nothing more than an example of the tyranny of men, for it utterly disregards the woman's worth. Isn't it more proper that the mother should not only teach her son but also rule him? What is more unnatural than for the parent to submit to the child?" Pyŏnguk's face became flushed as she spoke vigorously against the old morality. "Miss Pak, you have suffered all these years for nothing because you were enslaved to such obsolete beliefs. You must free yourself from their bondage. You must awaken from this false dream. You must become a woman who lives for herself. You must seize your own freedom," Pyŏnguk said. Her face appeared grave as she spoke these words.

"What shall I do then?" Yŏngch'ae asked, for she felt extremely confused. To her it now seemed entirely natural that she had come to rely on Pyŏnguk to tell her what to do with her own life. It was as if her fate hung on Pyŏnguk's words. So Yŏngch'ae fixed her gaze on Pyŏnguk's eyes and mouth.

"A woman, too, is a human being," Pyŏnguk said, "and she should therefore take on all the roles of a human being. She may become a daughter, a wife, a mother . . . these are her roles in life. She may also find her place in religion, science, or the arts, or work for the nation or our society. But traditionally in our country the woman's role has been limited to that of somebody's wife, and even that choice was made by someone else. Up until now a woman has been nothing more than a man's accessory, one of his possessions. You, Miss Pak, were your father's property, and you were about to become Mr. Yi's, as if you were a thing transferable from one hand to another. But we, too, must become human beings. Of course we are women, but before that we must become human. There's much you must do, Miss Pak, for you were not born solely for the sake of your father or Mr. Yi. You were born not only for the millions upon millions of Koreans who lived before us but also for the millions upon millions of our people who are now living as well as for all those who will come after us. You have, Miss Pak, obligations not only to your father and Mr. Yi but also to your ancestors, fellow Koreans, and descendants. To die before you have fulfilled all these obligations is a sin."

"What must I do then?"

"Begin a new life today," Pyŏnguk said, smiling.

"How do I begin it?"

"Begin everything anew. Forget everything that's past, and start all over. In the past you lived your life bound to the will of other people. From now on . . .," Pyŏnguk said, and she paused for a moment looking at Yŏngch'ae.

"From now on . . . how shall I . . .," Yŏngch'ae said, hanging on Pyŏnguk's every word. Her face had become flushed and she was nearly breathless.

"From now on . . . we live for ourselves, according to our own will."

The train had come out of the mountains and was now racing through a broad plain. A clear limpid stream ran alongside the train, sometimes on the left, sometimes on the right.

The two women gazed out of the window wordlessly.

[*The novel concludes with all the main characters assembled at a flooded railroad river crossing. Having just given an improvised benefit concert for the local flood victims, Hyŏngsik, Pyŏnguk, Yŏngch'ae, and Sŏnhyŏng pledge themselves to work for the well-being of the Korean people.*]

Meanwhile all those who had lost their homes to the floodwater sat in a daze as before on the bare ground. Even though they were racked by hunger, they had no way to help themselves. They could only wait for nature to play out its destined course. For who could defy the violent outbursts of nature? Yet these people were pathetic, indeed, for hadn't they lost the very foundation of their livelihood, the accumulations of a lifetime, to the rains of a single night? It was as if their lives had been built on sand.

Now, as the rains cease and the floodwaters recede, they can rebuild their lives, gathering up the few handfuls of scattered sand like the ants that build their colony in the ground by digging up the earth with their thin, frail legs.

Having lost everything to the rains of a single night, they were now shivering from hunger and cold. . . . In a way they were to be pitied, but, in another way, they seemed feeble and foolish. Their faces showed no glimmer of wisdom. Rather, they looked stupid and dull. All they knew was how to work the land with a little knowledge of farming. And, if lucky, in four or five years they'd save up a few bushels of unhulled rice, only to lose them to a flood. They would never become rich; they would only get gradually poorer, growing ever feebler in body and mind. Left to themselves they would eventually end up the remnants of a race like those aborigines of North Japan. Therefore, they must be given power, they must be given knowledge, so that they could strengthen the foundation of their lives.

"Science! Science!" Hyŏngsik cried out to himself when they returned to their room in the inn and sat down.

The three women stared at him.

"We must give science to our people before anything else. We must give them knowledge," he said, jumping up with clenched fists and pacing the room.

"What did you think about what we saw today?" he asked.

The three women did not have a ready answer to the question.

"I pitied the people," Pyŏnguk said after a long pause. "Didn't you?" she added, smiling.

Working together, they had come to feel much closer.

"Yes, they're pitiful. What do you think is the cause?"

"It's the backwardness, of course. They have no power to improve their lives."

"Then how could they . . . no, not they but we, I mean . . . how could they be saved?" said Hyŏngsik, looking at Pyŏnguk.

Yŏngch'ae and Sŏnhyŏng looked at Hyŏngsik and Pyŏnguk in turn.

"We must strengthen them! We must enlighten them!" Pyŏnguk cried out confidently.

"How do we do that?"

"We must teach them! We must lead them!"

"How?"

"Through education and through our own examples!"

Yŏngch'ae and Sŏnhyŏng did not understand all that was said by Hyŏngsik and Pyŏnguk. But what was taking place before their own eyes was giving them a living education, an education neither school nor great oratory could have bestowed.

"Yes, you're right. They must be taught, must be led by education and example," Hyŏngsik said. "But who will lead them and teach them?" he asked, and then he shut his mouth tightly.

The three women felt shivers run through them.

"Who will do it?" he asked once again, looking at them one by one.

For the three women it was as if they were undergoing an inexpressible spiritual awakening they had never before experienced. They trembled simultaneously.

"We will!" came a spontaneous chorus of answers from the three women.

Now all four of them felt as if a flame had blazed up before their eyes; as if the ground beneath them shook from a violent earthquake. His head lowered, Hyŏngsik sat for a long time.

"Yes, you're right," he said after a long silence. "We will have to do it. And it is for this we are going abroad. For who is giving us the money so that we can ride on this train and go abroad to study? It is our country, of course. Why? So that we may bring back power, knowledge, enlightenment . . . so that we may help our people build a firmer and stronger foundation for their lives in a more enlightened society. Isn't this our goal?"

And then he took out his wallet from his vest pocket. Holding up the blue train ticket, he said: "This ticket is soaked in the sweat of those people over there trembling from hunger and cold . . . the sweat of that young peasant[5] also . . . their hope that they may never suffer such a calamity again." And he shook himself as if trying once again to confirm what he had resolved to do.

The three women, too, shuddered as Hyŏngsik did.

In that instant, lightning-like, the same thought flashed through the mind of each: "That's what I must do!" and they felt united in body and mind, all differences among them vanishing entirely.

TRANSLATED BY KICHUNG KIM

---

[5] A young farmer and his pregnant, fever-racked wife they helped earlier in the day.

Kim Tongin

Kim Tongin's stories censure a society that does not permit the pursuit of pleasure. His characters disregard morals and customs while trying to create a utopia of luxury and dissipation. As the quintessential character Pŏngnyŏ in Kim's most realistic story, "Potato," illustrates, this hedonistic outlook originates from contradictions in Kim's view of life. His characters' hedonism comes not from their vibrant life but from their separation of life and man—hence Kim's decadent idealism, which fails to illuminate the real world. Kim's chief contribution to the form is his skillful use of dialect, but exaggerated details and sensational grotesquerie must be regarded as defects.

POTATO

Strife, adultery, murder, theft, begging, imprisonment—the slums outside P'yŏngyang's Ch'ilsŏng Gate were a breeding ground for all the tragedy and violence of this world. Until Pongnyŏ and her husband moved there they had been farmers, the second of the four classes (scholars, farmers, artisans, and merchants) of society.

As a young girl, Pongnyŏ had been strictly reared in a poor but moral farm family. Although the strict code of conduct of the scholar class was said to have disappeared from Pongnyŏ's family when it fell to farmer status, the family's sensibilities were still slightly higher than those of the older families, and the household canons remained in force as of old. Of course Pongnyŏ, though reared in this manner, did regard it as customary to strip down in summer and go swimming in the creek like the other girls, or to go around the village half-dressed. Still, in her mind she felt a certain concern with morality, however vaguely.

At the age of fifteen she was sold to a village widower for eighty *wŏn* and thus married off. Her bridegroom was twenty years her senior. Originally, in his father's time, his people had been farmers of considerable means, owning several plots of land. But by the time he married Pongnyŏ, his family was sinking and losing its possessions one by one; the eighty *wŏn* he paid for Pongnyŏ was the last of his estate. He was an extremely lazy fellow. The village elders had used their good offices to obtain a sharecropper's plot for him, but he merely threw the seeds about and let his plot fall into neglect, neither tending nor weeding it. When autumn came, he would harvest lackadaisically, giving nothing to the landlord and consuming the whole crop himself. "The harvest was bad this year," he would say. Because he acted like this, he never lasted two years in succession on the same field. He persisted in his ways, and within a few years he had so totally undermined his own reputation that he could obtain no more field space in the village.

Pongnyǒ and her husband managed to survive three or four years after they were married, thanks only to the help from Pongnyǒ's father. But even he, the last of the old-time scholars, began bit by bit to feel hatred toward his son-in-law. Thus the couple came to lose credit even with Pongnyǒ's family.

The couple discussed the situation this way and that. Having nothing better to do, they went to P'yǒngyang to become day laborers. Because of his laziness, however, her husband could not even succeed as a laborer. With his A-frame[1] on his back he would go to Yǒngwang Pavilion and moon at the Taedong River all day long—who could be a day laborer that way? The couple worked as day laborers for three or four months. Then, through sheer luck, they made their way into a household as live-in servants.

However, they were expelled from the household before long. Pongnyǒ looked after the house diligently, but she could do nothing about her husband's laziness. She looked daggers at him and pestered him, but she could not cure him of his slovenly habits.

"Why don't you put away the rice sack?"

"I'm getting sleepy. You do it."

"You expect me to?"

"You've only been living your useless life for twenty years or so. Can't you do it?"

"Ah, drop dead!"

"What did you say, bitch?"

This kind of bickering went on incessantly, and in the end they were dismissed.

Where could they go now? So it was that for want of anywhere else, they were forced into the slums outside Ch'ilsǒng Gate. The main occupation of the slum's inhabitants was begging, and their second-

---

[1] A-frame: a backpack in the shape of the letter A with which Korean workers carry heavy loads.

ary pursuits were thieving and whoring among themselves. All manner of other terrible and sordid vices were practiced as well. Pongnyŏ began begging with the rest.

But who would give money to a young girl in the prime of her life? "What's a healthy young person like you doing begging?"

Whenever she heard this kind of response she made various excuses, saying that her husband was dying of a disease or some such, but she failed to elicit the sympathy of the people of P'yŏngyang, hardened as they were to such tales. And so it came to pass that even in the slums, they were among the poorest. In their circles, a man with a good income was one who could start his day with a mere half chŏn² in coins and return home with one wŏn and seventy or eighty chŏn in cash. In one exceptional case, there was a man who went out one evening to earn some money and returned that very night with more than four hundred wŏn. He soon began selling cigarettes in the neighborhood.

Pongnyŏ was now nineteen years old, and good-looking as well. If she were to follow the usual example of the other girls in the district and visit prosperous houses, she could make fifty or sixty chŏn a day. With her upbringing, though, she could not bear to do such a thing.

The couple remained impoverished; it became common for them to go hungry.

At that time the groves of pines surrounding Kija's tomb³ were alive with pine-eating caterpillars. The city government of P'yŏngyang decided to have the caterpillars caught by hand. As if bestowing a benefice, the government allowed the slum girls to apply to work as laborers.

All the girls applied for the jobs. However, only fifty were accepted. Pongnyŏ was among them.

She caught caterpillars diligently. She placed her ladder against the trees, climbed up, seized the caterpillars with tweezers, and dropped them into a bucket of insecticide. She kept working steadily, and soon her bucket was full. For one day she received a wage of thirty-two chŏn.

---

²chŏn: the Korean cent. In most cases, the cent is used. 100 chŏn make one wŏn.
³Kija (Chi Tzu in Chinese): uncle of the last monarch of the Shang dynasty who is said to have fled to Korea in 1122 b.c. and built a capital at P'yŏngyang.

However, after working like this for five or six days, she noticed a strange phenomenon: a certain group of girls never caught any caterpillars, but were always chattering and laughing below her ladder, just playing around. Not only that; when the pay was distributed, the girls who had been idling received eight *chŏn* or so more than those who really had been working.

There was only one supervisor. He not only tolerated the girls' loafing, but he also occasionally joined in their frolic.

When lunchtime came one day, Pongnyŏ climbed down from her tree and ate. As she was about to climb up again, the supervisor called to her.

"Pongnyŏ! Hey, Pongnyŏ!"

"What is it?"

She put down her bucket and tweezers and turned around.

"Come here a minute."

She went silently to the supervisor.

"Listen, Pongnyŏ, uh . . . Let's go back over there."

"What for?"

"Oh, you'll see . . ."

"Okay. Hey, Sis!"

Turning around, she shouted toward the spot where the other girls were gathered.

"Hey, Sis, let's go."

"Nah, I don't wanna. You two are going for kicks—why should I go too?"

Pongnyŏ's face reddened, and she turned to the supervisor.

"Let's go." The supervisor started off. Pongnyŏ lowered her head and followed.

"Atta girl, Pongnyŏ! Lucky you!"

Pongnyŏ heard these jibes coming from behind her. Her downcast face grew redder still.

From that day on, Pongnyŏ, too, became one of those who did no work and yet were paid good wages.

Pongnyŏ's sense of morality and her view of life were never the same after that day. Until then, she had never even considered having sexual relations with a man other than her husband. She had considered such acts not as human behavior, but as that of beasts. She was certain that if she did such a thing, she would be struck dead.

But how could one account for what had come to pass? Since

Pongnyŏ herself, who was certainly human, had had this experience, it was by no means out of the range of human possibilities. Besides, though she did no work, she received more money. There was a guilty thrill in this, and it was much more dignified than begging for a living. To describe it in other terms, it was a waltz through life. Nothing could match this enjoyable experience. Was this not, then, the secret to human existence? Moreover, from the time this happened, Pongnyŏ acquired, for the first time in her life, the self-confidence of a real individual human being. From that time on, she began to powder her face.

A year passed. Pongnyŏ's savoir-faire enabled her to steer a smooth course through life. And as for her marriage, now the couple was not quite so destitute. Her husband was usually at home lounging on the warmest spot on the floor and chuckling as if it were a fine thing after all.

Pongnyŏ was more beautiful than ever.

"Hey, man, how much did you make today?"

When Pongnyŏ saw a beggar who looked as if he had made a lot of money, she would solicit him this way.

"I had a bad day."

"Just how bad?"

"Only thirteen or fourteen yang."[4]

"You did pretty well. Why don't you lend me five yang?"

"Well, today I . . ."

When she carried on like this, Pongnyŏ invariably followed the man, clinging to his arm.

"Now that I've caught you, you have to lend me the money."

"How come every time I meet you, you make such a stink? Well, I'll lend it anyway. In exchange for something, huh? How about it?"

"I dunno. Ha, ha, ha!"

"If you don't know, I guess I don't hand it over."

"Well. You know I know what you want."

Her character had developed to this extent.

Fall came, and with it, the slum girls began to go about at night carrying wicker baskets, the better to filch sweet potatoes and Chinese cabbage from the vegetable fields of the Chinese living in the area.

---

[4] yang: an old Korean dime.

Pongnyŏ also was adept at stealing her share. One night she was carrying a basket of stolen potatoes. Just as she was about to make her getaway, a dark shadow loomed up behind her and grabbed her tightly. It was old Wang, the Chinese owner of the garden. Pongnyŏ couldn't say a word. She just temporized, flirted, and stared down at her feet.

"Let's go into the house," he said.

"If you say so, I'll go. Sure, why not? You think I wouldn't?"

Pongnyŏ, with a wag of her bottom and a toss of her head, trailed after Wang, swinging her basket.

Pongnyŏ left Wang's house about an hour later. Just as she was coming out of the fields onto the road, she heard someone calling her from behind.

"Pongnyŏ, isn't that you?"

Pongnyŏ turned around with a start. There was her next-door neighbor holding a basket under her arm and groping her way out of the dark fields.

"Is that you, Sis? Did you go in there, too?"

"Were you there, too?"

"In whose house, Sis?"

"Me? Nuk's. How about you?"

"Me? Wang's . . . How much did you get, Sis?"

"Just three head of cabbage. That Nuk's a tight-fisted bastard."

"I got three *wŏn*."

She answered as if boasting.

About ten minutes later, after she had laid out the three *wŏn* in front of her husband, the two of them laughed and laughed about old Wang.

From then on, Wang came over for Pongnyŏ whenever he felt the urge.

Whenever Wang paid his visits, he would sit and fidget for a time. Then Pongnyŏ's husband would acknowledge the situation and go outside. After Wang left, the couple would rejoice in their one or two *wŏn*.

Pongnyŏ gradually curtailed the sale of her charms to the village beggars. When Wang was busy and couldn't come to her, Pongnyŏ would go to his house of her own accord.

By this time, she and her husband were among the wealthy folk of the slums.

Winter passed, and spring arrived.

Then it happened that Wang purchased a virgin as his wife for one hundred *wŏn*.

"Hunnh!" Pongnyŏ just snorted.

"Pongnyŏ looks jealous."

Pongnyŏ harrumphed and laughed whenever the slum women spoke like this. "Me, jealous?" She always denied it vigorously. But she could not keep the dark shadows out of her heart.

"You bastard, Wang. I'll get you for this."

The day Wang was to bring home his new bride drew closer. Wang cut his long hair, of which he had always been quite proud. A rumor spread that he had done so at his bride's suggestion.

"Hunnh!" Pongnyŏ just sneered all the more.

Finally came the day when the bride, dressed in all her nuptial fin-ery and riding in a sedan chair, arrived at Wang's house, out in the district's vegetable fields.

Later that night the Chinese who had gathered in the house plucked their curious lutes, sang their native songs, and merrily cele-brated the wedding. All the time, Pongnyŏ stood in hiding around a corner of the house, a murderous intent gleaming in her eyes as she listened to the merriment within.

The Chinese celebrated until about two in the morning. Pongnyŏ entered the house after she saw the last of them leave. Her face was dusted with white powder.

The bride and groom stared at Pongnyŏ in surprise. Glaring all the while with frightening eyes, Pongnyŏ went up to Wang, grabbed his arm, and hung on. A strange laugh bubbled from her lips. "Come on! Let's go to my house."

Wang could not say a word; his eyes just bulged impotently. Pongnyŏ shook him once again.

"Hey, come on!"

"We're busy tonight. We can't go."

"Business in the middle of the night? What kind of business?"

"Private business."

The strange laugh that had been coming from Pongnyŏ's lips sud-denly dwindled into silence.

"You low-life bitch." Pongnyŏ raised her foot and kicked out at the head of the finely attired bride.

"Come on! Let's go, let's go!" Wang was shaking all over. He broke free from Pongnyŏ's grip.

Pongnyŏ fell, but she got right up again. When she rose, she held a glittering sickle in her hand.

"I'll kill you, you Chink bastard! You son of a bitch! You hit me, you hit me! You bastard, you're killing me!"

Screaming at him, she brandished the sickle. A violent scene ensued, its setting the Wang home, that house standing alone in the desolate fields outside the Ch'ilsŏng Gate. However, even this violent scene soon came to an end. The sickle that had been in Pongnyŏ's hand somehow found its way into Wang's, and Pongnyŏ fell dead on the spot, blood gushing from her throat.

Three days passed before Pongnyŏ's corpse could be taken to be buried. Wang went to see Pongnyŏ's husband several times. Pongnyŏ's husband in turn visited Wang a number of times. Some manner of negotiations took place between them.

In the dead of night they moved Pongnyŏ's corpse from Wang's house to her husband's. Three people then gathered around the body. One was Pongnyŏ's husband, one was Wang, and the third was a certain herbalist. Without a word, Wang reached into his money bag and handed three ten-*wŏn* notes to Pongnyŏ's husband. The herb doctor received two ten-*wŏn* notes.

The next day Pongnyŏ, having been pronounced dead of a cerebral hemorrhage by the herbalist, was carried out to the potter's field.

TRANSLATED BY CHARLES ROSENBERG AND PETER H. LEE

Han Yongun (1879–1944) was a patriot, revolutionary, reformer, and prophet. In 1894, at the age of fifteen, he took part in the Tonghak (Eastern Learning) rebellion—a movement to expel foreigners in order to preserve native ways and beliefs and to liberate the masses from oppression. He then became a monk and realized that Buddhist reform could not be brought about without personal regeneration. He strove to revive the Buddhist faith, in which he saw the spiritual foundation for the salvation of Korean society. At the time of the 1919 independence movement, he helped draft a "Declaration of Independence," which was written mainly by Ch'oe Namsŏn, the author of "From the Sea to Children," and signed the document as one of thirty-three patriots. In prison he wrote another essay in which he said that the desire for freedom and independence is instinctive, that aggression would eventually fail, and that Korean independence was vital to the preservation of peace in East Asia. He also predicted that if Japan continued its military aggression, it would eventually clash with the United States and China.

In *The Silence of Love (Nim ŭi ch'immuk)*, Han rediscovered the complex Korean word *nim*. In love poetry it refers to the beloved; in allegorical poetry, the king; in religious verse, God. In Han's poetry, *nim* is the object of one's love, be it the nation, life, the Buddha, or enlightenment. His poems are built on the dialectic of engagement and withdrawal, motion and stillness, action and nonaction, life and death, nirvana and samsara, enlightenment and illusion. The situation in the poems in *The Silence of Love* and the identities of the speaker and listener signal the reader that more is intended here than just love talk. Semantically, the poem's controlled indeterminacy allows the reader to explore other interpretive horizons—for example, the range of meaning and connotation of the word *nim* in a given

24

context and in the literary tradition and the Korean collective experience. Syntactic changes, repetition of key words *(ploce)*, and special connotations imparted to certain words through manipulation of the sounds of Korean help the reader experience the manifold significance of the narrative situation.

Kim Sowŏl (1902–1934) is another poet who explored to the fullest the multiple meanings of *nim*, as well as other words with the same weight. Kim is not a seeker of the absolute but an interpreter of mood. Unfulfilled love, unhappy life, and unquenchable longing permeate his work, underscoring the gulf between desire and fulfillment. His is a poetry of lasting regret—as, for example, in "My voice goes aslant rejected, / Lost between heaven and earth" ("The Summons of the Soul"). Rather than confronting life directly, Kim's poems are subtle and sometimes passive. Kim said that his poetic line corresponds to the rhythm of human breathing, and his poetry expresses in new rhythms the world of traditional regret of the Korean people, fashioning a new folk poetry that answers to contemporary reality.

Han Yongun

THE SILENCE OF LOVE

Love is gone. Ah, my love is gone.
Sundering the mountain's green color, severing our ties, love is gone
     down a path leading to a maple grove.
The old vows, firm and glowing like a gold blossom, have turned to
     cold dust and flown away in the breeze of a sigh.
The memory of a keen first kiss reversed the compass needle of my
     fate, then retreated and vanished.
I am deafened by love's fragrant words and blinded by love's blossoming face.
Love, too, is a man's affair. We feared parting at meeting, warned
     against it, but parting came unawares and the startled heart
     bursts with new sorrow.
Yet I know that to make parting the source of vain tears is to sunder
     myself my love, so I transformed the unruly power of sorrow
     and poured it over the vertex of new hope.

As we fear parting when we meet, so we believe we will meet again
    when we part.
Ah, love is gone, but I have not sent my love away.
My song of love beyond song shrouds the silence of love.

I CANNOT KNOW

Whose footstep is that paulownia leaf that falls quietly in the windless
    air, drawing a straight wave?
Whose face is that piece of blue sky flickering between ominous black
    clouds, chased by the west wind after a rainy spell?
Whose breath is that unnameable fragrance that brushes by the still
    sky, born amid the green moss in the flowerless deep forest and
    trailing over the ancient stupa?
Whose song is that small winding stream gushing from an unknown
    source and breaking against the rocks?
Whose poem is that twilight that adorns the falling day, treading over
    the boundless sea with lotus heels and caressing the endless sky
    with jade hands?
The ash left after burning becomes oil again. For whose night does
    this feeble lantern keep vigil, my heart that never stops
    burning?

ARTIST

I am a clumsy painter.
Lying on the bed without sleep, my fingers on my chest, I drew your
    nose, your mouth, even the dimples on your cheeks.
I tried to draw your eyes that always wear a little smile but rubbed it
    out a hundred times.

I am a shy singer.
When my neighbor had left and the chirping of insects was stilled, I
    tried to sing the song you taught me, but I became shy of a doz-
    ing cat and could not sing.
So I quietly sang with the thin wind when it skirted the paper screen.

I don't seem to have the temperament of a lyric poet.
I don't want to write on such things as joy, sorrow, and love.
But I wish to write about your face, your voice, and your carriage just
as they are.
I will write about your house, your bed, even the tiny stones in your
flower garden.

A FERRYBOAT AND A TRAVELER

I am a ferryboat,
you are a traveler.

You tread on me with muddy feet,
I embrace you and cross the water.
When I embrace you, I can cross deeps, shallow, or rapids.

When you don't come, I wait from night to day, exposed to the wind,
wet with snow and rain.

Once across the water, you never look back at me.
Yet I know you will come sooner or later.
Waiting for you, I grow older day after day.

I am a ferryboat,
You are a traveler.

SECRET

A secret? What secret? What secret would I have?
I have tried to keep a secret from you, but I could not.

My secret has entered your sight through my tears;
My secret has entered your hearing through my trembling heart.
Another secret has become a red heart and entered your dreams.
I have yet a final secret. But I cannot express it, because it is like a
soundless echo.

INVERSE PROPORTION

Is your voice silence?
When you are not singing a song,
I hear your melody clearly.
Your voice is silence.

Is your face darkness?
When I close my eyes,
I see your face clearly.
Your face is darkness.

Is your shadow light?
Your shadow shines upon
The window after the moon has set.
Your shadow is light.

TRANSLATED BY PETER H. LEE

Kim Sowŏl

LONG FROM NOW

Long from now, if you should seek me,
I would tell you I have forgotten.

If you should blame me in your heart,
I would say "Missing you so, I have forgotten."

And if you should still reprove me,
"I couldn't believe you, so I have forgotten."

Unable to forget you today, or yesterday,
but long from now "I have forgotten."

AZALEAS

When you leave,
weary of me,
without a word I shall gently let you go.

From Mount Yak
in Yŏngbyŏn,
I shall gather armfuls of azaleas
and scatter them on your way.

Step by step
on the flowers placed before you
tread lightly, softly as you go.

When you leave,
weary of me,
though I die, I'll not let one tear fall.

MOUNTAIN FLOWERS

Flowers on the mountain bloom,
the flowers bloom.
Fall, spring, and summer through,
the flowers bloom.

On the mountain,
the mountain,
the flowers blooming
are so far, so far away.

A small bird sings
on the mountain.
Friend of the flowers,
it lives on the mountain.

Flowers on the mountain fall,
the flowers fall.
Spring, summer, and autumn through,
the flowers fall.

THE ROAD

Again last night
at a country inn
grackles screeched at dawn.

Today
how many miles
again lead where?

Away to the mountains,
to the plains?
With no place that calls me
I go nowhere.

Don't talk of my home,
Chŏngju Kwaksan,
for the train and the boat go there.

Hear me, wild geese in the sky:
Is there a road of the air
that you travel so sure?

Hear me, wild geese in the sky:
I stand at the center of the crossroads.
Again and again the paths branch,
but no way is mine.

TRANSLATED BY DAVID R. MCCANN

MODERN FICTION
II

Sim Hun

Sim Hun was born in Seoul in 1901. While still a high school student, he took part in the 1919 independence movement and spent four months in jail. Upon returning from his studies in Shanghai (1922–1923), Sim worked for the Seoul Broadcasting Company (1923–1930) and also wrote scripts for motion pictures. Sim died of typhoid fever while reading the proofs of *The Evergreen,* a prizewinning novel composed on the occasion of the fifteenth anniversary of the founding of the *Tonga Daily.* The rural enlightenment movement in the early 1930s was sponsored by the two leading Korean dailies and comprised two campaigns: the eradication of illiteracy *(Chosŏn Daily)* and "To the People" *(Tonga Daily).*

Modeled on the true story of Ch'oe Yŏngsin (1909–1935), a student sent by the YWCA in 1931 to Hwasŏng, Kyŏnggi province, the novel's main characters, Miss Ch'ae Yŏngsin and Pak Tonghyŏk, take part in a student rural enlightenment campaign during the summer vacation. Meeting for the first time at a reception, they become friends and soon fall in love. Upon graduation, Pak goes to Hangok village and Ch'ae to Ch'ŏngsŏk village to conduct their work. Using the village church as a night school, Miss Ch'ae teaches youngsters the Korean alphabet. Her pedagogic skill and powerful personality attract many children, but the local Japanese police allow only eighty out of one hundred and fifty to be admitted. Miss Ch'ae then raises funds to have a new school built, but she collapses from exhaustion on the day the new building is to be dedicated. The excerpt presented here illustrates the twin obstacles she and her coworkers had to confront: the Japanese oppression and the farmers' reluctance.

THE MULBERRY TREE AND THE CHILDREN

[FROM *THE EVERGREEN*]

The number of children at the school increased almost daily. The small church, built roughly with a galvanized roof and planks, had not been repaired and its walls were falling apart; whenever it rained, the ceiling leaked and because the rowdy children ran about shaking the building, even the floor had fallen through in three or four places. Whenever the aging elder observed this, he stuck his head out and said, "We can't raise funds for repairs, and you run around ruining the church!" Moreover, the children, who were just learning to write, scribbled everywhere, inside and outside the church, with chalk and pencil, and they drew pictures besides. The elder and the minister frowned whenever they saw these markings.

Yŏngsin felt very bad, and several times a day she admonished the children until it seemed her lips would wear out. However, she was proud of the fact that some of the pupils she taught with great effort were, by ones and twos, beginning to learn their letters. "Elder, since we are to build our own facilities and move out, please bear with us until this autumn," Yŏngsin begged for forgiveness. Then the elder would stroke his bald head and mumble, "Well, Miss Ch'ae, don't worry. Everything will turn out the way God wants it. Yours is a noble undertaking." Yŏngsin felt uneasy about staying in a rented building, and pondered every conceivable plan to build a school and move out as soon as possible.

The village was poor, however, and money was particularly scarce at the time; not even one-tenth of the pledged contributions came in. The mutual assistance guild raised spring silkworms, and one group managed to gather thirteen or fourteen pecks; but the price of silk cocoons dropped sharply and they didn't make as much as they'd anticipated. Every home was raising chickens by more advanced methods these days, but when the price of feed and the cost of Western-type hens such as the Leghorn were calculated in, the income from eggs barely covered the costs.

Thus, it was not possible to build the school, which would cost, conservatively speaking, at least five or six hundred *wŏn*. When Yŏngsin, frustrated by the slow progress of the building project, pressed the issue, the other members said, "Food eaten fast will not digest well. Our teacher is too impatient . . ." and consoled her more than once or twice.

Sometimes five or six children were added to the school in one day. At other times more than ten at a time came. The grammar school was fifteen *ri* away,[1] and since the two-year temporary school was just as far away as the marketplace, the children who wanted to learn gathered around Ch'ŏngsŏk village, like moths flying about the lamp-light because they could not go anywhere else. Including the most recent entrants, the pupils numbered more than a hundred and thirty. However, unable to send away the children who were already there, she gave as an excuse that the school was too small when she tried to turn away new applicants.

Yŏngsin sang to herself a phrase from a hymn, "Anyone can come, anyone can come," and said, "Yes, until the church bursts, gather around. When summer comes, we can sit in the shade of the trees; on a moonlit night, we won't need lamps." She accepted pupils as they came and enlisted the aid of the young graduates from the grammar school—men and women—and dividing the group into beginning and advanced classes she began to teach. Three or four good youths respected and helped Yŏngsin, and Wŏnje, the only son of the land-lord, was devoted to her. He lived in the same house as Yŏngsin, and because he could not go to an advanced school, he faithfully studied middle-school materials from Yŏngsin in his spare time.

Thus, the inside of the crumbling church was full of children—as if it were growing bean sprouts. It was filled so tightly that there was no room for the teacher to move in and out. In the beginning class, as they repeated, "Add *kiŭk* to *ka*, make *kak*, add *niŭn* to *na*, make *nan*,"[2] the children could not stretch their legs; and holding their heads erect and gazing at the blackboard, they opened and closed their mouths like swallows. Then from the advanced class, as they spread open their *Farmer's Reader*, came, "Those who sleep, awake! / Those who are blind, open your eyes! / Do your work diligently, / And find out the means to live." They repeated this after their teacher at the top of their voices. If one were close by, the din was enough to break one's eardrums, but when one listened from afar, one would think, "Ah, now your eyes are opening, aren't they!" and Yŏngsin danced with joy.

It was the evening of one such day. A policeman, who had been watching her, appeared and abruptly said:

---

[1] A common Korean measure of distance, about one-third mile.

[2] Here the children, choosing the first consonant and vowel in the Korean alphabet, are learning how to combine the letter *k* with the syllable *ka* to make the syllable *kak*, and the like.

"The chief wants to see you. Please report to the police substation tomorrow." Relaying his message without waiting for a reply, he turned his bicycle around and rode off.

For what reason was she being summoned? Hadn't they already granted her permission to increase the school contribution to 500 wǒn?

Yǒngsin was at a loss what to do. If it were an ordinary matter, it would be enough for the policeman himself to take care of it and go; but she could not understand why a summons had come from such a distance.

Ever since Yǒngsin first came to the village, she had met with interference over this matter and that, but had eventually made the authorities understand the purpose of the school and the women's mutual assistance guild. So this summons was all the more worrisome.

All kinds of thoughts arose in Yǒngsin's mind and that night she could not sleep. The following morning after breakfast, she set out. For the first twenty ri, the road was level, but after that she had to cross a steep pass, and got blisters on her feet. Her underclothes were soaked with perspiration.

I will not record here the conversation between Yǒngsin and the police chief or anything else relating to it. However, the main points of the summons were as follows:

1. Since the church is small and falling apart it is dangerous; no more than eighty children should be accepted.
2. A request for contributions, if too strongly worded, is in conflict with the law.

So the police chief firmly warned her. Yǒngsin defended herself, pleaded that she could not reject the children who came. But the chief threatened, "It is an order from above. If you do not comply, we will close your school." Helpless, Yǒngsin held her tongue and left the substation. She returned dragging her sore feet. She did not eat her supper and stayed up all night.

"Persevere! I have withstood worse. Surely I can bear this sort of thing!" Even as she said this, she regretted that she had not spoken her mind to the police chief. However, she realized that if, unable to control herself, she had shouted back, she would not have been allowed to teach even the restricted number of children, so she took a deep breath. "Since it is an order that cannot be disobeyed, from tomorrow only eighty children will be allowed, and the rest must be sent away. I must do it." "I cannot do it. I'd rather go nail up the church door—I cannot bear to do such a thing myself." Yŏngsin cried out and collapsed to the floor. For some time she tossed and turned in agony.

Putting out the light, she turned her blanket over and lay down. She could not bring herself to tear down the tower she had built with devotion and painstaking effort in the face of hardship and affronts. She could not abandon halfway the language class, one of the most serious efforts she had begun since coming to Ch'ŏngsŏk village—and the one with the finest results. "How can I send away the fifty extra students? Up to now, without complaint, I have been instructing them. What pretext can I suddenly give for not being able to teach?"

She would rather die than tell a lie, but the situation was such that she was compelled to concoct an excuse. She racked her brains, but could come up with nothing, and she could not sleep a wink.

When the morning star gradually dimmed, Yŏngsin washed up and set out for the church. Earthly creatures had not awakened from their dreams; heaven and earth were still. Yŏngsin knelt down on the dew-drenched stairs and prayed reverently: "Lord! According to your wishes these precious and beloved sheep are gathered here. Today one-third of them will lose their shepherd. They can do nothing but wander again in darkness. Lord! So that each will receive new hope, please don't allow this pitiful herd to lose heart, do not abandon even one. Without a day's delay please bestow that light. O Lord! My heart is bursting!"

As the sun on her back climbed the skies, Yŏngsin lay choked with tears.

That day, two children arrived who had been expelled from the primary school because they could not pay the sixty cents tuition and had fallen behind several months. They were carrying their books in a bundle, their school insignia attached to their caps.

"Children, I'm sorry," Yŏngsin said. "But since there's no place for you to sit I cannot accept you. Come back in the fall. In a little while a larger school will be built. Then I will be sure to call you." She wrote down their names, patted their backs, and forced herself to send them away. And before other children could arrive, she went into the church.

Because she had not slept at all, her head felt heavy and her eyes could not focus. Going to the center of a classroom, she stood listlessly for a while, as though in a daze. Her head was reeling, but after pressing her forehead she was able to go and stand before the blackboard. Picking the chalk up in her hand, she paced off one-third of the distance from the front platform to the back of the class. Then she drew a straight line from the east end to below the west window. After waiting for the children to come, she opened only one side of the church door. As usual the children, chattering all the while, came scrambling in noisily. Yŏngsin quietly seated the first comers by ones and twos inside the line. Before she knew it, eighty pupils filled the space.

"Those of you who have come in late, please sit outside the line. And don't make any noise."

Not understanding the teacher's order, those who came late wondered what it was all about. They studied the expression on her face, went outside the line, and squatted on the floor.

She could not have the children draw lots. Nor could she indiscriminately turn away the beginners. So Yŏngsin turned away those who came late. They came only ten or so minutes late, but there was no other way to do it.

Not until after the children were turned around and seated did she quietly intimate this to Wŏnje and the other helpers. If the other children heard the news, things might get out of hand.

Hearing her words the faces of the young helpers suddenly turned ashen.

"Say nothing and put the room in order just as I tell you. I shall explain in detail later on."

Since they had absolute trust in Yŏngsin, they just bit their lips and wore a grave expression.

Calmly, Yŏngsin stood up on the platform, her complexion greenish, like one about to collapse.

The children asked one another, "What is she trying to tell us? Why is she behaving like that?" And they studied her appearance, which they found unusual. No one coughed. They just stared at Yŏngsin.

Yŏngsin stood there, her lips trembling, unable to open her mouth. She looked down at the line drawn on the wooden floor, like a sword that cuts with a single blow the affection between teacher and pupil. When she gazed at some fifty children huddled together outside that line—those innocent faces which seemed to be waiting, wondering what sort of frightening verdict was to fall—Yŏngsin, close to tears and choked up, could not say a word.

It was only after a few minutes that she got the courage. Then, in a downcast voice she said, "Students, listen quietly. Today I have something very difficult and sad to say. . . ." Faltering again she continued, "Those of you sitting outside that line, from today on— it's come about that I cannot teach you any longer." This bolt out of the blue fell on the heads of the innocent children. Countless eyes that had been fixed on the teacher blinked and became round as cherries.

One whose hair was rather thick asked, "Why? Why won't you teach us?"

Yŏngsin said imploringly, "The building is so small that no more than eighty pupils can be taught. When the new building is finished this fall, I shall not forget to call every one of you."

"Well, then, how come you've managed till now to teach us in this small place?" The question was raised by a boy whose voice had changed. Yŏngsin's heart was pierced, as if shot by an arrow. She couldn't answer. She felt dizzy and stood there holding her forehead. By ones and twos the children sitting outside the line began to creep on their hands and knees. Drawing together, they pushed their way inside the line:

"Teacher!"

"Teacher! Teacher!"

As they called continuously, they even clambered on top of the platform. Yŏngsin was surrounded by at least fifty of them.

"Teacher!"

"Teacher!"

"I came earlier."

"I went to the bathroom and came just a little late."

"Ch'asun saw me come before Maktong."

"Teacher, I'll be on time from tomorrow. I'll even come before you."

"Teacher, look here. Look at me! From now on I'll even come without eating breakfast. Don't tell me to go. Please! Please!" The children fell down pell-mell, scrambled for the front, and climbed up on the platform. Yŏngsin felt dizzy from the pushing and falling children, and from those who were being stepped on and crying. Her headache made things worse, and she stood there with difficulty, grabbing a corner of the table. Now she was no longer standing on her own—

rather, her body, surrounded by children and on the verge of collapse, was forcibly being held up.

"Teacher!"

"Teacher!"

The children's touching outcry continued until her ears rang. Still, Yŏngsin, closing her eyes and biting her lower lip, said:

"Get down! Hurry, get down and go. If you don't listen, I'll chase all of you out."

The youths assisting Yŏngsin tried to drag the children down and threatened them with a pointer, but the children clung to Yŏngsin like leeches, and did not fall off.

Yŏngsin's shirt was turned into a rag; even the folds of her skirts were torn to shreds. One girl wrapped her arms around Yŏngsin's legs and, lying flat, immobilized her.

Yŏngsin, taking hold of her torn skirt, said, "Let go, let go! All of you go over there. Please, I'm choking!" Wrenching her body away, she carefully shook off the children clinging to her. The children, fearful that if they fell off they might be left out, hung on tenaciously. The church staff viewing this spectacle entered and drove out those who had been sitting outside the line. Boys and girls, as if taken away from their mothers' breasts, were forced out, sniffling until their eyes turned red, or sobbing bitterly.

Behind the children's backs, gazing at their sad plight, tears began to trickle down Yŏngsin's cheeks. Lest the children see her tears, Yŏngsin covered her face with her sleeve and turned around. After calming herself she regrouped the remaining eighty, who sat with bowed heads, embarrassed by the fact that their classmates were chased out in order to make room for them. Yŏngsin walked in front of the blackboard with faltering steps. She was too depressed to begin a new lesson, so she said, "Today, let's review," and spread open the *Farmers' Reader* as a textbook. "Let everyone come to school. One must learn in order to do any work," they began to recite in dejected voices.

Yŏngsin loathed hearing their lifeless voices, and in order to avoid looking at the empty corner of the classroom, unsightly as a mouth with several missing teeth, she turned her gaze toward the glass window.

Yet the sight outside the window made her even sadder. Those driven out were clinging by their legs to a low fence around the church, their heads sticking out, looking over the fence! And hanging from the boughs of the withered mulberry tree were human fruits. Also among them were the small children who, unable to climb the tree, had flopped down on the ground, sniffling and crying.

Yŏngsin swung open the window and, together with the youths, moved the blackboard, propping it on the rise of the window so that it could be seen from outside the fence. She wrote in large letters: "Let everyone come to school. One must learn in order to do any work." The children up in the tree and those clinging to the fence opened their mouths wide and, shouting at the top of their voices, repeated the phrases written on the blackboard. They seemed to shout not so much to memorize the phrases as to register their bitter complaints.

TRANSLATED BY PETER H. LEE

Yi Hyosŏk

Yi Hyosŏk graduated in English literature from Keijō Imperial University in 1930. During his early career as a fellow traveler of the proletarian literary movement, Yi dealt with the urban poor. But his second phase is marked by his dislike of the city with its dissolution, fear, strife, betrayal, and decadence. Excoriating the artificial life of the city, Yi retreats into mountains and fields with their trees and animals. It is significant that, while stressing man's harmony with the cycles of nature, Yi omits winter. "The Buckwheat Season" (1936) is original in conception, lyrical in style, and careful in plot. Its symbolic parallels between the donkey and its mare and old Hŏ and his son Tongi create an aesthetic of karma: life inseparable from relation.

THE BUCKWHEAT SEASON

The summer market was bound to be unpopular. With the sun still in mid-sky, the market grounds were nearly deserted. Even under the cover of the stalls, the sunlight scorched the backs of the vendors. Most of the villagers had gone, except for a few lingering fagot vendors who had not done well. There was no point staying longer just for those who would want only a bottle of kerosene or a string of fish. Swarms of flies and village troublemakers were a nuisance. So the left-handed, pockmarked dry goods vendor Hŏ Saengwŏn finally turned to his fellow trader, Cho Sŏndal, and broke the silence:

"Shall we close up?"

"A good idea. Have we ever had a good day at Pongp'yŏng Market? Let's go. Maybe we'll have a better day at Taehwa tomorrow."

"We might have to walk all night."

"The moon may come up, though."

Seeing Cho begin to count up his earnings, making little clinking sounds, Hŏ set to taking the curtains down from their stakes and gathering up the goods spread before him. Rolls of cotton, silk, and satin filled two wicker trunks. Pieces of cloth lay scattered about on the mat. Other vendors were also closing their stalls, and some impatient ones were already departing. No trace could be found of the vendors of dried fish, taffy, and ginger. Tomorrow, markets would be held at Chinbu and Taehwa. To reach either one, the vendors would have to trudge some twenty to thirty miles[1] during the night.

The marketplace was littered, like a courtyard after a festival. Someone was already squabbling in a tavern. The shrill, unremitting cries of a woman mingled with the curses of a drunk. Without exception, the evenings of market days began with the shrill cries of a tavern woman.

"Saengwŏn, you play it cool, but I know just how you feel about that Ch'ungju woman," Cho Sŏndal said with a grin, as if the woman's cry reminded him of the woman from Ch'ungju.

"She's like a cake in a picture. You know we can't compete with the young fellows."

"That's not always so. True, they're much attracted to her. Take Tongi, for example—he seems to have made a conquest of her."

"What, that greenhorn? He must have bribed her with his goods. I thought I could count on him."

"You never can tell in this kind of affair. Let's stop guessing and go and see. I'll treat you."

Hŏ was not enthusiastic, but went along. Hŏ had little luck with women. With his pockmarked face, he lacked the courage to approach them; they, in turn, showed no real interest in him. Hŏ had spent half of his life lonely and without direction. Yet at the mere thought of the Ch'ungju woman he would flush like a child, totter, and then stand numbly, as if glued to the ground.

When he entered the Ch'ungju woman's tavern and found Tongi seated at the table, he grew angry in spite of himself. He could not contain himself when he saw Tongi flirting with the woman at the wine table.

"You're quite the playboy," he said. "What an ugly sight it is to see a fellow as young as you drinking and flirting with a woman while the sun is still up. You go around disgracing the name of us traveling vendors, but you still want a share in our trade." "It's none of your business," Tongi's bloodshot eyes seemed to retort. When he met the young man's gaze, Hŏ could not resist an impulse to slap his face.

Tongi rose indignantly, but Hŏ went on: "I don't know where you come from, but you too must have a father and mother. They'd be delighted to see you acting this way, I'm sure! Business is business;

---

[1]In the original, distance is given in the Korean measure, *ri*, which corresponds to one-third mile. Here, the mile is used.

you've got to give it your whole heart. What use is a woman to a petty vendor like you? Now get out! Be off this moment!"

Hŏ felt a measure of sympathy for Tongi as he watched him leave the room dejectedly and unprotestingly. "He and I scarcely know each other. I went too far." Hŏ was seized with remorse.

"You two are my customers, but how dare you berate the kid like that! He may be young, but he's old enough to father a child," the Ch'ungju woman protested. Her lips formed a pout as she poured wine gracelessly.

"It's good medicine for a greenhorn like him," Cho cut in, trying to patch up the situation.

"You're infatuated with him, aren't you? It's a sin to drain a kid."

After this, Hŏ grew more confident. He also felt a boundless urge to get drunk, and he began to empty the cups offered him. As tipsiness overtook him, Hŏ began to think more of Tongi than of the woman. What on earth would he do with that woman even if he could snatch her away from Tongi? He began to reproach himself for rebuking Tongi. Therefore, when Tongi came helter-skelter to call for him after some time had passed, Hŏ threw his cup without a second thought and rushed out of the tavern.

"Saengwŏn, your donkey has broken his tether and is raging."

"The troublemakers must have teased him."

Hŏ was anxious about the animal, but was more moved by Tongi's concern. As he ran across the deserted market ground after Tongi he felt his eyes moistening, though he was laden with wine.

"What can be done about those incorrigible troublemakers?"

"I won't let them get away with being cruel to my donkey."

The animal had been Hŏ's companion for half of his life. The two had traveled together from market to market, bathing in the same moonlight and lodging in the same inns. These twenty years had made them both old. The donkey's disheveled mane was coarse like its master's hair, and its moist eyes were gummy like its master's. The donkey's tail, short as a broom made from a stump of wood, scarcely reached the donkey's legs, no matter how hard it was brandished to drive away flies. How many times had Hŏ removed the donkey's worn shoes and replaced them with new ones? The donkey's hooves had stopped growing, and blood oozed out from under the worn shoes. The donkey knew its master by smell, and it brayed out a welcome at Hŏ's approach as if to appeal his own case.

Hŏ stroked the donkey's scruff as if he were calming a child, and the donkey twitched its nostrils and snorted. Its nose was running. Hŏ suffered greatly because of the animal. Unable to cool off, the animal's damp, weary body trembled—it must have been through a lot. The bridle was loose, and the saddle was on the ground.

"You rascals," Hŏ shouted. Most of the boys had made off already. The few who remained began to quaver at Hŏ's shouts.

"It's not our doing," a sniveling boy shouted back from a distance. "It's a mare that made him go wild."

"Listen to that talk . . ."

"When your donkey saw Kim Ch'ŏmji's mare leave, it began to kick and foam like a mad bull. We couldn't help watching the spectacle. Look under its belly!" The boy shouted again in a cocky tone and burst into laughter.

Hŏ felt the blood rush to his face in spite of himself; he wanted to stand in front of the animal's belly just enough to screen it from the boys' gaze.

"That old animal still wants a mare!"

The boy's derision caused Hŏ to falter momentarily. He could take it only so long, though, and he brandished his whip to chase the boys away.

"Come on, catch us if you can. Lefty's trying to beat us!"

There was no hope of overtaking these market troublemakers. A left-handed man was no match even for a boy. Hŏ threw down his whip. He felt himself burning as the wine began to work on him.

"Let's leave. There's no end to squabbling with those fellows. The kids are harder to deal with than the adults, you know," Cho urged.

Cho and Tongi saddled their donkeys and began to load them. The sun seemed to have sunk considerably.

In his twenty years as a traveling vendor of dry goods, Hŏ had seldom missed the market days at Pongp'yŏng. He had traveled to such neighboring counties as Ch'ungju and Chech'ŏn, and even to the far-off Yŏngnam area; but now he seldom ventured out of his county except for sorties to Kangnŭng to replenish his stock. Since markets were held every five days, Hŏ traveled from one town to another, constant as the moon in the sky. Though he might speak proudly of his birthplace, Ch'ungju, he seemed never to have visited it, much less gone back for a prolonged stay. His home was the beautiful hills and waters near the market towns. Each time Hŏ and his animal approached a market town after a half-day's walk, the weary donkey would give a resounding fanfare of braying, and Hŏ's heart would leap with joy, especially at dusk with lights swimming in the distance.

When he was young, Hŏ had economized and saved a fair amount of money. He gambled extravagantly, though, at the All Soul's Day Festival and in three days he lost everything he had. He thought of selling his donkey, but his love for the animal intervened, and he gritted his teeth and gave up the idea. Thus he ended up back where he had begun and had to resume his itinerant vendor's career, following the markets. On the day he fled town with the donkey, he caressed the animal and cried, saying that he had done well not to part with it. His debts compelled him to forgo the idea of making money, and he wandered from market to market, living hand to mouth.

He had once had a taste of luxurious dissipation, but he had yet to win a woman. To him, a woman was a creature without feelings. "Am I fated to live this way?" Hŏ felt bitter. The only thing close to him was the faithful donkey.

Nevertheless, he could not forget the first incident of his life, his only strange affair with a woman. It had taken place when he was beginning to frequent Pongp'yŏng market. He had been young then, and his life still had some meaning.

"It was a night with a bright moon, but I still can't figure out how it all happened." Hŏ was about to tell the story again. Cho had heard it often enough since making friends with Hŏ, but he could not bring himself to reveal his boredom. Hŏ, on his part, feigned indifference and went on as he pleased.

"This kind of story goes well with the moon." Hŏ glanced at Cho, not because he felt sorry for his friend, but rather because he was moved by the moonlight. It was just after the fifteenth of the month; and the moon was no longer quite full, but it still shed a faint light that caught Hŏ's fancy. Taehwa lay at the end of a twenty-five-mile-long journey through the night, over two mountain passes and one river, and then a plain and a mountain path. The road appeared suspended from the waist of a hill. It was past midnight, and in the stillness around him, Hŏ caught the sound of the moon breathing like a beast within arm's reach, and bean stalks and ears of corn, drenched in moonlight, appeared bluer than usual. The waist of the hill was all planted in buckwheat, and the fresh flowers, as serene as salt sprinkled under the soft moonlight, were breathtaking. The red buckwheat stalks were as tenuous as a fragrance, and the donkey's gait was refreshing. The road was narrow, and the three rode single file. The jingle-jangle of the bells floated lightly over the buckwheat fields. Hŏ rode at the head and Tongi at the rear, so that the former's story scarcely reached the latter's ears. Yet Tongi, sunk in his own reverie, was not lonely.

"It was the night of a market day, just like tonight. The tiny room in the inn was so stuffy I couldn't sleep, so I got up about midnight and went out to have a dip in a nearby brook. Pongp'yŏng was the same then as it is now, buckwheat fields everywhere, as far as the eye can see, with white flowers thick around the brook. I could have removed my clothes in the river's stony bed, but the moon was so bright I went into a nearby water mill. Funny things do happen. There I stood face to face with Sŏng's daughter, the prettiest in all Pongp'yŏng. Luck must have favored me."

Responding to his own remark, Hŏ paused and sucked on his cigar for a while, as if he begrudged his story. Fragrant blue smoke wafted up and melted into the night air.

"She hadn't been waiting for me, nor for anybody in particular, for that matter. She was weeping. I could guess what it was about. The Sŏng family was then in sad straits, at the verge of ruin. She must have been worried about her family's affairs, too. They wanted to marry her off to a suitable man, but she was dead set against a match like that. A girl is most attractive when she weeps. At first she looked startled, but I suppose when you're in trouble, your mind softens easily. We came to an understanding. It was a fabulous, breathtaking night, come to think of it."

"Then, the following day, she took off to Chech'ŏn or some such place, right?" Cho chimed in.

"The whole family vanished before the next market day. The market was filled with gossips. The best for the family would be to sell her off to a tavern, they chattered. I searched Chech'ŏn market in vain time and time again; there wasn't a sign of the girl. Our first night together was our last. Since then, Pongp'yŏng has caught my fancy. I can't forget it, not even after half a lifetime."

"You were lucky," Cho said. "Things like that don't happen often. Think of getting an ugly wife and having children; your worries would only grow. The mere thought of it is enough to make me sick. But wouldn't it be a strain to make the rounds of the markets until

I'm old? I'm going to change careers this fall. I'll open a little shop near Taehwa and send for my family. It's quite a job to stay on the move the four long seasons through."

"I may settle down when I find my girl again. I'll be plodding along this road and viewing the moon till the end of my life."

The mountain path opened onto a main road. Tongi came up front, and the donkeys trotted three abreast.

"Young man," Hŏ turned to Tongi. "You're in the prime of life. I went too far at the Ch'ungju woman's tavern. I'm sorry. Please don't make too much of it."

"Not at all. It is I who am ashamed. There's no room for a woman at this stage of my life. Awake or asleep, I think only of my mother." Tongi's feelings having been softened by Hŏ Saengwŏn's story, his tone was a shade subdued. "When you said, 'You too must have a father and mother,' I felt my heart break. I don't have a father. My only flesh and blood is my mother."

"Is you father dead?"

"I never knew him."

"Who ever heard of such a thing?"

The two men's laughter made Tongi reply all the more earnestly.

"I'm ashamed to tell you this, but it's true. My mother gave birth to an illegitimate child and was thrown out of her house. It may sound strange, but I've never seen my father's face, and I don't know where he is."

A pass appeared before the three, and they dismounted. The path along the ridge was rugged, and it was difficult to talk; the conversation lagged for a long while. The animals slipped often. Short of breath, Hŏ had to rest his legs several times. Perspiration bathed his back. Every time he crossed a hill, he revealed his age. He envied a young man like Tongi.

Beyond the hill was a brook. The plank bridge, carried away by a flood during the monsoon, had not been replaced, and the men had to strip to wade across. Strapping their baggy trousers to their backs, they rushed into the water half-naked and ludicrous. They had been sweating profusely, but the nighttime chill of the water soon penetrated to their bones.

"Well, then, who on earth reared you?" asked Hŏ.

"My mother was compelled to take a husband. She started a tavern. My stepfather, a heavy drinker, was useless. Once I cut my wisdom teeth, there wasn't a day he didn't beat me. When Mother tried to intervene, he would kick me and beat me, and even brandish a knife—it was a wretched household, you can imagine. I left home when I turned eighteen, and here I am, an itinerant vendor."

"I thought you were quite grown up for your age. But your story tells me you've had a hard life."

The water was now waist deep. The swift current and the slick pebbles made the crossing hard. Cho and his donkey were on the far bank already, but Hŏ and Tongi, who had to assist the old man, lagged behind.

"Was your mother's home originally Chech'ŏn?"

"Not exactly. Though she never made it quite clear, I understand she was from Pongp'yŏng."

"Pongp'yŏng? What was her maiden name?"

"I never heard her mention it."

"I suppose she's doing right," he mumbled as he blinked his weak eyes and lost his footing. He fell forward and immediately plunged into the water with a splash. The more he pawed the air, the less control he had of the situation. Before Tongi could come shouting to his rescue, Hŏ had been carried away a good distance. With his clothes dripping, he looked more miserable than a drowned dog. Tongi carried the old man on his back with ease. Though wet, the lean old body was light on Tongi's stout back.

"Sorry to trouble you so much. I must have been out of my mind."

"Don't worry about it."

"By the way, did your mother look for your real father?"

"She wanted to see him, even if only just once, she used to say."

"Where is she now?"

"She's separated from my stepfather and living in Chech'ŏn now. I'm planning to send for her this fall. If I work hard, sweating and grinding, I might manage to support the family."

"That's a great idea, for sure. This fall, you say?"

Tongi's broad shoulders seemed to warm Hŏ's bones. When they had crossed, Hŏ wished to be carried a bit farther and regretted having to dismount.

"You've been making blunders all day. What's the matter with you?" Cho asked.

"It's the donkey. The thought of it so distracted me that I lost my balance." Hŏ looked at Cho and burst into laughing. "Didn't I tell you? Old as it is, my donkey had a colt by the mare of a woman in Kangnŭng. Could there be anything cuter than a colt prancing about with pricked ears? I sometimes go out of my way and visit the place just to see that."

"It's an extraordinary colt all right. It nearly drowned a man," Cho laughed.

Hŏ wrung out his wet clothes and put them on. His teeth chattered, his body shook, and he felt chilly, but he was in high spirits for some reason.

"Let's hurry to the inn. We'll build a fire in the yard and settle down for a warm rest in the warmth. We'll boil water for the donkeys, too. After tomorrow's market at Taehwa, Chech'ŏn will be my next stop."

"You're also going to Chech'ŏn, Saengwŏn?"

"Yes. I feel like visiting it after all this time. Will you join me, Tongi?"

When the donkey began to trot, Tongi held his whip in his left hand. Hŏ's eyes were weak and dim, but this time he could not fail to notice Tongi's left-handedness.

The donkeys' steps were light, and the tinkle of their bells resounded over the dark plain.

The moon sank considerably.

TRANSLATED BY PETER H. LEE

Yi Sang

"Wings" by Yi Sang concerns a hermetically sealed life. Intent on escaping from the everyday world of frustration and negation, the central figure lives a life of uneasiness, suspicion, and boredom, a life without money or ambition. He learns that he cannot possess the other—his existence is a continuous hide-and-seek between a desire for possession and a denial of being possessed. Is a true meeting possible? Are love and marriage expressions of what the existentialists call *mauvaise foi?* The other remains unknowable; only misunderstanding and deceit exist between two lives. There is no dialogue between the "I" and his wife. Indeed, she exists only through his eyes. There is no escape from his imprisoned self. Yi's protagonist illustrates the bankruptcy of one who severs all traffic with society. The wings might represent a liberation of the self and release of a tormented consciousness. Although Yi's resistance to any accommodation with reality is passive and traditional, he refuses to simplify the problem and struggles to confront it. The insanity of society is the cause of the protagonist's plight, and Yi Sang transforms the modern intelligentsia into an objective correlative of the social and economic contradictions of the 1930s.

WINGS

Have you ever heard of the "genius who became a stuffed specimen"? I'm cheerful. Even love is cheerful at times like this.

My spirit shines like a silver coin, only when my body is so tired my joints creak. My mind prepares a blank sheet of paper whenever the nicotine filters into my roundworm-ridden stomach. On a blank sheet I spread out my wit and paradoxes, as if placing the pieces in strategic positions in a game of chess. This is the horrible disease called common sense.

Again, with a woman, I draw up a plan of life, a scheme of one whose spirit has gone mad after a glimpse of the ultimate reason, a man whose lovemaking technique has grown awkward. What I mean is that I plan to design a life in which I own half a woman—half of everything. The two halves, like two suns, will keep on giggling face to face, with only one foot in life. I must have been fed up with all mankind. Goodbye.

Goodbye. It might do you some good to practice the irony of devouring the kind of food that you dislike the most. Wit and paradoxes . . .

It would be worth your while to put on your mask. Your mask will feel noble and at ease—think of something ready-made that no one has ever seen before.

Shut off the nineteenth century if you can. What is called Dostoevsky's spirit is probably a waste. It is well said (although I don't know by whom) that Hugo was a slice of French bread. Why should you be deceived by the details of life or by its pattern? Don't let disaster catch you. I'm telling you this in earnest.

If the tape breaks, blood will flow. The wound will heal itself before long. Goodbye.

Emotion is a kind of pose. (I suspect I'm only pointing out the elements of the pose.)

The supply of feeling comes to a sudden stop when the pose advances to a state of immobility.

I've defined the purport of my view of the world by recalling my extraordinary growth.

The queen bee and the widow . . . Is there any woman in the world who has not become a widow in daily life? No. Would my theory of looking at every woman as a widow offend women? Goodbye.

This number thirty-three looks like a house of ill repute. Eighteen families live in this compound labeled thirty-three, where all the rooms are lined up shoulder to shoulder, their paper windows and furnaces identical. Everyone who lives in them is young, a budding flower.

No sun ever shines into the rooms, because their inhabitants ignore the sun. On the pretext that they must hang out their soiled bedding on the clothesline in front of their rooms, they block the sliding doors off from the sun. They take naps in the darkened rooms. Don't they sleep at night? I don't know, because I sleep day and night. Daytime is quiet for the eighteen families in compound number thirty-three.

But they remain quiet only in the daytime. At dusk they take the bedding down. And when the lights come on, the eighteen families become much more animated than in the daytime. Then I hear the doors opening and closing all through the night. I begin to notice all sorts of odors: the smell of herrings being broiled, the odors of women's makeup, the smell of water that has been used to wash rice, and the fragrance of soap.

What amuses me most here are the name plates posted on each door.

Standing all by itself there is a front gate that represents the eighteen families. But the gate, like a thoroughfare, has never been closed; all sorts of peddlers come in and out through it at any hour of the day or night. None of the eighteen families bother to go out to buy bean curd: they do their buying in their rooms, just by sliding the door open. It would be meaningless for the eighteen families to post their name plates at the gate for number thirty-three, so they have devised a system of pasting their name cards on their doors. The cards bear names like "The Hall of Patience" or "The Hall of Blessing."

Above the sliding doors of my room—my wife's room, I mean—is pasted her small name card, one quarter the size of a playing card, purely as a concession to the custom in the compound.

I do not play with anyone in the compound. I never greet anyone. I don't want to greet anyone other than my wife.

I think it would hurt my wife's reputation if I were ever to greet the others or play with any of them. I am that devoted to her. I am this devoted because she, like her name card, is the smallest and the most beautiful of all the women in the eighteen families. Because she is the most beautiful of eighteen flowers, she shines radiantly, even in this sunless spot under a galvanized roof. And I keep this most beautiful flower; no, I live clinging to her, and my existence must be an indescribably awkward one.

I like my room very much. I find its temperature comfortable, and the semidarkness suits my eyes. I wouldn't want a room any cooler or warmer, or any brighter or darker. I keep on thanking the room for maintaining such an even temperature and brightness. I'm pleased to think that I was born to enjoy this kind of room.

But I don't want to calculate whether I'm happy or unhappy. I don't need to think about that problem. All was well as long as I spent day after day in idleness, with no purpose. Wanting to be happy or unhappy is a mundane calculation. This way of living is the most convenient and comfortable one.

This unconditionally suitable room is the seventh from the gate—

"lucky seven." I love number seven like a decoration. Who would have guessed that the partition of one room into two with sliding doors would symbolize my fate?

The outer part of the divided room gets some sun. In the morning, the sunlight enters in the shape of a wrapping cloth; in the afternoon, it goes out the size of a handkerchief. I do not need to tell you that I live in the inner part of the room, the half that sees no sun. I don't remember who decided that I would occupy the sunless part and my wife the sunny part, but I don't complain.

As soon as my wife goes out, I go into her room and open the window to admit the sun. The sunlight brings out the colors in the bottles on her dressing table. Watching the bright colors is my favorite pastime. I play by singeing tissue paper, which only my wife uses. If I focus the sun's rays with a magnifying glass, they become hotter and begin to scorch the paper. Presently a small flame begins to spread, accompanied by thin smoke. This happens quickly, but the anxious waiting for that moment, akin to wishing oneself dead, interests me.

If I get tired of this game, I play with my wife's small hand mirror, which has a handle. A mirror is useful only when one looks into it; otherwise it is nothing but a toy. Soon I get tired of the mirror, and my zeal for play leaps from the physical to the mental. Throwing the mirror down, I go to my wife's dressing table and look into the beautifully colored perfume bottles lined up in a row. These are more attractive to me than anything else in the world. Selecting and uncorking one, I bring it under my nose and inhale it as gently as if I were holding my breath. My eyes close themselves at the exotic sensual fragrance. Surely it's my wife's body odor. After recorking the bottle, I reflect: from which part of her body have I detected this particular fragrance? But this is unclear, because her odor is a composite of many fragrances.

My wife's room is always splendid. In contrast to my bare room, without even a nail on the wall, her wall has a row of hooks under the ceiling on which are hung her colorful skirts and blouses.[1] Their many patterns regale me. When I dream of her naked beneath her skirts, and of the various poses she might take, my mind loses its dignity.

---

[1]"Blouses" in translation stands for chŏgori (tops), the Korean jacket worn by both men and women and tied in front.

However, I have no clothes to speak of. My wife doesn't give me any. The Western suit I wear serves at once as my Sunday best, my ordinary clothes, and my pajamas. My undershirt for all seasons is a black turtleneck sweater. The reason for black, I presume, is that it doesn't require washing. Wearing soft shorts with elastic bands around the waist and the two legs, I play without complaint.

The sun has gone down without my knowing it, but my wife has not returned. Tired playing my own games and knowing that it's time for her return and that I should vacate her room, I creep back to my own room. It's dark. Covering myself with a quilt, I take a nap. The bedding, which has never been stowed away, has become a part of my body. I normally fall asleep right away, but sometimes I can't sleep even if I'm dead tired. At such times, I choose a theme and think about it. Under the damp bedding I invent and write. I've also composed poems. But as soon as I fall asleep, all these achievements evaporate into the stagnant air that fills my room.

When I wake up, I find that I'm a bundle of nerves, like a pillow stuffed with cotton rags or buckwheat husks. I loathe bedbugs. Even in winter I find a few in my room. If I have any problem in the world, it's my hatred of bedbugs. I scratch the bites till blood oozes out.

In the midst of a contemplative life in bed, I seldom thought about anything positive. There was no need to. If I had, I would have had to consult with my wife, and she would always have scolded me. Not that I feared her scolding, but it bothered me. Trying to do something as a social creature or being scolded by my wife—no, idling like a lazy animal suited me better. I sometimes wished to tear off my mask if I could, this meaningless human mask.

To me, human society was awkward. Life itself was irksome. All things were awkward to me.

My wife washes her face twice a day.
I don't wash at all.
At three or four in the morning, I go to the lavatory across the yard. On moonlit nights I used to stand in the yard for a while before returning to the room. Although I have never met any one of the eighteen families, I still remember the faces of almost all the young women in the compound. None of them rival my wife's beauty.

My wife's first washing, at eleven in the morning, is simple. Her second washing, at seven in the evening, is more elaborate, and she puts on far cleaner dresses at night than she does in the daytime. She goes out day and night.

Does my wife have a job? Perhaps, but I don't know what it is. If, like me, she has no job, there is no need for her to go out, but she does. And she has lots of visitors. When she has many visitors, I have to stay in my room all day long, covered with a quilt.

On such days I cannot play at making flames, or smell her cosmetics. And I am aware of being gloomy. Then my wife gives me some money, maybe a fifty-*chŏn* silver coin. I like that. But not knowing how to spend the coins, I at first put them beside my pillow, and they accumulated. Seeing the pile, my wife bought me a piggy bank that looked like a safe. I fed the coins into it one by one, and then my wife took away the key.

I recall putting silver coins into a box thereafter, but I was too lazy to count them. Sometime later, I espied a beehive-shaped hairpin in my wife's chignon; does this mean that my safe-shaped piggy bank has become lighter? In the end, however, I never again touched that piggy bank beside my pillow. My idleness didn't call my attention to such an object.

On days she has visitors, I find it hard to fall asleep, as I do on rainy days. On such days, I used to investigate why my wife had money all the time, and why she had a lot of money.

It seems that the visitors are unaware of my presence behind the sliding doors. Men tell jokes so easily to my wife, jokes that I would hesitate to tell her. Some visitors, however, seem more gentlemanly than others, leaving at midnight, while others stay on the whole night, eating. In general, things went smoothly, however.

I began to study the nature of my wife's job, but found it difficult to fathom because of my narrow conceptions and insufficient knowledge. I'm afraid I may never find it out.

My wife always wears new stockings. She cooks meals, too, though I've never seen her cooking. She brings me three meals a day in my room without fail. There are just the two of us, so it is certain that she herself has prepared the meals.

I eat alone and sleep alone. The food has no taste, and there are too few side dishes. Like a rooster or a puppy, I down my feed with no complaints. But deep within me I sometimes feel that my wife is unkind. I became skinny, my face grew paler, my energy visibly weakened day by day. Because of malnutrition, my bones began to stick out. I had to turn my body dozens of times a night, unable to remain for long on one side.

Meanwhile I kept on investigating the provenance of her money and what kind of food she shares with her guests. I could not fall asleep easily.

I perceived the truth at last. I realized that the money she uses must be given her for doubtful reasons by the visitors, who appeared to me nothing less than frivolous.

But why should they leave money, and why should she accept it? I could never understand the notion of such etiquette.

Well, was the transaction merely for etiquette's sake? Would not the money be a kind of payment or honorarium? Or did my wife seem to them one who deserved sympathy?

Whenever I indulge in such probing, my head swims. The conclusion I had reached before I fell asleep was that the subject was unpleasant. But I did not ask her about it, not only because it would be a nuisance, but also because, after a sound sleep, I used to forget everything.

Whenever visitors go away or when she returns from outside, she changes into a negligee and pays me a visit. Lifting my quilt, she tries to console me with strange words I can't understand. Then with a smile that is neither sneering, nor sardonic, nor hostile, I gaze at her beautiful face. She gives me a gentle smile. But I do not fail to notice a hint of sadness in her smile.

I know she notices that I am hungry. But she never gives me the leftovers in her room. It must be that she respects me. I like her respect, which is reassuring even when I am hungry. When she leaves me alone, not a word she has spoken remains with me. I see only the silver coin she has left behind, shining brightly in the electric light.

I've no idea how full the piggy bank is now. I never pick it up to see how much it weighs. I keep on feeding the coins through the button-hole-like slit with no volition, no supplication.

Why she should leave me coins is as difficult to determine as why her visitors leave money with her. I do not dislike the coins she gives me, but the feel of one of them in my fingers gives me a brief pleasure from the moment I pick it up till it disappears through the slit of the piggy bank. That's all there is to it.

One day I dumped the piggy bank into the latrine. I didn't know how much money was in it. How unreliable everything seemed to me when I realized that I was living on earth revolving fast like lightning through endless space. I wished I could quickly get off the speedy earth that makes me dizzy. Having pondered thus inside my quilt, putting the silver coins into the piggy bank became bothersome. I had hoped my wife would carry the piggy bank away. In fact, the piggy bank and money are useful to her, but they were meaningless to me from the start. I hoped she would take it away, but she didn't. I thought of putting it in her room myself but I had no chance because of her numerous guests. Having no alternative, I dumped it into the latrine.

With a heavy heart I awaited my wife's scolding. But no. She kept on leaving coins in my room. Without my knowing it, the coins began to pile up in a corner of the room.

I resumed my probing—the reason for my wife's giving me coins and her guest's leaving her money. It dawned on me at last that it had no other reason than a sort of pleasure. Pleasure, pleasure . . . Unexpectedly I began to acquire an interest in the subject. I wanted to experience the existence of pleasure.

Taking advantage of my wife's absence, I went out to the streets. I brought along all my coins and changed them into paper notes—five *wŏn*. Pocketing them, I walked and walked, heedless of where I was going, in order only to forget the reason for my walking. The streets that came into view after so long stimulated my nerves. I began to feel tired in no time, but I persisted. I kept walking till late at night, heedless of where I was going and oblivious to my original purpose. Of course I didn't spend a penny; I could not conceive the idea of spending money. I've completely lost the ability to spend.

I couldn't stand the fatigue any longer. I staggered home. I had to pass through my wife's room to reach my own. Thinking she might have a visitor, I stopped in front of the door and clumsily cleared my throat. To my consternation, the door slid open, and my wife and a man behind her glared at me. The sudden glare blinded me, and I fidgeted.

Not that I didn't see my wife's angry eyes, but I had to pretend I didn't, because I had to pass through her room to reach my own.

My legs gave out, and I could not stand. I covered myself with my quilt. My heart throbbed, and I was on the verge of fainting. I was out of breath, though I had not been aware of it on the streets. Cold perspiration broke out on my back. I regretted my adventure. I wanted to sleep in order to forget the fatigue. I wanted a sound sleep.

After a rest, lying on my belly, my heart's wild beating subsided. I thought I was alive again. Turning to lie on my back, I stretched out my legs.

However, my heart again began to beat rapidly. I listened through the sliding doors to my wife and her man whispering. In order to sharpen my hearing, I opened my eyes and held my breath. But by that time I heard my wife and the man getting up, the man putting on his coat and hat, and then the noise of the door opening, the loud thud of the man's leather shoes on the ground, followed by my wife's rubber shoes softly treading, and their steps finally receding toward the gate.

I'd never seen my wife act this way before. She had never whispered to a man. Lying in my room, I used to miss what the men said when they were drunk, but I always caught every word my wife spoke in her even clear voice, neither too loud nor too low. Even when she said something that went against the grain, I felt relieved at her composed tone.

But there had to be some reason for her present attitude, I thought, and I felt displeased. But I made up my mind not to probe anything that night and tried to sleep. Sleep did not come for a long while, and my wife did not return until late. I must have slept at last. My dreams roamed amid the incoherent street scenes I had witnessed.

Someone shook me violently. It was my wife, and she had sent off her guest. I opened my eyes and stared at her. There was no smile on her face. After rubbing my eyes, I looked at her more attentively. Her eyes were filled with anger, and her lips trembled convulsively. It seemed her anger would not subside quickly, so I closed my eyes. I awaited her tirade. But presently I heard her rise, breathing gently, and swishing her skirt; then there came the sound of the sliding doors opening and closing. Lying still like a frog, I regretted my sortie more than my hunger.

Inside the bedding, I begged my wife's pardon. I told her it was a misunderstanding. I had returned home thinking it was past midnight —indeed not before midnight, as she had said. I was too tired. I had walked too far and too long, and that was my fault, if fault there must be. I wanted to give five *wŏn* to someone in order to feel the pleasure of giving away money. That was all there was to it. If you think that sort of wish is wrong, it's all right with me. I concede I was wrong. Don't you see I am repenting?

If I could have spent five *wŏn*, I would not have returned before midnight. But I could not. Because the streets were too complex, swarming with people. Indeed I could not figure out to whom I should give the five *wŏn*. And in the midst of it all, I ended up staggering with exhaustion.

The first thing I wanted was rest. I wanted to lie down. Hence I returned home. I'm sorry I miscalculated—I thought it was past midnight. I'm sorry. I'm willing to apologize a hundred times. But if I failed to dispel her misunderstanding, what good is my apology? What a disheartening thing!

For an hour, I had to fret like this. I pushed aside the quilt, rose, slid open the door, and staggered into my wife's room. I almost lost consciousness. I remember throwing myself down on her quilt, producing the five *wŏn* from my trouser pocket, and shoving them at her.

When I awoke the following morning, I found myself inside my wife's bedding. It was the first time I had slept in her room since we moved to compound number thirty-three.

The sun's rays were filtering in through the window, but my wife was already out. Well, she might have gone out last night when I lost consciousness. I did not want to investigate. I was out of sorts and had no strength left to move my fingers. A spot of sunlight the size of a kerchief dazzled my eyes. Countless particles of dust danced wildly in the bright sunbeam. I felt my nose stuffing up. I closed my eyes, covered myself with the quilt, and tried to take a nap, but my wife's odor was provocative. I twisted and turned, and in the midst of recalling all the cosmetic bottles lined up on her dressing table and the perfume that wafted up the moment I uncorked them, I could not fall asleep, however desperately I tried.

Unable to calm down, I kicked the quilt to one side, got up with a jerk and returned to my room. I found a tray of food neatly laid out, already cold. She had gone out, leaving my feed behind. At first, I was hungry. But the moment I scooped up a spoonful of rice, I felt a sensation akin to putting cold ashes into my mouth. I threw the spoon down and crept into the quilt. The bedding that had missed me the previous whole night welcomed me. Covered with my quilt, this time I slept a deep sleep for a long while.

It was only after sunlight came in that I awoke. My wife didn't seem to be at home yet. Or, she might have returned but gone out again. But what was the use of examining the matter carefully?

I felt refreshed. I began to recall what had happened the night before. I cannot adequately tell of the pleasure I felt when I thrust the five *wŏn* into my wife's hand. I think I've discovered the psychology of the guests who leave money for my wife and my wife's state of mind when she leaves coins for me. I was delighted beyond measure and smiled to myself. How ludicrous I'd been not to understand their feelings. My shoulders began to dance.

Therefore I wanted to go out again tonight, but I had no money. I regretted having given my wife the five *wŏn* all at once. I regretted having thrown the piggy bank into the lavatory. Disappointed, but out of habit, I put my hand into the trouser pocket that had once contained five *wŏn* and searched around. Unexpectedly my hand came out with something. Only two *wŏn*. It didn't have to be much money. I mean, any amount would do; I was grateful.

Oblivious of my shabby suit and the hunger that assailed me, I went out to the streets swinging my arms. Going out, I wished time would fly like an arrow so that it would soon be past midnight. Handing money to my wife and spending the night in her room were fine in every respect, but to return home mistakenly before midnight and provoke her into looking daggers at me was terribly frightening. I kept watching the street clocks while roaming about, heedless of where I went. I did not tire quickly this time. Only time's slow progress frustrated me.

After ascertaining by the Seoul railway station clock that it was past midnight, I turned toward home. That night I encountered my wife and her man standing at the gate talking. Assuming an unconcerned air, I brushed by them and went straight into my room. Presently my wife returned to hers. Then she began to sweep the floor, which she had hitherto never done. As soon as I heard her lying down, I slid open the door, went into her room, and thrust the two *wŏn* into her hand. She stole a glance at me, as though she thought it strange that I had returned home again without spending the money. At least she allowed me to sleep in her room. I would not exchange that joy for anything in the world. I slept well.

When I woke up, my wife was already out again. I then went to my room and took a nap. When she aroused me by shaking me, light was already streaming in. My wife asked me to come to her room, the first time she had ever bestowed such a favor. She dragged me by the arms, smiling all the while. I was apprehensive lest a terrible conspiracy lurk behind her changed attitude.

Leaving everything to her, I let her drag me into her room. There was a neat supper table. Come to think of it, I had gone two days without food. Forgetting that I was starved, I equivocated.

I began to think. I wouldn't regret it even if she raised hell soon after this last supper. In fact, I'd been bored to death by the world of man. With my mind at ease and in peace, I ate the strange supper with my wife. We two seldom exchanged a word, so after supper I returned to my room. She did not detain me. I sat leaning against the wall and lit a cigarette. And waited for a thunderbolt. Let it strike me if it must.

Five minutes, ten minutes . . .

But no thunderbolt. Gradually the tension subsided. I thought of going out again tonight and wished I had money.

Of course, I had none. What pleasure could there have been in going out? I felt giddy. Incensed, I covered myself with the quilt and tossed and turned. My supper seemed to rise up in my throat. I felt nauseous.

Why doesn't paper money—even small amounts of it—rain down from heaven? Sadness overtook me. I had no way of obtaining money. I must have wept in bed, asking why I didn't have money.

My wife came into the room once more. Startled, I crouched like a toad and held my breath, anticipating her thunderbolt. But the words she spoke were tender and friendly. She said she knew why I wept. I wept because of the lack of money, she said. I was taken aback. How does she read others' minds? I was a trifle frightened, but I hoped, from the way she was talking, that she might give me some money—if so, how happy I would be. Wrapped in the quilt, I did not raise my head, but awaited her next move. "There," she said. Then came the sound of something falling beside my pillow. Judging from how light it sounded it had to be paper notes. Then she whispered into my ear that she would not mind if I returned a bit later than last night. That wouldn't be too difficult; what made me happy and grateful in the first place was the money.

At any rate, I went out. Since I am night-blind, I decided to walk around the brightly lit streets. Then I dropped in at the coffee shop next to the first- and second-class passengers' waiting room in Seoul station. That shop was a great discovery.

First, no acquaintances of mine patronize the place. Even if they came in, they left right away. I made up my mind: henceforth I would while away my time there.

Also, the shop's clock, more than any other in the city, must tell the correct time. If I tactlessly trusted incorrect clocks and returned home ahead of time, I would faint again.

Occupying a whole booth, I drank a cup of hot coffee. Travelers seemed to be enjoying their coffee in the midst of the bustle. They drank it quickly, gazing at the walls as if they were meditating, and then went out. I felt sad. But the melancholy mood pleased me more than the intrusive atmosphere of other coffee shops in the city. The occasional shrill or thundering steam whistles were louder than the

Mozart played in the shop. I read and reread, up and down, down and up, the menu with its meager selection of dishes. Their exotic names, like the names of my childhood playmates, entered and left my vision.

I had no idea how long I had sat there, my mind meandering, when I noticed that the place was almost deserted, and the boys were tidying up the shop. It must have been time to close, at a little after eleven. This was no haven after all! Where could I spend one more hour? Worried, I left the coffee shop. It was raining. Heavy sheets of rain fell, intending to afflict me, who had no raincoat or umbrella. Looking as weird as I did, loitering in the waiting room was out of the question. A bit of rain would do me no harm. I stepped out.

Soon I felt an unbearable chill. My suit began to drip, and in no time the rain had soaked through to my skin. I tried to keep on wandering about the streets braving the rain, but I reached the point where I could no longer endure the chill. I shivered with cold, and my teeth chattered.

I quickened my gait and thought: probably my wife would have no visitors on a wet night like this. I decided to go home. If, unfortunately, there were guests, I would explain the unavoidable circumstances. They would understand my plight.

No sooner had I got home than I discovered that my wife did have a guest. I was cold and wet and, in the confusion, I forgot to knock. I witnessed a scene that my wife would have liked me not to. With my soaking-wet feet I strode across her room and reached my own. Casting off my dripping garments, I covered myself with the quilt. I kept on shivering; the cold became intense. I felt as if the floor under me were sinking. I lost consciousness.

When I opened my eyes the next day, my wife was sitting beside my pillow, looking concerned. I had caught cold. The chill and headache persisted, and my mouth was full of bitter water.

Pressing her palm on my forehead, she told me to take some medicine. Judging from the coolness of her palm, I had a fever. She reappeared with four white pills and a glass of lukewarm water. "Take them and have a good sleep. You'll be all right," she said. I gulped the pills down and covered myself with the quilt. I fell asleep at a stroke, like a dead man.

I was laid up for several days with a running nose, during which time I kept on taking pills. I got over the cold, but a bitter taste like sumac lingered in my mouth.

I began wishing to stir out again, but my wife advised me not to.

She told me to keep on taking the pills every day and rest. "You got a cold by roaming about to no purpose, causing me trouble," she said. She had a point. So I vowed not to go out, and planned to take the pills just to build up my health.

I kept on sleeping day and night. Strangely, I felt sleepy day and night and could not stand the feeling. I believed it to be a sure sign that I was regaining strength.

Thus I must have spent almost a month sleeping. My too-long hair and moustache were uncomfortable, so I went to my wife's room while she was away and sat before her dressing table. I decided to cut my hair and smell her bottles of cosmetics at random. In the midst of the various aromas I detected her odor which made me lose my composure. I called her name to myself: "Yŏnsim!"

Once again after a long while I played with her glasses. And I played with her hand mirror. The sun filtering through the window was very warm. It was May, come to think of it.

I had a good stretch, laid myself down on her pillow, and wished to boast to the gods of my comfortable and joyous existence. I had no traffic with the community of man. The gods probably could neither punish nor praise me.

But the next moment I caught sight of a strange thing: a box of Adalin—sleeping pills. I discovered the box under her dressing table, and thought they looked very much like aspirin. I lifted the lid and found four tablets missing.

I remembered taking four pills that morning. I had slept the day before, the day before that, and the day before that . . . I was unable to resist sleep. My cold was over, but she kept on feeding me aspirin. Once, a fire had broken out in the neighborhood while I was sleeping, but I had slept through it. I had slept that soundly. I must have been taking Adalin for a month, thinking it was aspirin. This was too much!

All of a sudden I felt giddy and nearly fainted. Pocketing the Adalin box, I left home. I climbed a hill. I loathed seeing all the things in the world of man. Walking, I resolved not to think about anything related to my wife. I thought about flat rocks, about azaleas I'd never seen before, about larks, and about the rocks laying eggs to hatch. Fortunately, I did not faint on the way.

I found a bench. I sat in meditation, thinking about aspirin and Adalin. My head was too confused to think coherently. In five minutes, I became frustrated and cross. Taking the Adalin box from my pocket, I chewed down all six tablets. What a funny taste! I then laid myself down on the bench. Why did I do such a thing? I do not understand. I just wanted to. I fell asleep right there. In my sleep, I heard the faint gurgling of a brook among the rocks.

When I woke up, it was broad daylight. I had slept one day and one night. The scene around me looked yellowish. Even in such a state, a thought flashed through my mind: aspirin, Adalin.

Aspirin, Adalin, aspirin, Adalin, Marx, Malthus, Madras, aspirin, Adalin.

My wife had cheated me into taking Adalin for a month. Judging from the Adalin box I had discovered in her room, the evidence was indisputable.

To what end had she put me to sleep day and night? After putting me to sleep, what did she do day and night?

Did she intend to kill me bit by bit?

On the other hand, it might very well be that what I had taken for a month was aspirin. She might had taken it herself in order to sleep away something that troubled her. If so, I was the one to be sorry. I was sorry to have harbored such a great suspicion.

I hurriedly climbed down the hill. My legs gave in, my head was dizzy, and I barely made my way home. It was shortly before eight.

I intended to apologize for my perverse thoughts. I was in such a hurry the words failed me.

Oh, what a disaster! I witnessed something I should absolutely never have laid eyes on. In my confusion, I closed the door and stood leaning against the post, my head lowered and my eyes closed, trying to allay my dizziness. In a second the door opened, and out came my wife, her clothes still in disarray. My head swam, and I fell head over heels. Astride me, she began to bite me all over. The pain nearly killed me. Having neither will nor energy enough to protest, I remained prostrate, awaiting what would come next. A man came, took my wife in his arms and carried her into the room. I loathed her for so docilely submitting to his embrace. I loathed him.

"Are you spending the night prowling and whoring around?" she reviled me. I was mortified. I was dumbfounded, and words failed me.

I wanted to shout back at her, "Didn't you try to kill me?" My allegation might prove to be groundless, which would bring disaster. I'd rather keep silent in spite of my undeserved poor treatment. I stood up, dusted myself off, emptied out my trouser pocket—God knows what made me do it—and stealthily pushed a few paper notes and coins under my wife's doorsill. Then I ran out.

Narrowly escaping a collision with some passing cars, I managed to find Seoul station. Sitting in an empty booth, I wanted to remove the bitter taste in my mouth.

Oh for a cup of hot coffee! As soon as I stepped into the station hall, I realized that I had forgotten that I was penniless. Dazed, I loitered helplessly, heedless of direction, not knowing what to do. Like a half-wit, I wandered here and there . . .

I could not recall where I'd been. The moment I realized that I was on the top floor of the Mitsukoshi department store, it was almost noon.

I sat down in the first seat I could find and recalled the twenty-six years of my life. Nothing emerged clearly in my dim recollections.

I asked myself: what desires have I had in my life? I did not want to answer. I disliked that kind of question. It was hard for me to recognize even my own existence.

Bending over, I looked at some goldfish in a bowl. How handsome they were! The little ones, the big ones—all of them looked fresh and wonderful. They cast their shadows in the bowl under the May sun. The movement of their fins resembled those of people waving handkerchiefs. Trying to count the number of fins, I remained bent over. My back was warm.

I looked down into the bustling streets. The tired pedestrians jostled wearily, like the fins of the goldfish. Entangled in a slimy rope, they could not free themselves. Dragging along my body which was crumbling from fatigue and hunger, I too must be swept away into the bustling streets.

Coming out, a thought flashed through my mind: where would my steps lead me?

We had a misunderstanding. Could my wife feed me Adalin in place of aspirin? I couldn't believe it. There was no reason for her to do so. Then, did I steal and whore around? Certainly not!

As a couple, we are destined to go lame. There is no need to see logic in my wife's behavior or my own. No need to defend ourselves either. Let facts be facts and let misunderstandings be misunderstandings. Limping through life endlessly, isn't that so?

However, whether or not I should return to my wife was a trifle difficult to decide. Should I go? Where should I go?

At that moment, the shrill noon whistle sounded. People were flapping their limbs like chickens; the moment when all sorts of glass, steel, marble, paper currency, and ink seemed to be boiling up, bubbling—noon with extreme splendor.

All of a sudden my armpits began to itch. Ah, these are the traces of where my man-made wings once grew, the wings I no longer possess. Torn shreds of hope and ambition shuffled like dictionary pages in my mind.

I halted, wanting to shout:

> Wings, grow again!
> Let me fly, fly, fly; let me fly once more.
> Let me try them once again.

TRANSLATED AND ABRIDGED BY PETER H. LEE

Kim Tongni

As a defender of humanism, Kim Tongni (b. 1913) interprets the incursion of foreign civilization not as a historical necessity but as a conflict between ideology and ideology. To him enlightenment is not political or economic, but cultural. In his earlier works that concern the crumbling of traditional society, he views the family as its nucleus. His characters are closed people controlled by fatalism and nihilism. They solve their relations with others and nature by precedent and custom—for to extricate oneself from folkways means death. When tradition is gone, we should seek our true home in a timeless mythic age. Kim seeks the ur-form of experience in Korea's incantatory indigenous beliefs. His attempts to transcend history, however, lead him to neglect the problems of the real world.

Originally published in May 1936, "The Rock" was revised twice, in 1947 and 1976. The leper's ritual of grinding rock is not so much for a miraculous healing but for a reunion with her son Suri. Throughout his stories, Kim's stress on maternal love and the mother's role in the family is consonant with the place of matrimony in indigenous shamanism. The leper's grief and her merciful prayer for reunion may very well stand for Korea's sorrow under Japanese rule and the country's appeal for liberation.

THE ROCK

The cry of the wild goose is in the northern sky. Autumn is coming. The firefly is no longer on the wing, not even at night, and the Milky Way is gradually drifting near the dome of the sky. But for some people the cry of the wild goose is an unwelcome sound, people who have no homes and who are used to falling down and spending the night wherever it happens to find them.

A group of cripples, beggars, and lepers has gathered beneath a railway bridge a little way from town. The coming of autumn is a worry for all of them—for the man lying with his feet wrapped in coarse straw matting, the man lying with his body buried in sand, the man sitting with a sack thrown around his shoulders.

"The nights have got really chilly," an old cripple says, and immediately a man with a twisted arm takes him up on it.

"Chilly is it! My limbs are all caught up in a ball!"

On one side a tremendous racket accompanies the teaching of one of those songs beggars use on market day.

I may look like a beggar, but I'm the son of a minister of state.
I could be governor of a province, yet here I am singing for pennies.

When they get about this far in the song, the "teacher" raises his hand, stops the performance, and proceeds to deliver a lecture.

"Body movement is everything. Whether you are wriggling your backside or swinging your head or dribbling excited spits as you swagger with the music, it's all got to match the rhythm."

The lecture ends and straightaway two beggar kids sing out lustily:

Who is your teacher? He's better than me.
Has he read the *Book of Songs* and the *Book of History?*[1] His style is cultivated.
Has he read the *Analects* and *Mencius?*[2] Every verse is really fine.

This time everything is fine—head and arm action, the swinging of the hips.

"Ah, ha," they cry and laugh in unison. Everyone seems pleased.

A train goes by and immediately the group of lepers gathered in the lower corner has a new subject for discussion.

"Do you hear word of your son often, missus?"

The woman just shakes her head. She is the most recent arrival to the group.

Silence for a while and a black gloom wraps them round.

"They say the Japs are going to kill off everyone suffering from paralysis."

"They're not going to kill people who've done no wrong."

It was the latest arrival who comments—the woman who had come from the village.

"Ah, the weather's got right cold now, all right."

---

[1]*Book of Songs:* China's oldest anthology of poetry containing three hundred and five poems; one of the Confucian classics. *Book of History (Book of Documents):* a collection of didactic speeches, exhortations, and debates attributed to rulers and ministers of ancient China from the legendary Emperor Yao to the return of the defeated army of the Ch'in in 626 B.C.

[2]*Analects:* a record of conversations between Confucius (551–479 B.C.) and his disciples as recorded by the latter. *Mencius:* a record of Mencius's (372–289 B.C.) opinions expressed in the form of interviews and conversations.

The young man beside her mutters again, and immediately thoughts of her son run through the village woman's head. Up till last year she too had had a husband and a son.

Her son's name was Suri. Although he still hadn't got married by the time he was nearly thirty, he had saved up well over a hundred *wŏn* and was an object of envy among his own friends. They say he always maintained that he would get married and set up his own place when he had saved up two hundred *wŏn*. Because of this he never allowed himself the drink he always felt like having; in winter he generally got by without wearing heavy woollen socks. In all probability, he would have got himself a wife and lived out a quiet, respectable life, had not the dread hand of disease reached out to his mother.

In one single night's drinking and gambling, Suri threw away the twenty-odd *wŏn* that still remained of his savings, money not yet spent on medicine for his mother, and from that day on he was like a man deranged. He would wander around the streets with two raging, bloodshot eyes, cursing and fighting with the villagers for no reason at all, and he was liable at any moment to set fire to his mother's hut. Then in the middle of all this, quite without warning, he just took off somewhere. That was this year, early in spring, when the buds were about to come out in the trees.

After he lost his son, the old man became more coarse and violent with every passing day. He came home drunk every night and beat his wife. Quite often he would forget to get food for her for several days at a time, and he was forever at her to die.

"Why can't you just die?"

" . . ."

"I still have the strength left to bury you snug."

His wife cried bitterly every time she heard him say this. He hadn't always been this way. Up to a few months ago he would click his tongue in compassion when he offered her rice, the wine, and the scraps of meat he had managed to find.

"Eat that up and it'll make you better."

This was after they had been thrown out of servants' quarters. He had built a hut behind the village and installed his wife there, while he himself wandered around from house to house working as a day laborer and running errands for a tavern.

It was early summer this year, when the barley was about to ripen. Ugly rumors—of a wolf that carried off a child in a faraway village, of a leper in a barley field—began to spread through the village. The old man, well drunk, came to his wife's hut. Under his shirt, wrapped in newspaper, he had a lump of rice-cake mixed with arsenic. It was evening. His wife had the straw mat that shaded the door pulled aside and was busy scraping bean paste stew from the sides of the pot with the stump of a spoon. As soon as she saw the old man she waved her hand and shook off the flies that were crawling on her face. She tried to force a smile on her sad face.

The old man, tense with excitement, fingered the lump of rice-cake under his shirt. Even after going inside the hut he continued for some time to gaze silently at his wife, his eyes unnaturally bright with alcohol. Suddenly he felt once again under his shirt.

When she first got the rice-cake she looked up gratefully at the old man. But she knew the color of arsenic when she saw it, and when she discovered the dark-red substance mixed in the rice-cake she glared at the old man for a long moment, and her look was frightening.

The cry of the cuckoo came from a distant mountain ridge. Finally, the woman understood everything and bent her head. Tears rolled down her black, blotchy, corpse-like face.

The old man, as if embarrassed, ignored her. He spat and got up. "Die, can't you. You're only trouble."

He spat once again to hide his discomfort.

The next day the villagers whispered the following story. For a while after her husband had gone off, the woman continued to cry by herself. In the end she ate the rice-cake all right, but death was not so easy to come by. Eventually she just had to go somewhere and, they say, she left the rice-cake thrown up all over the hut.

The woman wandered around all the villages, wherever her strength would carry her. This wasn't because begging was easier in the villages than in the marketplace, but because she thought she just might happen to meet her beloved son. A summer of begging and sleeping out of doors went by in vain. In fact the idea that she might meet her son before autumn was completely hopeless. It was about this time, too, that she began to be lonely for the old man.

"I still have the strength left to bury you snug."

She thought of how the old man used to force death on her until she couldn't bear it, and yet she felt that if she were to meet him now, he'd build her some sort of hut for the winter.

One day, in desperation, the woman built a little hut on a hillock with her own hands. "Hut" is an exaggeration; it was nothing but sand and mud thrown on a three-pole frame, with a coarse straw mat spread over it—about enough, at best, to keep off the frost. It wasn't much, but she had had to wrestle with it for many days. Dirt lodged in her mouth, her nose, her eyes, everywhere there was an opening. Her skin couldn't be any more chapped; her bones were numb with pain.

She was ill for two days, just lying there, not knowing where she was. On the third day the owner of the field came. He cursed at her for some time and then roared.

"You've got today to pull your hut down, and if you don't I'll set fire to it and burn it down."

He then left. Now it wasn't only that she hadn't the strength to build again—although this was true—but there just wasn't another suitable place in the area. So she couldn't take the hut down, not even to save it from the flames. And in actual fact she didn't want to leave the vicinity of the railway bridge under any circumstances. This was because of a huge rock at the entrance to the village, right on her way from the railway bridge to the market. The rock had many names —the Rock of Blessings, because it was said to dispense blessings; Wishing Rock, because the people said it granted wishes; Tiger Rock, because it was shaped like a tiger lying down. These were only a few of its many names. There was a continuous stream of young women right through the four seasons who came to implore these blessings. They would sit on the rock all day long, rubbing it with a stone about the size of one's fist, and if the stone stuck to the rock it meant that the wish would be granted. There were even women who used to wrap up some rice and spend day after day rubbing the Rock of Blessings.

It wasn't only the women that came to implore blessings who dearly prized the rock. The local children used to play horse there, and the old people used to view the fields from there, with their backs resting against the rock. All the village people, without exception, set great value on the rock.

Suri's mother was no exception; the rock was important to her, as well. She believed that by rubbing the rock she would get to meet her beloved son. There's no knowing how many times she rubbed that rock and called Suri's name while managing to avoid being seen by the villagers.

About two weeks after she began rubbing the rock, it came about, whether by chance or as an answer to her prayer, that she met the son whom day and night she had so longed to see. It was in the morning when the marketplace was jammed with traders. Suddenly there was someone pulling her sleeve as, gourd in hand, she was about to go into an eatery. In that moment she knew instinctively that it was Suri. She lifted her head, and she saw her son's face. For a brief moment the mother's long, white bucktooth was visible.

The son grasped his mother's hands and they began walking. There was an old ruined castle a little way from the market and beside it a lane that had been there since olden times. The lane was covered with autumn grass so that not even the shadow of a passerby could be seen.

The two of them sat on the grassy lane holding each other and calling each other's name.

"Mother."

"Suri."

Streams of tears flowed from their eyes.

"Mother, where . . . how have you been? How have you been able to live? . . . Mother!"

The mother, her long bucktooth bared, could only cry. Even if flesh and blood itself were rotting, her tears were as plentiful as ever.

"Mother, how I've searched for you! How . . ."

Suri buried his head in his mother's lap and wept.

A red dragonfly lit on the flower of a buckwheat stalk which had sprung up in the middle of the wild grass. A snake on the hill opposite, its back a maze of designs, disappeared through a crack in the rock.

"I'll go try and raise some money quickly, Mother. You must come live with me. And please, please, you mustn't die till I come with the money."

He was stroking his mother's shoulders and arms as he made this request. Tears of dejection streamed down from his red eyes.

They went back to the marketplace. Suri pressed four *yang* into his mother's hand and promising to come back in four days he left her at the rice-cake stall. The sun was already high in the sky. The marketplace was filled with the shouts of people coming and going. People driving cattle; people carrying wood; women standing there with babies on their backs and small wooden barrels balanced on their heads (what did they contain?); youths flying around on bicycles; a Jap upstart sitting in a swaying rickshaw—all laughing and chattering, or at each other's throats fighting, or crying as they ate. . . . It was like the buzzing of swarming bees, and Suri, head bent, wandered vacantly in the middle of it all.

"The railway bridge beyond the Rock of Blessings."

He muttered this a few times as he wandered around the market, an empty A-frame pack slung on his back. It was a long time since he had been to the market, and he really wished he could go away with news of his father. But no one could give him clear information. Some said that the old man was half-paralyzed and wandering in the streets, others said he had asthma, could hardly breathe, and was running errands for some inn in town. There was nothing comforting in the news he got.

From the time Suri's mother had succeeded in meeting her son, her thoughts more than ever centered on him. She roamed the market every day, craning her neck to spot him again. But the promised four days went by, then two weeks, then a month, and still he didn't appear.

With the passing of time her whole faith and trust became more and more bound up with the rock. It was as if she would always have the hope of meeting her son again so long as the rock stood on the ground, and perhaps even her own illness might somehow be completely cured.

"Come rain, come snow, just keep rubbing the Rock of Blessings."

Deep in the night, when everyone was asleep and she wouldn't be seen, she used to drag her sick, leaden body to the rock and caress the rock with her hand.

But this time it wasn't as before. The Rock of Blessings didn't so easily produce an answer to her prayers. She thought she was probably rubbing the rock in the dead of night and not using it properly. Beginning the next day, she decided that insofar as she could she would take advantage of moments when no one was looking, and rub the rock in the daytime.

It's very difficult to avoid people's eyes in the daytime, however. One day as she was rubbing the rock, imploring it to grant her request to see her son, she was noticed by some of the villagers. Suddenly a straw rope was wound around her. She fell bodily from the rock. Dragged along like a dog, her legs trussed up in the rope, her whole body burst into one bloody wound. She lost consciousness. When eventually she opened her eyes, barely conscious, a workman from the local village office was washing the rock with water.

After that she never passed beside the rock without stopping dead in her tracks and staring at it fixedly for a moment. To anyone standing nearby it looked as if her feet had somehow stuck to the ground of their own accord. For her the rock represented something she longed for and missed indescribably, and at the same time something hateful and spiteful. She regarded all her happiness and misfortune as tied up with that rock.

On this day, too, she was on her way back from the market where she had been roaming all day long. It was evening. Mountain, stream, and village were all clothed in twilight. As always she had a gourd clasped to her breast as she passed the village. In the gourd she had a whole mess of rice, rice cake, taffy, overripe persimmon, buckwheat paste, jujubes, noodles, bean sprouts, cod heads, dried pollack tails, and the like, all in a lump. Her head had fallen far forward and she was pulling her legs heavily. Every now and again she would turn her head, stand for a moment, and then after a quick glance in the gourd force her steps forward again.

"Why didn't I press the point and ask just now?"

She muttered this to herself several times. "Just now" referred to when she was getting the bean paste at the bean paste stall and the old man beside her selling persimmons was saying to someone else:

"Did you know that Suri is getting out for good?"

"Didn't he get six months? Is he getting out already?"

She had heard secondhand stories like this only too often before. This time she had been too busy getting her bean paste to concentrate on what people beside her were saying. Besides, it seemed so unlikely that anyone would be talking about her son that the conversation had only half-registered with her. But now as she was coming down the village road looking at the Rock of Blessings, what had been said in the market suddenly came into her mind. Now it seemed quite clear that those people had in fact used Suri's name.

"Ah, surely it was Suri they were talking about."

The more she thought about it, the more certain she was that they had been talking about him. It was as if she could still hear Suri's name in her ear. She stopped, stood, hesitated for a moment whether she should go back to the market, and then continued on down toward the rock. Her whole body throbbed with pain; her legs felt heavy enough to fall off. Her head swam dizzily.

When she got to the rock it was after sunset, those first moments of evening when darkness begins to spread its wings in the corners of distant fields. As always she stopped when she came face to face with the rock. She lifted her head and stared at it. Then, turning her head again, she looked in the direction of the hut. Then it happened. What she saw was not the tiny hut that she usually saw there; this time she saw flames leaping up into the sky. For a second she doubted her own eyes. She looked again and still she saw flames. Behind closed eyes the flames continued to roar. Eyes closed—flames; eyes open—flames. Flames, flames, flames. She collapsed on the rock like a stick of wood.

She groped the rock with hands that were already without feeling. Then, embracing it, she rubbed her black, corpse-like face against it, seemingly content.

One cold tear rolled down the rock.

The following day the villagers gathered beside the rock. They spat as they spoke.

"The dirty thing would have to die here."

"A leper dying with her arms around the Rock of Blessings."

"Our precious rock."

The tears of the woman on the rock had dried into crystals.

TRANSLATED BY KEVIN O'ROURKE

MODERN POETRY

II

Yi Sanghwa (1900–1943), Sim Hun (1904–1937), Yi Yuksa (1904–1944), and Yun Tongju (1917–1945) knew how to express in poetry their encounter with history and to expand the poet's consciousness and establish his authority. The speaker in Yi Sanghwa's "Does Spring Come to Stolen Fields?" (1926) wishes to return to the earth as a child might return to his mother. But the mother as land, or land as the mother, are both unattainable.

Sim Hun, in "When That Day Comes," reveals his aspirations to independence in impassioned language. The speaker says he will "soar like a crow at night / and pound the Chongno bell with [his] head," and "skin [his] body and make / a magical drum and march with it / in the vanguard." Couched in the language of impossibility, the poem is an affirmation of the speaker's unshakable belief in the day of liberation. The Chongno bell was struck on festival days in the past. The speaker looks forward to the day when the bell will resound and the "thundering shout" of his people will greet the restoration. In his claim that nature will share his joy and rise and dance with him, Sim uses the ancient trope of a moment so rapturous, a joy so extreme, that the speaker will burst the confines of his body.[1]

Yi Yuksa was imprisoned seventeen times for political crimes against the Japanese and perished in prison in Beijing. All the lines in "The Summit" (1939) have four stresses and are metrically self-contained. The poem's power comes from the use of personification ("season's whip"), metaphor ("vexed steps"; "sword-blade frost"), metonymy ("bend my knees"), and oxymoron ("steel rainbow"), as well as a

---

[1]See Maurice Bowra, *Poetry and Politics 1900–1960* (Cambridge: Cambridge University Press, 1966), pp. 92–93.

combination of harsh aspirated consonants that creates the rhythm and enriches the meaning. The fusion of sound and sense evokes the encroachment of winter, as the speaker struggles to "outface / The winds and persecutions of the sky." The speaker is modern in that he reveals a vision of a moment of time, a new way of viewing human existence. Like certain of Hemingway's heroes, the speaker makes no pretense of sentiment or self-pity; he is faithful to his experience, which is universally valid.

The recurrent concerns of Yun Tongju, who perished in Fukuoka prison on February 16, 1945, are the sorrows of the oppressed, the reality of death, and the predicament of the sensitive and frustrated individual overwhelmed by existential despair and spiritual desolation. At times he feels a nostalgic dismay and pity at the image of his divided and displaced self, which the age erodes and obliterates, as in "Confessions" (1942). Dispassionately viewing an immense void, he realizes that it is futile to seek an elusive relief. Tormented by exile and unfulfillment, these poets led brief but meaningful lives. Their pessimism was finally balanced by affirmation, the celebration of a triumph of the self that was purchased with sacrifice.

Chŏng Chiyong (b. 1903) left behind him a legacy that every aspiring Korean poet continues to learn and imitate. The creator of arrestingly modern poetry in its sensibility and an alchemist of words with dazzling verbal and imagistic dexterity, Chŏng's first collection (1935) was followed by *White Deer Lake* (1941). The title poem, comprising nine sections in prose, presents the poet's experience in a vivid colloquial style. The theme may be conventional (for it belongs to a body of works on the same theme), but the poet's use of the right words in the right context produces an effect that is utterly modern. Compact phrasing and a judicious, and very distinctive, blending of Sino-Korean and native words suggest the speaker's "discovery of his thought in the process of saying it." Upon seeing a motherless calf, the speaker thinks of having to "entrust [his] children to a strange mother" (section 6). He also contemplates his ultimate homecoming: "I won't mind turning white as a birch after death" (section 3). The audacious listing of alpine plants, included primarily for their sounds, may be unpoetic in itself, at least in the hands of a lesser poet. Here, however, the enumeration is given new life (section 8).

Yi Yuksa

THE SUMMIT

Beaten by the bitter season's whip,
I am driven at last to this north.

I stand upon the sword-blade frost,
Where numb sky and plateau merge.

I do not know where to bend my knees,
Nor where to lay my vexed steps.

I cannot but close my eyes and think—
Winter
    Winter is a steel rainbow.

DEEP-PURPLE GRAPES

In July in my native land
Purple grapes ripen in the sun.

Village wisdom clusters on the vines
As distant skies enter each berry.

The sea below the sky opens its heart,
A white sail moves toward shore.

The traveler I long for would come then,
Wrapping his wayworn body with a blue robe.

If only I could share these grapes with him
I wouldn't mind if the juice wet my hands.

Child, take out a white linen napkin,
Spread it on our table's silver platter.

THE LAKE

My mind would dash and run
But my eyes, wind-washed, still meditate.

At times I invite swans, and unloose them;
Embracing the shores I weep at night.

As I ponder the shadow of a dim star,
Purple mist settles like a thinking cap.

THE WIDE PLAIN

On a distant day
When heaven first opened,
Somewhere a cock must have crowed.

No mountain ranges
Rushing to the longed-for sea
Could have dared to invade this land.

While busy seasons gust and fade
With endless time,
A great river first opens the way.

Now snow falls,
The fragrance of plum blossoms is far off.
I'll sow the seeds of my sad song here.

When a superman comes
On a white horse down the myriad years,
Let him sing aloud my song on the wide plain.

FLOWER

In the east where the sky ends
And not even a drop of rain falls,
A flower blossoms red—
O endless day that will shape my life!

In the northern tundra at cold dawn
A bud stirs in the snow,
Waiting for a blinding flock of swallows.
O solemn promise!

Where waters seethe in the middle of the sea,
The flower castle erupts, fanned by the wind—
Today I summon you here,
My mob of memories drunk as butterflies.

A TALL TREE

Stretching to the blue sky,
Burned by time but standing tall—
Don't put on blossoms in the spring.

Brandishing old spiders' webs,
Fluttering on the path of an endless dream,
Your mind has no regret.

If you find dark shadows gloomy,
Tumble down into the lake's bottom
Where no wind can shake you!

TRANSLATED BY PETER H. LEE

Yi Sanghwa

DOES SPRING COME TO STOLEN FIELDS?

The land is no longer our own.
Does spring come just the same
to the stolen fields?
On the narrow path between the rice fields
where blue sky and green fields meet and touch,
winds whisper to me, urging me forward.
A lark trills in the clouds
like a young girl singing behind the hedge.
O ripening barley fields, your long hair
is heavy after the night's rain.
Lightheaded, I walk
lightly, shrugging my shoulders, almost
dancing to music the fields are humming—
the field where violets grow, the field
where once I watched a girl planting rice, her hair
blue-black and shining—

I want
a scythe in my hands, I want
to stamp on this soil, soft as a plump breast,
I want to be working the earth and streaming with sweat.

What am I looking for? Soul,
my blind soul, endlessly darting
like children at play by the river,
answer me: where am I going?
Filled with the odor of grass, compounded
of green laughter and green sorrow,
Limping along, I walk all day, as if possessed
by the spring devil:
for these are stolen fields, and our spring is stolen.

TRANSLATED BY PETER H. LEE

Sim Hun

WHEN THAT DAY COMES

When that day comes
Mount Samgak will rise and dance,
the waters of Han will rise up.

If that day comes before I perish,
I will soar like a crow at night
and pound the Chongno bell with my head.
The bones of my skull
will scatter, but I shall die in joy.

When that day comes at last
I'll roll and leap and shout on the boulevard
and if joy still stifles within my breast
I'll take a knife

and skin my body and make
a magical drum and march with it
in the vanguard. O procession!
Let me once hear that thundering shout,
my eyes can close then.

TRANSLATED BY PETER H. LEE

Yun Tongju

SELF-PORTRAIT

I go round the foot of the mountain seeking a lone well by the field, to
look into it without words.

In the well the moon is bright, clouds flow, sky spreads open, a blue
   wind blows, and there is autumn.

A young man is in the well too. Hating him I turn away. But as I go
   on, I come to pity him.

When I return and look in the well again, that young man is still
   there. I start to hate him again and turn away. But as I go on, I
   come to long for him.

In the well the moon is bright, clouds flow, sky spreads open, the blue
   wind blows, autumn reigns, a young man stands there.

ANOTHER HOME

The night I returned home,
My bones followed me to bed.

The dark room merged with the universe,
The wind blew like a voice from heaven.

Poring over my bones
That glow quietly in the dark,
I don't know whether it's myself that weeps,
My bones, or my beautiful soul.

A faithful dog
Barks all night at darkness.

The dog that barks at darkness
Must be chasing me.

Let's go, let's go,
Like someone pursued,
Let's go to another beautiful home
That my bones don't know about.

CONFESSIONS

My face reflected
In the rusted blue bronze mirror,
Full of disgrace—
Which dynasty's relic am I?

Let me shorten my confessions to a line
—Twenty years and one month,
With what hope have I lived?

Tomorrow, the day after, on that joyful day,
I must write another line of my confessions.
—In that youthful age,
Why such a shameful declaration?

Night after night let me polish
The mirror with my palms and soles.

Then a sad man's retreating figure,
Walking alone below a meteor,
Will emerge from the mirror.

EASILY WRITTEN POEM

A six-mat room in another country;
Night rain whispers outside the window.

To be a poet is a sad mandate.
Shall I scribble a line?

The envelope holding my college fees
Smells of sweat and love;

Clutching my notebooks,
I head for an old professor's lecture.

Come to think of it,
I've forgotten my childhood friends.

With what hope
Am I moving forward alone?

Life, they say, is hard,
I am ashamed
To have written a poem so easily.

A six-mat room in another country;
Night rain mutters outside the window.

With a lamp I drive out darkness,
The last "I" awaiting morning that will come like an era,

I stretch out my small hand to myself,
In a handshake of tears and comfort.

TRANSLATED BY PETER H. LEE

Chŏng Chiyong

POMEGRANATE

Coals in the brazier burn lovely as a rose,
Spring night smells of dry burning grass.

I crack a pomegranate that passed a winter
To savor its kernel stones one by one.

O clear recollection, rainbow of new sorrow,
Soft and quick as a goldfish.

This fruit mellowed at the last harvest month
When our small story sprouted.

Young girl, frail friend, stealthily
A pair of jade rabbits doze on your bosom.

Fingers of a white fish in an ancient lake,
Silver threads tremble, lithe and lonely.

Holding a pomegranate grain against the light,
I dream of a blue sky, Silla's myriad years.[1]

SUMMIT

On a sheer bluff,
Embossed cinnabar.
Dewy waters flow,
A red-plumed bird,
Perched perilously,
Pecks a berry.
Grape vines move past,
A scented flower snake
Dreams a plateau dream:
The granite brow, tall as death,
Where birds of passage return countless years,
Where a young moon sinks
And a double rainbow throws open a bridge—
Looking up, high as Orion.
Now I stand on the highest peak
Where star-sized white blossoms dangle,
My dandelion legs planted evenly.
As the sun rises, the eastern sea
Like a far flag fronting the wind
Flaps around my cheeks.

---

[1]Silla: one of the three ancient Korean kingdoms, the traditional dates of which are 57 B.C. to A.D. 935—hence a round number, one thousand.

WINDOW, I[2]

Something cold and sad haunts the window.
I dim the pane with my feverless steam.

It flaps its frozen wings, as if tamed,
I wipe the glass, wipe again—

Only black night ebbs, then dashes against it,
Moist stars etched like glittering jewels.

Polishing the window at night
Is a lonely, spellbinding affair.

With your lovely veins broken in the lung,
You flew away like a mountain bird!

WINDOW, II

I look out
Into a dark night.
A giant pine tree in the courtyard climbs.
I turn back and return to bed.

I'm thirsty.
I go back to the window
And peck the glass with my mouth,
Like a goldfish stifled in a bowl.

No star, no water, windy night—
The window rattles like a steamship.
Translucent purple hailstone,
Pinch my body, pound, shatter me!

---

[2]Composed on the occasion of his child's illness and subsequent death.

My fever mounts.
Like a stricken lover,
I rub my cheeks against the glass
And drink in cold kisses.

O burning tinkle!
A distant flower!
A lovely fire breaks out
In the capital.

WHITE DEER LAKE[3]

1

Nearer the summit, the fainter the scent of gaudy flowers. As I climb, their waists vanish, then their necks, and finally only their faces peek, etched in patterns. Where a chill air matches that of the north, plants vanish, but are resplendent like stars strewn in the August sky. Fall evening shadows, stars light up in the bed of flowers. Stars move, I am bone-tired.

2

I have revived after wetting my throat with the lovely fruit of mountain orchids.

3

A white birch turns into a skeleton beside another white birch. I won't mind turning white as a birch after death.

4

In a demon-deserted desolate corner, ghostly flowers[4] turn blue in the face.

---

[3]A lake in the crater of Mount Halla on Cheju Island.
[4]ghostly flowers: *toch'ebi* in Korean.

5

At 6,000 feet, horses and cows mingle with men. Horse with horse, cow with cow, a pony follows a cow, a calf a mare—but they part.

6

A cow had a hard time at first calving. In confusion she ran a hundred *ri* downhill to Sŏgwip'o.[5] The motherless calf moos, following persistently after a horse or a climber. Thinking of having to entrust our children to a strange mother,[6] I wept.

7

Orchids' fragrance, orioles' call, whistle of Cheju birds, sound of water skittering over the rocks, pines at the ruffle of a distant sea. Among the ash trees, camellias, and overcup oaks, I missed my trail and emerged on a path winding around the white rock covered with creepers. I run into a mottled horse, which does not back away.

8

Flowering ferns, bracken, bellflowers, wild asters, umbrella plants, bamboo, manna lichens, alpine plants with starlike bells—I digest them, am drunk on them, and fall into a doze. Yearning for the crystalline water of White Deer Lake, their procession on the range is more solemn than clouds. Beaten by showers, dried by rainbows, dyed by flowers, I put on fat.

---

[5]Sŏgwip'o: a town in the south of Cheju Island.
[6]a strange mother: refers to the Japanese colonizers.

9

The sky rolls in the blue of White Deer Lake. Not even a crayfish
stirs. A cow skirted around my feet disabled with fatigue. A wisp
of chased cloud dims the lake. The lake that reflects my face all day
is lonesome. Waking and sleeping, I forgot even my prayers.

TRANSLATED BY PETER H. LEE

Hwang Sunwŏn

Hwang Sunwŏn was born in 1915 in Taedong, South P'yŏngan, and graduated in English literature from Waseda University in Tokyo in 1939. His literary career began with the publication of a collection of verse in 1934, but since 1940 he has written mainly short stories and novels. A member of the Korean Academy of Arts since 1957, Hwang is currently a professor at Kyŏnghŭi University in Seoul.

A master of the modern short story, Hwang has attemped to capture the images of his people in lyrical prose and delicate natural imagery. In his early stories, Hwang dealt with children and their rites of passage, the impact of their discovery of death, the consciousness of beauty and ugliness, the knowledge of good and evil, and the awakening of love and sex. In these stories Hwang either employs traditional symbols or creates his personal symbology. Hwang's novels encompass such local and universal topics as the conflict between land-owner and tenants (*The Descendants of Cain*, 1954) and the alienation of a member of the untouchable butcher class (*The Sun and the Moon*, 1964) to show how one "must endure and overcome one's own loneliness." All Hwang's works are characterized by his ear for the speech patterns of all classes and ages, an eye for telltale gestures, narrative sophistication, and beautifully chiseled prose with seductive rhythm. The background of "Cranes" (1953) is the Korean War. Two young men, childhood friends from the farm, are now in different roles: one is a security officer and another, a prisoner suspected of underground activity for the North. But like the crane that soars high into the sky, friendship transcends ideological differences.

CRANES

The northern village lay snug beneath the high, bright autumn sky, near the border at the Thirty-eighth Parallel. White gourds lay one against the other on the dirt floor of an empty farmhouse. Any village elders who passed by extinguished their bamboo pipes first, and the children, too, turned back some distance off. Their faces were marked with fear.

As a whole, the village showed little damage from the war, but it still did not seem like the same village Sŏngsam had known as a boy.

At the foot of a chestnut grove on the hill behind the village he stopped and climbed a chestnut tree. Somewhere far back in his mind he heard the old man with a wen shout, "You bad boy, climbing up my chestnut tree again!"

The old man must have passed away, for he was not among the few village elders Sŏngsam had met. Holding onto the trunk of the tree, Sŏngsam gazed up at the blue sky for a time. Some chestnuts fell to the ground as the dry clusters opened of their own accord.

A young man stood, his hands bound, before a farmhouse that had been converted into a Public Peace Police office. He seemed to be a stranger, so Sŏngsam went up for a closer look. He was stunned: this young man was none other than his boyhood playmate, Tŏk-chae.

Sŏngsam asked the police officer who had come with him from Ch'ŏnt'ae for an explanation. The prisoner was the vice-chairman of the Farmers' Communist League and had just been flushed out of hiding in his own house, Sŏngsam learned.

Sŏngsam sat down on the dirt floor and lit a cigarette.

Tŏkchae was to be escorted to Ch'ŏngdan by one of the peace police.

After a time, Sŏngsam lit a new cigarette from the first and stood up.

"I'll take him with me."

Tŏkchae averted his face and refused to look at Sŏngsam. The two left the village.

Sŏngsam went on smoking, but the tobacco had no flavor. He just kept drawing the smoke in and blowing it out. Then suddenly he thought that Tŏkchae, too, must want a puff. He thought of the days when they had shared dried gourd leaves behind sheltering walls, hidden from the adults' view. But today, how could he offer a cigarette to a fellow like this?

Once, when they were small, he went with Tŏkchae to steal some chestnuts from the old man with the wen. It was Sŏngsam's turn to climb the tree. Suddenly the old man began shouting. Sŏngsam slipped and fell to the ground. He got chestnut burrs all over his bottom, but he kept on running. Only when the two had reached a safe place where the old man could not overtake them did Sŏngsam turn his bottom to Tŏkchae. The burrs hurt so much as they were plucked out that Sŏngsam could not keep tears from welling up in his eyes. Tŏkchae produced a fistful of chestnuts from his pocket and thrust them into Sŏngsam's. . . . Sŏngsam threw away the cigarette he had just lit, and then made up his mind not to light another while he was escorting Tŏkchae.

They reached the pass at the hill where he and Tŏkchae had cut fodder for the cows until Sŏngsam had to move to a spot near Ch'ŏn-t'ae, south of the Thirty-eighth Parallel, two years before the liberation.

Sŏngsam felt a sudden surge of anger in spite of himself and shouted, "So how many have you killed?"

For the first time, Tŏkchae cast a quick glance at him and then looked away.

"You! How many have you killed?" he asked again.

Tŏkchae looked at him again and glared. The glare grew intense, and his mouth twitched.

"So you managed to kill quite a few, eh?" Sŏngsam felt his mind clearing itself, as if some obstruction had been removed. "If you were vice-chairman of the Communist League, why didn't you run? You must have been lying low with a secret mission."

Tŏkchae did not reply.

"Speak up. What was your mission?"

Tŏkchae kept walking. Tŏkchae was hiding something, Sŏngsam thought. He wanted to take a good look at him, but Tŏkchae kept his face averted.

Fingering the revolver at his side, Sŏngsam went on: "There's no need to make excuses. You're going to be shot anyway. Why don't you tell the truth here and now?"

"I'm not going to make any excuses. They made me vice-chairman of the League because I was a hardworking farmer, and one of the poorest. If that's a capital offense, so be it. I'm still what I used to be—the only thing I'm good at is tilling the soil." After a short pause, he added, "My old man is bedridden at home. He's been ill almost half a year." Tŏkchae's father was a widower, a poor, hardworking farmer who lived only for his son. Seven years ago his back had given out, and he had contracted a skin disease.

"Are you married?"

"Yes," Tŏkchae replied after a time.

"To whom?"

"Shorty."

"To Shorty?" How interesting! A woman so small and plump that she knew the earth's vastness, but not the sky's height. Such a cold fish! He and Tŏkchae had teased her and made her cry. And Tŏkchae had married her!

"How many kids?"

"The first is arriving this fall, she says."

Sŏngsam had difficulty swallowing a laugh that he was about to let burst forth in spite of himself. Although he had asked how many children Tŏkchae had, he could not help wanting to break out laughing at the thought of the wife sitting there with her huge stomach, one span around. But he realized that this was no time for joking.

"Anyway, it's strange you didn't run away."

"I tried to escape. They said that once the South invaded, not a man would be spared. So all of us between seventeen and forty were taken to the North. I thought of evacuating, even if I had to carry my father on my back. But Father said no. How could we farmers leave the land behind when the crops were ready for harvesting? He grew old on that farm depending on me as the prop and mainstay of the family. I wanted to be with him in his last moments so I could close his eyes with my own hand. Besides, where can farmers like us go, when all we know how to do is live on the land?"

Sŏngsam had had to flee the previous June. At night he had broken the news privately to his father. But his father had said the same thing: Where could a farmer go, leaving all the chores behind? So Sŏngsam had left alone. Roaming about the strange streets and villages in the South, Sŏngsam had been haunted by thoughts of his old parents and the young children, who had been left with all the chores. Fortunately, his family had been safe then, as it was now.

They had crossed over a hill. This time Sŏngsam walked with his face averted. The autumn sun was hot on his forehead. This was an ideal day for the harvest, he thought.

When they reached the foot of the hill, Sŏngsam gradually came to a halt. In the middle of a field he spied a group of cranes that resembled men in white, all bent over. This had been the demilitarized zone along the Thirty-eighth Parallel. The cranes were still living here, as before, though all the people were gone.

Once, when Sŏngsam and Tŏkchae were about twelve, they had set a trap here, without anybody else knowing, and caught a crane, a Tanjŏng crane. They had tied the crane up, even binding its wings, and paid it daily visits, patting its neck and riding on its back. Then one day they overheard the neighbors whispering: someone had come from Seoul with a permit from the governor-general's office to catch cranes as some kind of specimens. Then and there the two boys had dashed off to the field. That they would be found out and punished had no longer mattered; all they cared about was the fate of their crane. Without a moment's delay, still out of breath from running, they untied the crane's feet and wings, but the bird could hardly walk. It must have been weak from having been bound.

The two held the crane up. Then, suddenly, they heard a gunshot. The crane fluttered its wings once or twice and then sank back to the ground.

The boys thought their crane had been shot. But the next moment, as another crane from a nearby bush fluttered its wings, the boys' crane stretched its long neck, gave out a whoop, and disappeared into the sky. For a long while the two boys could not tear their eyes away from the blue sky into which their crane had soared.

"Hey, why don't we stop here for a crane hunt?" Sŏngsam said suddenly.

Tŏkchae was dumbfounded.

"I'll make a trap with this rope; you flush a crane over here."

Sŏngsam had untied Tŏkchae's hands and was already crawling through the weeds.

Tŏkchae's face whitened. "You're sure to be shot anyway"—these words flashed through his mind. Any instant a bullet would come flying from Sŏngsam's direction, Tŏkchae thought.

Some paces away, Sŏngsam quickly turned toward him.

"Hey, how come you're standing there like a dummy? Go flush a crane!"

Only then did Tŏkchae understand. He began crawling through the weeds.

A pair of Tanjŏng cranes soared high into the clear blue autumn sky, flapping their huge wings.

TRANSLATED BY PETER H. LEE

O Sangwŏn

Born in 1930 in Sŏnch'ŏn, North P'yŏngan, O Sangwŏn graduated in French literature from Seoul National University and has subsequently been an editorial writer for the *Tonga Daily*. Since "A Respite" (1955) his recurrent themes have been war, revolution, death, and man's fate. Perhaps the true subject of this story is not the Korean War but the protagonist's struggle against his fate as a South Korean platoon leader taken prisoner by the enemy and about to be executed. The strong current of humanism running through most of his successful works poses questions about the enigmas of man's fate and the boundaries of human capabilities.

A RESPITE

He lay shivering in the darkness. Everything would come to an end within the hour. His hands and feet were frozen. Frost-caked dirt walls closed him in, and he could glimpse the icy sky through a crack in the trapdoor above. He was lying in a hastily dug, underground prison. A faint body odor was in the air. It couldn't be more than three days, he thought. Then he recalled what one of the men had said when they pushed him down the ladder into this hole: "This fellow will fare no better than the last." Who could that other fellow be? Could he be the same one he had seen outside awhile ago just before they shot him? If not, who could he have been? He began to shiver even more; he was frozen to the marrow.

What group do you belong to? What is your educational background? Your motive for enlisting? What do you think of communism? What are your feelings toward the United States? What? Comrade, what you are saying lacks sense! You are still class-conscious, dear comrade. Of course, we know you cannot help having been born to the class to which you belong, make no mistake about that. But we hate the pride and consciousness of your class. We will give you another chance to think it over. We will hear your answers in exactly an hour, and your answers will decide everything.

These remarks, exchanged during the investigation, came back to him piece by piece. In an hour everything would end. The sound of snow trodden underfoot as he was marched from the interrogation room to this underground prison, led by a soldier of the People's Army and followed by another with a Russian tommy gun pointing directly at his back, still sounded in his ears.

In an hour I will be led out to the same place. After a brief conversation the leader of the band will say: "Very well, dear comrade, walk straight along this river bank without looking back." Then I will hear the sound of snow under my feet as I pace along. No, they might strip me of my uniform before they send me off. (Although my combat fatigues are somewhat torn they're American-made and still good. I will walk along the white river bank, my skin red from the cold. Several rifle shots will ring out and I will slump to the ground. Soon the red of my blood will dye the white snow and everything will come to an end. They will march back to the headquarters, their rifles slung over their shoulders, muzzles pointing down. They will file into the warm office kicking the snow from their boots and rubbing their hands to warm them. After a few minutes they will forget about me altogether, warming their hands at the stove, rolling cigarettes, or lazily stretching out on chairs.

It really doesn't matter who dies once he is dead. These things are daily routine. I'll be the only one who will die neglected and forgotten, bleeding and clutching snow in my hands.

He felt a sudden cramp in his muscles. Was it the cold? He smelt the odor again. He wasn't the first, he thought, just a link in an endless chain. . . .

We fight and we die in the end, that's all. There is nothing else. We are for or against nothing, nor are we after anything. We fight as human instinct directs us, and we die as a result.

The front line had pushed steadily northward. Several contacts were made with the enemy. The reconnaissance platoon, which he led, was far ahead of the other troops, deep behind enemy lines. Communications with headquarters were lost.

The soldiers in the platoon watched the radio operator anxiously. Friendly forces retreating all along the line! All roads blocked by the enemy. Where should we try to make a breakthrough? Now the number of skirmishes began to increase. He was losing his men one by one. He decided to take to the mountains, avoiding contact with the enemy as much as possible. Hunger and fatigue. The number of men steadily decreased while the remainder had to fight their way through the cold and snow not knowing exactly where they were heading. Lost in the knee-deep snow of a blizzard, they made their way into a small village. Deserted houses lay half-buried in snow. There was no sign of the enemy. The famished soldiers scattered throughout the village in search of food. All they were able to find was a sack of frozen potatoes. They ate them raw. Then they all slumped down exhausted. The hunger and fatigue weighed on them. Every toe was frostbitten. At sundown the blizzard became even more furious. Night sets in quickly in the mountains. The platoon sergeant was sitting up, leaning against the door frame, but hearing the storm outside, even he finally fell asleep. It was on nights like this that one might expect a surprise attack.

But nothing happened.

The fight against cold, hunger, and snow resumed with dawn. One by one, platoon members fell victim to the elements. He watched the last stare of those who fell. He knelt beside them when they went down in the snow, unable to follow the others. His hands, searching their pockets for possible mementoes to send back to their families, were even colder than their dying bodies. Murmuring "Lieutenant . . ." they died, their eyes turning, cold, wandering off into the void.

"Lieutenant, I was born in North Korea. . . . I am alone, and I don't have anybody in the South. . . . This is my address in North Korea."

He was handed a frayed piece of paper. He held the dying soldier's hand and squeezed it without a word. What else could he do?

Now only six were left.

They pushed through the snow, leaving the bodies of the dead behind. Fear began to take over. The rugged terrain gave way abruptly to a plain. They could see a highway ahead of them. The platoon sergeant, who had gone on to scout, ran back.

There were innumerable hoof marks, wheel tracks, and boot impressions, he reported. He carried back horse dung. It was soft—proof that troops had passed by not very long ago. There was nothing they could do except wait for nightfall and cut across the plain to the mountain range on the other side. So they waited.

They got to the other side of the highway without difficulty. They made their way along the ditch, taking great care to remain concealed. They slowed down as they drew near the mountains. Just then it happened. The sound of a shot and one of them dropped with a shriek. They all hit the snow.

They wondered from which direction the shot had come. As he cautiously raised his head to look around, another shot rang out. It was from the left flank. They all faced that direction.

Their predicament was obvious. The enemy knew where they were, but they did not know where the enemy was. They could not remain there like sitting ducks. They stood out in the snow even though it was dark. They started to crawl toward the mountain. Bullets whined around them. One of them shouted, "Lieutenant!" with a shriek. He closed his eyes. He was sweating profusely. He crawled forward with his eyes closed. He felt weak and at times he feared he might faint. The dark silhouette of shrubs that girded the foot of the mountain appeared ahead. The enemy fire slowed down. The platoon sergeant was hit just as they reached the foot of the mountain. The lieutenant dragged him behind some rocks.

He did not realize how far he had dragged the sergeant when he himself slumped to the ground exhausted; it was almost daylight.

It was getting even colder in the cell. He moved a little. He was numb all over from the cold. Soon everything would come to an end. The same rank odor pervaded the damp hole. Footsteps could be heard in the snow. They drew near. Maybe the hour had come. He sat up. A few moments of suspense. Then the footsteps faded away. Nothing. Just someone passing by. Very cold. Did the man turn back on his way here? He felt weak again.

"What was your major subject? Why did you choose to study law? The fact is that you've been soaking up the conventional ideas of your class since childhood. You must abandon the habit."

"We think very highly of fellows like you, comrade. I'm always prepared to welcome fellows like you."

The draft through the crack in the door brightened the light from the fireplace.

"Comrade, I think you're a fine young man. Go ahead, help yourself to a cigarette." He poked the fire and the embers burned brightly.

"My dear comrade, I think you're the most pitiable young man in the world for that very reason. I'm truly sorry that you won't change your attitude."

"Comrade, why do you stare at me so coldly? You say nothing. . . . I see. I understand what you're trying to tell me with your silence. I am sorry you won't reform."

The words came back to him as if in a dream. He stirred a little in an effort to warm himself. His thoughts wandered further into the past.

It was nearly daylight when he and the sergeant finally slumped onto the snow. The dawn was beautiful. The snow-covered scenery was even more beautiful. The snow on the trees glistened in the early morning sun.

The sun was quite high when he finally sat up. The sergeant lay unconscious in the snow clutching his bloody leg. He had more bloodstains on his shirt, at the shoulder, and on his back. The lieutenant propped him up.

The sergeant slowly opened his eyes. Seeing the lieutenant, he smiled a bitter smile. The lieutenant embraced the sergeant, rubbing his cheek against the other's. They were the only ones left.

"It seems it's my turn now, sir," said the sergeant quietly. He looked down at the sergeant's face, but he could detect no sign of gloom: only a hard-boiled determination that had survived long years of military service. The sergeant had served with the Japanese army during World War II in the South Pacific and later in northern China. Following the liberation he had spent two months in a prisoner-of-war camp. Then he had served in the Chinese communist army and subsequently in the nationalist army before returning to Korea only to enlist again in the Korean army. He was a career soldier and said there was nothing more interesting than life in the army. The moments of mortal risk in battle were the only times he felt he was truly alive, he used to say.

"Men are born to kill each other. What else is history but a record of the massacre of man by man? I like fighting. When I hear battle cries, my heart leaps. When I've got an enemy in my gunsight, I'm overwhelmed with joy. I feel history is being made at that very moment. The meaning of life is fighting and dying fighting."

That was how he lived. Now he lay dying. He knew it was his turn to go.

In his damp hole he now recalled the sergeant's words. He tried to rise but fell back on the ground. He had a cramp in his right arm. He clenched his teeth and waited for the pain to pass. Soon everything would end. He thought of the sergeant again.

"Sir, I've made up my mind where to die." The sergeant had crawled to a sunny spot and propped himself against an old oak.

His serene face with closed eyes showed no trace of sorrow or loneliness. Only the solitude of the snow-covered mountain reflected in his face. Then he slowly slid sideways and slumped down in the snow. The lieutenant rushed to help him sit up but the sergeant, half opening his eyes, said with a small smile, "Leave me be . . ."

The sergeant closed his eyes again. His breath came slowly. The lieutenant walked on alone in the knee-deep snow heading south. Often he collapsed. He wandered around in snowstorms not knowing his direction. His feet were numb from the cold. Fear and despair began to take hold of him. *Am I heading in the right direction? What is my present position?* There was nobody to consult, but he couldn't very well stay put in one place. He staggered on through the snowstorm. *How far do I have to keep going like this? When will I get somewhere?* He slept in the snow. With the dawn he walked again. After many slips and falls he was a mass of cuts and bruises. Fatigue and hunger, cold and loneliness, plagued him at night. *Am I going to be buried in the snow like this for eternity?* The night would somehow end and the dawn would break. He got up because he had to walk. The terrain became rougher. Once he slipped over a cliff and fell four or five meters. When he came to, his whole body ached with indescribable pain.

He got up. His clenched fists were shaking violently. He had to climb back up the cliff from which he had just fallen. Its four or five meters seemed an insurmountable height, but he had to get up them. He began to climb, his teeth clenched; he sweated profusely, the sky began to sway above him. He clung to the roots of a tree and closed his eyes; the root came loose, snow and dirt blinded him, but he reached the top. Once there he passed out.

As soon as he came to his senses, he began to walk again. Walking south, step by step, was the only thing left for him to do. The carbine had become too heavy and so he tied it to his back.

A week passed and finally one evening, as dusk slipped quietly in, he conquered the mountain. When he awoke the following morning, the sun was high and he was startled to find a small village practically under his nose. He had slept in the snow when a village was so near! A warmth, a new desire to fight on, welled up in him. He slid down the slope to the village, his eyes brimming with tears. He reached the edge of the village. Its houses, with their open doors, looked deserted. The snow in the village was fresh and untrodden. Pigsties and cow barns . . . this must be a place where people live! He stepped through a door . . . a pillaged chest of drawers, scattered rags, and dirty clothes. He scooped up an armful of old clothes and held them close. Ah! The human odor! He looked around the room . . . it was deserted.

Just then he heard footsteps outside. He jumped up and took cover against the wall. He found a peephole through a crack in the wall. Nothing seemed to stir outside. *Was I just hearing things?* The next moment he distinctly heard people talking. He became alert, expectant. He peered out intently. About fifty meters away, behind another small house, a group of people were marching along a path. They halted.

There was no mistaking they were soldiers, even from that distance. There seemed to be some American-made uniforms among them, too. *Am I already behind friendly lines? No, that couldn't be. . . . Wait, what about the other uniforms? They look familiar.* To get a closer look at them he had to move to the adjoining hut. He moved deftly and speedily, using haystacks, barns, and such for cover. From his new position he could observe them much better through an opening in the stone wall. Now he could even pick up some of their words.

Comrade, firing squad . . . these two words met his ears. *They are communists!* He listened more carefully. He could now see a barefooted man, clad only in his underwear, standing in the middle of encircling soldiers. His hands were bound behind.

"Comrade, do you have any objection to what the people do?" said the man who seemed to be the leader of the group.

"A human being is not a tool. What more need I say? But I can tell you this much: I realized for the first time that I was a living, breathing man the moment I was captured. I am happy because I am not a tool or a machine but a living man and I am going to die like a man. I am unable to describe my joy!"

"Very well." A derisive smile curled the leader's lips. "You walk straight down this embankment. It will lead you to the south. Since that is the direction you want to take so much, I am sure you'll be very happy."

The victim turned around. He began to walk slowly and deliberately. Two soldiers raised their rifles. Hearing the sound of cocked rifles, the man walked on, calm and manly, his bare feet treading the snow. With the sound of rifle shots he would drop, still facing the south.

Now the lieutenant knew what it was all about. He felt that the man walking out there on the embankment was none other than himself. The whole scene began to sway and reel in front of him. Almost instinctively he gripped his rifle butt. *It's cowardly to avoid a fight for the comforts of tomorrow. The man walking out there now is nobody but me. I am now being slaughtered, and I'm not going to let that happen.* He took aim at the two riflemen. The next moment his carbine went off. He saw the two drop to the ground. He squeezed the trigger again and again. They started to shoot back at him. Sweat began to run down his forehead. Things became blurred. They stopped shooting; now they had him completely encircled. They inched closer. Something hard hit him on the shoulder. Then he heard a shot. He jumped up only to slump down again immediately. He knew he was going to faint, but another shot rang in his ears. He felt a numbing pain in his right arm. He felt a warmness flowing down it. He could sense people approaching him, then he felt a blow on his head. He lost consciousness completely.

How long did he lie unconscious? When he came to he touched his arm with his fingers and looked at them. They were stained with dark blood. He could hear people talking in low voices. The place was filled with cigarette smoke. He could see a dusty ceiling covered with cobwebs. It was a room, then, he thought. From time to time he could hear someone's footsteps outside treading the snow. Just as those footsteps came close and then moved away, his consciousness returned and retreated off and on for a long time.

Repeated interrogations followed. The ultimatum was given. Everything would end soon. The floor of the underground cell was getting even colder. His head was clear now. His muscles convulsed at times with a numbing pain. He heard people approaching. This must be it, he thought. *The trapdoor will soon open with a squeak. A ladder will be pushed down through the darkness like the hand of fate. Quiet. Nothing happens. Why? Am I just hearing things? No, it's those people all right. They are coming to get me.* He tried to sit up in the darkness. He looked up and a bright shaft of light came down the ladder.

"We haven't got all day. Get moving down there. Come on up!"

He climbed the ladder rung by rung. He had difficulty controlling his knees because they were numb and weak. When he reached the trapdoor they grabbed him and dragged him out. He slumped down on the snow. The cold snow melting under his face brought him round. *Now I must get up and must walk firmly. I must do everything with exactitude till the moment I die.*

Grasping the snow he got up. He walked slowly but steadily toward the office, his eyes shining intelligently.

Brief formalities over the order for his execution were given.

They went out to the snow-covered embankment—that same embankment! How many people had taken this route south? Across the wide, rolling plains he could see a mountain range on the other side. It too was clothed in snow. It was a beautiful winter scene. "Walk straight ahead. It leads to the south. Since you so desire to go that way, I am sure you'll be very pleased." He began to walk. Each step made a footprint in the white snow. *Now I must walk with firmness.* Squad, ready! He heard the cocking of their rifles. He could see nothing but white snow ahead. *Now everything is going to end. I must do everything exactly right till the moment I die. I must control myself . . .*

He walked steadily on, firm step by firm step. *I am approaching death step by step, but I must not abandon myself to fear or despair. The rolling plain with the white mountain on the other side. Then the sound of rifle shots. But they sound different, like something from another world. It's nothing; I must walk on.* He felt a spasm in the back of his head and around his waist. *No, it's nothing, nothing . . .*

The white snow gradually turned gray, then black. The end had come at last. *They will march back to their headquarters, their rifles over their shoulders, muzzles pointed down. They will file into the office rubbing their hands together. After a few minutes they will completely forget all about me, roll their cigarettes, and stretch out in comfort. It won't matter who has just died. There is nothing more commonplace than that.* His mind gradually blurred. He was lying on white snow. The sun shone brightly.

TRANSLATED BY KIM CHONGUN

Kim Yisŏk

Born in P'yŏngyang in 1914 to a wealthy Christian family, Kim Yisŏk received his early education in P'yŏngyang before coming to Seoul to attend Yŏnhŭi College (now Yonsei University) in 1936. After two years, however, he left college without taking a degree and began his writing career. Until 1951 he worked in a company and taught at a girls commercial school and an art college in P'yŏngyang. In January 1951, together with two brothers, he evacuated to the South but had to leave his own family behind. Settling first in Taegu and then in Seoul, he led a refugee's life in a rented room until his remarriage in 1958. In Seoul he worked as an editor of the journal *Munhak yesul* (Literary Arts) and was a high school teacher.

After his literary debut in 1938, Kim published stories, novels (*Tale of Hong Kiltong*, 1964), a manual of composition (1961), and children's stories (1964). He was awarded the Asian Freedom Literature Prize (1956) and the Seoul City Cultural Prize (1964). He died of a heart ailment in 1964 in Seoul.

In his stories Kim attempted to portray the doubts and anguish of conscientious intellectuals unable to find an adequate code of ethics to live by. He once said, "Nothing is more fearful to the writer than stagnation. One must conquer his own life with a new discovery—otherwise he cannot stand firm in his own convictions." The trials and hardships of the unemployed after the Korean War are movingly captured in "The Cuckoo," which was first published in *Munhak yesul* (May 1957).

THE CUCKOO

Village H is four hundred *ri* from Seoul. They say it takes eight hours to get to Village H, even when the bus runs at full speed. Before boarding the bus, I could not help sighing at the thought of a daylong bus ride. It was not to visit a dear friend that I was going, but to look for a job. Of course, there wasn't anything lined up for me; I was just going to see if by chance I could find some work. I had to go whether or not I wanted to; I had been out of a job for nearly a year.

In my last job I had worked as a clerk with an American war supplies company. My salary was very good, but since the number of U.S. troops had been cut down, the company had to go, too, leaving me jobless. During the first few months after that, I did not worry about my future. I had received a bonus in a lump sum from the company and decided I could live on that for a while. "In the meantime, I'll look for a suitable job," I thought. But that suitable job did not turn up after two months, or after three.

Frankly, it is not easy for a man in his forties to find a job. In the first place, the employer feels that he has to pay considerably more for an older man. In addition, employers are uneasy giving orders to someone over forty. Therefore, prospective employers would refuse to interview me as soon as they found out my age.

I learned of possible jobs here and there with the help of my friends. They all seemed hopeful at first, but nothing ever came of these leads. One long year went by this way, and, needless to say, my life became a big mess in the meantime.

Then I met an old classmate from middle school by chance one day in a tearoom.

"Let me write a letter of introduction for you," he said. "Go at once to Village H. There's a big construction job going on. They're building a dam there. The man in charge of personnel is a good friend of mine, an American called M. Nine chances out of ten, a letter from me to him will get you a position."

My classmate took out his fountain pen and busily wrote the letter for me. But even with that letter in my hand, his "nine chances out of ten" sounded more ominous than hopeful to my ears, for my hopes had been dashed many times before. At the same time, I did entertain a dim hope that something might turn up in Village H, for it was a secluded place and far away from Seoul. Having been sustained by that dim hope for three or four days, I finally took the bus to Village H.

Once on the bus, I thought I had done well after all, just by getting out of Seoul for a while. I was already under the spell of the scenery outside, receiving the full blast of the wind as the bus sped up. The April air still felt chilly, but it cleared my head, wearied as it was by the tumult of Seoul street life. At the sight of a farmer tilling the field with an ox, I felt that I had tapped some vital life force. I could almost catch the smell of that dark soil as it lay freshly overturned. At the entrance to a village stood an apricot tree in full bloom. It seemed so strange to see tall poplars appear to bob up and down, full of life, as I approached them, when my eyes had scarcely registered the image of the apricot blossoms. After curving around the foot of a mountain, the bus went along a clamorous mountain stream. When I caught sight of a waterfall cascading over the rocks, my heart was relieved of a burden that it had borne for ever so long.

The snow-crested mountaintops made me recall my hometown in a deep valley, surrounded by hills, thirty *ri* from the railway. I had to walk home in the snow when school closed for winter vacation. I had once seen a villager frozen to death on the way home; his body was as hard as iron, and white icicles clung to his beard. But despite this unpleasant memory, my hometown still remains dear to me. I closed my eyes for a time in an attempt to visualize my home. There appeared in my mind a scene in which black soil began to show its face, emitting steam in the midst of a snow-covered world. I could see the face of all my fellow villagers, one after another. They welcomed spring joyously, not because their miserable snowbound existence had come to an end, but because they could now go out once more in search of new life. With these thoughts I suddenly had a vision of returning home to welcome the spring, and thought that some unexpected good fortune might be awaiting me somewhere. "If only I could live in a deep valley such as this, with a fishing rod in my hand, how joyous life would be!" With these thoughts came the feeling that contrary to my earlier misapprehensions, my present destination might be well suited for the way of life I envisaged. This made me more impatient and anxious. Would there really be a job for me? I felt like a pupil waiting to learn the outcome of an entrance examination.

Fewer people remained in the bus as we went deeper into the mountains, with green buds coming out on big old trees. A fat middle-aged man sprawling across two whole seats next to me suddenly roused himself from his doze and asked me the time. I did not want to tell him that I had no watch.

"Some time around three or four, I think," I answered, judging from the position of the sun in the sky. As if he could not trust my answer, he asked a woman opposite in Western clothes. She shook her head to say that she had no watch, and her gaze returned to the magazine on her lap. She had been sitting as if bored, occasionally glancing at the magazine without really reading it. I could tell at a glance that she was no ordinary woman. Probably she was going to the same place I was, the big construction site where many Yankees were supposed to be working. Once again she lifted her eyes from the magazine and gazed out at the scenery.

It was already dusk when I alighted from the bus on a bridge that went to the H power plant. The driver told me that this was my destination. The steep mountain slope was shot across with huge pipes from the dam, beneath which the northern reach of the Han River flowed steadily. Even in darkness like india ink, I could sense that spring had come.

As I reached the end of the bridge, it grew darker and a cool breeze crept up my sleeves. From where I was I caught sight of a young man in a helmet watching the river flow by at the foot of the mountain, about a hundred meters from the bridge. I started toward him.

Then I heard a cuckoo. I stopped suddenly to look toward the mountain ridge. I saw no bird—only the quiet forests standing snug and serene, hidden in the dark.

The young man was wearing an army jacket and a yellow helmet inscribed with the letters S.G. From his attire, I could tell that he was a watchman for the dam construction field of H electric plant, which was operated by an American company.

I greeted the young man and asked, "Is this the X American Contract Company work site?"

"Yes, sir! Can I help you?" His reply was courteous.

"I came to meet an American named M. How can I see him?"

"Mr. M? Well, work has ended for the day, and he'll be hard to find. He's in the field office, about five *ri* farther up the mountain. His quarters are there, too. It would be better if you came back tomorrow morning."

"Oh, I see."

Having had some experience earning my bread under Americans, I know how they hate to see people after working hours. I knew I had to turn back, but I was worried about finding a place to spend the night.

"I'm afraid I'll have to stay overnight here. I'm sorry to bother you, but could you tell me where I can find an inn?"

"A place to stay? There's no decent inn here like there would be in Seoul. In the village down by the power plant there are several shacks that take overnight guests. But all the Americans' prostitutes are staying overnight there tonight. The company president is here from Seoul, and those Yankee harlots were driven out of the camp, so it won't be easy to find a place tonight. Still, I'm glad to see them get chased out of camp. They're a real eyesore!" The guard sounded as though the problem of my lodgings was no more than a side issue. He hawked and spat in disgust.

I was uneasy at the thought of spending the night outdoors. But as I was about to turn back, the guard called to me.

"By the way, sir, in about ten minutes a shift truck will be here with a night watchman. There'll be an American in the truck. You might ask him."

Such being the case, I might as well wait until the truck comes and get more information from this guard in the meantime, I thought.

"In Seoul the people say business is booming here and the Koreans get good pay. Is it true?" I asked, offering him a cigarette.

"Oh, so you're looking for a job, too. You want to work as an interpreter?" He grinned as if he had known this all along. "Well," he continued, "I suppose the interpreters are well paid, but not the day laborers. I can see why rumors like that get started. Judging from the number of job hunters swarming around here, they must imagine that business is booming. But that's all nonsense. There isn't a single place where the Americans are that's any good anymore. It's really a mess. I've worked for them for four years since I left the army, but look at me! They've been around this country quite some time now, and they're as stingy as can be. At the beginning, the food was good and the pay was reasonable. But now it's just beyond words. People come here because they hear you get free room and board, but nothing is free. They don't realize it's being taken out of their own wages. Well, maybe for farmers without their own land, this is the place to give it a try."

The guard went on with his lament for a time, and then his tone changed. "The interpreter's work up here is different from what it is in the army. You have to work as a foreman, too, so you have to know something about field work. When the work isn't done right, they blame the foreman rather than the laborers." And then as if to spare me unnecessary worry, he went on, "But the field work is nothing once you get used to it, and everybody gets the hang of it after a week or so. When you're asked if you have any field work experience, just tell them yes. I wouldn't worry too much."

After a few more words of encouragement, the guard exclaimed, "Oh, that man coming over here is from Seoul, looking for a job like you," pointing somewhere behind my back with his chin.

A tall, thin man in his late twenties had emerged from the darkness carrying an old bag in his hand. As he came up to us he said, "Oh, I'm in trouble. My friend's out of town. Goddammit!" Spitting out the "goddamn" in a man-about-town manner, he went on, "If I come, things'll be okay, they say, so I come hubba hubba with a one-way bus ticket. But it's a sonovabitch. Dear Mr. Guard, I've got no other choice. I'll stay here with you overnight. Jesus Christ!"

Stretching out his arms toward the guard with a meaningless gesture, the newcomer crouched down and made a sad face. "That really is a problem, isn't it? It gets quite cold at night here, not like Seoul. It's impossible to . . ."

As he saw the headlight over at the foot of the mountain, the guard said quickly, "Oh, here comes the truck with the night shift guard, sir. Please ask the American." He took one step forward, stood at attention, and then saluted.

I explained to the American driver why I had come, and he gave me the same answer the guard had given me, that I should come back early the next morning. He took the friendly guard off with him, leaving a night-shift replacement.

The man squatting down looked more restless than before, now that our sympathetic friend had gone. He had come penniless all the way from Seoul, hoping to meet a friend so that he might find a job here. I can't very well leave him in that condition, I thought. Come to think of it, it could happen to anybody, even to me. I couldn't go off by myself to find a place and leave him behind.

"Why don't you come down with me to find a place for the night? It's too cold to stay up here."

The man leaped to his feet as if he had been waiting for just such an offer.

"Oh, indeed, that's true. Thank you! Thank you very much!"

He bowed several times.

"I don't have much money either, but let's go together anyway. There should be a way to live just as there is a way to die."

"Well, yes! I was told to come up right away by a friend of mine, and here I am."

As if to make an excuse for his present situation, he continued, "If only I can meet the guy, it'll be okay! Goddamn!" he murmured to himself. Then, as if reminded of something important, he suddenly said, "Uh . . . by the way, I'm glad to meet you."

Drawing close to me, he introduced himself as a Ch'oe of Wangsimni, in Seoul.

In this manner we started in search of lodging, down the hillside path toward the H electric plant. Night had fallen and the stars were out.

"By the way, you look very familiar," he said suddenly, his eyes trying to find my face in the dark. I wondered why the man was starting out on this strange tack and found him amusing.

"I live in Seoul, so you must have seen me somewhere there," was my unenthusiastic reply. Ch'oe continued with his questions.

"You go to Myŏngdong often?"

"Once in a great while."

"Then which tearoom do you usually go to?"

"None in particular."

"Still, have you been to a place called the Azalea by any chance?"

I remembered having been there a couple of times, so I told him that I had. As if this were a major discovery, and as if to assure me that he was no hoodlum, Ch'oe said, "Oh, I know! That's where I met you. You and I are no strangers to one another, then. It's just that we haven't been introduced till now. We're in the same difficult situation, and I mustn't make myself a burden to you. If I meet my friend in the morning, everything will be all right."

Ch'oe explained that his friend was a section chief here, and the chief of a very nice section at that. He seemed anxious to make a good impression on me by bringing his friend into the conversation.

"Do you happen to have a cigarette?" Ch'oe finally blurted out the request that he had been holding back for some time. I gave him a cigarette and was about to light one for myself when he quickly gave me a light.

"I'm even out of cigarettes. Goddamn! By the way, you came here to get a job, didn't you? Let's try to work together, even though it's a small village. I'm really not a bad guy once you get to know me."

Ch'oe grinned, but he began to look discouraged when I made no reply. He puffed on the cigarette several times. Then, after taking two deep drags, he crushed out the glowing tip and put the butt carefully into his pocket.

"You ever worked in a Yankee company before?" he asked me. I did not think it necessary to recount my whole life story and answered simply, "No, I haven't."

"Oh, then you've been at a university, as I thought."

"I've been nowhere near such a place," I answered.

Ch'oe looked disappointed and shook his head once or twice. He walked on without a word for a while, probably trying to figure out what line of business I might have been in. He evidently thought it rude to ask any more questions.

Then he began speaking again, in a solemn tone. "If you want to work in a Yankee place, you've got to learn to be smart from the very beginning. You must push yourself into a nice position and make sure you know how much you'll be getting paid. Otherwise you'll be fooled. If you don't look sharp from the beginning, that's the end of it. We Koreans think modesty is a virtue, but these guys sure as hell never appreciate that. The best thing to do at a Yankee place is to make your pocket fat doing monkey business with them." He sounded as if he knew everything about Yankee work camps.

"You seem to be quite an expert on the Yanks. How long have you worked with them?" I asked this pointless question to avoid appearing rude.

"Since before the Korean War. It's been about ten years now. After ten years this is what I've become. But it was fun fooling around. By the way, your words are too polite, sir. Regard me as your younger brother. I'm glad to have met a nice gentleman like you, a person like my elder brother. Incidentally, sir, it's simply no good working for the Yanks in peacetime. First of all, there are no supplies coming in like there used to be during the war. It was great during the war. The food was good, and we got paid overtime, too. You could make easy money smuggling out army stuff. But the pickings have got pretty goddamn slim since the war ended!"

Ch'oe cracked his knuckles.

"Did you work as an interpreter in the army?" I asked.

"At first I started as a laborer, and I had to do what those guys told me. Then I learned the language and started working as an 'inter.' To make a long story short, the inter's job is a matter of knowing how to act sharp. No matter how well you speak the language, you've got to act nice to the Yanks first and foremost. People with no English never know what I'm babbling about anyway, and the Yanks can't understand what I'm yapping about in Korean. So this is where an inter can play it smart. Everything's okay as long as you please both sides. You just roll your tongue smoothly, shrug your shoulders, and keep talking. Then they all think you're a number-one inter. And when they ask you something, you should always act like you understand, whether you do or not. You just keep saying 'Yes, okay,' pretending to know everything, and you'll get away with it. Ha, ha . . . The first thing you have to learn in this world is how to play it smart."

"You seem to know that pretty well," I said.

"Don't say that, sir. In fact, I've survived that way all my life. Shall I tell you a funny story? It was when I was working as an inter for an army division behind the front line. The mess sarge had a dog, but it disappeared. He claimed the village people killed the dog to eat it and asked me to go around the village with him to check. I told the sarge that we Koreans never eat dogs. He wouldn't listen and asked me to go out with him. It wasn't my lucky day. When we came to one of the houses, about seven or eight men with their sleeves all rolled up were busy eating the meat off that dog. It had just come out of the oven all hot and steaming.

"No sooner did the sarge see this than he got really mad. 'That's my dog!' he shouted at me. He shook his clenched fists.

"Then those young guys turned on me because they couldn't do anything to the Yank. 'This dog bit a child so we're eating it. What's wrong with that? Hey, mister interpreter, is this the dog's owner? Good. We'll just make him pay for the dog-bite medicine!'

"Under the circumstances I couldn't very well tell the sarge what the men were saying. I had to play it smart. First, I reprimanded the young men very solemnly. 'This gentleman here is in charge of the mess hall. He works with Koreans and he is a nice person. If he knows it's his dog, you'll be in trouble. In America, if you kill somebody's dog you're sent to prison. But you'll all keep quiet; I'll try to deal with him.' I gave them all a solemn warning and then turned to the sarge. 'You're wrong; this isn't your dog. They're all angry because they think you're insulting them by calling them barbaric dog eaters.'

"The sarge yelled in reply, 'If that's not dog meat, what is it?'

"What could I tell him on the spot like that? I just let my mouth do the talking. 'It's the *meat of a noru*.'[1]

" '*What's a noru?*' he asked, his eyes wide.

"I didn't know the word for 'deer' in English, but I couldn't let him know that. So I calmly announced, 'It's a *small tiger!*' with a loud 'goddamn' after the sentence. At this his wide eyes grew even wider.

---

[1]Italicized passages originally appeared in English transliterated into Korean script.

'*Small tiger, goddamn, big party is wonderful!*' he said, adding several 'goddamns' of his own and shaking his head. If I hadn't played it smart that time, he would surely have made trouble by saying, '*Koreans chap chap dogs.*' I really acted smart and took care of things quick." Ch'oe grinned.

"It's an interesting story," I said.

"Oh, there are plenty more where that came from," he said. Then, after hesitating again, he asked me for another cigarette.

We were stopped by a policeman as we passed the gate of the H power plant. We showed him our ID cards and explained why we had come.

"This is no ordinary place, so we pay extra attention to security. Please don't feel offended; it's just a routine check," he said kindly. To our inquiry about lodging, he said:

"As you can see, there's no inn as such here. But if you go down a little farther, there are some chophouses. If you ask there, they may put you up for the night."

We thanked him and walked down the hill toward the village of small shacks, now glittering with lights.

"The policeman quite nice, okay. If all police like that, democracy number one here. But every guy sonovabitch. I am sure you support the opposition party, no? Opposition's okay, too, but they haven't got no money. Jesus Christ," Ch'oe said half in Korean, half in his broken English.

As we reached the village, Ch'oe motioned me to silence. Clearing his throat with some unnecessary coughing, he solemnly asked for the proprietor of the chophouse. A man nearing forty who looked like the owner of the place came out of the back room.

"We have come from Seoul with supplies for the construction project. We are wondering if we could impose ourselves on you for the night. As a matter of fact, we are well acquainted with that policeman in front of the power plant. It was he who directed us to your place. He'll soon be here himself."

Ch'oe told his story with a straight face to the very end, and the owner adopted a humble manner. "The rooms are too filthy for gentlemen like yourselves, but please do come in and have a look." He lit the lamp for us.

"We didn't come here looking for a first-class hotel. Thanks anyway," Ch'oe replied.

Glancing around the room, Ch'oe turned to me and said, "The room's dirty, but what else can we do? We're in an isolated village deep in Kangwŏn province. I am afraid you'll have to bear it for one night."

He spoke to me as if to a superior. I went into the back room of the chophouse where he and I were destined to spend the night together.

"Have you noticed the change of that man's attitude toward us? Country guys are easy to handle. The best way is to make them feel low by claiming to have connection with authorities. Ha, ha . . ."

Ch'oe seemed anxious to lighten my mood by laughing at his own cleverness, but I did not feel like joining in. All I wanted was to lie down. I was very tired. But even if I lay down, it didn't seem possible that I would fall asleep easily. Probably a drink or two might help, I thought, and ordered a bottle of wine with our supper. When the table was brought in, Ch'oe painstakingly asked the proprietor the cost of a night's stay, our supper, and the bottle of wine I had ordered. This he did by inserting "goddamns" and "sonovabitches" after almost every word.

He sat down very politely in front of the table and once again brought up the same subject. "Er . . . I really don't know what to say, sir. Anyway, if I meet him, it's going to be okay. I am quite certain."

It made me uneasy to see Ch'oe in an uncomfortable position. I bade him to make himself at home, and went to pour him a large draft of wine.

"Oh, no, no. I should pour a drink for you first, sir. I don't drink much, in fact."

He politely took the glass in both hands and tossed it off in one gulp.

"You seem to be doing pretty well," I commented.

"As a matter of fact, I learned to drink in the army. Before that, I couldn't touch a drop. In the army, we used to drink beer; we had enough of it to drown ourselves in. Not only beer; there was Coca-Cola, lemon juice, and everything. Those Americans have a different constitution from ours. They drink their beer ice cold, even when it's freezing outside."

Ch'oe emptied his second glass.

"*Korea makkŏlli very nice.* It's bootleg, I know. In Seoul, you don't find such good wine as this. It's almost as good as the Canadian whiskey Americans are crazy about."

Now, with alcohol in his system, Ch'oe no longer felt the need for his humble manner. He began to cram food into his mouth with his chopsticks.

"Talking about whiskey, did I ever fool those guys when I passed off Korean whiskey as Canadian. When they ran out of whiskey in the PX, they would ask us to buy them some. Who's gonna buy them real whiskey? I made them drink fake stuff. I could make ten bottles with one bottle of Canadian. But what do those guys know? They simply couldn't tell the difference. Oh, it makes me laugh just to think of it. They thought Korean whiskey would kill them, but once it was in a Canadian bottle it was the greatest. And they just went right on saying Korean whiskey is rotgut. Goddamn!"

Ch'oe's voice grew louder as the alcohol went to his head. By now I was tired of listening to his "goddamns." I decided I had had enough to drink and began to eat my rice.

"Why start on the rice so soon? Let's have another bottle," Ch'oe said.

Just then a woman went past our room into the next. She was wearing Western clothes, which was quite unusual in such a remote country village. Ch'oe became tense all of a sudden, and his eyes began to sparkle.

"Yah, nice, goddamn!" Ch'oe slapped his knee and summoned the proprietor. With an insinuating gesture toward the next room, he asked who the woman was. The proprietor replied that the woman lived on the construction site with an American and had just been chased out the day before. At this Ch'oe spat out more of his "nice" and "goddamns." The owner, who had been laughing as if he understood exactly what Ch'oe meant, saw an opportunity here to sell more liquor and offered to bring another bottle of wine.

"Goddamn! We're free to drink or not, as we like. Why be so pushy?"

"Aren't I free to ask you if you want more? You don't have to yell at me!"

"Oh, *funny guy, of course, freedom is freedom, goddamn!*" were Ch'oe's comments in English.

Banging the table with his fist and winking at me, Ch'oe shouted for more to drink.

"We can't sit here like this when there's a flower in the next room. Why don't we call that *female* in here?"

And then, not even waiting for my answer, as if he didn't care what I said, he shouted, this time to the next room, in his broken English:

"Good evening lady. We have number one party okay. Come here!"

There was no reply from the next room. Ch'oe repeated some more "goddamns" and then came out with something like a laugh, as if embarrassed.

I was simply dumbfounded.

"I think you go too far, young man. Let's go to bed now. We've had enough to drink." I leaned against the wall, feeling very tired.

"Big brother, please leave everything to me!" His "sir" had now become "big brother." Suddenly he leaped to his feet.

"You don't even know her. What do you think you're doing, anyway?" I was upset and felt somewhat angry. But Ch'oe acted as if my words mattered not in the least to him.

"Leave it to me!" Throwing these words at me, he went to the door of the next room and knocked.

There was no reason for me to worry, but my heart beat faster with fear that the drunken Ch'oe might cause some trouble. But contrary to my fears I heard whispering in the next room. It must be working, then, I thought. Then Ch'oe returned, now full of life. "Okay!" he said and winked at me. Then he quickly lowered his voice and said, "Now don't forget, big brother, you are supposed to be a big contractor connected with an American firm. Once they smell your money they're all yours, these girls. Whether they're college graduates or ignorant prostitutes, they're all *same same*, all *same same* when it comes to money. Big brother, why don't you play it smart tonight? If you do, you might just end up in bed with her."

Ch'oe's body was quivering with excitement. When he went as far as this, I could not help thinking that he was rather charming. But my words were severe.

"Your joke is going to far. Why do you do such things?"

"You don't have to worry, big brother. Why don't you just watch the show and enjoy the refreshments afterward? Anyway, I told her you came from Seoul to neogtiate with the Americans here about a subcontract for the dam project. I asked her to act as a mediator between you and the Americans. She looked quite interested. She says she has to make herself look pretty for you, and that's what she's doing now."

After a time the lady in question opened the door with an "Excuse me." She had ample breasts and was wearing a green dress. I could tell at first sight that she was not at all bad looking.

Ch'oe got up quickly to welcome the woman with his *"Welcome, Welcome,"* in English. She answered, *"Thank you,"* also in English, and nodded. Without the slightest hesitation she took a seat at the table.

"Let's introduce ourselves before the fun begins. My name is Tony Ch'oe. This is the gentleman I just told you about. He has always looked after me, just like an older brother."

"I am Jackie. I hope you'll come to love me a lot."

"Don't worry, Miss Jackie, I'll do the loving."

"No, not that kind of love." Jackie sent Ch'oe an appealing look which was not at all unpleasant.

"Miss Jackie, you take care to please my big brother tonight. There gonna be many parties. I hope you do well. I know it's gonna be okay; you speak such a good English."

Ch'oe handed Jackie a glass.

"I hear you came from Seoul." Her speech sounded very ladylike, as though she knew that this was the proper sort of question to be asking. "You must be tired after the journey," she added. "There isn't even a decent inn here. I am sorry you have to stay at a place like this."

Finding no words for a reply, I simply offered her a glass of wine. She took the glass in a reserved manner. However, I noticed that she had a capacity for drink.

As the wine flowed, Jackie became quite drunk. She began to argue with Ch'oe about the American army, mixing in English phrases like "you know" and "I know."

"After all, the army is the best. And the best of all's the marines. But these civilians—they're no good. They're so stingy they tremble over a pack of cigarettes. Mr. Tony, I'm down and out. I've been living on memories only. In Masan I used to live happy with Johnny, a major, but he *gone home.* Mr. Tony, I cannot forget that man."

"Yes, those were the good old days!"

"Of course. Every day we had parties. But now, it's just awful!"

"If you go to the *Eighth Army* in Seoul, you'll find some business, still."

"Never mention that place! Those guys got spoiled in Japan. I lived with some of them a couple months; it makes me sick just to think of them."

"But that depends upon the individual. Even now if you find a nice guy, you can make money. You know black marketing?" He said the last sentence in his usual broken English.

"That, too, is an old story. In those days, some boys would bring me a truckful of cigarettes. How I miss the good old days!"

"Goddamn, let's drink, let's forget," Ch'oe said.

"Let's do that! Hope that guy Honey turns up tonight. I'm gonna get drunk, act crazy to that stupid boy, and then run off to Seoul. And after that, *whas's-gonna-do?*"

"You run away with me!"

"*Mr. Tony*, you really will?"

"Where *Miss Jackie* go, I go too."

"Why don't you stop your joking and finish your drink," I butted in.

"Okay!" Ch'oe answered. But finding the bottle dry, he ordered another with a quick glance at me. If one must drink more, one must eat more food, too, he said, and called for another order of side dishes. Then he whispered something in my ear.

"Don't worry about the money. I have a watch. When we meet my friend, everything will be okay."

If I let him go on like this, I won't even have my return bus fare, I thought. Besides, I was too tired to go on any longer.

"I'm afraid I must have some sleep. I cannot lie down in front of a lady."

I let my discomfort show in my face. For a minute Ch'oe looked as if all the fun was over. Then he went to whisper something to Jackie. He was probably suggesting that they move to the next room and start afresh there. Jackie nodded, and Ch'oe shouted, "Okay." He told me to go to bed, and that he was going to have some more fun with Jackie in the next room. Then he moved the table there.

I had the owner bring me an army mattress. I lay down but felt too cold to fall asleep, due perhaps to the small amount of alcohol I had consumed. The *you know*'s and *I know*'s went on in the other room. It seemed quite late now. They were both very drunk in there. Their words amounted to nothing but mumbles and were not at all clear. Finally a jazz song by Ch'oe and squeals of laughter from Jackie were accompanied by the pounding of chopsticks on the table.

Ch'oe became exultant when Jackie told him he had a "*beauty voice.*" Now the song lyrics were "Quick, quick, slow slow; quick quick, slow, slow." Apparently the two were now staggering about the room, trying to embrace and dance at the same time. I felt an impulse to yell at them, but instead turned my face to the wall. Still, I could not sleep.

In the next room the chant of "quick quick" came to a halt, and there was silence. I imagined the two to be kissing.

I regretted having let Ch'oe come with me and concluded that he really did know how to play it smart.

I somehow managed to drop off to sleep, but soon a loud noise like a wall collapsing awakened me again.

There was a fight going on in the next room. I heard the sound of something breaking, along with Jackie's screams of "Honey! Honey!" and some strange sounds from Ch'oe. Indeed, he sounded as though he were being choked to death. I knew instantly that Jackie's Honey had come and started a fight, which sounded like a one-sided affair. Once again I heard something like a head striking the wall. Perhaps Jackie's Honey had seized Ch'oe by the collar and was using him as a battering ram. Jackie's sobs and Ch'oe's desperate cries were as one now, both louder and more frequent than in the beginning. It seemed that Ch'oe was being murdered. In a daze I sat upright in the dark room, my heart pounding. Even in my agitation, I was able to recall the beer bottle that had served as a candleholder and now lay beside my pillow. I knew I must take that bottle and rush into the next room.

But somehow I could not do that. "One of us is being killed by a foreigner," I thought. Yet I just kept sitting, breathing hard. Ch'oe, at the end of his endurance, uttered a strange sound. At that instant a door slammed, sounding as if the whole house were coming apart, and a voice yelled out, "Son of a bitch!" Evidently Ch'oe's assailant had loosened his grip on Ch'oe's collar and pushed him away.

"Don't you wanna go?" I heard the American say in his coarse, angry voice. He was speaking to Jackie.

"I'm sorry." Jackie sounded tearful. I heard the American kick open the door as Jackie followed him out of the house. From the street, I heard an engine start. The car drove off. Even before the sound of its engine was lost in the distance, I heard from Ch'oe in the next room sobs but snores. The snoring grew louder, and once again I found it impossible to sleep. I felt cheated in having lavished my concern on such a person.

Dawn had broken some time before when I arose. I opened the window and saw a steep mountain path winding up a slope before my eyes. The ridge was covered with dark, heavy clouds, and it looked as though it were about to rain. But the newly budding trees outside refreshed me. For a time I gazed at the green buds, and then called out to Ch'oe in the next room. There was no answer. Thinking that he was still in bed, I went and opened the door to his room. However, Ch'oe was gone, leaving all the mess of the night before untouched. I came back to my room to see if his bag was still there, but it, too, was gone.

I called the owner of the chophouse and asked him what had happened to Ch'oe. Ch'oe had gone off early in the morning, it seemed, saying that I would pay the bill. The bill was twice as steep as I had anticipated. Asked why it was so expensive, the proprietor replied that he was charging me for the dishes broken during the fight. I was dumbfounded—no, I was more than dumbfounded, for if I paid the full amount I would be unable to return to Seoul. I tried to convince the proprietor that I should not be forced to pay for dishes another had broken. But as I expected, he would not hear of it. "Stop talking nonsense. I missed a good night's sleep on account of you two!"

I had lost a night's sleep, too, for that matter, but I could not very well use that as an argument in my favor. I had to empty my pockets. I was now determined to find Ch'oe and stick close to him. Otherwise, I would have no way of going back to Seoul.

I left the chophouse, started up the mountain path of the night before, and headed for the construction site. All the way I was haunted by the thought that I might not be able to find Ch'oe. My heart beat all the faster as this thought assailed me, and I hated myself for having been such a fool.

I heard someone call me from behind as I approached the field office. Turning around, I found Ch'oe following me, bag in hand.

"I'm sorry about last night, sir. I overdrank myself, for sure. I was completely *knocked out. Sonovabitch.*"

He did not even try to hide the black eye the American had given him.

"You left early. Where have you been?" I asked him.

"Oh, did you have to ask me that? You know where I've been." Ch'oe laughed as if embarrassed. But since I appeared not to understand him, he went on to explain, "Miss Jackie isn't at all a bad girl at heart. She went off with that man last night, but she really didn't want to. Since she had decided to leave the guy anyway, she just went along with him in order to get money for her trip."

I cast a quick glance at his swollen face and asked once again, "So you saw Miss Jackie this morning?"

"That guy is still flat on his back, I suppose. I haven't been able to see her. But I did manage to find my friend's place. Goddamn, my friend didn't come home last night. But please don't worry. He's sure to come back some time this morning. How much did you have to pay?"

"I'm broke. I had to pay for the broken dishes as well."

"Why did you have to pay for that? I wasn't the one who broke them, sonovabitch. By the way, you're going back to Seoul today whether you get the job or not, aren't you?"

"I have to leave on the ten o'clock bus whether I get the job or not. I'm afraid you'll have to come up with my bus fare."

"Of course, I'll be responsible for that. When my friend comes back, there'll be no problem."

About thirty to forty farmers were milling about in front of the field office in hopes of getting work for the day. Every one of them looked pale.

I met Mr. M and showed him the letter of introduction my friend had written. He did no more than to ask me how well I knew my friend and tell me to leave my address. He gave me a sheet of paper, adding that there were no jobs open at the moment, but that he would let me know if anything came up.

I was aghast to think of all that I had endured just to be given this curt reply. But I wrote down my address anyway, hoping for some unforeseen lucky break, and left the office. Ch'oe, who had been waiting outside, rushed to ask me about the job. "No such luck," I answered.

As I shook my head, Ch'oe's face fell, and he asked an unnecessary question. "Then you will have to leave anyway?"

I remained silent, and Ch'oe looked apologetic. "If I meet my friend, I'll stay here even if I don't get a job today. But, sir, you need money for your lunch besides the bus fare, don't you? You didn't have breakfast either."

Ch'oe's solicitude was palling on me, but at the same time I had no choice but to remain until his friend appeared.

We decided to go to the guard's checkpoint to wait. That way we could not miss the friend even if he came by car, since all vehicles were stopped at the checkpoint.

At the checkpoint, Ch'oe lifted his hand, shouted "Hey!" and peeped inside. He was trying to see whether or not his friend was there. Even in his disappointment, Ch'oe reassured me that his friend would be back before noon and that everything would be all right.

The guard on duty was the same we had met the night before. He looked pleased to see us again.

"How did it go?" he asked about my job.

"There's no opening now, so I'm on my way back to Seoul. Do you think I could get a lift as far as Village H?" I spoke in a discouraged tone, and the guard's look was sympathetic. He assured me that many cars went in that direction from the work site, and that I should wait for a while. We went to the same spot where Ch'oe had sat last night and squatted down there. It was funny to think that we, the outgoing passengers, should be waiting for an incoming car.

"If he doesn't come back today, what are you plannning to do?" I asked Ch'oe. As worried as I was about myself, I felt sorry for him, too.

"I don't know. Anyway, he's got to come back. Oh, yes. He'll be back for sure."

Quite impatient now, he was talking to himself.

During this time several cars came and went through the check-point. Whenever a car drew near, Ch'oe would jump up to look inside and mumble to himself, "It's quite strange! He was supposed to be back before noon, they said." He had even discarded his beloved "goddamn" by now.

Whenever a village-bound car happened to arrive, the guard would let us know about it without fail. Each time Ch'oe would answer in my behalf, "We have to meet someone who will be coming into the camp before we can leave."

Every time a car came through that was headed for the village, I would ask Ch'oe the time. And whenever I asked him the time, Ch'oe looked embarrassed. He must have remembered the drunken promise he had made the night before, that he would give me his watch should I end up spending all my money on his account. For my part, I had no choice but to ask him the time since if I did not leave the site by one o'clock at the latest, I would miss the last bus for Seoul.

The mountain slope was now deeply veiled in mist. A soft rain began to fall, and I began to feel hungry. From boredom I began to count the rain drops falling onto the river.

Just then the guard told me that a truck was leaving for Village H. I immediately asked Ch'oe the time. Again with an embarrassed look on his face, he told me that it was already one o'clock. In that case I had to give up the idea of going back that day whether I liked it or not, I concluded. I thought how stupid I had been to take Ch'oe at his word. Then quite suddenly the thought dawned on me that I had a fountain pen with me. If I sold it at the village, I might be able to get enough for bus fare, I thought.

I hurled myself onto the truck, which had already started to move. Ch'oe, too, started suddenly to run after me. "How can you go? How can . . . ? Take this with you. Take it!" he shouted at me as he removed his wristwatch. But the distance between Ch'oe and the truck grew steadily wider as he ran doggedly after, waving the watch in one hand. I lost sight of him as the truck turned a corner of the mountain road.

Suddenly I heard a cuckoo. I could not tell where its song came from; I merely gazed at the flank of the mountain. And the call of the cuckoo, too, gradually died out. My ears followed that sound intently as it receded in the distance. I wondered if it was not merely to hear the song of that cuckoo that I had come here all the way from Seoul.

TRANSLATED BY PETER H. LEE

Ch'oe Inhun

Published in the magazine *Free Literature* (October 1958) as a prize-winning story, "The Gray Club" was Ch'oe Inhun's maiden work. The club is "a solitary island" in the middle of a metropolis, a sanctuary where Hyŏn, K, M, C, and later Miss Han (Kitty) gather to pursue their studies in the arts. Hyŏn represents a new generation which finds society indifferent, history malicious, government oppressive, and all gods dead. Rejecting ordinary domestic life and social order, Hyŏn seeks solitude and an enclosed place—he likens the Gray Club to the Bamboo Grove where seven worthies withdrew from a turbulent political world in third-century China. With a few select friends, he can indulge there in literature, music, and philosophical conversation.

Such a mode of life was nothing new for creative young intellectuals in Korea, but Ch'oe was the first to write about it. Aspiring writers, mostly university students, would frequent coffee shops (*tabang*, literally "tearoom") to meet with a few boon companions and established writers. Usually a writer held court in his favorite coffee shop at a certain time of day, and young writers would gather to discuss the books they had read or their own works. Often a group would move to another place to meet a different circle of friends or writers. If one member had a large house, they would gather regularly there. This has been a life-style of aspiring writers and artists for many decades in Seoul, the center of literary activity in Korea, and the author captures an essential aspect of the literary life. Rich in fancy and attentive to detail, his narration and dialogue are witty and refreshing. For more on Ch'oe Inhun, see the headnote to *Away, Away, Long Time Ago*.

THE GRAY CLUB

Engulfed in an inky darkness that was unusual for a late spring night, the desolate mountain path seemed empty and cold. Hyŏn heard a dog bark. He rummaged through his pockets as he walked, took out a cigarette, and put it in his mouth. The light of the match, struck on his fingertips, left a faint trail and faded into the darkness. Hyŏn felt an indescribable exhilaration. To Hyŏn, who had neither anticipated the unknown nor indulged in or been swayed by anything foolish for some time, this was clearly a departure.

Hyŏn liked to think he had outgrown feeling excited. How much he used to read—all night long, his eyes bloodshot. . . . In those days it seemed that some horrible calamity would strike immediately if he did not keep reading twenty-four hours a day. He felt that the moment he put down a book in the middle of a certain scene, a demon would devour him. He struggled from book to book, obsessed with the notion that if he put down his books, even for a minute, he would be left in a void. But those days when Hyŏn was seduced by books were actually a time of salvation. To Hyŏn, the problem was his belief that if he persisted in anything he would be saved. What followed and how that related to his present mental condition occupied his mind. In the end Hyŏn threw down the books. No matter how much he read, he could not obtain what he sought. To know the uselessness of books was their usefulness. It seemed like a paradox, but it was true. Hyŏn's eyes acquired a new vision and he saw the world as it was. Everything became clear. Once the true nature of history, philosophy, and literature stood revealed, these matters lost their charm. Hyŏn thought he had found the last thread of the world, a world made of glass thread, all tangled and twisted. He realized that he knew nothing, and knowing clearly that he knew nothing, he saw himself caught in a contradictory trap.

It had happened several days before. That day, Hyŏn sat and idled the time away at his favorite coffee shop. He was browsing through the newspaper when his eyes suddenly stopped. He stared at a small item concerning government appointments at the bottom of the front page: "Kim Mansul Appointed Consul-General to Marseilles." "Marseilles," Hyŏn uttered the name of this foreign city to himself. It was by no means an unfamiliar name to Hyŏn. Judging from the many associations it evoked, it must have meant more to him than those of the many Korean cities he had never visited.

"Marseilles' consul-general. Hmm, not a bad job. Better than an ambassador. Ambassadors can't use their ability or charm. They're mere transmitters—like parrots—to the Ministry of Foreign Affairs. A consul—that sounds like an easy job for a citizen with a little initiative. Korean consul-general to Marseilles. Neither too complicated nor too shabby. Kim Mansul . . . Hmm, if I were the consul, I would do ten times better than he. Pass Yokohama and Hong Kong, head for Calcutta through the Indian Ocean, cross the Mediterranean Sea (the sea route is more attractive than a plane journey)—the cobalt-colored waters of the Mediterranean, sunken slave ships bearing the bones of Greek and Roman soldiers and sailors.

"Would I reach the harbor of Marseilles? Absolutely. A distinguished Parisian and prominent ladies of Marseilles stand and watch my ship drop anchor. Ladies with parasols like a cluster of cosmos blossoms; the conventional brief reception and interview at the pier. Ride with the mayor and his wife; attend a party sponsored by the Chamber of Commerce; listen to the people with a correct and unaffected smile. Presently they will realize what a diplomat I am.

"The official business of the consul in France is merely to stamp the visas of travelers. The rest of the time, I would gradually work my way into circles of artists and scholars—Stendhal, Maupassant, Zola, Camus—and with my knowledge of literary history and philosophical criticism win their respect and obtain their friendship. Finally I would become an intimate of artists and intellectuals in Paris, and they would probably ask me to give a lecture somewhere or to teach comparative philosophy at the university, if only for an hour a week. Or my novelist friends would beg me to write a novel. Who says Koreans cannot become world famous? Their only disadvantage is being born in a backward country. I would write a long, beautiful poem using the anxiety of modern man in the symbolist vein. When translated into English and German it would become an instant best-seller and be imported into Korea, contrary to normal procedure. Hmm, what great works are there in Western literature? If I created a hero who personified the subtle East Asian mind, all other masterpieces would pale before it. There would be a congratulatory party in the bustling Parisian artistic community. The sound of champagne corks popping. The chatter of guests. The tuxedos of the gentlemen. The dazzling breasts of the ladies. And then . . ."

Hyŏn's happy dream might have continued endlessly and made him a member of the French Academy, but he felt a pain in his fingertips and came to his senses abruptly. His cigarette had scorched his fingertip. The grayish spot began to throb. Hyŏn, his composure shattered, gave a shout and kicked a chair aside as he ran out of the coffee shop.

Nursing the cigarette burn with his good hand, Hyŏn roamed through the dark streets like a madman. Added to his physical pain was the pain of selfmockery, which came like a needle prick and was more excruciating. "How disgusting. I am utterly disgusted with myself. I am nothing but a caricature."

Hyŏn disliked himself to the point of loathing. His was not the healthy dislike that induces reflection or justifiable self-reproach, but the kind of self-loathing one feels when he sees the yawning of discontented lovers, a feeling of helpless self-disgust. "I have no skills. I'm lazy and haven't the generosity to love another person. Even as I put on airs, I become irritable. . . ."

"Your Excellency must have swallowed something foul. Your manner of spitting is very unusual." K, a painter, tapped Hyŏn on the shoulder with a waggish gesture.

"Oh, it's good to see you."

"It doesn't seem to be a propitious meeting."

"I don't feel very confident these days," Hyŏn said to K as he walked beside him wearing a bitter smile.

"Self-confidence, isn't that something one gains or loses?"

"You pig! Why do I have an insensitive friend like you, huh?"

"You didn't have to say that," K replied sullenly without cracking a smile. Sitting across from Hyŏn at a tavern, K spoke again.

"Come to think of it, if you go out and walk around everyday, your nerves suffer and you become gloomy. A friend of mine is taking care of a big house all by himself. We use it as a place to get together and idle away our time. He and I have agreed to keep off the streets for a while, and now we're in the midst of recruiting members. Hyŏn, you must join us. My friend likes to collect records, and it's a wonderful place to listen to music. There's no comparison with a shabby coffee shop. You don't know what it's like to be in a big house. Why, aren't there a lot of artistic movements springing up in the form of private circles? It may sound funny, but we feel the sort of excitement one feels when founding a secret organization. The purpose of the organization is to avoid useless contacts with reality through hibernation." With these words, K leaned on his elbow, gazed out the window, and stylishly whistled a catchy tune.

"A secret organization? Right! Secret meetings in flickering lamplight. An armed guard at the gate. Dark streets. Creeping spies. Blind corners. Melting shadows. . . . Bravo! It's agreed. A secret organization sounds good. Let's drink a toast to our secret organization." Startled, the other guests in the tavern turned to stare at the two men, who now were drunk.

K drew Hyŏn a map as the two parted, adding that it was easy to locate. But Hyŏn knew the area quite well.

So it was that Hyŏn found himself climbing a desolate path smoking a cigarette. He came to a house with high stone walls like a fortress. Once it had been the property of some Japanese.

Looking beyond the house, Hyŏn could see the streetcar tracks and the illuminated downtown area. This was a very choice location. Hyŏn read the nameplate by match light, and then casually shook the dust from his shoes and calmly pressed the bell attached to a pillar.

The eight-mat room within the house was cluttered with Western furniture. At the center was an enormous round table, upon which a stuffed owl had been placed. Three men sat around this table looking like a picture. Although there was no power failure, the lights were off and a thick candle was burning. To anyone just entering it, the room resembled a gloomy cave. The eyes of the owl perched on the table glittered. The spectacle filled Hyŏn with a vague uneasiness.

K pointed to a seat next to himself with an oddly aloof expression, as if he had just met Hyŏn for the first time. Hyŏn sat down and looked at the two men with strange detachment. One of the two winked as soon as his eyes met Hyŏn's. The greeting didn't seem audacious—Hyŏn felt that he was indeed part of the group. K rose.

"The members are all present. I request that M read the declaration of our organization," K said, and then plopped down. M, who was seated to Hyŏn's right, was very pale. He got up and began to read aloud from a prepared speech.

"When the path to action is blocked, then nonaction takes its place. When one hesitates to say yes rather than answer no, silence may be the best thing. The worldling freely chatters about 'easy escape.' Is that not an easy way out? We challenge this easy way out. Creation is ended. Only mechanical repetition remains. God constantly conceives, and men replicate. If the genius plays a solo, the mob accompanies him. We reject this phenomenon, which is an illusion. We see history as it really is. History is a shimmering illusion of time. We reject time. We gather here to praise empty-handedness. We curse action. Evil and hatred arise from action. The wise preside over a gray twilight where history begins to repent of a day's action and prostrates itself in penitence. We step forward as lovers of gray. Why do the masses fear 'youthful ardor'? We proclaim with clear minds that we reject action. Only at dusk does the wise owl of Minerva open its eyes. This bird is our symbol. Our principle is a spiritual one; let us cherish the inner emotions that bind us and support our awareness of living in a land of purity. We know that to the select few, this kind of youthful openness is no passing fever, but a feeling that underlies their entire lives. He who transgresses this unwritten law must withdraw. He who divulges the truth to the outside world will be subject to spiritual assassination, whereby we will brand him a philistine and refuse him our friendship. Our club shall be called the Gray Club."

As soon as M sat down, K introduced the members. When he realized that M's friend C, and even K, were meeting each other for the first time, Hyŏn was surprised again. At first, Hyŏn smiled wryly at the tone of the declaration as it was read. Toward the end, however, he began to feel differently. This was a pure attachment, at least, and though naive in spirit, it was a valuable one. Hyŏn's pretense that he was on a higher plane than his fellow men began to give way before the innocence of these people. Does not the devil's cruelty pale before a child's smile? The contempt for sentimentality that Hyŏn kept buried deep within him began to weaken in this atmosphere, allowing him to reveal his true self. Hyŏn's self-consciousness was dispelled, and he clearly felt his unbearably sick mind—the self-mockery springing from that other self which surpervised, ridiculed, and mocked his own thoughts and actions—shattered and again reformed with a click.

"Salvation." He heard a voice whisper. Hyŏn gazed around at the faces of the members and discovered others of his own kind. A boundless, warm tide welled up in his chest and urged him to eloquence. Is eloquence not evidence of confidence? The eyes of the stuffed owl grew limpid and the night deepened.

More than a month after its formation, the Gray Club acquired a new member. It happened this way:

It was as if Hyŏn had assumed the role of a hero. One day he dropped in at his favorite coffee shop. After becoming a member of the Gray Club, Hyŏn, like the other members, practically stopped going to the coffee shop and the music hall where he used to spend all his time. To its members, the Gray Club was as essential as breathing. They could not bear to miss a single meeting. If they met, they made it a point to spend the whole day and even sat through the night. It was strange, but there seemed to be an unwritten law that forbade participation in any other group and prohibited close friendships with outsiders. It closely resembled the desire of two lovers to monopolize one another. Thus, it had really been a long time since Hyŏn had entered this coffee shop. Hyŏn nodded briefly toward the counter, where the owner acknowledged the greeting and inquired after him. Hyŏn's old friends rushed up as soon as he took a seat.

"Where have you been?"

"You haven't been around much at all lately."

"You must be in love."

A girl passed by as Hyŏn's friends greeted him with these words. One among the group said, "It's been a long time. Anything new?"

"Nothing new," she replied and quickly moved on.

Hyŏn felt a strange admiration for her simple, clear answer. Had another girl uttered the same words in a situation like this, she might have appeared common or ridiculous. But this girl was different. What's more, his friends seemed to take it for granted that she would act like this.

"Who is that girl?"

"That's Miss Han, who attends B University. Don't let her looks deceive you. She's a wonderful girl. Are you interested? I'll introduce you."

Hyŏn sat down, forcing a smile, and saw the girl coming his way again. He glanced sidelong at her as she passed by and took her original seat. After a while the group rose and invited Hyŏn to go drinking with them, but he shook his head. He had an idea. When the last of his friends had departed, Hyŏn stood up abruptly and moved to a seat right across from Miss Han. That was not so unusual, but he took out a piece of paper and wrote the following:

> I feel an extraordinary interest in you. Please do not naively inquire as to the meaning of my interest. Perhaps you know that one can make a strong impression upon first meeting because of his distinctive looks or bearing. This could be a source of pride for you and joy for me. I am a member of a secret organization, and I strongly urge you to join it. By no means will your honor be compromised. I request a prompt reply.

Without a word, Hyŏn pushed the sheet toward the girl. She looked surprised but made no attempt to rise. Hyŏn felt pride in his estimation of her character and uttered a cry of satisfaction.

Casually turning the note over she smiled reproachfully. "What if I refuse?" she said.

"I am sorry, but now that the secret is out, you must be ready for the worst. How's that?"

"What woman could resist such intimidation?"

Hyŏn uttered a cry of satisfaction for the second time. When he reported his actions to the Gray Club, a dispute arose with the members, criticizing his rash and thoughtless act.

First K said, "I am absolutely against it. Our club has been able to flourish and maintain its purity down to this day only because its membership is restricted to men. If we include women, a split will surely develop. Even if that doesn't happen, we'll have to be so careful that we won't be able to continue in our old ways. I'm opposed to this! Hyŏn has acted independently, and we must take disciplinary measures!"

C reiterated K's argument. "From times past," he said, "women have brought about the downfall of secret organizations. Can't you see the example of Stendhal's 'Vanina Vanini'?[1] Hyŏn says that she is very smart and fitting; how can she breathe alone among strange men? This is improper, and I'm opposed to it!"

Walking slowly away from the record player, M said, "Think it over. If we reject her, our secret will be exposed. You seem to be nervous about the opposite sex, but aren't you yourself demonstrating your vulnerable character? The problem is how to deal with this accomplished fact. A discussion of principles is meaningless here."

While the senior members argued pro and con, Hyŏn, who had caused all the trouble, was deprived of his right to speak and remained seated in the corner. The members decided to accept Miss Han after an interview, with the following reservations:

First, they would not consider her as a woman.

Second, intimate contact with her was forbidden.

Third, they would always act with the honor of the club in mind.

From the first day, Miss Han made such a good impression upon the members that their anxiety was completely dispelled.

"I was about to leave when he pushed the paper forward so abruptly. But the moment I saw his face, I knew that he was not a scoundrel," she said, submitting the note for inspection. K pulled out one of the eyes of the stuffed owl and took from within it the declaration made at the founding of the organization. This he read aloud.

---

[1]This story of Stendhal, pen name of Marie-Henri Beyle (1783–1842), tells of how Princess Vanini of Rome falls in love with Pietro Missirilli, a member of a secret political association in nineteenth-century Italy plotting to establish a republic. In order to possess him wholly, however, she betrays him and has him incarcerated by the authorities. See C. K. Scott-Moncrieff, *The Shorter Novels of Stendhal* (New York: Liveright, 1946), pp. 239–269.

After the girl took the oath, K declared that Hyŏn's note to her possessed historical value. He pushed it, together with the original declaration, into the owl's socket and replaced the eye. "Hmm. Hyŏn is quite a fellow. What an amazing love letter," K said in admiration.

C reported on the details of the club's past and added, "You must respect its senior members and defend the interest of the club. Do not forget to help with the cleaning." In the midst of this Miss Han shrieked, "I have been kidnapped as a maid!"

They all went to a movie as a welcome reception for the new member. The movie was a dramatized version of *Alt-Heidelberg*.[2] With its portrayal of life similar to theirs and its youthful romanticism, it was a fitting metaphor for their present state of mind.

That night, the members gave Miss Han the nickname of "Kitty." This was to be her official appellation among the members.

The Gray Club was at its brilliant apogee. It exceeded its members' expectations as an unfailing asylum. It had neither fixed meetings nor a fixed schedule. One person at a time came and went, and there certainly were no regular general meetings. Whether anyone came or not, M would sit rummaging through his phonograph records while K brought his drawing materials and sketched. The stove near the window was always lit, and Hyŏn's habit was to pace restlessly up and down between the stove and the window. He was not sensitive to cold, but it was his habit to gaze at the flame rising from the stove for an hour or two without feeling bored. "If I said gazing into the fire is a habit, one might laugh. But anyone who laughs at me may be more shallow than I am. My delight is no different from that of T'ai-kung Wang's joy in fishing,[3] Bodhidharma's gazing at a wall,[4] or a pimple-faced youth's pleasure in playing billiards. It is democratic to understand the interests of others and show a generous consideration for them, and such generosity would make this world a much better place to live." Such was Hyŏn's cherished belief. For this reason, he

---

[2]*Alt-Heidelberg*: dramatization (1903) by W. Meyer-Förster (1862–1934) of his sentimental novel *Karl Heinrich* (1899). As a film it was shown all over the world.

[3]T'ai-kung Wang: the wise fisherman who was discovered by King Wen of the Chou dynasty during a hunting expedition. The king invited him to serve as preceptor.

[4]Bodhidharma (fl. 470–520): The first patriarch of Ch'an Buddhism in China was an Indian dhyāna [meditation] master and champion of the *Laṅkāvatāra sūtra*. He arrived in Canton about 470 and then moved north, where he stayed until about 520. He is said to have sat and gazed at a wall continuously for nine years.

acquired the honorific title "Knight of the Stove," which somehow turned into "Custodian of the Stove"—he brought in the firewood and removed the ashes.

Kitty was a great lover of peanuts, and she always sat cracking the shells as if she had been born to eat peanuts. Kitty's peanuts had great appeal. With three or four of them, she was able to make others work for her. None of them had the moral courage to resist the temptation of her peanuts. One day, K exchanged a volume of Degas's paintings[5] bound elegantly in cloth for a bag of peanuts.

The night that this happened, Kitty saw K browsing through the book page by page. Kitty had been watching him, but refused to be generous with even a single peanut. Unable to reason with her, K made the deal. The next day, K claimed that it was invalid, but he soon became an object of blame and censure, and his argument was shattered to pieces. The members had been bribed with peanuts.

C considered his sacred daily work to be taking his afternoon nap and begging for a single peanut. When M's grandmother peeped in, which she often did, it was common for Kitty to present her with a heap of peanuts. The atmosphere was unusual. We might liken it to the attachment of adults to Tom Sawyer's Cave of Pirates.

"There is a human type which has no hands or feet for action, but who possesses a window for observation. The person who loathes lifting a finger but finds meaning in all kinds of colors and forms is a window type. The functions of a window are complementary. A window presupposes a building that isolates one from the outside world. It is the part of the building that shields one from the complexity of tangled actions and movements. Drawing a blind or a curtain, closing shutters, locking the door—all these acts symbolize obstruction of the window. On the other hand, a window allows a building to communicate with the outside world. Communication with the outside world through a window can be effected only by means of the eye. The mediation of the eye is indirect and calm. A window person gazes out at the genial spring of life and the cruel winter of strife. He does not burn his body in joy, nor does he lament any misery. He does not admit that it would have been better if the world had not been created. It is just as well that it was—this is his aesthetic and ethics. A

---

[5]Edgar Degas (1834–1917): French master of drawing the human figure in motion, a great colorist working mainly in pastel.

person without such a window is like a windowless building. He will suffocate from prejudice and solitude and will probably go insane.

"The Gray Club is a club composed of 'Knights of the Window.' The members approve of a world filled with praise, rather than one of discontent. The scene viewed through the window is mostly beautiful. A person viewed through the window is like a protagonist in a novel who lives in a harmonious balance between inside and outside. A window is a telescope for the wise and a comfort to the foolish. This is the philosophy of the Gray Club."

This passage is an excerpt from a speech that Hyŏn attempted to deliver in defense of his position near the window when he received the title "Knight of the Stove." The Gray Club possessed a window, but it was unlike any other. It was the eye of the club. After talking, everyone would go to the window. Through the large window in the east wall, one could take in a wave of tiled roofs and even the base of faraway South Mountain in a single glance.

This had the effect of drawing the viewer deep into himself. Tiles of various forms and hues, the colors of walls, and tints of buildings in Seoul, all had become varied in recent days. It seemed that our ancestors did not like to paint their houses in bright colors, but the situation had changed. The abundant colors of the undulating tile roofs spread beneath the clear autumn sky. Is there a life that burns so intensely as an apple blossom beneath that red galvanized roof? Is there the breathing of a girl like the emerald sorrow of an iris under the blue roof? All these roofs put on a gray veil, however, when twilight came.

"When man is lonely, he stands by the window," Hyŏn said to K.

Pressing his face against the window and gazing outside, K replied, "I think it would be more accurate to say that a man stands by the window only when he is lonely."

"Do you mean to say that you're lonely when you have friends and the Gray Club?"

Instead of answering, K looked Hyŏn in the eye.

"Do you ask that thinking you know the answer?"

"I seem to know the answer and yet not know it."

K plopped down on the sofa. "To speak of solitude is to speak of women."

"Women?"

"Certainly."

"Is that all?"

"It is a trivial Freudian fad, already outmoded. A man can feel lonely even without women. What else was the loneliness felt by Don Juan?"

"It's a plausible enough rebuttal, but not in the case of Don Juan. The void in Don Juan could only be filled by a woman's heart. A woman is a gate in the blind alley of our existence. We can't go beyond that. The gate is a passage to something beyond it."

"But since the gate is locked eternally, it's the final object, isn't it?"

"Right. It amounts to seizing an opportunity to usurp unjust authority."

"Women did not usurp it. It is rather that men have given them that epithet."

"Women still bear it without rejecting it."

"Not because they're intelligent but because they are shameless."

At this moment a voice from behind said, "Gentlemen, you are greatly mistaken." Since there had been no one else in the room, the two were surprised. They saw Kitty standing beaming at them. She looked uncommonly ladylike in her new homespun overcoat and a shawl wrapped about her so that only her eyes were exposed. She took off her coat.

"I thought you fellows were different. You're old-fashioned." With that, she pointed to her head with a finger.

"Ha, ha, ha," Hyŏn and K could only laugh.

"To use arbitrary definitions when discussing women will do men harm in the long run. How can anyone who can't see things clearly hope to perform meaningful acts? I tell you, women are exactly like men. A woman can apply your theory to men also. Hasn't it been clear from Ibsen's time? Men and women have been the same creatures since the creation. To judge human nature by superficial matters, such as social position in this case, is very foolish. You gentlemen seem to see me that way, don't you?"

"Absolutely not. You are my equal. You, our queen, understand this well."

"It's becoming worse. If you don't appreciate me, I'll withdraw." Kitty deliberately changed to her usual tone and placed her hands on her hips.

The embarrassed Hyŏn sought some clever retort, but he could think of nothing. K, however, was on top of the situation.

"What nonsense. You know quite well the fate of one who withdraws willfully from the organization. On a certain pitch-black night, without anyone's knowledge . . . like this!" So saying, he feigned stabbing empty space with an imaginary dagger.

"I take back what I said. It was only a joke." Then she brought out her bag of peanuts. At this moment, M entered. M, the caretaker of the house, went out whether there were guests or not. He came in at any time, and it was difficult to know whether M was the host or a guest; such was the atmosphere of this anarchistic club. Kitty rose and put on a record. A lovely melody poured forth, as if to express their present mood. As she leaned against the record player, Kitty's face appeared as milky white as a gourd flower in the dim room. Suddenly, Hyŏn asked himself if he had loved Kitty from the start. Then he became gloomy.

Summer passed unnoticed, and once more the needles fell one by one from the fir tree by the window.

Hyŏn and Kitty were walking side by side toward the club, thinking about the people they had just left behind, a group of Jehovah's Witnesses. "Please attend at least once. After you've studied our doctrine, you may believe or not as you wish," an evangelist who came to the house had urged Kitty. She had not wanted to go alone and so invited Hyŏn to accompany her. There was clearly a fresh religious atmosphere at the Witnesses' meeting. They were as excited as if this business about Jesus had happened yesterday.

"1. Christmas has no biblical foundation.
2. The portrait of Christ is a historical fabrication.
3. Christ's scaffold was not a cross, but a straight plank. To harbor the cross as the symbol of faith is ignorance on the part of the church and deception on the part of the clergy.
4. The soul is mortal.
5. The kingdom of Jesus will appear on earth in the near future."

They maintained this kind of dogma in their study of the Bible and claimed that they accepted as the literal truth every word in Revelation, which up to now had been interpreted allegorically. It was said that the sect was founded toward the end of the nineteenth century. Their publication, *The Watch Tower*, was central to them; they published it in their headquarters in America. Their chief function was the study of the Bible, but they didn't have professional clergy-men. The pedantic interpretation of the Scriptures, however, pro-voked antipathy in Hyŏn.

"They seem to feel a tremendous sense of mission. They earnestly try to persuade you," said Hyŏn.

"They're rather unusual people, different from normal churchgo-ers. Seeing that the majority of them are people who have broken away from established denominations, they clearly aren't easygoing."

"But their assertion that the most important point in the Old Tes-tament, the creation of heaven and earth, coincides with the present theory of physics is too nonsensical. They are trying to support each word of the Bible with scientific proof, but does the Bible need scien-tific authentication?"

"They should just go on insisting that everything happened, instead of trying to prove it scientifically."

"How can we rest easy if biblical interpretation follows every change in scientific theory? There is nothing more disheartening than a scientific interpretation of the Bible."

With that, Hyŏn gazed casually up at the sky. It was a radiant, star-lit night. Kitty, too, looked up at the sky.

"So I feel that only those who have witnessed Jesus walking on water and have seen people speaking with Jesus after his resurrection can believe. Buddhism is entirely different. One is fact; the other is a philosophy. Philosophy remains philosophy even after a thousand years, but the record of a fact is not the fact itself."

"You cannot believe because you haven't witnessed these things?"

"One who believes without witnessing is a monster."

"There are countless things we believe without seeing them. Have you ever *seen* that the earth is round?"

"Women are empty after all. How are that and this the same?"

"Look—here you are speaking about women again. Your feudalistic attitude is just incurable."

Hyŏn put a hand to his brow and nodded regretfully.

"That's that, Kitty. But why do men want to know God?"

"Haven't you read the Catholic catechism? It probably amounts to 'Why was man created? Man came into the world to know and wor-ship God!' "

Hyŏn nodded at her answer, which was not an answer at all. He did not want to construe the perplexing problem of God as only the result of excessive consciousness. As time passed and he matured, and if the urgency of this question melted away of its own accord . . . but then, he did not want to live a life of compromise. He had no ability, however, to produce an answer by force. When a nebulous doubt arose that he could neither believe nor disbelieve, he again had to wage a war of self-persuasion to appease his struggling self. His predicament even led him to the exotic assembly of Jehovah's Witnesses with their fantastic stories. When they reached the club, M was not to be seen, but C was lying alone on the sofa.

Without even turning his head, C immediately recited as if from memory, "Why must man live?" Hyŏn replied, in an intonation that seemed appropriate for chanting some scripture, "We live to know and to worship God."

Then C said, "Where is God, then?" Hyŏn did not answer and lay down on the sofa. There came the sound of peanut shells cracking, and C awoke with a start.

"Give me some peanuts." He stuck out his hand. Hyŏn was surprised. When did she buy the peanuts? It was like the workings of a ghost.

"Just one peanut. Thanks to you, our noble catechism session is ruined. As a compensation . . ."

"Why so rude? Can't you be nice? No wonder you cannot comprehend Providence."

"I know, I know. I am weak to temptation, to that crunching sound."

"The catechism has gone out the window."

"Exactly. I must have one in a fit of anger."

"Ho, ho, ho. One in a fit of anger. Here it is . . ."

Hyŏn felt an indescribable happiness. If one stayed in the club, everything seemed to be all right. With that unfounded thought, he felt a tremendous chasm between Kitty as she was with him and as she was when in the club.

It was Christmas Eve. People bustled by carrying presents, and snow fell profusely upon them. In the streets, filled with picturesque neon signs and decorations, Christmas carols flowed from loudspeakers everywhere, enhancing the festive mood.

In front of a corner toy store, Hyŏn and his party of five stood gazing into the shop window. French dolls, cupids, puppies, giraffes, white bears, Mickey Mouse, elephants, and midgets displayed in the show window breathed silently. Their expression uniformly expressed nostalgia for home. Originally they were not citizens of this world. In truth, the giraffe's neck was not as long as that; the white bear's mouth in reality was much smaller; and where in the world is a mouse like Mickey Mouse? A beauty of exaggerated traits was the beauty of fairyland. They were the prisoners of a faraway land, kidnapped to console man in his loneliness. Because man grew up in intense solitude, does he not wander about in search of dolls even in adulthood? Buddha, Jesus, Marx . . . There was a purity in the ordered beauty of the toys. Therefore Hyŏn felt a sense of kinship with them.

Was it a form of sentimentality caused by the emptiness of a pagan on Christmas Eve? It may have been that, but that was not all. Hyŏn felt melancholy. The Gray Club was falling apart. For the first time Hyŏn realized how difficult it is for men to assemble and undertake something together. How can he explain the subtle complications and repulsions of sensitive young nerves? It was like the state of mind of lovers who, bored with each other, contemplate a way to rupture their ties. Where did the trouble start? No, curse the man who asks such a calculating question! It isn't a question of where the trouble started. The only important thing was that the Gray Club was falling apart, if indeed its purpose was to cherish the inner emotions that bound the members together and supported their consciousness of living in a Land of Purity.

Hyŏn was a traitor. His mind turned like the tide toward Kitty. Hyŏn could not check that tide, and he was miserable. Yet there was another Hyŏn who obstinately opposed his loyalty to the club. It could not but be reflected in the spirit of the members. Kitty stood immediately next to Hyŏn. Hyŏn put his hand into her overcoat pocket and groped for her hand. Kitty quickly put a warm, round object into Hyŏn's hand, and he knew instantly that it was a roasted chestnut. Kitty's blithe attitude, pretending not to recognize Hyŏn's feelings toward her and substituting a roasted chestnut, made Hyŏn impatient. When they returned to the club it was past twelve.

"Let's celebrate the Christmas of the pagans." Singing, K emptied out his package onto the round table. Hyŏn also poured out peanuts and doughnuts, and shouted joyfully.

"Yes, a pagan Christmas, a party to send off the old year. Oh, beloved Gray Club!"

Kitty looked out and said, "The snow is getting heavy. Everything is white, and I can't see a thing."

M put on Tchaikovsky's *Pathétique*, and C lit the five candles. After K bade everyone be seated, he raised his beer mug.

"To the glory of the Gray Club."

Five glasses clinked together.

"Hey, is there enough beer?"

"Don't worry. Will two cases do?"

"Hurrah! Let's toast Mr. M!"

Kitty alone remained silent. "Kitty, what does this mean?" K bellowed.

"What shall I do among drunkards, if you're going to finish off two cases of beer?"

"I see! Gentlemen, we are sold off at wholesale. Our queen implies that we can be trusted only to the extent of two cases of beer," K said heaving a deep sigh.

M was more resolute. "We have the honor of withdrawing from this disgraceful place," he said.

A crisis was narrowly averted by Kitty's endless pleading. Hyŏn had never been more elated. Even at that, the merriment seemed a frantic, mindless effort on the part of each member. At that instant a voice said, "Hey, you. That's your crooked mind. You, who are calculating the downfall of the club."

Hyŏn wondered whether M or C had spoken. But in fact this was his own mind that was reprimanding him. He felt that he would go mad, and he abruptly stood up and shouted, "Ladies and gentlemen, I would like to recite an impromptu poem for the club." There were applause and cheers.

> We know why there must be,
> In a deep green jungle,
> Ambition like a deluge,
> A sun burning like bloody hatred.
>
> We know the leopard's indomitable spirit
> That leaps over the ridge
> With his mate
> In the driving rain.
>
> We have found
> Demiurgus's[6] records that he lost
> On the day of creation.
>
> Living in the Pure Forest,
> Drinking the nectar of wisdom,

---

[6]Demiurgus: the creator of the world in Platonic philosophy.

The wise knows
The message of white clouds
Scattered in the boundless sky.
You who sorrow because you love life,
Come to the waters of purity
In the endless grove of gray.

O boundless youth!
Because love is intense,
We roll about in hatred
Glimpsing eternity through a cup of wine.
Let us laugh and cry,
O Gray Club!

You are my love,
You are my life.
A flag of youth
Fluttering in the wind,
O Gray Club!

Confusion ensued. K squeezed Hyŏn's neck and kissed him, while M pulled his leg impulsively. C poured beer down his throat until he nearly choked, and Kitty threw doughnuts and peanuts in his face. The night deepened.

Toward dawn, a song was suddenly heard in the neighborhood. All rushed to the window, opened it, and looked out. The snow had stopped, and a Christmas carol resounded through the dazzling white snow. This chorus in the middle of the night had an indescribable freshness.

"It's a chorus."

"We must give them presents."

"Good, good."

"Hurry!"

The members clattered down the stairs, passed through the garden, and ran toward the back gate. As he turned at the corner, Hyŏn saw Kitty running with her bag of peanuts. He seized her arm, and she merely gazed at him. He leaned against the pine tree in the yard, pulled her close, and kissed her. Her bag of peanuts slipped from her hand, and a clump of the snow that studded the branches above fell and scattered over her shoulder. In a dreamy rapture, Hyŏn dispelled the thought that Kitty, too, would soon be gone.

It was several days after Christmas when Hyŏn went to the club again. How could he face Kitty? It was a question of whether to remain in the club or withdraw from it.

In the end, however, he could reach no conclusion, and he decided to go anyway. The instant he opened the door, he was transfixed by a bizarre spectacle. Kitty stood nearly nude, behind the halo-like blaze of the stove, while K leaned on the wall in front, setting up his art equipment. M and C were lying on the sofa and gazing up at the ceiling as usual. Hyŏn feigned composure and sat on a corner of the sofa with his eyes closed. (*Slut, that incident the other night was nothing. This shows that I shouldn't misunderstand.*)

"Why are you so serious?" Hyŏn heard Kitty right next to him. She had donned her clothes and was standing there smiling. "Since he wanted to enter a picture called 'Nude' in the exhibition, I decided to be his model," she said. "If he wins, we'll divide the prize money fifty-fifty." Hyŏn felt that Kitty had suddenly begun showing off and had become a giant that he was unable to confront. The only problem now was when and how to withdraw.

But catastrophe was unexpectedly swift in coming. At dusk that day, Hyŏn walked toward the club with a heart as heavy as the weather had been in recent days. He had turned down an alley and gone about five paces off the main road when a man approached him and said, "Hey, you."

That short phrase sent a chill down Hyŏn's spine. The man who stood before him was a stranger.

"I'm a detective from P station." After identifying himself, the stranger confirmed Hyŏn's name. "Let's go to the station," he said then.

"Why?"

"You'll find out when you get there."

"I'll find out when I get there? Please show me your warrant."

"What? You wise guy!"

Hyŏn heard the sound of his cheeks being slapped. He was again surprised when he reached the police station. K, M, and C were already there. To Hyŏn's question they answered silently with their eyes. They were questioned separately.

"Why don't you confess now that . . ."

Hyŏn was amazed. He remained silent.

"Why are you so silent? Okay, then, let me ask you something. You know these men, don't you?"

He pointed out some names on a list lying beside him as he stared at Hyŏn. The names were unknown to Hyŏn.

"I don't know them."

"You don't, huh?"

The detective gasped and abruptly stood up from his chair. Hyŏn instinctively retreated a step. The detective sat down again and motioned Hyŏn to a chair.

"Sit down. Don't be that way. Listen to me. You know well enough that detectives have ways of finding things out. Depending on your attitude, the tone of the report can change. If the suspect stubbornly refuses to answer the question or continues to lie . . . Do you know how disadvantageous it will be when you go to court?"

"I don't even know what this is all about. I'm silent because I have no other alternative."

The detective narrowed his eyes.

"I know you guys aren't easy to deal with." He rested his chin on his hand and stuck his face closer.

"What did you do in Mr. M's house?"

"What do you mean?"

"Hmm."

He shook his head several times and went out the door. Left alone, Hyŏn became conscious for the first time of his fear and anxiety. It was Hyŏn who spoke first when the detective returned.

"There must be a mistake. Please explain why we were brought here."

"What impudence! . . . Didn't you gather every day to study seditious books and to contact these people who were plotting to overthrow the government?"

"What!" These words were so unexpected that Hyŏn could not reply at once. For the first time, Hyŏn could vaguely comprehend the nature of the detective's suspicion.

"This is a complete misunderstanding. It was nothing more than a gathering in a big house to chat and amuse ourselves with discussions of literature and philosophy."

An unbearable feeling of humiliation swelled up within Hyŏn even as he spoke. Was this his own definition of the Gray Club—chats for amusement's sake? The humiliation was followed by hatred for the man who had extracted this explanation from him.

"Well, then, let me ask you one more question. Why did you keep your meetings secret? In other words, why didn't you ever speak to anyone else about the meetings? There are indications that you attached extreme secrecy to them."

Hyŏn was speechless. How could he convince the detective of the intricate nature of the club? Yet he could not be silent, either. He vulgarized the whole affair, managing to swallow his pride. Unexpectedly the detective, though he nodded his head and asked questions once in a while, heard Hyŏn out. As soon as Hyŏn stopped speaking, the detective went out. He came back half an hour later. He then went out again and returned after thirty or forty minutes. This time he took Hyŏn to the detectives' room.

Presently K, M, and C entered.

"I don't think there's anything serious. Spend the night here and we'll send you back home in the morning," the detective said. Then he went out.

They pulled the chairs near the stove and sat in silence. They felt as though they were meeting after having committed some foul deed. In an extreme sense, their dismal mood was akin to that of a traitor who has just been released after betraying his friends.

The members were discharged about nine o'clock the next day. They split into two groups, K and C returning home while Hyŏn followed M to the club. When they were released the detective said that though it could not be revealed yet, they had been suspected of connections to a subversive group. Kitty had not been taken in for questioning so that the police could use her as bait.

"Because you all seem to be understanding, don't be upset." He tapped Hyŏn's shoulder.

As soon as M went downstairs to see his grandmother, Hyŏn was left alone. He opened the door and found Kitty standing in the middle of the room. Her expression was strained.

"I heard what happened from M's grandmother."

Hyŏn looked at Kitty without making any reply. He was restless, thinking constantly of how stupid he was. It was a confused and divided feeling.

"It was nothing. They mistook us for student dissidents."

"Student hoodlums?" Kitty wore an expression of doubt.

"Ha, ha," Hyŏn laughed a hollow laugh despite himself.

Kitty, concerned, was annoyed by Hyŏn's attitude. Just then an idea occurred to Hyŏn.

"That's that. But I have a problem."

"A serious problem?"

"Uh huh."

Hyŏn's long silence seemed to irritate Kitty more.

"Why are you acting like this?"

Hyŏn raised his head. "The club has asked me to ask you to withdraw voluntarily."

At that moment Kitty turned pale.

"That is . . ."

"It was all a miscalculation. At first, when I helped you get into the club, I was acting rashly. It wasn't your fault. As you know, the harmony of the club has been disrupted by your presence. We have discussed . . ."

Hyŏn's speech was interrupted by Kitty's hysterical laughter.

"Ha, ha, ha." Kitty just laughed and laughed.

"Oh really! Pardon me, sir. An order from the Gray Club. How about that! That's even more cruel than killing me. If I am driven away from this house of the wise, where can I find wisdom? Sophisticated salon of the greatest masterminds, how cruel of you to drive me away from the secret chamber of my soul. Ho, ho, ho . . ."

Kitty abruptly stopped laughing.

"Don't make me laugh. What is the Gray Club? It's a caricature of a small incompetent man, a ward of patients suffering from delusions of grandeur and boastful assertions. A Land of Purity. Don't make me laugh! Such unmanly hypersensitivity. Such authoritarianism that won't allow a woman to breathe freely. You looked down on me because I was nude, didn't you? On the contrary, I challenged you physically to show you how much I despise you all. I can just see you all confused and fluttering, not knowing what to do! The principle of the Gray Club is nothing more than spiritual paralysis. What good is it to pursue knowledge when you can't stir or move a single blade of grass in reality? Does reality retreat just because you close your eyes? I have been ruined on account of all of you. I don't ask you to share the responsibility. Wandering is a valuable experience, too. I stayed a step behind, not realizing until now. How about that? Isn't this fate too, old friends? Adieu, then. But last of all, praying for the glory of the Gray Club, my eternal love . . ."

Her incessant shouting and theatrical tone left Kitty pale and out of breath. As if in a trance, Hyŏn stood silent for some time. Slowly he opened his mouth.

"Kitty . . ."

Hyŏn's tone was heavy and evinced overwhelming strength.

"Kitty, we met in good faith. Why are you breaking my heart and leaving bad feelings between us?"

He was cautious and grave, trying to keep Kitty from becoming more frivolous.

"It was done for your benefit. But this kind of separation is unbearable. After all, you are a woman. You really have very little feeling. Do you know what I mean?"

Without giving her a chance to reply, he said, "You got angry without finding out the truth about us—M, K, C, and I; all of us were arrested. I said hoodlums, but are we really? Do you think that's possible? Judging from your contempt, we are less than hoodlums, but you at least know that our direction is different."

Kitty's face showed confusion.

"Kitty, are you really an admirer of putting theory into practice? Listen, the Gray Club was a cell of a secret organization devoted to terrorism and anarchy. Are you surprised? Do you think it's a joke? Kitty, man is a complex animal. Did you know that Cromwell's able secretary was Milton?[7] Why did Byron die in Greece and Heine sympathize with the revolution?[8] Poets glorify power. Deep within the consciousness of poets exists a dream of the emperor. Why did Plato seek to elucidate politics? Man is infinitely complex. It's a fact that after the liberation, we still don't know who the real assassins of political leaders were. Some suspect it to have been the work of the communists. It was the work of our club. While we approve of Plato's *Republic* as an ideal, we do not refrain from terror. We recognize Marx's utopia, but we oppose the manipulation of human beings. Even among the present academic circle . . . Oh, this is useless! Let me express first of all my heartfelt apology. But briefly, drawing you into the club was a means of deception. We meant to disguise the heavy color of steel with pastel pink. Don't be angry; that would be unreasonable. Part of our organization, the cell closest to our club, was arrested. Although we were released deliberately, K and C are

---

[7]John Milton (1608–1674): While serving as Latin secretary to the Council of State (1649–1660), Milton described Oliver Cromwell (1599–1658), Lord Protector from 1653 to 1658, as "the defender of conscience and liberty."

[8]Byron at Missolonghi: Lord George Gordon Byron (1788–1824) tried to rally the Greek insurgents against the Turks but died of fever before any military action in April 1824. Heinrich Heine (1797–1856): German poet whose writing during his stay in Paris was concerned mainly with politics and social questions; in 1835 his works were officially branded as subversive; in 1843 he met Karl Marx.

still being held. We think it's a trick. It is our purpose to confuse the authorities and thereby gain time. We have innocently pretended to be members of a literary club, but our friends seemed to doubt it. That, too, is a question of time. Kitty, you will not be harmed, since you really knew nothing. If you tell the truth, there will be no problem later. Our intention was a good one—to stop you from coming to the Gray Club anymore and to save you from unnecessary suffering during the coming days of disorder. I cannot possibly part from you in this manner. Man is complex and profound. You say you've been exploited by crooks, but isn't being free to wander something precious? Well, Kitty, I hope you take back the last part of your speech about action. Ha, ha, ha. I'm tired. I even loved you a little."

Hyŏn held his head and staggered.

Kitty was lying flat on the round table and crying.

Hyŏn fixed his gaze on her heaving shoulders. How long had he been watching her thus?

"Ha, ha, ha!" This sudden outburst of loud laughter caused Kitty to raise her head.

"Ha, ha, ha!"

Hyŏn laughed with his eyes wide open and his hands on his stomach. Kitty stood up quickly. She was exhausted by Hyŏn's repeated acrobatic leaps between truth and falsehood.

"Ha, ha, ha. How was that? I'm going to try out for a part in a movie. A convincing act, wasn't it?"

With a shriek, Kitty seized the legs of the stuffed owl and hurled it at Hyŏn's face. His face was stained with blood. It all happened in an instant. Kitty fell to the floor in a faint, but Hyŏn went on laughing and gazing at the feathers that littered the floor. He laughed on as if unaware of the blood flowing down his face.

"Ha, ha, ha . . ."

M opened the door and came in.

Hyŏn woke up suddenly sometime later. A dim fog was spreading thickly through the room, and silence surrounded him. Kitty's fainting, M coming in after that, Kitty having a fever and deciding to stay overnight—recollections of the events that had occurred before he fell asleep slowly returned to Hyŏn, as if to fill in the gaps in his consciousness.

Hyŏn rose silently from the sofa on which he had been sleeping. M appeared to be sound asleep, his face turned toward the wall. Hyŏn looked across at the sofa where Kitty was lying. He saw her pale face clearly in the moonlight coming through the window.

Hyŏn tiptoed to a spot directly above Kitty. Her nose appeared unusually prominent in the moonlight, like some toy, and Hyŏn felt a vague clumsiness and pity.

Hyŏn stood there as if waiting for Kitty to awaken. His mind was quite calm. Was he dazed, just awakened as he was from sleep? No, this was nothing physiological. Hyŏn had discovered women for the first time in the face of the sleeping Kitty. Until now, Kitty had been a talented person to Hyŏn, rather than a female. That talent was her charm. It had been the same when he kissed her on Christmas Eve. It was difficult for Hyŏn to love an unintelligent woman. This Kitty, however, who had suffered greatly from Hyŏn's psychological manipulations and who had fallen asleep on a stranger's sofa, was just a woman. Hyŏn also realized that he was just a man, a human being. It was beautiful, mysterious, but now was the time to strip away the mask, he thought. *(Not a wise woman, not a philosopher or princess, but just another human being. How good, how attractive!)*

Hyŏn tiptoed to the window and stood looking out. The view of the capital under the moonlight, from nearby roofs glistening like dewdrops on a rock to the faraway roofs like billowing clouds, appeared as if he were seeing it for the first time.

Hyŏn had no regrets. Everything had turned out well. He turned to look at M and Kitty and sighed. *(Why is being alive so interesting?)*

Hyŏn heard a rooster crowing. He imagined the radiant sun rising above the rooftops outside. He wanted only to see the bright morning. He suddenly felt sleepy. He returned to the sofa quietly and lay down once more. The moment before he fell into a deep sleep, he saw before his eyes the bright rays of the dawning sun.

TRANSLATED BY PETER H. LEE

MODERN SIJO

The three-line *sijo* is the most popular, elastic, and mnemonic of classic Korean poetic forms. Each line consists of four metric segments with a minor pause at the end of the second group and major pause at the end of the fourth. An emphatic syntactic division usually falls in the third line (the first group of the line is invariably of three syllables) in the form of a countertheme, paradox, resolution, judgment, command, or exclamation. The introduction of a deliberate twist in phrasing and meaning is often a test of a poet's originality. The only classic poetic form alive today in Korea, the *sijo* is still an oral art for the lettered and unlettered alike. Poets in the twentieth century have written individual *sijo* and *sijo* cycles. The classic form is retained in every respect except the number of lines. Influenced by Western versification, modern poets have often extended the number of lines to as many as ten. It is no accident that major modern poets in the form have championed the revival of Korean tradition. *The Hundred and Eight Passions and Delusions (Paekp'al pŏnnoe)*, the first modern *sijo* cycle of importance, was produced in 1926 by Ch'oe Namsŏn (1890–1957), who declared that the *sijo* is "the glory of Korean literature and the main current of Korean poetry."

A historian and scholar of Chinese studies, Chŏng Inbo (1893–1950) went to Beijing where he studied for eight years (1910–1918). Upon returning to Korea, he wrote editorials for the daily newspapers and taught at several universities. Known for his incorruptible character, he was named the first director of the Inspection Committee of the Republic of Korea (1948). He was kidnapped by the North Korean army in 1950. His collection of *sijo* first appeared in 1948.

Yi Pyŏnggi (1892–1968), Yi Hŭisŭng (b. 1896), and Yi Ŭnsang (b. 1903) all shared a lifelong dedication to the Korean language and literature. At the time of the Korean Language Research Institute incident (1942), all three were imprisoned and tortured, and their manuscripts for a dictionary of the language were confiscated by the Japanese. Yi Hŭisŭng was freed only after the liberation. Both Yi Pyŏnggi and Yi Hŭisŭng taught at Seoul National University and produced scholars who are active in the field today. Since his publication of "What Is *Sijo?*" in the *Tonga Daily* in 1926, Yi Pyŏnggi has not only systematized the rhetoric of *sijo* but modernized its tone and content by fresh, realistic diction.

Yi T'aegŭk (b. 1913), currently a professor at Ewha Women's University, has edited the journal *Sijo munhak* (June 1960) and helped nurture a number of poets in the form. Chŏng Hun (b. 1911), Yi Hou (1912–1969), and Pak Hangsik (b. 1917) have all contributed to the modernization of *sijo*. Pak Hangsik looks at reality in plain diction, while Pak Kyŏngyong has retained the classic touch in refined lyricism.

Yi Pyŏnggi

MOUNT ACH'A

Crossing ridge after ridge
    the landscape is desolate.
Grass, frost-covered rocks,
    red berries, violets—
I stop to look around,
    how could I be lonely?

RAIN

The day she packed her bags
    to leave me,
The rain fell gently
    from the dark hours.

Let it fall tomorrow,
    keep falling day after day.
         *

Please don't leave
    on that long, long road.
The rain falls gently
    far into the night,
Tenderly dissuading you
    better than I can.
         *

Pulling loose the sleeve
    I had grasped, you leave.
I wake from a dream,
    the glad tattle of rain!
Seeing the pile of your baggage,
    I close my eyes again.

WINDOW

In this room
    the window does for seeing.
A sheet of paper
    hides the universe.
But you light with an endless glow
    when the sun shines.
         *
You know best
    my ugliness and beauty.
You know best
    my sorrows and joys.
At the last moment of my life,
    I want to be beside you.

Chŏng Inbo

EARLY SPRING

Beautiful traces of early spring,
 where do they not pervade?
When my thoughts congeal,
 the passing clouds linger—
Don't say your brush lacks skill,
 why not try a line?

Yi Hŭisŭng

POMEGRANATE

Hidden among the leaves,
 you peek out at the blue sky.
Your cheeks and lips
 burn with ruddy fire.
Is it only the rind so red?
 I'll split the fruit and see.

Yi Ŭnsang

THE DIAMOND MOUNTAINS

What are the Diamond Mountains?
  They're rocks and water.
If rocks and water,
  then they're mist and cloud.
If mist and cloud,
  sometimes they are, sometimes they are not.

Yi T'aegŭk

ELEVEN-FACED

BODHISATTVA OF MERCY

Tiptoeing with dignity
  upon her lotus throne,
Through dreamy eyelashes
  she gazes upon the Eastern Sea.
Enlighten me, merciful goddess,
  on the workings of causation!
      *
She makes no motion,
  yet the tinkle of swaying beads.
Her skin glows through
  from under the folds of robe.
The rounded breast, thrust forward,
  gently pulses.
      *

On spring nights every year
    the cuckoo sadly cries.
The long, long time flows,
    flows fleetingly by.
Wrapped in rapturous dreams,
    she smiles alone.

Chŏng Hun

QUIET

In the middle of painting a hill,
    I call for a cup of tea.
The faint fragrance of india ink
    wafts like a mist.
A bird gives ear
    to the sound of pouring tea.

Yi Hou

BLOSSOMING FLOWER

The flower opens petal by petal,
    a heaven is unfolding.
When the last petal quivers,
    at that awful moment,
The breezes and sunshine hush,
    I too tingle and close my eyes.

Pak Hangsik

PEACH

A picture is a false image,
    a song flows away and dies.
On a black tray,
    the shadows are bright.
Peaches lie there still,
    a poem without a design!

Chŏng Wanyŏng

MID-AUTUMN FESTIVAL

The chestnuts wish only to open,
    the jujubes wish only to ripen.
Grandpa's white hair was eminent,
    I was a little prince then.
Tonight the moon from my home follows me
    and makes me cry.

LARK AND GRANNY FLOWER

Last night's sweet misty rain
    moistened the hills and fields.
Opening the heaven's door on a new morning,
    a lark sings and says:
Lift up your head,
    granny flower[1] on the hill!

---

[1]granny flower: pasqueflower or windflower.

Pak Kyŏngyong

SUNFLOWER

The prince is withdrawing
    from twilight, from his kingdom.
Burned with fire, even yellow gold
    will leave no trace.
In the garden where the sun dies,
    ah, another sun is setting!

TRANSLATED BY PETER H. LEE

MODERN POETRY

III

Sŏ Chŏngju (b. 1915) led a wandering life before the liberation. His early poetry in *Flower Snake* (1938) was characterized by sensuality and diabolism in a specifically Korean setting. With *The Cuckoo* (1948) Sŏ returned to broader East Asian emotions and themes involving eternal life. In subsequent volumes, Sŏ presented a vision of an idealized Silla kingdom in which man and nature were one. Sŏ forged the themes of Buddhist tales and legends into new forms and presented a view of life imbued with a dark, mysterious stillness. His most recent poems show him delving into native shamanism to transform intractably unpoetic elements into works of art.

Pak Tujin, born in Ansŏng to the south of Seoul in 1916, made his literary debut in 1939 with a group of original nature poems. His silence between 1941 and 1945 was inevitable, as the Japanese prohibited the use of the Korean language except in writings that promoted the Japanese war cause. Since the publication of his first collection of poetry in 1949, Pak has been a prolific and prizewinning poet. To Pak nature has always been "the source of God's love, light, truth, goodness, and beauty," and his paeans to the beauty of the created world and his Blakean innocence became imbued with a moral vision as he came to view the world in terms of moral conflict. As political corruption and repression increased in South Korea, Pak's moral consciousness came to the fore and his poems from the mid-1960s reveal a strong historical and cultural consciousness that bears testimony to contemporary reality. An aging eagle whose fidelity to his vision remains unshaken, he has withdrawn into nature to discover its creative power in water-washed stones—the topic of some two hundred of his poems, Pak's homage to nature as a creative force.

Pak Mogwŏl, born in Kyŏngju in 1916, made his literary debut in

1939. Until his death in 1978, he published poems, essays, translations, and children's poems. His early poems, written in folk song rhythms, recreated the local color of the south with effortless elegance and control. But from the late 1950s he turned to open forms and looser measures and a plain, often powerful, diction. The poetry he finds in daily urban life is sometimes precarious and marginal, but his more successful poems transform incidental experiences into flashes of discovery.

Sŏ Chŏngju

LEPER

Saddened by the sun
and blue of the sky

the leper ate a child
at moonrise by the barley fields

and through the night cried out
his sorrow red as a flower.

MIDDAY

A path through a field of red flowers
that plucked and tasted bring dreaming death;

along the path winding like the yellow back
of an opium-stunned snake
my love runs, calling me after

and I follow, receiving
in my two hands
the blood flowing sharp-scented from my nose.

In the broiling midday, hushed as night,
our two bodies burn.

SELF-PORTRAIT

Father was a serf;
he never came home, even late at night.
The only things standing there were grandmother, withered
and pale as the roots of a leek,
and one flowering date tree.
For a month, mother longed for green apricots, even one.
By the oil lamp set in the dirt wall's niche
I was mother's boy, with black fingernails.
With my large eyes and thick hair
I am said to take after grandfather on my mother's side
who went off to sea, the story goes, sometime
during the year of reforms, and never returned.

For twenty-three years it is the wind that has raised four-fifths of me.
Life has become more and more an embarrassment.
Some read a convict in my eyes,
some an idiot in my mouth,
but I will repent nothing.

On such mornings, at the magnificent dawn,
drops of blood mingle with the dew
of poetry settled on my forehead.
For I have come, tongue hanging out,
panting through sun and shade like a sick dog.

BESIDE A CRYSANTHEMUM

To bring one chrysanthemum
to flower, the cuckoo has cried
since spring.

To bring one chrysanthemum to bloom,
thunder has rolled
through the black clouds.

Flower, like my sister returning
from distant, youthful byways
of throat-tight longing
to stand by the mirror:

for your yellow petals to open,
last night such a frost fell,
and I did not sleep.

RHODODENDRON

A mountain is reflected
in each petal of the rhododendron.

On the mountain's skirts
a sad concubine's house is napping.

On the porch is set out
a chamber pot of brass.

Beyond the mountain,
shoals of yellow fish in the spring tide

and gulls that cry
at the pain of salt.

SNOWY NIGHT

On Cheju Island where I spent
Christmas night my sixtieth year
wandering about
and met that girl in a wine house
by the shore—
she had learned my poem
"Beside a Chrysanthemum"
from her high school language book
and still could recite it perfectly.
When some pesky drinking friend said
"Here, come meet the writer,"
she drew to my side and hid
her eyes in the folds of my coat,
sobbing—that child:
Is she crying somewhere as the snow falls this night?
Or have her tears dried? Has she learned to laugh out loud?

TRANSLATED BY DAVID R. MCCANN

Pak Tujin

CROSSING THE MOUNTAIN RANGES

The mottled mountain ranges are backbones of beasts,
I course up each ridge like blood spurting.

Ordering my disheveled hair with the wind,
Biting the morning sun with my blue teeth,

My roar is a scream, my roar spurts flame,
Setting fire to every dead sleeping valley.

Let an arrow come and pierce my heart,
Let a poisoned arrow pierce it,

There's a young sun growing in my heart,
My sun grows, tender and young.

Washing my ears with the howling waves
Of the madly rushing distant sea,

Let's weep once for the falling sun,
Let's weep once for the coming sun.

SOUL-SELLERS

Eighty percent servility and the rest is gall.
From the times of fathers, grandfathers,
Great-grandfathers, great-great-grandfathers,
North, south, east, west,
You kowtowed, bowed, beseeched on your knees,
Gold, silver, ginseng, pineseeds, tigerskins, virgins,[1]
What's more, blood and sweat,
What's more, vocal cords,[2]
Even your kin, ancestors, and brothers,
You sold them to Chinks, Japs, Russkies, Big-noses, . . .[3]

Lackeys, but among your own ferocious as wild beasts,
Biting and killing one another, wiped out by exhaustion.
Damn it, damn it!
In a land of beautiful sky and earth,
Who knows why you persist in
Spewing out your soul and gall,
"Korea in the world," "First-class backward nation."
You sold your souls to south, north, east, west,
Your housekeeping is dirty as a dog's,
Heaven fold upon fold, earth layer upon layer,
Wail with tears of blood.

---

[1]Gold, silver, . . .: traditional tributes sent to China by annual Korean missions.
[2]vocal cords: a metonymy for life.
[3]One line has been omitted at this point by the translator because it is superfluous.

HIGH MOUNTAIN PLANT

You live on a sheer riven cliff.
The dagger in my heart is a blossoming orchid
Curving through the thick fog and rain, shivering in the wind.
A fierce bird's torn wings mirrored in the cold moonlight,
The gorgeous flags, like a tide, engulfing the hill,
The mute roar, now fallen as flowers,
You live on the cliff this side of the silent abyss.
Gusts will blow again in the morning sky,
Revolution will overrun the earth, north south east west,
The dagger will stab the chain, the net, that night,
The creation's last light scattering flowers.
Orchid, you live on a cliff where the fog shivers.

APRIL

A dagger pointed at me,
A cup of poison to be drained,
I must embrace you.
I shall open my burning heart to you,
Digest you till my stomach turns,
And walk to the heaven at the earth's end.
One sun one moon
Inextinguishable
The timeless flow of water unending
Till my soles harden into paws,
This naked body will endure your lashes
Till flowers bloom everywhere.

TRANSLATED BY PETER H. LEE

Pak Mogwŏl

GREEN DEER

On a distant hill
Blue Cloud monastery
with an old tile roof

When spring snow melts
on Mount Purple Mist

Along the hill's twelve bends
elms break into leaf

In the bright eyes
of a green deer

A cloud
rolls

WILD PEACH BLOSSOMS

The stony hill
lapped by purple mist

Quiet
daylong

On such a day
wild peach blossoms

In a hillside village
the sounds of water

Clamorous, down the slope,
birds warble, mountain birds

A sun-drenched girl
crossing March.

ON A CERTAIN DAY

"Poet" is a title
That's always before my name.
Frayed hat on my head
I wander through rainy streets.
It's too small to cover my body,
Too absurd to shelter the little ones
Who always look up to me.
Man is not meant to wear
Dry clothes alone.
Only dry hair
Brings me to grateful tears.

A METEORITE

To bed.
When I turn to the wall,
A caress of forgetfulness.

That's the way it is.
A pleasant meteorite,
A burnt remainder is bound to be light.

My poems lighter than sponge,
Can they be called poetry?

I've no complaint about
My common days and nights,
My broad narrow taste!
Let me sleep.

When I turn to the wall,
Clouds and mist delight me,
Round my head a wind blows,

That's the way it is.
An inventory of conflagration,
A burnt remainder is always clean,
A light meteoritic stone!

My poetry of tomorrow,
Flavorless but free—
Evening of my life.

MY MIDNIGHT

Even metals gather rust,
The back alley is paved with cool shadow.

The world freezes,
Good faith
Buries the seed of inner fire.

I go down a stairway,
Arms folded.

Already
Those who must hide have hidden,
Those who must fall have fallen.
O clear world after such reckoning!

When I open my mouth,
It's breath not my words that steams.

Within that truth,
Nightly,
In a wilderness at our back
Which hands can't reach,
My midnight pole star!

ONE-COLOR ETERNITY

My shoelace comes loose
In the harvest month when ears ring clear.
Between meaningless lines
My shoelace comes loose.
Under the sky
Where the waterway of life
That can't be like hack work
Gushes out
To become clouds
To become stones,
No matter how you live, life can't be full.
In the one-color eternity of the harvest month
My shoelace gets loose.
Among stones
Some become monuments.
Among monuments
Some become stones.

TRANSLATED BY PETER H. LEE

Sŏ Kiwŏn

Sŏ Kiwŏn, born in Seoul in 1930, made his literary debut in 1956. He deftly portrayed the student soldiers in action during the Korean War who failed to provide a model for self-dedication or those who found themselves in a postwar society fraught with absurdity. A persistent inquirer into the inherent contradictions in traditional Korean society, Sŏ has written several historical novels. Built on the conflict between the old and the new, "The Heir" (1963) is an ironic story probing into the awakening mind of an innocent boy who fails to cherish the inherited values of traditional Korea, where the civil service examination was the only path to worldly success. The red certificate and jade pendants, symbols of old Korea's social and political ills, are meaningless in postwar Korean society.

THE HEIR

It was the monsoon season; rain was pouring down heavily, but he did not hear it. As he read to Sŏkhŭi, he was conscious of the smell of straw emanating from his cousin's hair.

"Why did the man leave his home? Sŏgun, brother Sŏgun?" asked Sŏkhŭi. They had come to the part of the story—the end of the first chapter—where the hero leaves home.

"Won't you let me break off here for today?" he asked her, closing the book. But she pestered him to go on, twisting at her waist.

He opened the book again and trained his eyes on the printed letters. On his cheeks he felt a blush appearing. He wished she would leave his room now. To be alone in a room with her made him uncomfortable.

Through the driving rain, he heard his grandfather's voice calling from across the courtyard.

"I think Grandfather's calling me." He raised his eyes from the book and strained his ears. Sŏkhŭi seemed not to care, whatever the old man might be wanting. She stared at his half-turned face intently. The call came louder.

"Coming!" he answered with a formal, grown-up voice and, leaving the room, put on the polite manner of a boy called to the presence of his elders. His name, Sŏgun, sounded much the same, in the inarticulate pronunciation of the paralytic old man, as those of his two other cousins, Sŏkpae and Sŏkkŭn. Often they answered to the old man's call together. His cousins, however, had not been seen around the house since morning.

"Greet the gentleman here," ordered the old man in the smoke-filled room, even before Sŏgun finished closing the double door. He bowed to the stranger who, like his grandfather, was wearing the old-style horsehair headgear. Sŏgun blushed as he did so, for he could never perform a kowtow without feeling embarrassment. He could not help feeling a momentary sense of disgrace whenever he had to kneel down on the floor with hands folded on his forehead.

"A fine looking boy he is! Sit down." The stranger spoke in a low voice, caressing his long beard, which looked like the silk of an ear of corn.

"He takes after his father. Do you remember my son?"

"Yes," answered the stranger, and then, to express his sympathy, he clucked his tongue.

Seated respectfully with bowed head, Sŏgun listened to them while they talked about his dead father. He stole a glance at his grandfather. The old man seemed reluctant to satisfy the other man's curiosity. The old man seemed to have mixed feelings of pity and resentment about his son, who had died in a strange place.

"You may retire now," said Grandfather.

The rainwater had gathered into a mud pool in the courtyard. The rain was not likely to let up soon. Standing in the gloom of the entrance, he looked across toward his room, where Sŏkhŭi was waiting for his return. He had a pale forehead and long black eyebrows.

Bashfulness lingered between his brows, which he knit narrowly, as if from biting a sour fruit.

To shelter himself from the rain, he stepped gingerly along the narrow strip of dry ground under the eaves. He entered the storeroom next to the room that stood beyond the garden, filled with the tepid warmth of straw decaying in the damp. The rafters stood out darkly from the mud-coated ceiling. He could smell the acrid odor of mud as the rats raced about the room. He looked up at the window set high in the wall. The paper was torn here and there, and a gray shaft of soft light entered, as at the dawn of a rainy day. The storehouse was divided into two sections. One of them served as a barn where farming tools lay scattered all around. Winnows and baskets hung on the wall where the cornstalk wattle showed amidst the mud plaster. It was damp and stuffy in the poorly ventilated storehouse.

Sŏgun picked up a weeding hoe and made a hoeing motion in the air a few times. A weeding hoe with its long, curved neck always amused him. He thought there was something attractive in its curious curve. Looking around the room, he saw the connecting door to the other section of the storehouse. There used to be an iron lock on the door ring. To his surprise, however, the rusty lock had come loose. His heart throbbed.

This room had been an object of curiosity ever since he had come to the country house—a vague fear and mysterious expectation mixed in his curiosity. Perhaps it was not right for him to enter the room without his grandfather's or uncle's permission. He hesitated a moment in front of the half-locked door, then finally took the lock off and stepped into the room. He assured himself that as heir of the family he was entitled to have a look at what was lawfully his. In fact, the word "heir" as it was said by Grandfather did not sound quite real to him. But now the boy once again uttered the word to himself.

Inside this part of the storehouse, it was darker than in the barn. There was a window the size of a portable table, but it opened on the dark entrance, providing no more illumination than a pale square of light like the night sky. There were soot-colored paper chests stacked one upon another on a corner of the shelf. He tiptoed to the shelf. At every stealthy step, the floor squeaked. Old books, tied up in small bundles with string and stacked high, were keeping a precarious balance. But the books interested him little. His attention was on the soot-colored paper chests. He did not hear the rain outside. The day after his arrival here, Grandfather had taken him to this room. From among the paper chests, the old man opened the one that best kept its shape. Taking out a scroll he said:

"This is a *hongp'ae*, which the king issued to those who passed the civil service examination."[1]

"What is a civil service examination?" asked Sǒgun.

"You had to pass it if you were to get an official position."

"Did you take it, Grandfather?"

"No, I did not."

"Why not?"

"By the time I was old enough for the examination, the Japanese were here, and the examination was banned."

There was embarrassment in the old man's tone. Later he found out that his grandfather as a youth had led a dissolute life and did not apply himself to study. It was not because of the Japanese but because of his own laziness that the old man failed to take the examination. All this he learned from his aunt, who, having heard it from her mother-in-law, passed it on to him like a family secret. The boy had a good laugh out of it.

"You are the ninth heir of a family with as many as five *hongp'aes*," the old man would say. But hearing his grandfather, the boy would picture a young man with a rambunctious crew of his schoolmates who abhorred books—juxtaposed with the present figure of his grandfather. Thinking about this amusing incongruity when he was alone, he would laugh to himself.

He carefully took down the paper chest his grandfather had shown him. It was full of scrolls. He ransacked them to see if there was anything else in the chest. But there was nothing except the grimy scrolls. He unrolled the one his grandfather had called *hongp'ae*, which looked like a sheet of flooring paper dyed red. A precocious boy who read difficult books beyond his age, he deciphered the faded characters. He found the three characters which made up his ancestor's name. They looked familiar to him.

He rolled up the paper and put it where it had been and shut the lid

---

[1]*hongp'ae*: a certificate on red paper given to those who passed the second civil service examination, held in the capital. The certificate was inscribed in black ink with the candidate's name and grade. In the original *taegwa*, the literature section of the civil service examination, the successful candidate became part of the civilian corps of the government, in contrast to the military corps.

of the chest. Then he took down a leather case from a peg on the wall. It was a roughly made thing, heavy as an iron trunk. The old man told him it was a quiver. There was a broken brass lock on it like the one on the rice chest, though smaller. The key was hanging on the corner of the case, but he did not need to use it.

Among various trinkets and knickknacks, he caught sight of a small wooden box. Out of the box he took a pair of jade rings strung together. The jade was a soft milky color.

He had no idea what these rings were for. The holes in the center would be too small even for the little finger of Sŏkhŭi. Maybe a kind of ornament for ladies, he thought.

He clicked the pieces of jade one against the other. They gave off a clear, sharp sound. Repeating the clicking several times, he listened to the sound intently. Then he strung the pieces together and put them into his pocket. His legs trembled. But hadn't he been told that everything in the room was lawfully his? As he closed the leather case, his pale hands shook. He did not look into the other relics. He stole out of the room. The rain was beginning to turn to a drizzle.

At every mealtime, Sŏgun sat alone with Sŏkpae at the same table with his grandfather. The country cooking, so different from what he had been used to in the city, tasted bitter. What was more, the boy hated to sit close to Sŏkpae, their shoulders nearly touching. He felt repelled by the occasional contact with other boy's skin. Sŏkpae, two years his junior, was an epileptic. That his cousin looked like him disgusted him. As he looked at Sŏkpae, a secret shame seemed to stir in him.

It was not until a week after his arrival that he had found out about Sŏkpae's condition; the fit occurred at dinnertime. The shredded squash seasoned with marinated shrimp gave off a foul smell. The soy sauce in the dark earthenware dish was no better. To swallow the squash, he had to hold his breath. A sense of loneliness choked him when he thought that he would be spending countless days from now on in this house, eating this food. Suddenly Sŏkpae fell over on his back, his spoon flung to the floor with a jangling sound. His eyes showing white, his foaming mouth thrust sideways, he struggled for air. Frightened, Sŏgun sat back from the table. The old man put his spoon down and sighed, turning away. The veins stood out in his eyes, either for grief or anger. Perhaps he was trying to keep the tears back.

Sŏkhŭi came in to serve the rice tea. Sŏgun felt pity for her. Perhaps the pity in his eyes touched her. He could see her eyes become moist. She hurriedly turned away and went out of the room.

Suddenly his uncle shouted angrily: "Take away the table!" He was moaning.

"What's the matter with you? Is he not your son, sick as he is?" Grandfather checked the outburst of the uncle. The uncle sat silently; a blue vein showed in the middle of his forehead.

"Don't be frightened, Sŏgun. He worries me so." His aunt tried to placate him in a tearful voice. Sŏgun wanted to run out of the room. But he felt that he had to see it through with the other members of the family until the fit was over.

Stiffness began to go out of Sŏkpae's twisted limbs, and he was breathing with more ease, but was still unconscious. He became soft like an uncoiled snake or a lump of sticky substance liquefying.

The boy gulped down some of the rice tea and left the room. The midsummer sun was going down, the clouds glowing in the twilit sky. Clear water, bubbling up from the well in the courtyard, prattled along in a little stream. They said a huge carp lived in the well among the moss-covered rocks.

His great-grandfather, returning from a long exile, had settled down here by the water, as his grandfather told the boy the story. Five ginkgo trees stood in line, dividing the path leading to the village and the outer yard.

"I wish he were dead!" Sŏkhŭi's sharp-edged voice came from behind his back. He wondered a moment whom she meant, but he did not care whom she wanted to be dead. He was feeling desolate enough to take it calmly, even if it were himself she was referring to. He watched Sŏkhŭi as she came near. He tried hard to be casual, but he felt as if he were choking; she looked grown-up, more grown-up than himself. She was smiling.

"Cousin Sŏgun, tell me about Seoul."

He did not answer. He merely smiled. Sŏkhŭi sat on one of the rocks by the well and stretched her skinny, red legs.

"I am the second tallest girl in class." She giggled, ducking her head. He wanted to find out more about her brother's illness, but he felt she feared any questions about it.

"You will be going to middle school next year. Perhaps the one in the county seat, right?" he asked.

"Grandpa won't let me go." Sŏkhŭi said in a thin angry voice.

"I suppose not," mumbled the boy.

"You don't know anything." Sŏkhŭi rolled her eyes and was going to add something, then seemed to give up. The air did not stir. Evening was coming on. A dry coughing broke the spell which had hovered over the scene. He recognized the dry coughs of his grandfather, which he heard early mornings, while still in bed. His eyes searched around in the gathering dusk.

The smell of wild sesame seed oil came drifting by; they must be frying something in the kitchen. He saw the white steam rising inside the dimly lighted kitchen. Grandpa had told him to get some sleep until called. Both his male cousins, Sŏkpae and Sŏkkŭn, seemed to like memorial services very much. They would poke their heads into the kitchen and get shouted at by their mother.

This was his first experience with sacrificial rites for the dead ancestors. He remembered his mother reminding his father about the rites and worrying. She would ask him if they shouldn't send some money to the country house to cover part of the expenses. Then his father would snap out sharply between his teeth: "How could we when they're having these rites every month of the year!" Sŏgun now seemed to understand why his father was so bitter about these rites. His uncle also looked angry and gloomy while getting the table and plates ready for the ritual. He could see his uncle considered these ancestral rites a burden.

Calming his restless spirit, he gazed at the tilted flame on top of the wooden lamppost. He made his bed and lay down, but sleep eluded him.

Sooty flames rose from the two candles burning in the discolored brass candlesticks set on either side of the sacrificial table. Through the thick wax paper covering the foods on the table came the pungent smell of fish. The grandfather, unwrapping a bundle of ancient hemp clothes, took out a long ceremonial robe and put it on.

The dusty robe wrapped around his thin old body, the old man knelt down before the sacrificial table and respectfully kindled the incense in the burner. Thin wreaths of bluish smoke began to writhe up from the age-stained burner. The stink from the fish on the round flat plate filled the room.

"The meat dishes should be set to the left. When will you learn the proper manner of setting the sacrificial table?" The man reprimanded his son and, holding up the sleeve of the robe with one hand, rearranged the dishes on the table with his free hand.

"This is for an ancestor of five generations ago," he told the boy for the third time this evening. The two elder men in the ceremonial robes made low bows; the children in the back rows did the same. Sŏgun nearly burst into laughter at the comic sight of the big flourish with which they brought their hands up to their foreheads before each kowtow. Yet his cousin Sŏkpae had a certain grace when he performed sacrificial bows. His soft and elastic body, unlike Sŏkkŭn's, fitted into the role with natural ease.

Sŏgun brought his hands up to his breast, but dropped them; Sŏkpae was bowing away ecstatically, flourishing his two limbs, which looked longer than his torso, as if performing a dance.

Grandfather cleared his throat, coughing a few times, before he started reading the prayer to the dead in a low, tremulous voice. Finished, he started keening, followed by everybody else. The grandfather's keening was the loudest and the saddest. The uncle was mumbling something in a low indistinct voice.

Sŏgun remained still, his eyes and mouth shut tight. Yet he was not indifferent; he was tense and felt an unexplainable chill running down his spine. He half-opened his eyes and looked up surreptitiously. Insects had gathered around the candle flames, which cast their shadows over the sacrificial table. He had an illusion of a strange figure squatting in the gloom behind the tablet bearing the ancestral name.

When he died, his father became like a stranger, the way he heaved a last chilly breath toward him, Sŏgun had had to draw his hand by force out of his father's tightened grip. He feared that the hand would come and grip him again. He could not bring himself to touch his father. He could not cry. But when he came out of the death chamber, an inconsolable sorrow seized him, and he cried with abandon.

The boy closed his eyes again. The keening went on. His body shook from suppressed crying.

When the rite was over, Sŏgun went out to the well. Stars glittered in the night sky between the clouds. The pale starlight played on the ripples in the well. He dipped his hands in the cool water. He washed and rubbed his hands until he thought he had scrubbed the last odor of the rite from his hands.

"Sŏgun!" His grandfather called him.

In the hall were placed three tables, where the family sat. "We are going to partake of the ancestral food and receive the blessing of the ancestors," said the grandfather, pointing with his chin to the seat opposite him for Sŏgun. The bronze rice bowl that had been placed on the sacrificial table was now set in front of the old man, almost touching his beard. Sŏgun could still see, in the center of the heaped rice in the bowl, the hole which had been dug by the brass spoon in the course of the rite.

Sŏgun tried a sip from the brass wine cup his grandfather handed to him. He grimaced. With a great deal of noise, everybody ate a bowl of soup with rice in it. The grandfather seemed displeased that Sŏgun did not eat like the others. He excused himself from the table, saying he had a stomachache, and returned to his room.

"How like his father!" he heard the old man say in a cracked voice.

The grandfather, donning a new ramie cloth coat the aunt had finished for him overnight, left for town early in the morning. The boy waited until he was sure his cousins were all safely out playing and then took his suitcase down from the attic storeroom. He took stock of its contents. The first time he was engaged with his things in the suitcase after he came here, his cousins stuck their noses in and pestered him. He wanted to keep his things to himself. In the suitcase were several novels, his school texts, a glass weight with a goldfish swimming in it, a telescope made of millboard, and a wallet which his father had given him the day before he died. They were all very dear to him. He placed on his palm the jade rings he had taken from the storeroom on that rainy day. He listened to the music the milky jade made when clicked together. The sound was as clear and sharp as before. The sound, in fact, had improved with the weather, which had cleared in the meantime.

Somebody came into the room unannounced.

"What are you doing?" It was Sŏkpae.

"Just checking on my things," the boy answered, very much confused and concealing his hand with the jade rings behind his back.

"Are you going somewhere?" asked Sŏkpae, drawing near.

"No."

Sŏkpae sneaked an eager look into the suitcase and then, grabbing at something, said:

"Won't you draw a picture of me, please?" The object Sŏkpae took hold of was a half-empty case of pastels. Sŏkpae's slit eyes winked at him.

"Oh, well." Sŏgun was pleased; he wanted to boast of his artistic talent. He felt much relieved that his cousin did not suspect anything. He spread out a sheet of paper on top of his suitcase and made Sŏkpae sit facing the doorway. He picked up a yellow crayon, taking a close look at his cousin. Sŏkpae sat, putting on an air of importance with his lower lip solemnly protruding. Sŏgun looked into the other boy's eyes and sat unmoving for a while, absorbed.

He felt dismay at a face that was so like his own. If Sŏkpae's features were taken separately, they would not noticeably resemble those of anyone in the family, let alone Sŏgun's. But when Sŏgun looked at the whole face, he could have been looking at his own.

"Aren't you going to draw?" Sŏkpae asked, only lowering his eyes.

Sŏgun began to draw. Sŏkpae's skin was darker, his features duller and thicker. From time to time, he slipped out a red, pointed tongue and licked his lips. Suddenly Sŏgun found himself wishing that Sŏkpae would have his fit there and then. A mixture of fear and curiosity came over him. He deliberately took time with his drawing.

"Here you are." The boy handed the finished picture over to his cousin, blushing.

"Why, it's you, not me, you drew!" Sŏkpae muttered.

"It's not true. It looks exactly like you!" he retorted angrily.

"Will you write down my name on this?"

He picked up a black crayon and wrote down the name.

Finally the grandfather found out about the missing jade. Sŏgun was sitting with his legs dangling on the low porch in back. The air was filled with the fragrant scent of balsam flowers, and beyond the mud wall towered the jagged ridges of the Mountain of the Moon against the cloudy gray sky. In the direction of the courtyard, he heard the grandfather's querulous voice. Now being used to the old man's intonation, he could follow the old man as he bawled out in fury.

"Why, you ignorant ones! You think it's a toy or something, eh?"

"Oh, please, Father. I'll take it back from the boy as soon as he comes home." His uncle tried to pacify the old man.

"It's all because you are so ignorant. You should have raised your boys to act like a gentleman's offspring. Instead, what do you have now?"

The old man did not attempt to choose his words in chiding his son, even when children were present. Sŏgun's heart sank. It was clear that Sŏkpae was being suspected of stealing the jade rings from the storeroom.

"That he could get so upset over such trash, after he has sold off every bit of property of any worth!" His uncle muttered after the old man disappeared into his quarters. Sŏgun trembled all over. He could not walk out of his hiding place and face the family. When he thought of what would take place after Sŏkpae came home, he felt an impulse to rush out to his grandfather and tell him everything. But still he could not move.

"I say, do you know what that is?" Grandfather, coming back, said now in a mocking voice.

"You told us it was jade beads, didn't you?" his uncle said.

"So you think it's just like any other jade, eh? It is no less than *tori* jade,[2] you hear?" The old man did not spare his son in taking him to task, as if they were not father and son but strangers to each other. Sŏgun did not know what jade beads were. They would not bring much money on the market, but they must still mean a great deal to his grandfather, the boy guessed.

He went out to the yard, dragging the rubber shoes which were too big for him. He was counting in his mind the money his father had left him along with that wallet. He thought he had enough to pay for board and room for four or five months. After his father died, his house, where he had a sunny study room, was sold by his uncle. He kept only the scuffed leather wallet and the bills in it.

"Let's go fishing together later on," said Sŏkhŭi, coming out to the yard with an armful of vegetables from the farm.

"It looks like rain again," he said.

Sŏkhŭi squatted down by the well and started washing the radishes.

"Pretty, isn't it?" Sŏkhŭi held out her wet hand, wiggling her pinky to draw attention to it. He noticed that it was dyed with balsam flowers. As he looked at the finger, she bobbed her head, puffing her cheeks, as she often did when she felt bashful. She was smiling. Sŏgun threw his head back and laughed like a grown-up. Looking at her from the back, in her white blouse and blue skirt, he could not think she was a cousin younger than himself.

---

[2]*tori jade:* jade rings or beads worn only by those in the senior and junior first ranks in the traditional Korean civil service.

"Do you know, Sŏkhŭi, what jade beads are?" asked Sŏgun, lowering his voice.

"Did you see the buttonlike things on Grandfather's headgear? They call them *kwanja*,"[3] Sŏkhŭi whispered back.

"They are not jade, are they?" He expressed his doubt.

"You hate my brother, don't you?" Sŏkhŭi too must be suspecting Sŏkpae of stealing the jade rings.

"Why should I?" Sŏgun feigned ignorance.

"I heard Grandpa once say that there has been no one else like him in the family." Sŏkhŭi looked up from her work, stopping her wash for a moment.

Sŏgun did not say anything. What he had just heard hurt him somehow.

"Do you know he had his head cauterized with moxa?"[4] said Sŏkhŭi wearily.

Sŏgun stood up and, leaving Sŏkhŭi to her work, walked toward the stream. He kicked at the small rocks on the roadside.

Rain started again toward evening; thunder clapped and rain began to pour down in streaming showers. It was only then that the house became topsy-turvy. The old man kept pacing back and forth between the inner and outer wings of the house, oblivious to the downpouring rain soaking his clothes.

"Where's your father? Of all the misfortunes of man!" The old man kept saying the same thing, wiping away the raindrops running down his beard. Sŏgun guessed the cause of all the commotion in the house. He saw in his imagination Sŏkpae's helpless body whirled in muddy torrents and then dashed against the rocks. His upturned eyes and foaming mouth were covered with the muddy water. "Grandfather, oh, grandfather! I didn't steal them!" But mud water filled his mouth, and not a moan came out of him. Sŏgun hugged his shaking knees. The uncle, who had just come back from the search, was going out again, this time taking Sŏkkŭn along with him.

"Let me go with you," asked Sŏgun.

"We don't need you." His uncle looked at him out of the corner of his eyes.

---

[3]*okkwanja* or *okkwŏn*: jade rings or beads, carved or uncarved, on the two strings on either side of the horsehair hat worn by officials. Other beads were made of gold, horn, or bone.

[4]moxa: dried moxa leaves, when used to cauterize the skin, act as a palliative.

"I want to go," insisted Sŏgun.

"I said we didn't need you," his uncle flung back an answer with anger in his voice.

The old man groaned with agony and said, "You had better take several men along with you."

"All right, all right," answered the uncle, exasperated.

A moldy smell pervaded the room. A millipede crawled up the door frame and then down into the room. The sound of rain did not reach him. He thought he ought to walk over to the male quarters and keep the old man company. He did not have the courage, however. He lit the lamp. He felt his forehead with his hand. Probably his hand was feverish too. His forehead felt almost cold against his palm. He felt a chill running down his back. He was too sick to sit up and wait. He made the bed and lay down.

He could hear the light, pleasant music of the jade rings in the rain. For a moment, he wished Sŏkpae's wrigging body would stiffen into a chunk of wood. He wished that Sŏkpae would never show up again. Even after he was gone from this house, Sŏkpae must not show up before the grandfather.

When he awoke from sleep, Sŏkhŭi was sitting by him. Her body, outlined against the lamplight, was almost that of a woman. He felt a cool hand on his forehead. He did not shake it off. The palm grew warm and sticky.

"Anything new about Sŏkpae?" asked Sŏgun, turning toward her.

"Sŏkkŭn came back alone," answered Sŏkhŭi. "Father went to the Mountain of the Moon with the village people."

Sŏgun remained silent.

"This happened before," said Sŏkhŭi. "Everybody was terribly scared. Sŏkpae came back the next morning. Even he himself didn't know where he had been."

The uncle came back toward midnight exhausted.

"Oh, that I might be struck dead!" The aunt wailed, beating the floor with her fists.

Sŏgun spent a sleepless night. Early in the morning, the villagers arrived with the news that Sŏmun Bridge had been washed away overnight. It was a wooden bridge on the way from the village to the county seat.

It was hard to tell whether his uncle was laughing or crying. He was scowling darkly. He sat on the damp floor and ordered the kitchen staff to prepare drinks for the guests and called in the people who stood around in the yard.

"Did you look into Snake Valley?" demanded the uncle.

"He can't have gone that far," said a man from the searching party, "and it rained so hard last night."

"The last time the bridge was washed out was five years ago," said another man and suggested: "Hadn't we better notify the police?"

The uncle stood up abruptly and, rolling up his trousers, started out. The rest of the men stood up too and, drying their wet lips with their hands, followed him out. The uncle disappeared out the front gate. But he seemed to have given up all hope.

"Oh, that I might be struck dead!" The aunt wailed in the main room. Her usual heartburn had gotten worse, and she had been fasting the previous day. When the heartburn got too painful, she nearly fainted but never forgot to exclaim: "Oh, that I might be struck dead!" as though it were some charm she had to repeat. She was not likely to recover from her mania unless Sŏkpae came back alive. She would rather cling to her sobbing, cling to her suffering, than seek a release from it, Sŏgun thought.

Sŏgun could not help feeling that Sŏkpae had gone out in the rain because of him. If only he had not come here, everything would have gone on in this moldy house as it had before his arrival. He was responsible for the untoward change in it.

Dark shadow covered the courtyard. No one stirred in the house. The whole place looked deserted. There was only the sound of heavy raindrops falling on the courtyard. The boy took up the jade rings in his hand and stole across the courtyard into the storehouse, shaking with excitement and fear. The rotten planks creaked and groaned under his light body.

He stifled an exclamation of surprise; a new lock was hanging from the quiver in place of the rusty old lock. The silver gleam of the new lock mocked him. A white, mean mocking was spreading all over the place: we have been waiting for you; we knew all along that you would come here to open the quiver again.

Sŏgun felt dizzy and had to lean against the muddy wall.

Sŏkpae's body was found lying among the rocks after the flood receded. It had once been as light and supple as a snake crossing the highway, but it was now as stiff and heavy as a water-soaked wooden tub, his once sleek skin turned yellow by the working of the muddy water. His uncle loaded the body on his A-frame and carried it down the slope with unsteady steps.

Sŏgun thought he must leave this house before Sŏkpae's body came home. He must get away quickly because he could not face the dead body of someone virtually killed by him.

Sŏgun ran to his room and took down his trunk. He fished out the wallet his father gave him and put it deep into his pocket.

"Are you going someplace?" Sŏkhŭi's voice called from behind. He was startled but did not turn his head.

"Don't go, please. Don't go." Sŏkhŭi implored with tears in her voice. Sŏgun turned his head around and looked into her eyes. He shook his head sadly. His lips were trembling, and his throat choked so hard that he could hardly breathe. Sŏkhŭi was crying with her head lowered.

The smell of dry straw drifted from Sŏkhŭi's hair. Sŏgun walked out, leaving her alone in the room. The rain suddenly poured down in torrents. All he carried with him was an umbrella, the wallet with the scuffed edges, and the pair of jade rings. He started slowly toward the highway, all the time feeling with one hand the cool jade rings in his pocket. Rain soaked him. He heard the voice of his punctilious grandfather saying: "Everything in here is yours."

Once he reached the highway, Sŏgun started running.

TRANSLATED BY UCHANG KIM

Kang Sinjae

Kang Sinjae, born in 1924 in Seoul, is one of Korea's leading writers. She has dealt often with relations between the sexes: a woman made unhappy by her oppressive and meddlesome husband; one who rebels against the patriarchal family structure and male-dominated society; one who withholds affection and love. Her fresh sensibility in handling the same theme can be seen, for example, in "The Young Zelkova" (1960), which concerns the eighteen-year-old Sukhŭi's relationship with her new stepfather's son from another marriage.

Kang has not only maintained an artistic distance between her characters and herself but has also refused to turn her characters into wailing women who curse all men. In the course of their attempts to discover the role of woman in family and society, however, some destroy themselves. In "Another Eve" (1965), the man-hating Agatha and the thirty-year-old child Nana are victims in the struggle to assert their rights.

ANOTHER EVE

I trudged along the walls of the Ch'anggyŏng Zoo and as I reached the road that turns off in the direction of Fourth Street, I felt so exhausted that I sat down on the curb.

Mrs. Ch'oe Aeja once said, "Agatha, your legs are so . . ." But what's wrong with my legs? Bowed or not they're strong as a bear's and can walk for miles. But now they're so tired they don't feel like mine at all. It's probably because I haven't eaten properly.

It's getting dark. It must be after eight. Where can I spend the night? If you don't watch your nutrition, it's bad for the eyes, they say. The thought made me angry. Once someone compared my deep-set eyes to those of an owl, but they see well. They're good, healthy eyes. In my forty years, they have never once given me problems.

After resting a bit, I have begun to feel chilly. It's going to be a cold night. The wind is tossing the fallen leaves around. I don't like it. All those houses and rooms shut tight against me; it doesn't leave a place for me to lay my head.

Far off I can see a large residence, its lights blazing. I can only sleep comfortably in a large, clean room. . . .

I had worked in many homes but I liked this one best. At last I had found a nice person to work for, I thought. As long as nothing particularly disagreeable happened, I was determined to stay there for a long time.

First of all, many interesting things happened in that house. Work is very important, but one must have some fun in life. Cooking, washing, and cleaning—you can't live on such a routine alone. There was something hilarious about that house.

Second, not a single man lived there, which pleased me very much. Of course there was that old husband of my mistress and that son of hers who was over thirty and worked in a bank, but since I had gone into service about a year ago, neither of them had been home more than two dozen times in all. So they didn't exist as far as I was concerned.

I don't like men. I don't see why any woman would want to live with one.

"But how did you manage to have those children of yours, Agatha?" Mrs. Ch'oe once asked me, teasingly.

I replied bluntly, "I got married, didn't I? I happened to bear them, that's all. But then, really, I don't see what's so wonderful about men that women go crazy over them."

I clicked my tongue with scorn and Mrs. Ch'oe stared at me and sighed, "You live with them because you're supposed to." She added with an uncertain smile, "But then, there isn't anything so horrible about them, either."

Though over sixty, Mrs. Ch'oe still retained much of her feminine beauty. But it was all useless now. Her husband kept a separate house with a mistress and came only once in a while to give her a living allowance. Still, it's better to be beautiful than to be square-faced and robust like me.

I shook my head at Mrs. Ch'oe, "I don't think so. All they do is tell you what to do. I wonder why some women go crazy over them."

"Not so loud! Lower your voice when you talk," Mrs. Ch'oe reprimanded me. Then she asked me how old I was. When I told her I was forty-three, she asked me I had been a man-hater when I was young.

I had always been like this and had never approved of those women who cling to their men. That was why I liked this place. There were no men around.

The third reason was that no one there treated me harshly. I'm not fool enough to be treated harshly by anyone. But in any household there's always one faultfinder who bosses everyone around, a person whose main job is to criticize and scold the maids. In this house Mrs. Ch'oe was supposed to take that role, but from the very start I put her in her place.

When told to do something, I'd deliberately put it off; when told to hurry, I'd pretend not to hear. When she became impatient and asked me if I hadn't heard her, I'd yell back at her twice as loudly, "I'll do it when I have the time!" That would silence her. She would remain quiet and just stare at me. Then I would add, "Can't you see? Do you ever find me standing around, my hands just folded? If you leave me alone I'll do it. Don't be so fussy!"

My face would turn red with anger. My owl eyes must have looked even uglier. As a matter of fact, I never like to be told what to do by anyone. If they'd only leave me alone, I would make my own judgments and manage things as they should be. You don't find many woman who do the housework as quickly and well as I do.

After several such lessons, Mrs. Ch'oe changed her tactics and started to flatter me. "Agatha, stay with us a long time, won't you? I'll get you a silk brocade jacket." I would just sneer.

It was true that I needed money because I had to provide my daughters with rice. But as for colorful silks, I never coveted them, even as a young woman. I always regarded them as tasteless. My two daughters are living in a shack at the foot of Nogo Mountain, sometimes starving, sometimes eating. One goes to middle school and the other to primary school.

Anyway my mistress had no other choice but to lower her head. She went out every day, what with the YWCA, relief work, or a charity bazaar. She had no time to manage a household. Besides, a dependable maid like me is hard to find these days.

At eight in the evening, I would stop my work and go into the living room to watch TV. Sometimes I watched with Mrs. Ch'oe or her daughter-in-law, but more often I was all by myself. At nine, I'd go to bed. I was usually too sleepy to pray, but never forgot to make the sign of cross before going to bed. I simply have to go to a better place in the next world.

My big comfortable room was just right for me. My girls, who sleep on soggy straw mats in that shack sometimes beg me to come back and live with them. I refuse because I can't stand their bedding.

In the morning, I'd wash and hose down the tiles in and around the house—I love splashing water around—and for kitchen work, all I did was cook the rice and wash the dishes after each meal.

This much work was just right for my constitution. It didn't tire me out. I made up my mind that I'd stay all my life.

Once in a while Mrs. Ch'oe and her daughter-in-law would have a confrontation. Of course they never used dirty words, but a fight is a fight. The cause of their quarrels never sprang from some occasional disagreement; it had always been part of that household.

That particular day, Mrs. Ch'oe brought home a bundle of imported bananas and out-of-season peaches from the opening party for the new Women's Assembly Hall.

"How is my Nana? Agatha, is Nana better?" she asked. Deliberately I did not answer, thinking that if she were so concerned about the girl she should have stayed home and taken care of her. The old woman handed me the bundle, motioning me to wash the fruit right away. She rushed off to the girl's room.

I couldn't help laughing. If she had only known how her precious little Nana was being treated at home in her absence she'd have had a fit!

"Nana, dear, Mummy is here. How's your cold? Is your fever over now?"

Mrs. Ch'oe threw aside her alligator handbag and, hands glittering with jade and diamonds, touched the girl's forehead as if she were a little baby.

Nana sat up in bed, fixing her uncertain eyes on the opposite wall. She was a spinster of thirty years.

"Have you had supper, baby?"

"Ah . . ."

Mouthing the affirmative, she shook her head. Mrs. Ch'oe turned to me for an answer.

"Of course she has eaten. You don't think I'd starve her, do you?" I replied bluntly.

The fact was, I had snatched the table away from Nana when she had had only a mouthful or two. She probably had no appetite with her cold. If she wasn't going to eat, why mess up the table, I thought. The girl burst out crying when I took away her supper. She went right back to bed. But it's no problem at times like these because she never tells on people.

"Nana, dear, eat these bananas and peaches. Hurry up and wash them, Agatha."

Nana touched her finely shaped forehead with white, transparent fingertips, her eyes still fixed on the same place as if watching something far away.

She was a beautiful girl. Whenever I looked at her face it made me wonder. Her figure, too, was just right, not too tall, not too short, with slender shoulders. She was neither too fat nor too slim, her pink skin just like a baby's cheeks. Her voice, when she spoke, was clear and beautiful.

If only she wouldn't do such strange things, even I would be attracted to her. At thirty, she didn't look a day older than twenty-two. It had happened when she was twenty-two, and probably her age had stopped with that sad incident which Mrs. Ch'oe told me about.

When I returned with the fruit tray, she urged the girl, "Eat these, dear. Quick!"

As if nothing else in the world mattered at the moment, Mrs. Ch'oe sat down, not worrying about her beautiful party skirt. She looked her age at such times. Her nose, supporting gold-rimmed glasses, was shining with perspiration.

Nana sat motionless, as if she didn't hear a thing. In her green French lace skirt and jacket, Nana kept on staring at the wall with her dark crystal eyes, her mind far, far away.

"Eat, child," Mrs. Ch'oe shook the girl.

Then suddenly raising her knees together, Nana covered her face with both hands and mumbled to herself. The ring on her left hand—they call that stone a "ruby" or something—sparkled.

She had nagged for an engagement ring and Mrs. Ch'oe bought her this expensive one. The ring always looked pure and beautiful, unlike the ones Mrs. Ch'oe wore on thin fingers that looked like the branches of a tree.

"Chunghyŏn, don't do that! I'm going with you. I'll run away from home. I'll go. I don't like it. Hold me tight. Squeeze me. What? My mother?"

Then all of a sudden Nana, pulling her hands from her face, emitted a piercing scream.

"What? Tell the bitch to die! The devil! You bitch, Ch'oe Aeja, you are a bitch!" With a fearful look, she spread all ten fingers as if to scratch her mother's face.

"Stop it, child. Eat these!"

I peeled a banana and held it right in front of Nana's eyes. Nana threw a quick glance at me and then once again hid her face in her hands and mumbled to herself. Her voice was now low and she was mumbling fast—all you could hear was something like "sh sh sh . . ."

"Now, eat!" I snatched her hand away from her face and forced the banana into her mouth.

"Don't, Agatha!" Mrs. Ch'oe's voice sounded like a plea from a dead person. Standing up she said, "Let's go, let's leave her alone, Agatha. . . ."

I followed her out, carrying her alligator bag. Nana's mumble became a little louder. "Chunghyŏn, darling, hold me tight. Don't leave me. I can't live without you." It would go on for hours like that.

If a sane woman were behaving the way she did, it would look awful and even dirty; but when Nana did it alone, it was a lot of fun to watch.

Mrs. Ch'oe's monologues were something too!

"My God, how did I make a girl like that?"

"Who knows? You did it yourself!"

Ignoring me, she went on: "Nana's right. I'm too evil to live!"

She then threw off her outer clothing and sat down, her legs wide apart, and began slapping her knees.

"Didn't you say it's your husband's fault?" I scoffed at her. Her agony amused me.

"That's true. I wouldn't give my girl away to any man; I saw what the old man did to me, chasing women all his life. I just couldn't see her get married, even if I were to die, I couldn't let her marry him."

"So you have fine results now. You locked her up and made her an old maid when she wanted her man so much. . . ."

Mrs. Ch'oe seemed too tired to notice my scorn.

"My Nana was too naive. It's all because she was too naive and gentle. If only she were a little wicked and aggressive, she would have gone off with that boy, no matter what I did."

"What does she see in that man, I wonder. Nana is a beautiful girl and I like her and all that, but I cannot understand her fussing over that boy," I said.

"If you can't understand, don't try! She's a sick child! . . ." she suddenly shouted at me.

I went off on another track, still sneering at her. "But not all husbands are like yours. There are many happy couples, aren't there?"

"You must miss your husband very much since you were one of the happy couples." She looked as if she had a bitter taste in her mouth.

"He's dead now, but he certainly didn't go after other women, and that's a fact. But I don't miss him, either." I told her the truth.

"Frankly, I didn't do so badly as a young girl," she went on as if in a dream. "I had a good education—went to college in Tokyo—and I was good-looking too. Several times I was asked to participate in beauty contests. And then, haven't I been fair to my husband? But despite everything that mean old man. . . . Oh, I grind my teeth just thinking of him. It's he who made our Nana so. Of course, that old man did it."

She blew her nose into a perfumed linen handkerchief. She was weeping; her eyes were red.

The daughter-in-law came in through the sliding door. "Are you back, Mother?" Her slow voice sounded sleepy. She always had the look of a person trying to suppress a yawn. Her plump, white face gave the impression of a good heart.

She had probably been lying with the baby, but she usually stayed in her room as long as she felt like it before coming out to greet her mother-in-law at night with her usual, "Are you back?"

Glancing at the heap of bananas and peaches, she said:

"Oh, you bought expensive things." She sat down beside the fruit.

Mrs. Ch'oe turned her eyes to me. Her eyes were scolding me as if to say, "Why didn't you put them aside for Nana? You shouldn't have left them there like that." The daughter-in-law plucked a banana from the bundle, paying no mind to her glance. (Of course, I paid them no mind either!)

"Well, let's see what this tastes like." Pushing the rest of the fruit toward her mother-in-law, she said, "Why don't you have some, too, Mother?" She sounded as if she had bought them herself. This woman had gall!

The daughter-in-law's mother would occasionally send some food. Her father had an influential position and received more gifts than his own home needed. And it's better to give it away than to throw it away. Anyway, she was generous and so why shouldn't she have a banana even if it had been bought for Nana?

Mrs. Ch'oe did not say a word. But through her glasses I could see there were daggers in her eyes.

The daughter-in-law swallowed the last bit of the banana and said, "Mother, when you go out please leave some money for groceries. The refrigerator's practically empty. There wasn't a thing to eat for supper."

"Why, didn't he give you some money?"

"Who's he?" she asked, holding up her white pug nose.

This woman was very indifferent to her husband. She never showed signs of jealousy even when he was away for days on end. Indeed, she seemed to ignore him completely.

Mrs. Ch'oe, on the other hand, could not bear to stay at home with her resentment toward her own husband. She went out every day in order to forget him. Whenever the old man stopped by, she wouldn't let him go without a squabble. She didn't quite know how to take her daughter-in-law's attitude toward her own son—whether to think of her as a generous woman, or to hate her for being arrogant.

The daughter-in-law's attitude toward her husband was: "You don't count. Do as you like." To her, the important things in life were her two sons—four and two years of age—good food and plentiful sleep. She was not interested in outside activities.

"Didn't he give you enough money to run the house?" Mrs. Ch'oe's voice became sharp now that she was in a bad mood.

The daughter-in-law answered in her slow, sleepy voice. "Why don't you ask him when you see him next? Ask him how much he gave me." Standing up she added, while straightening her skirt, "Anyway, the dessert was splendid after that beggar's porridge supper!" Giving another glance at the bananas and peaches, half of which were still in cellophane wrapping, she turned to go.

"What, exactly, are you insinuating?"

"What do you mean insinuating?"

"Weren't you sneering at me?"

"I wonder why it sounded like a sneer."

She went off to her room. A plump woman like that with a white face always leaves behind the impression of columns of clouds. Mrs. Ch'oe was mad, but being an educated woman, she didn't raise her voice. As fights go, it ended rather lamely, but all the same it was fun to watch her fidgeting in her anger afterward.

A day never went by for Mrs. Ch'oe without a bath. It was supposed to be good for blood circulation and beautiful skin. But that evening she went straight to bed, trying hard to control herself. Her eyes were bloodshot.

Nana was quiet now. She must have fallen asleep. The daughter-in-law remained in her room. Now a pleasant quiet prevailed in the house. It was at such moments that I felt I was the only person alive in the place, bustling about, talking loudly, and bumping into things.

Though it wasn't quite dark yet, I decided to lock every door and go to look in on Grandma. Her room was at the back of the kitchen, dark and dank, next to the storeroom. It must have been built for the maids originally. But I wouldn't have deigned to live in it even if they had begged me. The room was just right for Grandma.

From there you couldn't hear the noises she makes, nor did the smell of her reach us. As for Grandma herself, she couldn't even tell that the room was dark and dank.

Foolish old people are always very interesting to watch. They come up with the most absurd thoughts, do all sorts of fantastic things day in and day out. This old woman had a dignified and gracious manner and a charming smile. She sometimes called me "Her Excellency Kim" and bowed to me.

The next morning, as soon as Mrs. Ch'oe left the house, the daughter-in-law took the fruit basket out of the refrigerator and started to gulp down the fruit one by one. She gave some to me and her son but she did most of the eating herself.

"If she asks you, tell her you gave them to Nana," she told me, laughing, as she put back the leftover fruit. Nana had not eaten her bananas—more than a dozen—during the night. She had refused them even when I tried to force them down her throat the night before. If I were to tell the mistress Nana ate all the fruit in the refrigerator, she would not only believe me but would be delighted because her daughter had enjoyed them so much.

At about eleven o'clock, Nana walked out in the hall on unsteady feet. God knows what she had been doing during the night—or during the morning. Her green lace skirt was torn all the way down the front. Displaying her shapely, ivory-like bare feet, Nana stood staring into space in front of her.

"What on earth have you been doing? Messing up that well-combed hair . . .?" The daughter-in-law started teasing her with a mocking smile.

Mrs. Ch'oe did not usually leave the house until she had combed Nana's hair and watched her finish her breakfast. Today, Nana's waves were unusually messed up and her slip badly wrinkled. Part of it was wet and sticking to her body.

"What have you been doing? Show us." The daughter-in-law's chubby hands turned Nana's shoulders around. Nana, with a feeble smile, searched her sister-in-law's face. She looked pitiful. Probably it's such a look, her eyes and lips, that attract men.

"Sit down here and let me see! Quick, quick! Then you can have something delicious. . . ." She pushed the girl down on the floor. Nana, still with uncertain eyes, said nothing. I stopped cleaning the hall and barged in.

"She won't do it. Unless she feels like it, she won't do it," I said laughing.

"When you're ready to enjoy the spectacle, she won't comply," she said as she marched off to the pantry. She probably wanted to taste what she had been cooking all morning—steamed chicken or beef soup. She was always very enthusiastic about cooking. As for me, I never liked it—it's too troublesome. But I like to eat all the same; so I didn't mind her fussing about in the kitchen.

I took hold of the broom that had been standing against the sliding door. As we had often observed what Nana does in her room, the daughter-in-law and I could easily guess what funny things she had been up to.

Apparently the girl could see her old lover vividly in her mind's eye and did all sorts of things with that imaginary boy, hugging him, petting him, and whatnot. She would then talk the talk of love. When she was in one of those fits she didn't care if people were watching. Even when she was beaten to stop she would just keep on going.

"Oh, how can one be so crazy about a man? She should have gone off with that boy, as her mother says."

I had never seen this Chunghyŏn, but his name became so familiar that I almost felt he was my son. But to tell the truth, it gave me a sort of satisfaction that Nana had not eloped with him, and had become what she was.

"Move over, I must dust the floor," I said gently (at least, so I thought!) but the girl would not move an inch. So I hit her with the broom.

The daughter-in-law threw a rag through the kitchen door, "Wipe the floor with this, you crazy girl. You do nothing but waste good food." Even as she said this she looked kindly and gentle with a smile in her eyes. Her voice was soft and casual.

Nana had the habit of obeying her sister-in-law. She bent down over the floor and started to mop. As if afraid to soil her skirt she tucked it up and scrubbed the floor like a well-behaved girl.

"Why a thing like that should go on living, I don't know. She'd be better off dead."

"You're right!" I chimed in.

Nana was not only mentally sick. She had boils all over her body and her internal organs seemed to be out of order. That is why, when I saw her well mannered like this, I felt more convinced than ever that she would be better off dead.

One day, the daughter-in-law's maternal aunt came to visit us when Mrs. Ch'oe was away. This old lady saw how her own niece treated the crazy girl and, shocked by the harshness with which the invalid was handled, she reprimanded her niece.

"It makes no difference, Aunt. She doesn't know a thing." The daughter-in-law answered as if she cared nothing.

"Of course, it's all the same how she is treated. She doesn't know," I barged in. Nana herself did not know how people treated her and, since Mrs. Ch'oe did not hear anyway, it didn't matter what we did to her.

The old woman stared at me rather than at her own niece.

"Didn't she graduate from the best girl's high school with the highest honors? Wasn't she second in the college entrance examination?" Then she muttered to herself. "Oh, the poor dear. It's such a pity."

"Pooh!" I couldn't help scoffing at her remarks. What's the use of education, college or no college, when it comes to this? It's all useless. Whether you are educated, or have a beautiful face, it's all the same. (Both my girls attend school. If they learn how to write their own names and do some simple arithmetic, that's enough. Nothing else could be expected out of it.) The good Lord is watching over us. Everybody comes into this world according to His will and goes back to Him after a short life according to His will.

I never steal because He said, "Thou shalt not steal." It's written in the Bible, they say. But I also heard the bishop and Sister Patricia say we are not supposed to steal. And then there's a civil law which forbids it. Where would I go if I stole? Therefore, I remain an honest person.

I lead an honest life, say my prayers, and cross myself. I am fulfilling all that is required of me. He will have to reward me in the next world. There is no reason I should be punished there. There's nothing lacking in me. Haven't I always performed my duties faithfully? I've chosen work that suits my abilities. Many widowed women remarry, but I didn't do that.

When they get sick or something, my girls beg me to come back to live with them. Some neighborhood maids suggested that I live with my girls and peddle vegetables or something, but I won't do that because I don't like it. My living standards, including my food, must be at least as good as they were in the Ch'oe household, otherwise I cannot live.

I haven't been to church often and I cannot afford to be choosy about Friday meals. But it's all due to professional reasons and I have no other choice. If I had said I had to go to mass, I know Mrs. Ch'oe wouldn't have stopped me, and as for food on Fridays, it's up to me. But if I try to observe all these restrictions, I may get overtired and undernourished. So I just give up.

I am strong. I seldom get sick. But when I feel a little tired, or something goes wrong with my health, I feel miserable and get irritable. That is why I avoid anything that might endanger my health.

Excuse the digression. Anyway, since Nana was doing the housecleaning I had nothing to do for a while, so I sat on the hall floor and started talking to the daughter-in-law. The green leaves looked greener in the yard. There was a cool breeze blowing in.

"When you see Nana so engrossed with the opposite sex (I love big words!), how do you feel? Why aren't you more possessive of your husband? Otherwise, he may leave you for good."

As if uninterested in what I was saying, the daughter-in-law drew a wooden tray toward her and started to eat peanuts.

"Have some too, Agatha." Shelling a peanut, I continued my conversation. "Don't you think so? You are rather funny. Other women aren't like you."

"You ought to know why. You are a man-hater, aren't you?"

"Yes, I am, but I'm special."

Then, as if mocking, or just teasing, she went on with a smile in her eyes. "What can I do? He will come back to me someday, and I go on waiting."

Nana put her beautiful chin on her knees and looked at the green lawn outside. Thinking of Chunghyŏn, no doubt. There was nothing else in her head but that young man.

"Apparently the man was not quite so crazy about her. He didn't go mad like her, did he?" I changed the subject.

"Not at all. He married and lives happily with his wife and children."

"Oh, dear!"

"Doesn't he have his pride too? He's a perfect gentleman from a good family. He had to give her up when her mother went nearly crazy herself in opposition to the match, as if he were going to eat the girl up."

"No doubt."

"The daughter-in-law suddenly cried out, as if taken aback, "Oh, my God, what is *she* crawling out for?"

I turned to look out in the backyard.

Grandma, gracefully coming across the backyard with that charming smile on her face, stopped when she saw us. On a hot day like this, she was wearing a winter hat and a jacket.

Last night the old woman had peeled the oil paper off the floor, thinking it was dried beef. This morning she had probably been cleaning out her old chest.

"Mrs. Wŏnch'ŏn! Mrs. Wŏnch'ŏn!" she called to me in a thin, shaky voice.

"How come Her Excellency Kim has been degraded to Mrs. Wŏnch'ŏn all of a sudden? That was her husband's mistress!" the daughter-in-law said stretching out both her legs.

"Do I look like her?"

"Who knows? I never laid eyes on her!"

The shaky voice called out again, "Mrs. Wŏnch'ŏn, I want to talk to you."

Probably it's not so easy to know how to behave in front of one's rival. She forced a smile. Like a noble, dignified lady, Grandma nodded at me.

I don't know how she managed to open the door I had locked from the outside, but the sound of the old woman coming up the hall woke me up.

I am a sound sleeper and unless somebody shakes me hard I never wake up. When I opened my eyes, I saw a broken glass bowl near where my head was.

That cunning old bitch was going to sneak out with the bowl and had probably dropped it near my head. She was hiding behind the sliding door waiting to see what would happen next. I dragged the old thing to the back room and shut her in.

Oh, that crazy old hag ruined my nap.

I did not get enough sleep the previous night because I stayed up late to watch a historical play on TV. I simply had to make it up during the day.

"Now, who's making the noise?"

Clacking my tongue, I lay on the mat in the hall. The cool wind felt a bit chilly. The summer's almost gone now, I thought. I was about to fall into a sweet sleep again when something—something heavy falling—woke me up once more.

If it was that brat Sigi, he would run away if I yelled; but it didn't sound like him. I covered my head with the quilt trying to go back to sleep.

Then another heavy thud!

"Oh, you can't even get a moment's rest in this place!" I got up grumbling. I listened carefully. The noise was coming from Nana's room. The daughter-in-law did not so much as show her nose from her room in the other part of the house. The shade cast by the walls outside looked somewhat cool to my eyes, if not plain somber.

"Oh, hell!"

As I followed the corridor toward Nana's room, my head became clearer and my curiosity grew. I couldn't make out what the noise was—heavy thuds separated by short intervals.

I peeped through a chink in the sliding door. Nana had fallen on the tatami floor as if she heard somebody near, her body crouched on guard like a frightened mouse. She was hugging her pillow to her breast.

A small table had been drawn out from the corner of the room. A mattress and some cushions were folded on it. The thuds came when she fell down on the tatami floor from the top of this heap. Probably the pillow had come off with her and she was trying to put it back on the table.

All this was very fine with me, but one thing that really shocked me was that she was stark naked. There were boils on her body. They looked dirty—like king-size flies—but at the same time they made her silky skin look whiter, almost like sugar.

I held my breath and Nana, no longer on her guard, straightened the upper part of her body and started to walk on her knees. Putting the pillow back on top, she climbed on the table.

I had seen many crazy things in this room, but this was the first time I had ever seen her completely naked. I watched the rare spectacle until my eyes seemed to be popping out. She was a little heavier than I had imagined. Her body was well developed.

Once on the table, Nana stretched both her hands as far as she could and, as if she still could not reach high enough, jumped up. The next moment she came down on the floor again with a heavy thud.

"Oho! . . ." Now I knew. So this crazy girl wanted that medicine her brother had bought the other day. The son happened to be home that day—I don't know what wind had carried him in—and Nana was coughing and running a fever.

"Let's call the doctor."

"Doctor? She won't let him touch her. She'll raise hell, waking the whole neighborhood," his mother had said.

He went out without saying a word and soon returned with a bottle of cough syrup.

"It's strong medicine, Mother. She shouldn't take it more often than prescribed. Keep it in a safe place and give it to her according to the directions on the bottle."

Instructed by Mrs. Ch'oe, I had regularly given Nana a spoonful of syrup for a couple of days, and then, as it was a nuisance carrying the bottle back and forth, I decided to leave it on the top of the wardrobe in her room. I pushed it far back with a broomstick and stopped giving it to her.

"Well, the cough's getting better anyway."

Now she was set on getting that bottle off the top of the wardrobe. Climbing on the table, she fell again and again to land on the flat of her back, all four paws hanging in the air.

As the girl was not going to perform any more tricks, I opened the sliding door and entered the room.

"What are you doing? Aren't you ashamed of yourself, all naked? It's ugly."

Nana stood up, facing me, aghast. I poked my fingers at her soft skin here and there. She crouched, wriggling her body, then sat down.

"All right, then, I'll give you just one spoonful. Put your clothes on. What a mess you are in."

Swallowing the spoonful of syrup, Nana gave me a pleased smile. Perhaps it was the sweet taste of the syrup. Then a bright idea came to me.

"If you do as I tell you, I'll give you some more. Like this, okay! Go to it!"

I let Nana perform the love scene she so often presented—calling Chunghyŏn's name and making love. And I gave her a sip of medicine each time.

After a while I left the room. Back in the kitchen I realized that I had not put the bottle back. But I did not want to stop my work. If she wants to drink it up, let her go ahead. They say it's dangerous, but if she dies, so much the better. She knows no sorrow or joy in life, anyway.

As Mrs. Ch'oe came home late that evening, it was I who first noticed Nana's unusual condition. Since the afternoon performance, Nana had remained in bed sleeping, not making a sound. She usually crawls out when hungry, but she hadn't done so that evening. I almost went to bed without checking on her, but some prompting of humanity made me go see her. Her breathing was heavy and irregular.

"Nana! Nana!" I shook her hard. She didn't open her eyes. Her body was limp. I searched the room for the bottle. Sure enough, it lay empty in one corner of the room. There had been almost two cups of that thick black stuff in the bottle, but it was all gone.

"Nana!"

I shook her violently. I forced the spineless body up to a sitting position, but her eyes remained closed. Then some saliva oozed out from one corner of her mouth.

"Now, listen to me. Don't tell them I gave you that bottle. If you do, I'll give you a terrible time. Tell them you took it yourself from the cupboard in the hall, okay?"

There was no response. I became angry, shoved her back on the bed, and left the room. I decided I wouldn't say anything to Mrs. Ch'oe when she returned home.

But as soon as she stepped inside the house she insisted on going to her daughter. She wouldn't listen to me when I told her Nana was probably sleeping and it was better not to disturb her. She probably knew by intuition.

"My God, oh, my God! Agatha, Agatha, come quickly!"

I knew this was going to happen.

Phone calls soon brought the doctor and the son. Even the daughter-in-law, her hair mussed up, awoke and bustled around.

They made her vomit. Somehow I felt exalted. Forgetting it was time for bed, I helped them along.

Nana was all right now. She still did not speak but opened her eyes from time to time when shaken by someone.

I was not worried a bit. Nana hardly ever answers a question, and when she does nobody expects a true answer from her. So there was no danger of being found out.

It became very quiet. The night air turned chilly and the clacking sticks of the neighborhood fire watchmen added to the melancholy. As I was ready to fall asleep, the banker-son called me.

He was in Nana's room. At her head sat Mrs. Ch'oe with a serious expression. Even the daughter-in-law was there with her sleepy, swollen eyes.

The short and plump banker glared at me like a drill sergeant.

"Sit down there!" he growled at me angrily, pointing to the corner of the room.

I was very displeased and a little scared. I do not like men. I don't like them when they talk to me kindly, and when they growl at me I feel disgusted. I cast a quick glance at Nana. Her breathing was still irregular and her eyes were shut, but I was sure she was not asleep.

"You gave her that medicine, didn't you? Tell the truth!"

I felt I really must stand firm.

"What do you mean? Why should I have given it to her? That's the craziest story I've ever heard!"

"Be quiet! Where did you keep the bottle?"

"Oh, in the cupboard in the hall."

"You are lying. There's no use talking, Mother!" He turned his face toward Mrs. Ch'oe. I then raised hell.

"You don't need to question me! Why don't you ask her? She should know whether I gave it to her or not." Bending over Nana, I dragged her up in bed by the collar.

"Get up! Tell them! Did I or didn't I give you the bottle? Did I?"

Nana screamed. I shook her violently.

The son's hands gripped me and the next minute I was thrown hard against the wall.

"What do you think you are doing!"

"Agatha, the child's nearly dead. How could you . . .?" Mrs. Ch'oe shouted. I wouldn't let them get me down!

"You think I'd sit quiet when you blame me for something I haven't done? I must wake her up and ask her. Speak, you! Did you take the bottle yourself or didn't you? Did I give it to you?"

Once again I was after her. When a situation turned as critical as this, I wouldn't be satisfied until I heard what she had to say, even if I had to break her jaws open. I was determined.

I then heard something tearing at my back. Part of my jacket was torn away. I was shoved out in the hall where I fell on the floor.

"Mother, dismiss that person this instant! She's not human." The son spoke in a low but sharp voice. "If you must pay her something, do it now. You never know what she might do next."

"I owe her nothing. I advanced her salary for several months. It's she who should pay me back."

"Then it's all right. Just tell her to leave."

Mrs. Ch'oe kept silent. I could see that she was of the same opinion about me.

The only reason she didn't tell me to leave the house then and there was because of the late hour.

"You'll see!" I thought to myself. "Just wait and see in the morning, when your son leaves the house. Don't think I'll go away so easily."

I liked the place. I wanted to stay there the rest of my life. Since Nana could prove nothing against me, there was no reason I should quit. I would see to it that I had my revenge on Mrs. Ch'oe.

"It's two o'clock, did you say? All right! I'll sit up till four then. I don't want to look at her one minute longer. With such a fearful look can she be sane? She's worse than Nana. She's crazier than Nana and Grandma."

Neither his wife nor his mother spoke a word.

All right, you just rattle on as much as you like, I thought to myself. But the next instant I became all ears.

"In fact, we should report such a person to the police to teach her a lesson. . . ."

He wasn't just bluffing; he really meant what he was saying.

I hurried into my room and started packing. (Even then, I didn't steal anything.) I sneaked out in the backyard and opened the gate.

I was anxious to know what Nana had told them, what made the man so sure of my guilt—I wanted to find out all these things from Mrs. Ch'oe, but that word "police" gave me the chills.

I looked out in the alley, but I couldn't make myself go. It was so dark and the wind so chilly. I hesitated a little.

"Child, where are you going?"

The voice scared me to death. Grandma was sitting in the back hall. Even in the dark I could see she was all dressed up and held a white handkerchief in her hand.

"Is the exorcism over yet?"

I had forgotten to lock her door from the outside—I had not had the time—so there she was now. If I left her like that she'd be sure to make some trouble. But what should I care now? I left the gate wide open as I went out in the narrow street.

It was getting late; the wind blew harder. Autumn leaves blew over the walls of the zoo.

I cannot think of anywhere to go. I've been to all the places I could possibly go. I don't even know how far I walked today—from Tonam-dong to P'il-tong, to Noryangjin, to Map'o.

In my haste, I took a cab at one point, but after that I walked, since I had no money left. What a miserable state I'm in! I haven't even eaten. Aren't people really wicked? They won't even offer you a serving of rice. They'll probably all end up in hell.

I need a comfortable bed right now. It makes me so angry! I can't stand discomfort like this. . . .

TRANSLATED BY KIM SEYŎNG

Sŏnu Hwi

Sŏnu Hwi, born in 1922 in Chŏngju, North P'yŏngan, has been a prolific and prizewinning writer. Having given expression to a historical and cultural awareness hitherto dormant in postwar Korean fiction—for example, in his "Flowers of Fire" (1957)—he is known for his ability to discover beauty in the weak and ruined. His subjects include national consciousness, brotherly love that transcends political ideology, and those who are sacrificed to politics and society. The protagonist in "Thoughts of Home" (1965), the father of Yi Changhwan, wishes to recreate his old home and topography in the north in a village in the south. A perfectionist, he expends all his energy in building a replica, including the rats in the attic. But there is no faultless replica. While trying to relive his fishing experience, he drowns in a pond. Other monomaniacs inhabiting the world of Sŏnu's other stories show the victory of humanity over a cruel politics or the consequences of upholding vestiges of the past.

THOUGHTS OF HOME

I crossed the Thirty-eighth Parallel and came to the south in the spring of the year after the liberation. So it would now be some nineteen years I have lived here, making this other place my home.

I don't know why it is, but lately I've been having a dream in which I go back home. No, I find myself already there. For a long time I was too busy for such dreams. No sooner had I come to the south than I stumbled into the thick of a chaotic political battle between the left and right; then I was suddenly thrown into a war in 1950 that had me moving constantly all over the country. Even after that, with the endless struggle to make a living, I had no time for dreams. But this spring I found myself able to arrange for a small, subsidized house and found myself, at last, master of my own home. Perhaps that's the reason for the dreams.

Up to three or four years ago I had had no thought of getting my own house, even if the money had been available. After leaving the north, no matter where I lived I felt like a stranger in someone else's land—I always planned to go back to my own home one day. What sort of house—home—could I have here? But then, somehow, I happened into a large sum of money. Sick of the wretched life of a tenant —forced to move every six months or, at best, every two years—I arranged for this squat, little subsidized place near the edge of Koyang county on the far outskirts of Seoul.

My friends congratulated me, joking that at long last I had grown up and become a man of property. But even though the house belonged to me it didn't feel like my home. There was no change in the feeling that I would someday return to the old homestead I had left behind.

My longing for the north would explain why this little house—no bigger than the palm of your hand—has failed so to give me any real homelike feeling. And the more comfortable I have become, the more intense the thoughts of my old home. Perhaps this lies behind the dream in which I find myself back home again.

Several days ago I ran into my old friend Yi Changhwan who lives down near Ch'ungju in North Ch'ungch'ŏng province. When I learned that his father had died two months earlier I was once more put in mind of my old home. An intense feeling of nostalgia stung my heart. I wanted to slash out with a sharp knife at the invisible curtain that hung before my eyes. In the face of this thing I felt nearly suffocated with heartsick anger.

Just last night I couldn't shake the frustration that seized my heart as I lay in the darkness of my bedroom, thinking of home. I had to get up, light the lamp, and sit for quite some time, staring blankly into space. It took several deep breaths to ease the tightness I felt in my chest. I realized how similar I am at heart to Yi Changhwan's father who had died, yearning so to see his home in the north. While I sat there, arms folded, I thought again of what had happened a year ago spring when I was invited down to the country to see the new house that Yi Changhwan's father had built.

My friend Yi Changhwan had asked particularly that I go with him to see this house his father had built as his permanent home in a village near Ch'ungju.

"Father says I must bring you with me."

"Must? Why so?"

"He says he wants to see you come into the yard of his new house and then spend the night visiting and playing cards in the side room as you used to do back home in the north."

"But why?"

"Well, Father had some special reasons for building the house in Ch'ungju." Yi Changhwan explained why his father had gone down there and built a house.

A year earlier his father had gone without explanation on a tour of the countryside and returned to announce that he had found a fine spot where he must build himself a house.

When he came to the south the spring after liberation, his father had opened an automobile repair service that did well enough for him to buy an expensive house in Myŏngnyun-dong, but he suddenly felt he had to build this house in the country in spite of what people said.

"The shape of the mountains and the lay of the land are like it was back in the north. The only flaw is that it has no river flowing by. But the mountain ridges in the east at sunrise look the same. And the thick, dark pines in the hills out back with clumps of chestnuts here and there—it's all just like it was."

"What do you have in mind, Father?" Yi Changhwan asked with caution in his voice.

"Well, I'm going to build myself a home there."

Finally, Yi Changhwan understood why his father had been spending so much time in the countryside that his face had become darkly tanned. His father had thought constantly of his old home and now, after so much yearning, had found a spot that looked the same and was about to build a home like the one he had left behind.

This all seemed vain and useless to Yi Changhwan, but he knew his father's character well enough to realize he could never dissuade him.

Long before they had ever left their home in the north, well before liberation, Yi Changhwan had urged his father again and again to rebuild their house. It was a ramshackle building nearly a hundred years old that had sheltered some four generations. The rafters were rotting and the posts tilted, creaking as if about to collapse whenever the wind blew.

Once Yi Changhwan had gone up into the rafters to set a trap for the rats that had been tormenting him with their nightly rampages. His nose stung with the odor of mold and his feet sank in the frothy dust. Thought he walked carefully, the wooden planking creaked like it was about to crash down, unable to bear the weight of his body.

The earthen floor of the shapelessly long and cavernous kitchen was covered with more than a foot of hard, black dirt; people from the village would come and take a little from time to time—to use in making medicine, they said. The villagers knew well that his father would be displeased, believing that something auspicious was being lost, so they would wait until he was out to come like thieves and ask his mother's permission to dig up some of the dirt.

The stones placed under the downspouts to deflect rain, unmoved for one hundred years, had grown dark with age and spotted with moss; falling water from the roof, cutting the long years into them, had drilled holes deep enough to take an adult's ring finger with room to spare.

The village was open, without walls or front gates. Schools of minnows always played in the stream that flowed right by the house, and the large swamp a little further away swarmed with catfish and carp.

The low ridges that swept down from the mountains behind the house, sheltering it for some distance on either side, were shaped like what the geomancers call the Green Dragon of the East and White Tiger of the West.[1] Between the lower ends of the ridges where they merged with the fields stood a grove of willows, cutting across like a natural fence. The seven acres of paddies and fields lying within produced enough grain for a modest family to sustain itself comfortably by its own labor.

Before liberation a famous mineralogist once visited and offered to buy the land on which the house stood but left in surprise when he met with an angry response, bordering on insult, from Yi Changhwan's father.

"What? You want to buy this land where we have honored the spirits of our ancestors for generations? Do you think all it takes is money? Is that all you know?" the old man had roared.

Out on the broad, flat mountain ridge they called the Green Dragon of the East rested the spirits of five generations, counting back from Yi Changhwan's grandfather. Yi Changhwan had grown up to realize that their home was set on no ordinary ancestral land.

Sheltered as they were by the embrace of the back hills, the considerable west wind in the winter was deflected skyward, up over the house nestled in its basin-like site. With spring, the steady wind from the south seemed to circle round and settle into the basin with their

---

[1]According to the five elements (*wu-hsing*) theory, there are correspondences among the five elements (wood, fire, earth, metal, and water) and the seasons, organs, colors, notes, directions, virtues, planets, and the like. The Green Dragon is the guardian spirit of the east; the White Tiger is that of the west.

house. And the well water that rose beneath the juniper tree was warm in winter and cold in summer.

But the old house was so dilapidated that it somewhat gave the impression of an old clown. Yi Changhwan had proposed to his father that they rebuild the house.

"Why? Do you want something like Deacon Yi's foreign house?" he answered, adding, "All they did was stick in a lot of glass windows. What's homey about that? If you're so keen on tearing down this house and building a new one, wait till after I'm dead and gone. Then you may do as you please."

In the last of these words lay his father's unspoken warning not to bring the subject up again in his presence.

In the spring of the second year after liberation the old man had been thrown out of this house he so cherished. The day had come to leave—their possessions loaded into an oxcart—but Yi Changhwan's father did nothing to help. He just sat puffing silently on a pipe in the room where his father and grandfather before him had lived and died. Yi Changhwan had shouldered the last of their baggage.

"It's time to go now, Father."

"I know."

He struck his pipe on the ashtray to knock out the embers and then, coughing once loudly, slowly rose and went outside clutching his long arrowroot cane. After staring vacantly at the house for a while, he took a long, sweeping look around the grounds where it stood. Then, finally, he spoke.

"So much for that. Let's go now."

When they had crossed over the stepping stones in the stream in front of the house and reached the edge of the swamp on the other side, the old man stopped. He looked back again for some time, then stepped off briskly, cutting through the willow grove.

Now, some fifteen years later, Yi Changhwan's father had built a house shaped like the one he had left in the north. It was located in the countryside of North Ch'ungch'ŏng in a setting that recaptured the feeling of his lost homestead. He had asked me to come visit. As one of his son Yi Changhwan's oldest friends, I had been in and out of the old house since childhood.

I had no reason at all to turn down his request. So I set out with Yi Changhwan the following day to visit his father's house way down in the country beyond Choch'iwŏn and Ch'ungju.

We had walked some three *ri* over four steep passes when Yi Changhwan turned to me.

"Don't be surprised when you see it."

"Why should I be surprised?"

"Well, just don't be surprised," was all he would answer.

We passed over the last, lowish hill and I looked out over the broad expanse of fields that reached all the way to the mountains across from us. I gasped, capable only of silent but heartfelt agreement. I don't know if it was because I already believed what Yi Changhwan had told me, but the scene before my eyes felt somehow like what I had seen when I used to approach his old home in the north.

Though things weren't really the same, when you examined them carefully one by one—the high mountains in the distance, the ridges that swept down on either side, or the way a willow grove joined the ends of the ridges as they merged with the fields—the overall impression of the scene was still an extremely familiar one.

"I feel like I've been here before."

"Does it look familiar?"

"It's really close."

Our steps quickened and we passed a stand of acacias and drew nearer. But the closer we got, the fainter the impression of similarity I had felt. All the same, when I looked across to the house in that setting I could only sigh.

There was no question about it. This was surely Yi Changhwan's old house in the north that I had known so well. More than just the general shape of the house, this new building—hardly a month old—resembled the old one even to its ancient, run-down appearance.

I knew it well. I could see the hole for the dog in a corner of the straw fence around the country-style outhouse at the end of the west wing.

Even that.

As we got closer to the house I was swept with a growing sense of nostalgia and could feel the gooseflesh rising all over my body.

The narrow, twisting path that hugged the woods . . . the stepping stones in the stream that were held in place by wooden stakes and straw rope . . . the stagnant pool a little further downstream . . . ah! the tilting posts of the cowshed . . . and, inside, a calf, tied by a rope to a stake.

No sooner had we entered the yard than I found myself rooted in the center, peering at my surroundings. The tiles on the roof were not new. I wondered where they had come from. Even the downspouts were made of old tin.

The sides of the house were all plastered in clay, as was the fat chimney at one corner. The top of the chimney was finished off with pieces of wood, looking like a box had been placed up there. There was no wood-floored breezeway; in its place a wooden stoop stood over the stepping stones. On the doors hung crude iron pull-rings.

"What do you think of it?" Yi Changhwan had moved up next to me and spoke in a low voice.

"Hmm." I threw my shoulders way back and looked up in the sky. "When I came into this yard I really had the feeling I was in your house back north."

"You were surprised?"

"Umm, I was."

"Well, then . . ." Yi Changhwan began to speak but stopped.

"It's weird. The more it seems to resemble the old homestead . . . no, I mean the more I think of it as copied after the old house, the more unfamiliar it seems to me. I don't know why."

"The more similar, the less familiar?" he asked, confusion showing all over his face.

"Yes."

"Who's there? Isn't that Nongha?"

I heard a familiar voice behind my back. As I wheeled around, Yi Changhwan's father emerged suddenly into the yard from an opening between the cowshed and the main building. He wore a brown vest over the heavy cotton trousers that were tied off in the old way at the ankles.

"Ah! How have you been, sir?" I asked, bowing. Yi Changhwan's father beamed.

"You're here. You made it all right!" He approached and placed his hand on my right shoulder. He examined me for a while.

"You're beginning to get some wrinkles, son," he said. "Just a moment, now," he added and, releasing my shoulder, crossed over to the stoop and sat down.

"Now, I want to see you and Changhwan go out and then come back in again, together."

I was taken aback but, catching a glance from Yi Changhwan, I followed him all the way out to the stepping stones in the stream.

"Father wants to see you and me walking into the yard together as we did in the old days, back north." He looked a bit apologetic.

"Oh? Nothing difficult about that."

So the two of us directed our steps once more along the narrow path and into the yard.

Yi Changhwan's father, from his position on the stoop, watched our reappearance through narrowed eyes.

"Good! That's it!" he cried out, nodding his head up and down.

Yi Changhwan and I were standing in the middle of the yard, not knowing what to do next, when his father leapt down from the stoop and came out to us. He spoke to me.

"Nongha, what do you think? Doesn't it seem like you're home again?" he asked.

"Yes, sir," I answered. "Really . . . to be so much like the old homestead . . ."

I stole a look at Yi Changhwan. The look of confusion I had caught on his face a moment ago had faded now, but in its place shadows had gathered. His father's wrinkled face had a look of distant yearning.

"I tried to make it just the same. The workers had never done such a thing before, but they spared no effort." His head nodded with satisfaction and he took a long, careful look around the house.

"Here, you must be hungry! Why don't we go inside now?" he said, hopping up on the stoop and gesturing for us to follow.

I followed him into the room and there, inside, I met with another surprise when I saw the rush mat spread out on the floor.

"Where did you get this, sir?" I looked at the mat for some time and then sat down, running my hand over its smooth but fibrous surface.

"Make yourself comfortable," said Yi Changhwan's father as he reached for the long, bamboo-stemmed pipe which was resting against a wooden ashtray at the end of the room. He slowly filled it and put it into his mouth.

"I did have some trouble finding it," he said, and thoughtfully stroked the rush mat with one hand as if he were fondling a treasure.

"It's been fifteen years since we left and I now know that returning to the homestead is out of the question. I'm too old to wait any longer. I have no way to move those mountains down to me, so I built this house here. Of course I couldn't make it exactly the same, but it gives me the feeling I'm back home in my own house. That's a lot better than nothing."

He let his thoughts form a moment and spoke again.

"But, you know, there's no limit to a man's desire. The trouble is that once I had set out to imitate the old house, I found myself more and more caught up with minor details. Just placing a stone step. I would think it went one place but when I put it there it seemed wrong. So I'd stick it here and then there and after setting it and digging it up five or six times I would even end up going back to the spot where I had started. . . ." His eyes were filled with emotion.

In the evening Yi Changhwan and I had supper together in the same room with his father. While I was impressed by the old brass rice bowls, I was particularly struck by the fact that he served *toe piji* in addition to the usual foods.

To southerners, *piji* is what's left over when the wet bean curd is pressed into shape, but back home what we call *toe piji* is made by boiling up ham bones and pork with ground beans. This was not that common a dish even among refugees from the north, many of who had since developed more refined tastes.

As I picked out the generous ham bones to chew on I appreciated how intense were the old man's feelings for home. He longed for the reminders of home he could find even in the smell of *toe piji*. This tenacious yearning, this soul for which *piji* was a perfume! No—this heartrending scream of longing!

At first I had thought that Yi Changhwan's disapproval of his father lay in a fear that he would get inextricably wrapped up in this project of his, but when I came to understand I realized his concern lay elsewhere.

I played cards with Yi Changhwan until late that night and when we heard the sound of his father's snores from the inner room we put out the lamp and got into our beds. The oil lamp was a copy of the "room lamp" they had used in the old house back north before liberation. The next day Yi Changhwan and I went back up to Seoul.

A few days short of a year later I met Yi Changhwan and heard the sad news that his father had drowned in the swamp that had been dug out in front of his house. We had met and gone to a dark wine-stall and there, as we shared our cups, I heard several stories of his father's last days.

He told me of how his father had given a banquet on his birthday and invited down the few old friends of his who were still living in Seoul. He said the old men drank wine and exchanged stories about home and then sang nostalgic songs until late into the night.

"They hugged each other, laughing until they cried and crying until they laughed, acting like silly children again. I was waiting on them and heard the stories they told each other. It was mostly unimportant, pointless talk but I could sense one thing in particular—a lament that they could not see home again.

"A lament?"

"Uh-huh, a sad lament."

"A lament, you say. . . ."

"The old men stayed there two or three days and by the fourth day they finally had all left. After seeing the last of them off, Father seemed lost, like someone who had lost his soul."

"I can imagine."

"It was the last banquet Father would share with his friends."

Yi Changhwan paused a moment and sighed.

"After that he would become irritable very easily. Whoever went down to see him from then on—my cousin and his wife, or anyone— had to be extremely careful with him. And what's worse . . ."

He went on to tell how his father would get up all of a sudden in the middle of the night and, waking everyone, demand of his confused guests why there were no rats in his house.

"What's the trouble, Uncle?" they asked with caution.

At the sound of their questioning voices, he seemed to steady himself.

"Well, I was lying in bed and it seemed so quiet. I could hear the rattle of the ring the calf is tied to out in the shed, but then I suddenly realized there was no sound of rats racing around in the rafters. Why aren't there any rats?"

The next day Yi Changhwan's cousin went to a nearby village and bought five rats at fifty *wŏn* apiece and let them loose in the space above the ceilings in his uncle's house. Thinking they might run away, he even scattered rice and barley around for them to eat. He waited four days—each night expecting some reaction—but there was no indication that the old man had heard the sound of rats playing in the ceiling.

On the evening of the fifth day, just when the cousin was thinking that he had spent the 250 *wŏn* for nothing, as he was coming back through the yard from the outhouse, he heard what seemed like a scream from his uncle.

The startled cousin, fearing something had happened, dashed toward his uncle's room only to discover the old man out in the yard with his head pressed up against the crack between the sliding kitchen doors.

"What's the matter, Uncle?" he asked anxiously.

The old man turned and whispered to his nephew, narrow eyes filled with yearning.

"Quietly!" he admonished. Then, gesturing for his nephew to approach, he added, "Now come and listen here."

The younger man had no idea what was behind this but approached as he had been asked. He squatted down and pressed his ear to the crack between the doors.

"Can you hear the rats?"

"Sir?"

"Listen carefully. I just this moment heard a rat squeaking in there."

They were squatting face to face, but the cousin felt so sorry for the old man that he couldn't manage to look straight at him. He lowered his eyes to the ground.

A moment later the intolerable silence was broken as two squeals from a rat in a corner of the kitchen leaked out through the crack in the door. The old man's face lit up with satisfaction.

"Well? Did you hear it?"

"Yes. It cried twice," he replied like a schoolboy reciting his lesson.

"It looks like my father had longed even for the sound of rats. Even though it wasn't one from the old house." Yi Changhwan laughed bitterly.

"About three months ago, most of our close relatives went down to Father's house to join in memorial services for my great-grandfather. He was so very happy to see everyone together again—'Just like it was back north.' But when the services were over and the banquet was under way, father began to overdrink for the first time in a long while. He had the wine table removed and suddenly broke into sobbing lamentations. Everyone was startled by this and asked him why."

Yi Changhwan fell silent for a moment.

"What had started him crying was the thought of his older sister left behind in the north. He wasn't just crying, Nongha, he was sobbing and tearing at his chest. . . ."

"That's understandable."

"I came back up to Seoul the next day. But according to my cousin, he fell into the habit of talking to himself. My cousin told me he couldn't make out anything my father was mumbling even when he stood right next to him."

"Anything?"

"Umm. The only thing he said he could make out—and that just barely—was what Father would say as he pointed somewhere with his arrowroot cane: 'No, no. This isn't the way it was.' "

"Hmm."

"On the morning of the day he died, Father suddenly announced he was going to go fishing in the swamp. So my cousin asked if he wanted him to go into town and buy some hooks. But he said it wasn't that kind of fishing. Do you remember, Nongha, what we did when we were little? How we would get a piece of mosquito netting about one meter square and tie thin willow branches at the corners? Then we'd bind them in the middle where they crossed and put the thing on the end of a long bamboo pole. Remember?"

"Yes. And we'd hang squash blossoms and things from it."

"Right."

"Then we'd stick it out in the water and sprinkle bits of bean paste in the middle so the minnow and baby carp would collect in it. And when we pulled it out the net would be full of all those squirming little fish."

"That's it. That's what Father did that day."

"And then?"

"So my cousin sat beside him half the day, helping. At one point he left for a moment to go into the house, but when he got back he found my father with the upper half of his body thrust into the water."

"Had he fallen over?"

"Well, when they got him out he was already dead."

"How could he die like that?"

"It really doesn't seem a reasonable way to go."

"He'd never do such a thing. No, there was no sign of anything like that at all. . . . I raced down there as soon as I got the telegram, but all I found when I straightened up the things in his desk drawers was a note."

"What did it say?"

"It told where he wanted to be buried."

"Where was that?"

"In a sunny spot on the wide, flat ridge we called the Green Dragon of the East. The one that sweeps down by the left wing of the house. It's a pine grove like the burial ground back in the north." He said he buried his father there and came back up to Seoul.

He and I came out of the wine-stall and parted. Although it was late I purposely walked all the way to West Gate and there caught the last bus home. I don't know why, but I wanted to walk by myself. As I walked along in the night a weird idea came to me.

As Yi Changhwan's father sat by the edge of the swamp could he have seen something? Could he have looked across to the groves and fields in front of him, then turned his head to scan the mountains that embraced house after house, lifted his eyes to the skies and then lowered them again to look into the swamp? And there—blue skies and white clouds reflected in the peacefully still mirror of the water— could he have seen the reflection of his own face?

I understand. I remember the face of Yi Changhwan's grandfather when I was young. As Yi Changhwan's father had grown older his face came to look more and more like his father's—Yi Changhwan's grandfather.

And so, in the water . . .

TRANSLATED BY MARSHALL R. PIHL

Kim Sŭngok

Kim Sŭngok was born in Osaka in 1941 and graduated in French literature from Seoul National University (1965). As a spokesman for the generation of the student revolution in 1960, he attempted to form new values and introduce a new era in fiction. His characters are members of the younger generation, independent, inquiring, and cruel to themselves. They explore the sense of desolation and weariness in everyday affairs in search of a more vigorous and honest life. Kim's efforts to innovate the language and renovate sensibility have often been successful, as in the dialogue at the beginning of "Seoul: Winter 1964" (1965). A portrait of the inaction, self-deception, and boredom of the alienated generation, this prizewinning story is about three characters: the narrator, Kim, a graduate student named Ahn, both wanderers of the night in search of escape from their absurd existences, and a middle-aged man who has experienced a great crisis and comes to the realization that life is illusion and ultimately we own nothing. The three grope after the definition of man and his true situation in the modern world.

SEOUL: WINTER 1964

Anyone who spent the winter of 1964 in Seoul is probably familiar with those wine shops that appeared on the streets at nightfall, those stalls into which one stepped off a freezing, wind-swept street by pushing aside a flapping curtain. Inside, the elongated flame of a carbide lantern danced in the wind, and a middle-aged man in a dyed army jacket served up Japanese hotchpotch, roasted sparrow, and three kinds of wine. It was in one of these wine shops that the three of us happened to meet that night: myself, Kim; a bespectacled graduate student named Ahn; and a man who was about thirty-six years old and obviously poor, but about whom I could tell little else. In fact, I didn't care to know any more.

The graduate student and I began a conversation, and when the introductions were finished I knew that his name was Ahn, that he was twenty-five, was majoring in a subject I had never heard of, and was the oldest son of a rich family. He, in turn, learned that I was twenty-five and had been born in the country. After being graduated from high school, I had applied to the Military Academy but had failed and so had enlisted in the army, where I had caught gonorrhea once. I was now working in the military affairs section of a ward office.

With the introductions completed there was nothing else to talk about, so we quietly drank our wine for a short time. Then, as I picked up a charred sparrow, an idea occurred to me. After silently thanking the sparrow, I began to talk.

"Do you like flies, Mr. Ahn?"

"No, I've never—" he began. "Do you like flies, Mr. Kim?"

"Yes," I answered, "because they can fly. No, not just that. It's because they can fly, and at the same time they can be caught in one's hand. Have you ever caught in your hand something that can fly?"

"Well—just a moment." He gazed at me blankly from behind his glasses for a while, then screwed up his face a bit and said, "No, nothing—except flies."

Since the weather had been unusually warm that day, the frozen streets had turned into mud. But with nightfall the temperature dropped again and the mud began to freeze beneath our feet. My black leather shoes couldn't block the chill that rose from the ground. A shop like this is all right for someone who thinks he wants to stop for a quick drink on the way home, but it's no place for leisurely drinking and chatting with the man standing beside you.

Just as this thought was running through my mind, my bespectacled companion asked a commendable question. "He's quite a fellow," I thought and urged my cold-benumbed feet to hold out a little longer.

"Do you like things that wriggle?" he asked me.

"Yes, indeed," I answered with a sudden feeling of exultation. Reminiscences, whether sad or happy, can make one exultant. When memories are sad, one feels a quiet and lonely kind of exultation; when they are happy, the feeling is one of boisterous triumph.

"After I failed the examination for the Military Academy, I stayed for a while in a rooming house in Miari with a friend who had failed his college entrance exams. Seoul was a strange city to me. My dream of becoming an officer had been shattered, and I had fallen into deep despair. I felt I would never get over my disappointment. As you probably know, the bigger the dream, the greater the despair when you fail.

"About that time, I became intrigued with crowded morning buses. My friend and I would hurry through breakfast, then run, panting like dogs, to the bus stop at the top of Miari Ridge. Do you know the most exciting and marvelous things to a country boy's eyes when he first comes to Seoul? The most exciting thing, let me tell you, is the lights that come on in the windows of buildings at night. No. Rather it's the people moving about in the lights. And the most marvelous thing is finding a pretty girl beside you, not a centimeter away, on a crowded bus. Sometimes I would try to touch a girl's wrist and rub against her thigh. Once I spent a whole day riding around, transferring from one bus to another, trying to do just that. That night I was so tired I vomited."

"Wait a minute," Ahn interrupted. "What's the point?"

"I was going to tell you a story about liking things that wriggle. Please listen.

"My friend and I threaded our way like pickpockets into a crowded bus at rush hour and stood in front of a young woman who had found a seat. I grabbed a strap and leaned my tired head on my arm, then slowly let my eyes come to rest on the girl's stomach. At first, I couldn't see it, but in a few moments my eyes clearly detected the quiet rising and falling of the girl's stomach."

"Rising and falling? Because of her breathing?"

"Yes, of course. The belly of a corpse doesn't move. Anyway, I don't know why seeing the movement of that woman's stomach on the bus that morning delighted me so much. I really loved that movement."

"That's a very lewd story," Ahn said in an odd voice.

That made me angry. I had memorized that story in case I should ever get on a radio quiz show and should be asked, "What is the freshest thing in the world?" Others might say lettuce, or a May morning, or an angel's brow. But I would say that movement was the freshest thing.

"No, it's not lewd," I responded firmly. "It's a true story."

"What relationship is there between not being lewd and being true?"

"I don't know. I don't know anything about relationships."

"But that movement is just a rising and falling, not wriggling. It still seems to me that you don't love things that wriggle."

We both fell silent and just stood there toying with our glasses for a while. "All right, you son of a bitch," I thought, "if you don't think that's wriggling, it's all right with me."

A moment later, Ahn spoke again.

"I've been thinking it over, and I've come to the conclusion that your up-and-down movement is a kind of wriggling after all," he announced.

"Yes, it is, isn't it?" I was pleased. "It's undoubtedly wriggling. I love a woman's stomach more than anything. What kind of wriggling do you like?"

"Not a kind of wriggling. Just wriggling itself. For example—to demonstrate—"

"Demonstrate? A demonstration? Well, then—"

"Seoul is a concentration of every kind of desire. Understand?"

"No, I don't," I answered in a clear voice.

Our conversation broke off again. This time the silence continued for a long while. I lifted my glass to my lips and when I had emptied it I saw Ahn, glass at his mouth, drinking with closed eyes. I thought, a little sadly, that it was time to leave. So much for that! I was considering whether to say, "Well, see you again sometime," or "It's been interesting," when Ahn suddenly grabbed me by the hand and said, "Don't you think we've been telling lies?"

"No." The idea annoyed me a little. "I don't know about you, but everything I said was the truth."

"Well, I have the feeling we've been lying to each other." He blinked his reddened eyes a couple of times inside his glasses. "Whenever I meet a new friend about our age I always want to talk about wriggling. So we talk, but the conversation doesn't last five minutes."

I felt I could understand what he was talking about, but only vaguely.

"Let's talk about something else," he said.

But I wanted to give a hard time to this fellow who liked serious conversation so much, and I also wanted to exercise the drunk's privilege of listening to his own voice a bit. So I started to talk.

"Among the street lights in front of the P'yŏnghwa Market, the eighth one from the east end isn't lit."

I became excited as I saw that Ahn looked a bit stunned, so I went on.

"And on the sixth floor of the Hwashin Department Store, only the middle three windows have lights."

But this time I was taken aback, because Ahn's face began to glow with a look of delight. He began to speak quickly.

"There were thirty-two people at the West Gate bus stop. Seventeen of them were women and five were children. There were twenty-one youths and six old people."

"When was that?"

"At 7:15 this evening."

"Ah," I said. A feeling of desperation came over me for a moment, but I quickly recovered and plunged on.

"There were two candy wrappers in the first trash can in the alley beside the Tansŏng Theater."

"When was that?"

"As of 9 P.M. on the fourteenth."

"The walnut tree in front of the main gate of the Red Cross Hospital has one broken branch."

"At a certain tavern on Ŭlchiro Third Street there are five girls named Mija, and they're known by the order in which they came to stay there—Big Mija, Second Mija, Third Mija, Fourth Mija, and Last Mija."

"But other people know that, too, Kim. You're not the only one who has been there."

"Oh, yes. You're right. I hadn't thought of that. Well, I slept with Big Mija one night, and the next morning she brought me a pair of shorts from a woman who came around selling things on credit. By the way, there was one hundred and ten *wŏn* in the half-gallon wine bottle she uses for a bank."

"That's more like it. That fact belongs only to you."

Our manner of speaking showed increasing respect for each other. "I—." We would both begin speaking at the same time, and each would yield to the other.

This time it was his turn.

"In the West Gate area I saw a streetcar heading for Seoul station send sparks flying five times while it was within my field of vision. That was the streetcar passing by at 7:25 this evening."

"You were in the West Gate area tonight?"

"Yes, that's right."

"I was around Chongno Second Street. In the Yŏngbo Building, there's a fingernail scratch about two centimeters long just below the handle on the door to the toilet."

Ahn laughed loudly. "You made that mark yourself, didn't you?"

I was ashamed, but I had to nod my head. It was true. "How did you know?"

"I've had that experience, too," he replied. "But it's not a particularly pleasant memory. It's better to stick to things we happen to have discovered and secretly stored away in our memories. Manufacturing things like that leaves an unpleasant aftertaste."

"I've done many things like that and rather—." I was about to say I enjoyed it when a feeling of dislike for the whole thing welled up inside me; I just stopped without ending the sentence and nodded agreement with his opinion. Then a strange thought occurred to me. If there had been no mistake about what I had heard some thirty minutes earlier, the fellow in the shiny glasses standing beside me was surely the son of a rich family and was a highly educated young man. Then why did he now seem so uncivilized?

"Ahn, it's true that you came from a rich family, isn't it? And that you're a graduate student?" I asked.

"Well, you can call a man rich when he has about thirty million *wŏn* in real estate alone, can't you? But, of course, that's my father's property. As for being a graduate student, I have a student ID card right here." As he spoke, he rummaged his pockets and pulled out a wallet."

"An ID card isn't necessary. It's just that there's something a little strange. It just struck me a bit odd that someone like you would be in a cheap wine shop on a cold night talking to someone like me about trivial things."

"Well, that's—that's—," he began in a heated voice. "That's—but there's something I want to ask you first. Why do you roam the streets on such a cold night?"

"It's not a habit. A poor man like me has to have a little money in his pocket before he can come out on the streets at night."

"Well, what's the reason for coming out?"

"It's better than sitting in a boarding house and staring at the wall."

"When you come out at night don't you have a feeling of richness?"

"A feeling of what?"

"Well—something. Perhaps we could call it 'life.' I think I understand why you asked your question. My answer would be this: night falls, and I leave my house and come out on the streets. I feel like I've been liberated from everything. It may not actually be so, but that's the way I feel. Don't you feel the same way?"

"Well—"

"I'm no longer among things; rather, I watch them from a distance. Isn't that it?"

"Well, somewhat—"

"No, don't say it's difficult. In a manner of speaking, it's as if all the things that are constantly sweeping past me during the day are stripped bare and completely exposed before my eyes at night. Don't you think there is some meaning in that? Looking at things like that and enjoying them, I mean."

"Meaning? What meaning? I don't count the bricks in buildings on Chongo Second Street because there is meaning. I just—"

"You're right. There is no meaning. No, maybe there actually is some significance, but I don't know what it is yet. Since you don't know the significance either, let's go out and search for it together sometime. And we won't intentionally create some significance for it, either."

"I'm a little confused. Is that your answer? I'm a bit puzzled. All of a sudden this word 'meaning' appears."

"Oh, I'm sorry. Well, my answer would probably be that I came out on the streets at night because I feel a sense of fullness." He lowered his voice and continued. "You and I took different routes and came to the same point. If by chance it's the wrong point, it's not our fault."

Then he spoke in a jovial voice. "Say, this isn't the place for us. Let's go somewhere warm and have a proper drink, then call it a night. I'm going to walk around a while and then go to a hotel. Whenever I come out at night to wander around on the streets I stay at a hotel. That's my favorite plan."

As we reached into our pockets for money to pay the bill, the man beside us—who had put down his glass and was warming his hands over the coal fire—spoke. He seemed to have come in more to warm himself than to drink. He wore a fairly clean coat, and his hair, neatly combed and oiled, glistened in the fluttering light of the carbide lamp. Although I couldn't tell much, he seemed around thirty-six and had an air of poverty about him. Maybe it was because of his weak chin, or his unusually red eyelids. He just aimed his words in our direction, addressing neither of us in particular.

"Excuse me, but would it be all right if I joined you? I have some money with me," he said in a weak voice.

From that weak voice, he seemed to want sincerely to go, although he was not begging. Ahn and I looked at each other for a moment.

"Well," I said, "if you've got the price of the wine—"

"Let's go together," Ahn chimed in.

"Thank you," the man said in the same weak voice and followed us out.

Ahn's expression indicated he thought this a strange turn of events, and I, too, had an unpleasant premonition. I knew from experience that one could have an interesting and enjoyable time with someone he met unexpectedly over a glass of wine. These strangers virtually never came on with such weak voices, though. They were boisterous and overflowing with joy.

We suddenly forgot what we were going to do. A pretty girl beamed a lonely smile from a medicine advertisement stuck on a telephone pole and seemed to say, "It's cold up here, but what can I do?" A neon sign advertising liquor flashed incessantly on top of a building, and beside it another one advertising medicine would light up for long periods and then, as if it had forgotten, hurriedly go off and back on again. Here and there beggars lay like rocks on the hard-frozen street, and people walking hunched over intently passed swiftly by those rocks. A piece of paper driven across the street by the wind landed at my feet. I picked it up and found it was an ad for a beer hall touting "Service by Beautiful Hostesses" and "Specially Reduced Prices."

"What time has it gotten to be?" the listless man asked Ahn.

"It's ten till nine," he answered after a moment's pause.

"Have you had supper? I haven't eaten yet, so why don't we go together. I'll treat you," the man said, looking at each of us in turn.

"I've already eaten," Ahn and I replied at the same time.

"You can have yours," I suggested.

"I'll just skip it," he said.

"Go ahead and eat. We'll go with you," Ahn said.

"Thank you. Well, then—"

We went into a nearby Chinese restaurant, and when we were seated in a room the man again politely urged us to have something to eat. We declined again, but he suggested once more that we have something.

"Is it all right if I order something expensive?" I asked, trying to get him to withdraw his offer.

"Yes, by all means," he said, his voice sounding strong for the first time. "I've made up my mind to spend all the money I have with me."

I thought the man must have some secret plan in mind and felt somewhat uneasy with him. Nevertheless, I asked for chicken and some wine, and he gave the waiter our orders. Ahn looked at me in amazement.

At that moment, I heard a woman's warm moans coming from the next room.

"Won't you have something, too?" the man asked Ahn.

"No, thanks," he declined abruptly in a voice that seemed sobered.

Silently, we turned our ears toward the moaning sound that was growing more urgent in the next room. The faint rumble of streetcars and the sound of moving automobiles floated in like the rush of a flooding river, and now and again a bell demanding service rang somewhere nearby. Our room, however, was wrapped in awkward silence.

"There is something I would like to tell you." The man began speaking, apparently in better spirits. "I would be grateful if you would listen to what I want to say. During the day today, my wife died. She had been admitted to Severance Hospital—"

He looked at us searchingly as he spoke but there was no sadness in his face.

"Oh, that's too bad."

"I'm sorry to hear that."

Ahn and I expressed our sympathy.

"We were very happy together. Since she couldn't have children, we had all our time to ourselves. We didn't have a lot of money, but when we did get a little we would travel around and enjoy ourselves. During strawberry season we went to Suwŏn, and when the grapes were ripe we went to Anyang. During the summer we went to Taech'ŏn, and in the fall we visited Kyŏngju. We saw movies in the evenings and went to the theater whenever we could."

"What was wrong with her?" Ahn asked cautiously.

"The doctor said it was acute meningitis. She had had an operation for acute appendicitis once and had been sick with pneumonia once and got over those all right. But the next bad attack killed her—she's dead now." The man lowered his head and mumbled something. Ahn jabbed my knee with his finger and winked a suggestion that we leave. I felt the same way, but just then the man raised his head and continued talking so we had no choice but to stay.

"My wife and I were married year before last. I met her by accident. She mentioned once that her home was in the Taegu area but she had no contact with her family. I don't even know where her home is. So there was nothing I could do." He dropped his head and mumbled again.

"There was nothing you could do about what?" I asked. He didn't seem to hear me. After a few moments, though, he looked up again and, with eyes that seemed to be pleading, continued to talk.

"I sold my wife's body to the hospital. I had no choice. I'm just a salesman, selling books on the installment plan. There was nothing I could do. They gave me four thousand *wŏn*. Until just before I met you, I stayed around the wall outside Severance Hospital. I tried to figure out which building housed the morgue with her body in it but I couldn't. I just stood by the wall and watched the white smoke coming out of the chimney.

"What will become of her? Is it true that students will practice dissection on her, splitting her head with a saw and cutting her stomach open with a knife?"

We could do nothing but keep quiet. The waiter brought dishes of pickled radishes and onions.

"I'm sorry to have told you such an unpleasant story, but I had to tell someone. There's something I'd like to discuss with you—what should I do with this money? I'd like to get rid of it tonight."

"Spend it, then," Ahn replied quickly.

"Will you stay with me until it's all gone?"

We hesitated before answering.

"Please stay with me."

We agreed.

"Let's spend it in style," the man said, smiling for the first time since we had met. His voice, however, was just as enervated as before.

When we left the Chinese restaurant all three of us were drunk, one thousand *wŏn* was gone, and the man was crying in one eye while laughing in the other. Ahn was telling me that he was tired of trying to get away from the man and I was muttering, "You put the accents in the wrong places! The accents!" The streets were as cold and empty as those of colonial settlements in the movies, the liquor advertisement was flashing as relentlessly as before, and the medicine sign glowed when it could overcome its indolence. The girl on the telephone pole was smiling, "Nothing new here."

"Where shall we go now?" the man asked.

"Where shall we go?" Ahn asked, too.

"Where shall we go?" I echoed.

But we had no place to go. Beside the Chinese restaurant we had just left was the show window of a shop selling imported goods. The man pointed toward it and pulled us inside.

"Choose some neckties. My wife is buying them," he bellowed.

We picked out ties with motley designs, and six hundred *wŏn* was used up. We left the shop.

"Where shall we go?" the man asked.

There was still no place to go.

There was an orange peddler in front of the shop.

"My wife liked oranges," the man exclaimed, rushing up to the cart where the oranges were laid out for sale. Three hundred *wŏn* was gone. We passed the area restlessly while peeling the oranges with our teeth.

"Taxi!" the man shouted.

A taxi stopped in front of us. As soon as we got in, the man said, "Severance Hospital!"

"No, don't go there. It's useless," Ahn shouted quickly.

"No?" the man muttered. "Then where to?"

No one answered.

"Where are you going?" the driver asked with irritation in his voice. "If you don't have any place to go, then get out."

We got out of the taxi. We still hadn't gone more than twenty steps from the Chinese restaurant. The wail of a siren drifted from the far end of the street and gradually drew nearer. Two fire engines roared past us at high speed.

"Taxi!" the man shouted.

A taxi pulled up in front of us, and as soon as we got in the man said, "Follow those fire engines!"

I was peeling my third orange.

"Are we going to watch the fire?" Ahn asked the man. "We can't do that. There isn't enough time. It's already 10:30. We should find something more entertaining. How much money is left?"

The man searched his pockets and pulled out all the money, which he handed to Ahn. Ahn and I counted it: nineteen hundred *wŏn*, with some coins and some ten-*wŏn* notes.

"That's enough," Ahn said, returning the money to the man. "Fortunately, there are women in this world who specialize in showing off the particular characteristics that make them women."

"Are you talking about my wife?" the man asked sadly. "My wife's characteristic was that she laughed too much."

"Oh, no. I was suggesting that we go see the girls on Chongno Third Street."

The man looked at Ahn with a smile that seemed filled with contempt and then turned away.

By then we had arrived at the scene of the fire. Another thirty *wŏn* was gone.

The fire had begun in a ground-floor paint store, and flames were now leaping from the windows of a beauty school on the second floor. I could hear police whistles, fire sirens, the crackling of flames, and streams of water striking the walls of the building. But the people there made no sound. They stood like objects in a still life, the flames giving their faces the appearance of being flushed with shame.

We each took one of the paint cans rolling around at our feet, set it upright, and sat down on it to watch the blaze. I hoped it would go on burning for a long time. A sign saying, "Beauty School" had caught fire, and the flames had begun to burn the word "school."

"Let's continue our conversation, Kim," Ahn said. "Fires are nothing. We've just seen in advance tonight what we would have seen in tomorrow morning's newspaper—that's all. That fire isn't yours or mine or his; it's our common property. But fires don't go on forever, so I'm not interested in them. What do you think?"

"I agree," I said, giving the first answer that came to mind and, all the while, watching the flames consuming the word "school."

"No, I was wrong just now," Ahn said. "The fire isn't ours; it belongs exclusively to itself. We're nothing to the fire. That's why I'm not interested in fires. What do you think about that?"

"I agree."

A stream of water leaped at the burning "school," and gray smoke blossomed where the water landed. The listless man suddenly jumped to his feet.

"It's my wife!" he screamed, eyes bulging, and fingers pointing at the glowing flames. "She's shaking her head wildly. She's tossing her head back and forth violently as if it were about to crack from the pain. Darling—"

"Head-splitting pain is a symptom of meningitis," Ahn said, dragging the man back to his seat, "but that over there is just fire being blown by the wind. Please sit down. How could your wife be in the fire?" Then he turned to me and whispered, "This guy is giving us a good laugh."

I noticed that "school" had caught fire again after I thought it had been put out. A stream of water was reaching for that spot again, but the aim was off, and the torrent waved back and forth in the air. The flames licked vigorously at the letter B. I was hoping the Y would burst into flames, too, and that I alone among all the spectators would have known the entire process of the sign's burning. But then the fire became like a living thing to me, and I took back the wish I had made moments earlier.

From where we sat crouching, I saw a pure white object fly silently toward the burning building and drop into the flames.

"Didn't something just fly into the fire?" I turned and asked Ahn.

"Yes, it did," he answered and then turned to the man and asked him, "Did you see it?"

The man was sitting silently. At that moment, a policeman ran toward us.

"You're the one!" he said, grabbing the man with one hand. "Did you just throw something into the fire?"

"I didn't throw anything."

"What?" the policeman demanded, drawing back as if to hit the man. "I saw you throw something. What was it?"

"Money."

"Money?"

"I threw some money and a stone wrapped in a handkerchief."

"Is that true?" the policeman asked us.

"Yes, it was money. He has the idea that his business will prosper if he throws money into a fire," Ahn explained. "You might say he's a little odd but he's just a businessman who would never do anything wrong."

"How much was it?"

"A one-*wŏn* coin," Ahn answered again.

After the policeman had left, Ahn asked the man, "Did you really throw money?"

"Yes."

"All of it?"

"Yes."

We sat there for quite a while listening to the crackling of the flames. After a time, Ahn spoke to the man.

"You've finally used up all the money. I guess we've kept our promise, so we'll be going now."

"Goodnight," I said, bidding the man farewell.

Ahn and I turned and started to walk away, but the man followed us and caught each of us by the arm.

"I'm afraid of being alone," he said, trembling.

"It will soon be curfew time. I'm going to find a hotel," Ahn said.

"I'm going home," I said.

"Can't we go together? Please stay with me just tonight. I beg you. Please come with me for just a little while," the man said, shaking my arm like a fan. He was probably doing the same to Ahn.

"Where do you want us to go?" I asked.

"I'll get some money at a place near here, and then we can all stay together at a hotel."

"At a hotel?" I asked as my fingers counted the money in my pocket.

"If you're worried about the cost of the hotel, I'll pay for all three of us," Ahn said. "So—shall we go together?"

"No, no. I don't want to cause any trouble. Just follow me for a little while, please."

"Are you going to borrow money?"

"No, it's money that's due me."

"Near here?"

"Yes—if this is the Namyŏng-dong area."

"It certainly looks to me like Namyŏng-dong," I said.

With the man leading the way and Ahn and I following, we moved away from the fire.

"It's too late to be going around collecting debts," Ahn told the man.

"But I have to get the money."

We entered a dark alley and turned several corners before the man stopped in front of a house at which the light at the front gate was lit. Ahn and I stopped about ten steps behind the man. He rang the bell. After a while, the gate opened, and we could hear him talking with someone inside.

"I'd like to see the man of the house."

"He's sleeping."

"The lady, then."

"She's sleeping, too."

"I must see someone."

"Wait a minute, then."

The gate closed again. Ahn ran over to the man and pulled him by the arm. "Forget about it. Let's go."

"I've got to collect this money."

Ahn came back to where he had been standing. The gate opened.

"Sorry to bother you so late at night." The man stood facing the gate, head bowed.

"Who are you?" a woman's sleepy voice inquired from the gate.

"I'm sorry to have come so late, but—"

"Who are you? You look like you're drunk."

"I've come to collect a payment on a book you bought." The man suddenly screamed. "I've come for a book payment." Then he put his hands on the gatepost, buried his face in his outstretched arms, and burst into tears. "I've come for a book payment. A book payment—"

"Please come back tomorrow." The gate slammed shut.

The man went on sobbing for a long while, occasionally muttering, "Darling." We remained ten steps away waiting for the crying to end. After some time, the man staggered over to us. The three of us walked, heads lowered, through the dark alley and back out onto the main street. A cold, strong wind was blowing through the lonely streets.

"It's awfully cold," the man said, sounding worried about us.

"Yes, it is cold. Let's hurry to a hotel," Ahn said.

"Shall we each get a separate room?" Ahn asked when we had arrived at the hotel. "That would be a good idea, wouldn't it?"

"I think it would be better if we all shared one room," I said, thinking about the man.

The man was standing there blankly as if he didn't know where he was and looking as if he just wanted us to take care of things.

When we entered the hotel we experienced that same awkward feeling one gets when he leaves a theater after the show is over and doesn't know what to do next. Compared with this hotel, the streets seemed narrow and confining. All those rooms separated by the walls, one after the other—that's where we had to go.

"How about sharing a room?" I said again.

"I'm exhausted," Ahn said. "Let's each take a separate room and get some sleep."

"I don't want to be alone," the man mumbled.

"You'll be more comfortable sleeping by yourself," Ahn said.

We separated in the hallway and headed for the three adjacent rooms indicated by the bellboy.

"Let's buy a pack of cards and play a hand," I said before we parted.

"I'm completely exhausted. If you two want to play, please go ahead," Ahn said and stepped into his room.

"I'm dead tired, too. Good night," I said and went into my room. I wrote a false name, address, age, and occupation on the register and drank the water the bellboy had left, then pulled the covers over myself. I slept a sound and dreamless sleep.

Early the next morning, Ahn woke me. "The man is dead," he whispered, his mouth close to my ear.

"What?" I was suddenly wide awake.

"I went into his room just now, and he was dead."

"Dead—" I said. "Does anyone else know?"

"No, it looks like no one knows yet. We had better get out of here quickly before someone notices."

"Suicide?"

"No doubt about it."

I dressed hurriedly. An ant was crawling along the floor toward my feet. I had the feeling the ant was going to seize my foot, so I hastily stepped aside.

Outside, fine snow was falling in the early morning. Walking as quickly as we could, we left the hotel behind.

"I knew he was going to die," Ahn said.

"I couldn't have guessed it," I said truthfully.

"I was expecting it," he said, turning up the collar of his coat, "but what could I do?"

"There's nothing we could have done. I had no idea—"

"If you had expected it, what would you have done?" he asked me.

"Damn! What could I have done? How were we to know what he wanted us to do?"

"That's right. I thought that if we just left him alone he wouldn't die. I thought I was trying my best and that was the only way to handle it."

"I had no idea he was going to kill himself. Damn! He must have been carrying poison around in his pocket all night."

Ahn stopped by a bare tree that stood beside the street gathering snow. I stopped with him. With a strange look on his face, he asked me, "Kim, we're distinctly twenty-five years old, aren't we?"

"I certainly am."

"I am, too. That's certain." He tilted his head slightly. "I'm frightened."

"Of what?" I asked.

"That 'something'. That—" He spoke in a voice that was like a long sigh. "Doesn't it seem like we've become very old?"

"We're just twenty-five," I said.

"Anyway," he said, extending his hand. "Let's say good-bye here."

"Enjoy yourself," I said, as I took his hand.

We parted. I dashed across the street to a bus stop where a bus had just pulled up. When I boarded it and looked out a window I could see, through the branches of the naked tree, Ahn standing in the falling snow deep in thought.

TRANSLATED BY PETER H. LEE

Yi Ch'ŏngjun

Born in 1939 in Changhŭng, South Chŏlla, Yi lost his father and brothers before he was ten. He made his literary debut in 1965, a year before he graduated in German literature from Seoul National University. He won the 1967 Tongin Award for his story "The Deformed and the Fool" (1966) and the Yi Sang Award for a medium-length story, "The Cruel City" (1978). The predominant theme of Yi Ch'ŏngjun's work is people's incapacity to survive the ironies and contradictions of life in postwar Korea. His typical character does not believe in the solemnity of social norms and puts on a mask in his dealings with others. He knows the mask is a lie, but it is his only means of expressing himself.

A topic that has especially fascinated Yi is the decline of traditional arts in modern society and the collapse of the value system they represent. Alienated from the dehumanized world, his cast of characters—a rope walker, an artificial flower maker, an archer, a falconer, a stargazer—wish to return to normal everyday life but without success. The old arts are vanishing, and their practitioners must pay an exorbitant price for survival. The traditional artist may choose a comfortable and convenient life, but it appears to him false. Driven to the margin of society, residing between the old order and the new, he can belong to neither. He may be the epitome of social contradiction, but his lifestyle is a criticism of those who, refusing to acknowledge the implications of social cataclysm, are content to live in idleness. Yi once said that the modern writer is a fatalistic idealist who seeks truth and happiness. Some read "The Target" (1967) as an allegory of the archer as writer—the writer as craftsman—who questions the possibility of fiction given the nature of Korean—and modern—actuality.

THE TARGET

On an early summer morning the town park was enveloped in a heavy mist. Like a woman rolling up her white skirt, the park was unveiled as the mist slowly rose. The lower part of the park's bare grassy hill was revealed, and though no rain had fallen, the grass was fresh with dew.

The town was still deep in slumber. No rushing car or wagon was to be heard in the neighborhood. This weary slumber seemed to continue endlessly, undisturbed.

In this stillness, however, someone must have been up. The morning was not altogether silent.

Tak!

......

Tak!

......

From nobody knew where, the sound came at almost regular intervals, as though it would give an exact tally of the hours of the early morning. It sounded now like a drop of water striking the ground, and now like the moaning of a deity striving painfully not to sink into slumber here in the heart of stillness.

Tak!

......

Tak!

......

An inattentive mind might have missed the sound, and whoever did hear it could not tell whence it came. It seemed to come up from the town below, or from within the mist covering the park. Nevertheless, if one concentrated briefly, he would learn the origin of the sound. Moreover, he would surely be excited by the mysterious sight he would see, for even those who had lived in the town a long time rarely saw such a sight.

As the mist rose higher, a bower halfway up the hill appeared dimly. Its name, "North Tiger Arbor," could be read on its tablet as one approached.

Two people stood before the arbor, facing north. One was an old man with gray hair, and the other was a young woman whose age was not easily discernible because of her unusual hairstyle. Both were neatly dressed and wore colored belts over their white garments. The woman wore a blue belt, the old man wore a red one. The man's red belt seemed worn but clean. Long pockets hung on the couple's bags, and on the pockets were clearly embroidered the Chinese graphs for "North Tiger Arbor."

The two were not simply standing before the arbor. With bows they were shooting arrows over a small valley to a hill on the opposite side still covered by mist. They shot in turn: after the old man, the woman would shoot, and then the old man would shoot again. The interval between the shots was regular. With each shot, the sound *tak* . . .*tak* came from the opposite hill where the target was sited. To be more precise, it was mostly the old man's arrows that produced the sound of the target being struck, while the woman's arrows seldom did. The two seemed unaware of this fact, however. They simply shot by turns, never saying a word. At last the mist lifted, revealing the target on the opposite hill. On the target was painted a round circle in black. Laying down his bow, the old man shouted toward the arbor.

"Kŏn!"

A door was flung open, and a little boy came forth holding a fan. Silently the old man looked over at the opposite hill. The boy, Kŏn, ran to the hill and stooped beside the target. The old man took aim, and an arrow left his bow.

Tak!

Simultaneously with the sound, the boy raised his fan and moved it around with some skill. The fan resembled a large flower trembling in the air. The boy stopped and awaited the next arrow. On the opposite side of the valley, the old man gazed blankly at the quiet town below. Beside him the woman took aim. When the arrow was properly aimed, she held her pose briefly. Her left sleeve was rolled up halfway. Shortly the arrow flew, and once again the boy raised his fan high to trace a circular flower in the air. The woman looked at the old man.

"Second arrow!"

The old man spoke while still looking toward the town. The girl shot again, and the fan rose toward the sky.

"Third arrow!"

This time, however, the boy did not raise the fan high but put it beside his head, to the right. As if drawn by the movement of the fan, the boy leaned to the right with his left hand on his abdomen. All these actions took place in a moment. The woman's third arrow fell short of the target, and naturally the boy's pantomimed indication of the shot came the very instant the arrow left the bow. So perfect were the boy's judgments that he seemed already prepared while the woman was still taking aim. The boy slowly straightened.

"Fourth arrow!"

The man silently sized up the next arrow.

Tak!

The boy's fan was blooming.

"Fifth arrow!"

Still the old man gazed townward. The town appeared to be stirring, and vague sounds could be heard from below. The sounds struggled with one another to form a dense body of noise. A kind of impatience began to appear on the old man's face. The woman was hurrying slightly, though her movements proceeded in perfect order. At a shrill sound of the arrow cutting through the morning air, the boy stepped backward and raised the fan abruptly. The fan did not make a flower.

For the first time the old man turned his eyes to the woman. "You lose today. You got only three hits."

"I lose. Yes."

The woman still held an arrow and her half-open mouth seemed to have something to say to the old man. Pretending not to notice, however, the old man gestured toward the town with his eyes. His eyes seemed to carry a warning.

"They're awake."

The couple went back into the room in the arbor. Observing their action, the boy on the opposite hill hastened to gather up the scattered arrows. A moment later he too disappeared into the room.

The arbor stood serenely in the morning air, quite as if nothing had happened. Some time later the door to the room opened again. Wearing a change of clothes, the woman came forth to look around like one who has just risen from bed. The woman went into the kitchen. Soon the old man and the boy came out of the room as well. The old man went to the cattle pen in a corner of the plot and led a few goats off to the hill. The boy followed after, bearing a fodder-stick on his shoulder. Anyone arriving at this moment would think he was observing the morning routine at North Tiger Arbor.

But there was one man who had long since been watching the arbor attentively. On the hill above the arbor, now clear of mist, stood an old oak tree beneath which a young man had been seated for a long while. He could not see what was happening in the arbor until the mist dissipated, and when it did he seemed to have been deeply touched by what he saw. He had a dog by his side. He must have been lost in thought while viewing the archery match and subsequent developments in the arbor.

Sŏk Chuho was the man's name. He was aged twenty-nine. Sŏk was a public prosecutor who had come to this town a month ago on official assignment to a new post. For nearly the whole month he was busy taking over from his predecessor, getting acquainted with the public officials in town, and settling into his new residence. Now that these preliminaries were at an end, Sŏk had decided to resume his customary early-morning walks. Naturally he chose the town park for his excursions. On the morning of his first walk, he happened to discover the archery ground and the unusual events described above.

"What came of the game with the police chief?" clerk Kwŏn asked with a flattering smile when he came to Sŏk's office.

"What game?"

"You went out yesterday to play Korean checkers with the police chief, didn't you?"

This guy would do this to me, bringing up that game yesterday!

"Harmonious personal relations." Yes, that was their motto. But it was intolerable for Sŏk to be called *yŏnggam,* or "elderly man," by everybody in town.[1] And it was all the more unbearable to have to put up with this seemingly carefree clerk poking his nose into other people's business.

However, prosecutor Sŏk Chuho pretended not to hear the clerk. *I lost the game, of course. It's unpleasant even to think of it.* The way they had acted at the checkers game was disturbing. It would have been all the same even if they hadn't been playing for money, but they had insisted on betting every time. He was disgusted. Indeed, he had lost money to them. To make matters worse, he was in no position to propose something else in place of checkers. It was he who had at first suggested playing. And he felt ashamed at the prospect of giving up the game, because his opponents—the police chief, the head of the Agricultural Corporation Branch, the mayor of the town, and even the owner of three rental cars who acted like the boss of a great corporation—were thought to be distinguished men in town. The problem, then, was that he had not had enough practice at checkers beforehand. At present he could only endure the ordeal. And why on earth did the clerk have to remind him of it? Sŏk knew he would be ridiculed if he showed his displeasure. Harmonious personal relations. . . . This was the best policy for getting along in the world.

The clerk was silent, probably because he sensed what was going on in the prosecutor's mind. The official clerks . . . their talent for matching their mood to that of their elders! Shame on them! Prosecu-

---

[1] This paragraph has been abridged by the editor to eliminate inappropriate digression on the Korean word.

tor Sŏk avoided Kwŏn's eyes as if he feared being contaminated by such behavior. Still, he was impatient to say something to his clerk. Then the idea came to him.

"Ah, Mr. Kwŏn. Have you ever been to the archery ground in the park?"

"Yes, sir. There is one in the park." Kwŏn replied, somewhat embarrassed but still confident.

"I mean, have you ever seen people shooting?"

"You mean the archery ground in the park? I don't think so!"

Fool! Who could have lived long in the town and never known about the shooting in the morning? The indifferent mind notices nothing. A jewel is precious only to those who know what it is.

"Do you mean there is no archer in town?"

"Ah, they say there used to be many in the past. Recently I've heard that an old man, the owner of the archery ground, and his daughter shoot in the mornings. But I've never seen them myself."

"Then how does the old man earn his living?"

"By teaching archery to those who want to learn, they say."

Prosecutor Sŏk was pleased. This fellow, who at first seemed so ignorant, had much to tell him. That morning, he had been genuinely perplexed to see people shooting. But he could share his puzzlement with someone else.

"Will the old man teach anyone who wants to learn?"

"Of course. That's his work."

"By the way, why don't people take it up nowadays?"

"In the past, most of his students were officials in town. But these days the newly posted officials don't seem interested in archery."

"Should I prepare my own bow if I want to start practicing?"

"You could borrow one from the old man. They say he makes the bows himself. A good bow costs about twenty thousand *wŏn*, so it's too expensive to buy. Years ago, those who frequented the park often bought bows before they left town. Such things never happen nowadays, and the old man's bows must be covered with dust."

Sŏk Chuho was quite satisfied with this information.

"Mr. Kwŏn, you know a lot about this, though at first you pretended to know nothing."

"I'm just repeating what I've heard. I mean, I don't think about all this very much."

"You mentioned his daughter a moment ago. It seemed to me that she was too old to be his daughter." At last, Sŏk made his confession.

"Ah, so you've already been there!"

"This morning."

"She isn't really the old man's daughter. The girl and her brother were beggars. When they happened to start hanging around the hill, the old man took them in. The widower certainly intended to bring them up as his stepchildren. As you may have seen, the little boy is very obedient to him. By the way, it's strange that the girl is still unmarried, though she's a full-grown woman."

"Why hasn't she married?"

"I don't know. They say the old man is reluctant to marry her off, or she herself doesn't want to marry."

With this, Kwŏn gave an ambiguous smile. In his own way he must have conjectured what was going on in the prosecutor's mind. Sŏk quickly guessed Kwŏn's thoughts, and decided to take the initiative.

"Probably the girl has made you restless, eh?"

"Even if she willingly made me an offer, I'd turn her down. There's something I don't like about the idea of a female archer."

"Anyhow," the prosecutor said to change the subject, "would you inquire about archery lessons for me? I'd like to take it up."

"Sooner or later . . ."

The answer was not quite unwilling. Ah! Sŏk Chuho regretted asking. A man like Kwŏn would be unable to take a request for what it really is. For him, even a polite request from an elder was taken as an order.

"No, I'll go myself. It's my affair." He called off his request decisively.

"It'd be better," answered Kwŏn, straightening his bent back.

In the afternoon, Sŏk Chuho went up to North Tiger Arbor with his dog Paul following behind. He imagined that as an archer the old man would have a respectable air about him. To be humble before an old man lends dignity to a young man. It pleased Sŏk to picture himself taking a humble tack with the old man. He was in good spirits. He believed that the archery ground meant fortune for him. If he was alert, he could make it his fortune!

"I, Sŏk Chuho, am twenty-nine and now fully able . . ." He smiled contentedly as he said this to himself. And he looked around to see if anyone had overheard his words. Really, everything was in his favor. He had inherited a brilliant intelligence from his father, a distinguished judge on the Supreme Court, and had been reared in a good environment. Moreover, he had inherited a strong sense of pride from his mother, although he would not admit it willingly. He had graduated from so-called first-rate schools, from primary school through college, with no problems along the way. Unlike other boys, he had never experienced any hesitation in choosing his major at college. Eventually he had applied to law school, as his father had advised. As a senior in college he passed the competitive examination for judicial officer.

But college life was not altogether easy for him. He knew that his intelligence and favorable background were good in themselves. He sometimes felt, however, that these helpful circumstances might pose a threat in the future. It was unbearable to imagine that his future might be pedestrian. He must overcome any defects in himself. Deep in his mind was the proud feeling that he could defeat adversaries unconquerable by any other man. He spent the early part of his college life trying to improve himself in the liberal arts. If he thought it necessary, he did not hesitate to learn drinking, dancing, billiards, and mountain climbing. His friends often called him "smart," and he did consider the word applicable to himself. On the other hand, he did not fail to keep his pride in check. He tried to be humble. As he saw it, humility was more than the absence of pride. For instance, he had never maltreated his dog Paul. No doubt his attitude was not confined to Paul. He was to make up for his professional weaknesses as a prosecutor by trying to be humble and pious before all living things.

His career as a judicial officer had gone smoothly, as well. The only worrisome change was that his father, retired from his long judicial life, had suddenly embarked upon a political career with the opposition party. Sŏk considered this fact to be unrelated to himself.

His progress in his career, however, had started out with difficulty. That is, his new post was in a small town. At first he was disappointed. But he had the strength and the means to overcome this disappointment. He made up his mind not to waste time while he was there. His life in this town should be a more valuable experience than in a city. Although he could not devise a specific plan of attack in advance, he felt great confidence that he could do it himself. With this confidence, he arrived in town before the appointed day. As he had imagined, there were numerous difficulties awaiting him. Due to the provincial character of the place everybody began to call him by the deferential title *yŏnggam*, even at drinking establishments. In particular, the old police chief and mayor of the town used the term more often than anyone else. They themselves warranted the title, and it seemed that the people who most liked to use the term when addressing him were the very ones who deserved it themselves. Chuho had not yet become acquainted with anyone outside this elite circle.

Sŏk Chuho guarded himself against the influence of provincialism. He was confident he could avoid its constrictions. Moreover, he anxiously sought ways to make his life in the town more valuable than those of his friends in the city.

Perhaps this opportunity to learn archery was a great reward for his efforts. An unexpected event. A sensitive mind must not waste time. The worst enemy is lethargy. Climbing up the hill, Sŏk Chuho flattered himself. As he neared North Tiger Arbor, he could not erase from his mind the image he had of himself drawing the bow with great dignity. Those fellows in the checker game, I'll defeat them here on the archery ground! At the checker game they were all higher in rank than Chuho. But in archery he was sure of his advantage.

"Try it if you want," the old man in the arbor said after he heard Chuho. He was wearing a long belt with the logographs "North Tiger Arbor" embroidered on it. He brought out a bow as Chuho, now free from Paul, drew near.

"Have you ever been on an archery ground?" the old man asked, his eyes directed over the valley to the opposite hill where the boy was cutting grass. He seemed not to be interested in Chuho. The prosecutor thought it better not to have identified himself—the old man should be free to act of his own will.

"No, never."

"Then it would be better for you merely to watch today. You will come up again if you are so inclined." An almost imperative voice.

"Yes, I will." Chuho tried to be obedient.

"Kŏn!"

The boy, having cut the grass on the hill, ran up to the archery ground with a tuft of grass in his arms. Scarcely had the boy tossed the grass into the goat pen when he ran away scared. Wondering why, Chuho turned to the old man.

"The boy is afraid of dogs. He was once bitten by a wild dog."

Standing beside the pen, Paul was blankly watching the boy as he ran away. The dog must have approached surreptitiously to smell the child's leg. The dog had rarely gotten into mischief, but Chuho was obliged to concede. He tied Paul to a pillar of the arbor. But he need not have done it after all, for the boy, without being asked, was speedily crossing the valley with a fan in his hand. Leaving Chuho alone, the old man, having waited for the boy's arrival at the target, slowly took aim.

Tak!

The arrow flew almost straight at the bull's-eye. The fan was quickly raised and painted a whirling flower in the air. The next arrow flew in a curve. With such variations, the old man was slowly shooting with steadiness and precision. But what happened next? The sixth arrow flew far over the boy's head and the youngster bent to shake his fan backward from overhead.

"Did you watch the course of arrow? It was aimed higher than usual and flew farther than the other." Loading another arrow the old man turned his face to Chuho. Chuho was a little puzzled. He had not watched the arrow's flight carefully.

"So it seemed." Murmuring, he focused his eyes on the next arrow. The more carefully he watched, the more difficult it was to tell how the arrow was positioned. As soon as he lost sight of the arrow, the little boy over in the valley raised his fan. Chuho turned to the old man, but the latter did not see him. The next two arrows hit the right and left sides of the target respectively. Each time the boy's actions seemed to be quicker than the arrow. With the tenth arrow, the old man finished shooting. "On a still day like this, it is very easy to shoot." Thus said the old man as he made ready to end the session.

"Shall I try?" Chuho asked, feeling a little tense. The teacher looked at him uneasily.

"You should not try it too soon," the man answered, looking quite displeased.

"I'm sure I can manage. I have strong arms." He unconsciously stroked his arm as he asked once more. The old man blinked at him.

"It is one thing to have strong arms, but it is quite another to shoot," said the old man with dissatisfaction. But he delivered the bow to Chuho.

"Treat it carefully."

The old man gave him the belt, too. Chuho attempted to shoot in a brisk manner. But the bow was not easy to handle. It would straighten up as soon as Chuho bent it.

"Push up your chest. The strength of your arms alone is not enough."

When he did so, the arrow was fairly manageable. But he could not keep the attitude longer than a moment. His arms were shaking violently. The arrow started to fly. Without bothering to watch it, he quickly looked at the target. The little boy, who had been standing in the same spot since the old man began to shoot, seemed to search for the arrow in the air and quickly stepped aside from the spot. From there he began swinging the fan downward. On the other hand, the old man nodded his head three or four times as if he were struck by some idea. Chuho had no idea what was going on in the old teacher's mind.

"Should I bring my own bow?" Leaving the arbor, he was obliged to ask this question. Before the old man's suspicious eyes, he felt compelled to confirm his decision to learn archery.

"Do as you please. You can borrow one from me. In any case, while you practice shooting you should select one for your own use." Clerk Kwŏn was right.

"Would you show me some of your bows?"

"I will choose one for you later."

Chuho went down the hill.

After the young man had gone, the old man was struck by an idea and went up to the floor of the arbor. There he looked at the ceiling silently and sighed with his eyes closed. On the ceiling a number of bows were hanging in a row. Some were polished through long use, some were still fresh, and some were not finished. . . . He could see the bows clearly even with his eyes closed. He felt as if the bows were also looking down at him. How many dialogues had there been between the bows and himself! He could grow old with the comfort of the dialogue. He opened his eyes and pulled down a bow.

An elderly gentleman, Mr. Chang, used to visit the arbor regularly shortly before his death. He was innocent, like a child, and would get angry at anything that violated the art of archery. The face of his friend appeared in the old man's mind. He remembered, too, the Japanese county magistrate, now deceased, who had inquired after the arbor even after he had left town. Above all, he recalled the late owner of the arbor, that dignified and strict old man, his uncle. . . . His uncle's words were still fresh in his memory: "Nobody is qualified to keep this arbor except you."

The old man, having carefully examined the bows in turn, closed his eyes again. Memory was endless.

"Father, come to dinner!" At the little boy's summons, he opened his eyes and entered the room. In candlelight the dinner table looked dim. Soon the daughter entered from the kitchen. The family seated themselves around the table.

"Kŏn, you were scared, weren't you?" The old man smiled gently. The boy was quick to understand what his father meant.

"It was my mistake to allow a layman to shoot," he said to himself. He well knew how dangerous his boy's role was. An arrow can be fatal. Once skilled in the task, however, the boy could easily foretell where a flying arrow would fall. Thus it was not always such a fearsome task. But it was sometimes very difficult to know in advance where an arrow would fly, particularly when the archer was a novice.

The archery teacher knew all these things well through his own experience. When he was young, he used to wonder why on earth he had become a signal boy at an archery ground. But he had survived the ordeal and finally became the owner of this archery ground. He nodded again. Anyway the little boy should not lead the same life as mine; I must find a new life suitable for him, he said to himself.

Having finished his dinner, the old man watched his children gracefully eating their meal. Beggar though she was, the girl looked mild and virtuous. Having no child of his own, the old man had taken the girl and her brother in. At that time the girl had been sixteen years old. She used to carry her two-year-old brother around on her back. Twelve years had passed since then. The girl soon began to call him father, and like so many other little boys, the younger brother's first word had been "father." The girl managed to keep house well. Later the old man was informed that the boy was not really her brother but an orphan abandoned somewhere that she had decided to take with her. When the old man heard of this, the girl seemed to him prettier. Naturally the boy had not known about his true origin. His sister had great affection for him. And although the old man was strict in manner, the boy could always feel the irresistible warmth in his father's heart.

In any case, it was idle thinking. The problem was how to prepare a new way of life for the boy. During my lifetime he will be all right. But what will become of him then? The old man had never thought of the possibility that the boy might become an archer and the owner of the arbor after himself. Someday his sister would be obliged to leave here, and then they would go their separate ways. The old man knew it.

In reality it was more urgent to get his daughter married. Probably it was his fault for having taught her archery. Young women who were inferior to his daughter in character had already gotten married and had their own children. But no one had asked him for his daughter's hand. People turned aside their faces from both him and his daughter. The daughter of an archer . . . A female archer seemed to them offensive. It was for this reason that the old man began to shoot with his daughter in early mornings. She was indifferent in this matter, as if not knowing what was going on in the old man's mind. Sometimes a shadow might have passed over her face, but her father never caught sight of it. The old man sighed deeply again. The old maid carried the dinner tray to the kitchen silently.

The next afternoon, Prosecutor Sŏk Chuho came up to the arbor again with Paul. The old man informed him that he had not yet chosen a bow. The old man looked rather surprised to see the young man again.

"So you really want to try? Well, then, you are welcome any time."

The archery master brought out several bows. All of them were new. Chuho was unable to choose among them.

"Don't you have any used bows?"

"I have, but you had better train yourself with a new one."

"But please, show me an old one." The newly made bows seemed to him unreliable. Moreover, he had a superstition that anything old is valuable. He wanted to own a valuable bow and then show it to those town officials. For him it was always important to be a step ahead of others.

"This bow is made of good material, and until recently an old man used it," said the master, having brought out a polished bow. "The man who used the bow was an excellent archer."

"Is it suitable for me?"

"If you try to adjust yourself to it." Chuho decided to try it. The old man gave him a colored shoulder belt.

"What is this?"

"This is called an archery belt. It is used for carrying arrows. Although at present you need not carry arrows on your shoulder, you should wear it anyhow. That is the form you should hold on an archery ground."

From that day, Sŏk Chuho started to shoot. The teacher demonstrated shooting with ten arrows, and Chuho was allowed to shoot twenty. However, he could not see the boy beside the target on the opposite hill. At first Chuho imagined that the old man had forgotten; or perhaps the boy was busy with other things. But even when the child was lingering near the arbor, the old man did not send him over to the target. At last Chuho mentioned it to the old teacher, not so much because he enjoyed the boy's graceful movements; rather, he simply could not tell which way his arrows were flying. The old man's shots inevitably resulted in the sound of a direct hit, while Chuho was unable to decide how his next arrow should be aimed. But the old man flatly refused Chuho's request.

"Continue a little longer like this."

"I'm unable to aim exactly."

"At present, you are not trained in shooting. Proper archery is the outcome of spiritual discipline. Even though your arrows hit the target once in a while, it is simply an accident."

Spiritual dicipline—probably so. Again Chuho decided to follow the old man obediently.

Chuho tried and tried to shoot carefully. A week passed, but still the old man did not send the boy to the target. Chuho, who intended to display his skill in archery before his town fellows, became uneasy at this.

"I once saw them use a flag instead of a fan in Seoul. Which do you think is the proper means to signal?"

The old man answered bluntly, "A fan, of course."

"What is the boy called?"

"A signal boy."

"How far is it to the target?"

"One hundred and fifty? But the exact distance can be measured only by your eyes."

Chuho asked a lot of other questions as well and learned much about archery. For example, he was told that a bull's tendon is used for a good bow, that the arrow feather is very important in shooting, and the like. But the old man stopped suddenly and questioned Chuho with suspicion.

"Do you expect to learn archery through words?"

This question hit so pointedly that Chuho excused himself in embarrassment. "I thought I might introduce some of my friends to you tomorrow afternoon. I felt I had better have some knowledge about the way of the bow before bringing them here."

The old man still looked displeased and said, "Be that as it may, vain words are not required in learning archery. Words should be abandoned."

In departing, however, Chuho was obliged to ask, "If you don't mind, I would like to bring my friends tomorrow."

"I don't mind it, but . . ."

The next day Sŏk Chuho came up accompanied by four men. The upstart owner of business cars accepted Chuho's suggestion at once, for he was always on the lookout for anything that would give him an air of respectability; the rich brewer accepted for the same reason. The younger brother of a national assemblyman and clerk Kwŏn came too. The senior prosecutor, the police chief, and the mayor were not willing to come, but Chuho was content with the four men.

The old man, at first, seemed surprised to see that these four were treating the young man, Chuho, with a certain respect. But the old man's bearing toward both the prosecutor and his companions did not change.

Each time Paul was tied to a pillar of the bower for the little boy's sake. As before, the old man simply demonstrated shooting technique. As long as the boy did not go over to the valley, Chuho was all the same a novice like his companions, though Chuho was, in fact, a little more advanced than they.

When positioned on the archery ground, Chuho said few words, as if to emulate the old teacher. Giving some brief advice to his companions, he would silently shoot his arrows. Of course, the four men looked respectfully at his seemingly confident attitude.

Several days passed in the same way when an unexpected event happened. It began with a passing remark by one of Chuho's companions, but it suddenly filled the air with suspense.

"Old man, do you plan to let your daughter remain unmarried?" As they rested on the ground after shooting, the brewer idly posed this question. But the inquiry gave all the men a feeling that it violated a kind of taboo, even though it was natural for a disinterested party to ask such a thing. What they felt was vague and varied from person to person. They simply felt that the question would probably make the old man angry for reasons no one knew. Without knowing why they felt so, they turned their eyes to the old man. Contrary to their anticipation, he looked extremely indifferent. He said casually, "Is there any father who wants his daughter unmarried?"

"Then the woman herself does not want to get married?" Sŏk Chuho asked, realizing that the suspense had been groundless. But in a moment he perceived he was mistaken.

The old man answered bluntly, "No, though she has not said a word about it."

"Why, then, hasn't she married?" Recalling Kwŏn's earlier remark, Chuho pressed.

"You are wrong. Think over why you asked such a question. It is you who suppose that an archer doesn't want to marry off his daughter, or that the daughter herself has no desire to get married. I don't know why you have such a notion, but you obviously have."

The old man looked reproachfully at Sŏk Chuho. The reproach was not directed at Chuho alone. The old man closed his mouth in a frown. But he could not close it completely. Again he said in an anguished voice as if he were unable to endure something burning in his heart, "Is an archer or his daughter different from ordinary people? Since he loves archery, he may expect less of the world than they do. But he is also a man, and naturally wants to be fed and get married. The fault, if any, is not his, but of those who regard him as different from them."

This old man's character is extremely strict, Chuho thought. He was rather pleased by it. He recalled in his mind those Buddhist monks residing in the suburbs of Seoul, who have become like innkeepers or sight-seeing guides. This old man is surely different from them. He was lacking in humor and difficult to get along with. The old man reminded Chuho of a master he had read about in a novel. This thought contented him.

But his companions sitting there did not think the same way. If they had, the unexpected event would not have happened—though it is difficult to call it an event. The old man's severe and dignified manner caused a certain embarrassment among Chuho's companions. And his reproachful words exasperated one of them.

"You are different from other people so long as you live on your bow alone. Moreover, people say your daughter also practices archery."

Once the daughter's archery was mentioned, all the men asked to see her use the bow. The old man modestly refused, saying that her form was not good enough to be seen by others. As the old man spoke thus, nobody noticed his eyelids imperceptibly trembling. The men insisted on seeing her. Once again the old man refused, strongly this time. But Chuho's companions had dropped the discipline of the archery ground, and they did not give up.

Maintaining his silence, Chuho perceived a strangeness in their insistence. And it was even stranger to see the old man refusing strongly, as if he were insulted by the men's insistence. As for Chuho,

he could not suppress his desire to see the unmarried woman shoot—
something he had not seen since that foggy morning. What is beautiful should be displayed. And it must be praised and loved. It mattered little why his companions wanted to see it. In a sense, it is my duty to see it while I sincerely attempt to learn how to handle a bow, Chuho thought to himself.

Then he too asked the old man if they could watch the daughter shoot. At this, the teacher made a difficult face and proposed to postpone it until early next morning.

"But there is nothing to be ashamed of. What is beautiful must be displayed and praised," Chuho emphasized in a stately voice as if in a court of law.

The old man looked dejected, and called his daughter and the boy. The boy ran over to the valley to the target, and the young woman came out in white ramie clothes with a blue belt. And she shot her bow.

That was all that happened. That is why it is difficult to call it an event. Even Sŏk Chuho was exclaiming in praise, "Oh, wonderful, really wonderful!" on seeing her at archery against the dusky sky. All the men were quite content, whatever their first motivations might have been. And thus they came down the hill.

It must really have been an event for the family in the arbor, however, for the old man did not eat that evening and the maid did not enter the room after preparing and serving dinner. She just sat silently in a corner of the kitchen. The little boy alone enjoyed dinner with his usual relish. The old man, at times, gave a dry cough in vain to call his daughter, and made a low moan with eyes closed like a wounded animal. Nobody could tell what the afternoon event had really meant for the family, although they surely appeared deeply hurt by it.

But the next day the family acted undisturbed. The old man treated Sŏk Chuho and his companions as before. Noticing the old man's indifferent manner, Chuho recalled the old teacher's demeanor on the previous day. He had been greatly exasperated with something. And he said much more than usual, with an animated expression, before suddenly becoming dejected and summoning his daughter. Chuho felt that he had somehow insulted the man. But today the old man was as dignified as ever. He seemed no longer to show any excitement. Chuho felt sorry in some mysterious way.

Several days passed and still the old man did not send the boy to the target. Chuho had run out of advice for his novice companions. It seemed that they had all, including Chuho, become equal in the old man's eyes. But Chuho comforted himself with the thought that the day the boy was sent to the target would come earlier for himself than for the others. He waited.

And yet everything went on in the same way. The target without the signal boy, the dignified manner of the old man . . . everything went on unchanged. One day Chuho began to plot a little rebellion. He did not know exactly what was going on in the teacher's mind since the day he had made the mistake of showing his daughter's archery to the men. The old man was a giant. Chuho must be confident before the giant.

The rebellion was not just consciously plotted. During his visits to the arbor, his dog Paul had always accompanied him. The dog was rather a part of his body. And the dog got tied up whenever it came up the hill. Paul used to bark at first, but soon lay down. That afternoon, Chuho happened to see his dog unusually depressed. He saw in the dog's eyes a pitiable entreaty. At the sight of it, Chuho felt a strange rage toward the old man. The old man was the one who made Paul sad, he thought. He reflected also on how easily he accepted the old man's arrogance. He himself had never before mistreated Paul like this. His excessive feeling for the teacher was responsible for Paul's cruel treatment. And yet the old man would yield nothing. In spite of his justified sympathy for the gentleman, Chuho could not help getting angry at the sight of Paul's sadness. Suddenly he untied Paul. Once free, Paul started to run fitfully around the archery ground two or three times, and slowly back to the side of his master. At that moment the little boy, returning from tending the goats, caught sight of the dog and ran for his life. Chuho pretended not to notice it.

From then on Chuho did not tie his dog to the pillar. Paul began to sweep about the archery ground. Whenever Paul was running loose, the boy was nowhere to be seen. Long before Paul appeared, he would lead the goats off the grounds and escape speedily with a fodder-stick on his shoulder. When he had nothing particular to do, the boy simply sat alone on the hill above the archery ground. Chuho knew this, but he continued to pretend not to know. What he had done for Paul was absolutely right, he thought. Although he felt uneasy at times at the thought that his act meant a rebellion against the old man, he felt justified in his own way. But a dark expression sometimes passed over the old man's face when he saw his boy sitting alone on the hill with nothing to do. Chuho, however, did not catch sight of it.

Some days later . . .

"Boy, you are too afraid of dogs. Wouldn't it be better for you to go over and gather arrows?"

Chuho spoke jokingly to the boy on the hill. And soon the accident happened. At Chuho's joke, the old man suddenly made a merciless face and shouted up to the boy.

"Get over there!"

Chuho smiled faintly. He was aware that he was forming a conspiracy within himself. The conspiracy was already succeeding.

The little boy stealthily came down the hill, brought out the fan from the room, and ran over the valley. The old man, lost in thought after he summoned the child, turned his eyes abruptly to the valley. The boy already stood beside the target, waiting for arrows. Several expressions rapidly flashed across the old man's face. Then he appeared to be deep in thought.

At last Sŏk Chuho was allowed to shoot alone. He shot carefully with his first arrow. But he could not clearly discern the boy's signals. From the attitude of the youngster, he knew that his arrow had flown high over the target. He aimed his second. This time I will not miss. I will shoot straight to the bull's-eye, he said to himself. He shot. But this arrow did not hit the target either. No. The arrow flew straight. Another target was there. It seemed to him that a hidden target, until then lying somewhere, suddenly appeared, to be hit by his arrow. At that very moment, the boy fell on the hillside. His fall was strangely beautiful and for that very reason seemed all the more horrible. Perhaps the beauty lay in the successive movements of his fall: first he slowly sank to his knees, and then pitched forward, head first. A man of good memory might have recalled an image he had seen in a film: the dying of a little roebuck, shot by a hunter's gun and shedding blood in every direction.

TRANSLATED BY KIM CHONGCH'ŎL

MODERN ESSAYS

In traditional Korea there were two kinds of essays, formal and informal. Both were written in classical Chinese. Of the two, informal random jottings were the most popular form to which writers turned for their freedom, spontaneity, and diversity. Known as the literary miscellany, random jottings allowed the writer to question the official view of experience and explore a wider horizon of inquiry. While the familiar essay form ceased to be popular after the crisis of humanism in the 1930s in the West, today the essay, the descendant of random jottings, still flourishes in Korea and East Asia, though with certain differences in form and content.

Like its predecessor, the modern Korean essay offers a variety of narrative forms and content: accounts of trips, comments on current topics, lyrical or philosophical disquisitions, meditations on the seasons, to name only a few. Every daily or magazine has an essay column, and most writers have at least one volume of essays to their credit. The essay is also a favorite battleground for waging verbal warfare. Certainly the examples presented here demonstrate a variety of topics and diversity of style.

Chŏng Chiyong, one of the most influential modern Korean poets, is mentioned in Modern Poetry II. P'i Ch'ŏndŭk (b. 1910), who graduated from Huijiang University in Shanghai (1931), and Yi Yangha (1904–1963), who graduated from Tokyo Imperial University (1930), taught English literature at Seoul National University. After graduating in German literature from Hōsei University in Japan, Kim Chinsŏp (b. 1903) actively introduced Western literature, especially drama, to the Korean reading public before he was kidnapped by the North Korean army in 1950. Both Yun Oyŏng (b. 1907) and Yi Ŏryŏng (b. 1934), the editor of the monthy *Munhak sasang* (Literary Thoughts), studied and taught Korean literature. Yi's selections are from *In This Earth and In That Wind* (1963), which sold 300,000 copies.

Chŏng Chiyong

THE WARBLER AND THE CHRYSANTHEMUM

If I got hold of a twig of spring willow in which the sap still ran fresh, city dwellers would normally envy me my piece of nature. But recently I was able to find, even in Seoul, a place with a warbler in the front yard. Yet when I told my friends that I had moved into a place about a ten-minute walk from the streetcar stop by the district office outside the West Gate, they neither congratulated me nor were they impressed. My neighbors are more concerned with the stock market's condition and the rising price of land in the vicinity than with my warbler.

On a morning bright with rays of sunlight, the day after our move into the new house, I was surprised in bed by a sound like tinkling jade reverberating between the furrows in my tile roof. It was a warbler in the tree in front. I ran outside. If my wife, too, had darted out from the kitchen throwing down the fire tongs or just keeping them in her hand, the warbler in the tree would have been worthwhile. How could she be so dull and insensitive?

In my leisure hours in the evening I searched the area. I found not only warblers, but pheasant hens flying up from the brushwood and cock pheasants belling till the mountains responded. Eastern ring-doves came down to the entrance of our neighborhood in search of food, and "daughter-in-law birds"—said to be the soul of the daughter-in-law who hanged herself from a chestnut tree after carrying in a meal tray for her mother-in-law—were calling as well. This bird sings in secluded places and cries impatiently when the chestnut flowers are white as snow. It can usually be heard around breakfast and supper-time, as if to remind us of our daily food. Its plaintive cry trails off as though something had choked it. I learned about the origin of the bird when I was thirteen. Its cry conjures up the loneliness, sorrow, and fear of my boyhood, and even now I turn away from desolate nooks for fear of encountering it.

Having been planted by the authorities, the pine trees cannot but stand straight, and nothing matches the sound of wind blowing through pines, intimate and comforting, sad and joyous. It provides me solace when I face defeat. It is worth living outside the gates of Seoul just for the sounds of the wind.

Here no one criticizes me if I go about in shirtsleeves. I have discovered for the first time that I love the light, carefree feeling that comes with wearing shirtsleeves, a feeling that makes me flirt with nature and man. Sometimes I roll up my sleeves, but not with the intention of fighting. It is easier for me in my shirtsleeves to open my mouth, the constant object of my friends' disparagement. I can sit anywhere in any manner I like—I draw my knees up with hands linked under them. Even if I sit like this for half a day, you cannot attribute it to my laziness—I have clouds that blossom and fade, and a spring that bubbles in a valley throughout the seasons. Cuckooflowers and wild thistles are my treasure. Sitting beside them, my whole body, mind, and soul seem to expand. There is no reason to be immured in a decorated room. Here, where the purple flowers of cuckooplants are everywhere, even a thirty-year-old man without a sweetheart can live.

When the wind lulls, the golden barley field sends a warm scent of ripeness, pine resin gathers, and cuckoos call to each other. When I climb a hill, scattering the morning dew, the common dayflower beckons me. I am surprised anew by its lovely blue petals. What makes them so blue? When I crush them my fingertips are dyed blue. Soon the fireflies will light their lanterns and cling to the curled flowers.

Once I gathered dayflowers, made ink from them, and, like a lover, wrote letters to friends in that ink, informing them of the warbler in front of my room. A friend in Anak congratulated me, and another in Changsŏng came to visit. He had a double purpose: to meet the warbler and to see us in our new home. But on that very day the warbler seemed to be put out and did not sing. While beer foamed waiting for the bird to stir, my friend only smiled. One who wields the writing brush is often visited by such disappointment. Then I heard a siren that floated over smoke and dust and quietly died.

The warbler sings only in the right season. With the change of weather, not only the warbler but even the daughter-in-law birds have stopped singing. Only the Indian ringdoves are frantic. Flowers and leaves wither, one after another, and the wild chrysanthemums too finally succumb: only the pine wind is resolute.

When the season of the warbler returns, I will again invite my friend from Changsŏng, but can I stitch together the dying season? I will probably don an outer jacket with a silver button. As the warbler is to other birds, so is the Korean yellow chrysanthemum to other flowers. Soon I will be drunk on the yellow chrysanthemum!

TRANSLATED BY PETER H. LEE

Kim Chinsŏp

IN PRAISE OF POVERTY

The reader, hardly believing his eyes, might ask why I write about such a miserable subject as poverty. It is a pity that in this world, where money is the sole object, a man's sad plight compels him to praise untarnished poverty. One who is not rich cannot drive poverty away, so he praises it instead. It is his only weapon, the solace that keeps his body and soul together.

Where do wealth and poverty begin? In order for a man to be rich, how much must he have, and in order to be poor, how little? No one, of course, has the answer. There are rich who think they are poor; indeed, many of them walk around thinking so. Not knowing self-sufficiency, they crave unnecessary things. In other words, they never use the superlative. They look up to those who are better off than they and make a list of what they themselves lack. We cannot help people who have never heard of satiety or have forgotten the beautiful word "enough." Yet there are also people who think they are well off when they suffer hardships, people who live out their lives with such conviction. Not only do they not have a fortune to speak of, but they live from hand to mouth. They do not deem necessary what they do in fact need. They try to imagine those in circumstances more straitened than their own, and empathize with those on the verge of starvation. In this way, these champions of consolation make us feel as if their strength and love are directed not at themselves but toward others.

There cannot be objective standards to define wealth and poverty. A small pocket is easy to fill, but a sack with a hole is not. It is the man himself who determines whether he is rich or poor. Therefore, one who intends to leave a fortune to his children should teach them the talent for peering into the depths of poverty, and the art of the austere life, rather than leaving them perishable material. What makes a man rich is a taste for self-sufficiency and the mental ability to place himself in another's situation.

Can there be, then, no poverty in the world? Of course not. I think there are two kinds of poverty. The first might be called material poverty. That person is truly destitute who has become useless because he has nothing to do, who has lost the rights of action and existence, and for whom self-sufficiency and frugality do not avail. The second is spiritual poverty. One who suffers from this kind of poverty does not know there is a rightful and beautiful place where he can dedicate his talent and love, so he mocks the existence of such an alternative. And when his life has become meaningless, he becomes greedy rather than inquiring into his dissatisfaction. He who represents the second kind of poverty is poor indeed. It is sad to watch a poor man of the second type pass callously and arrogantly by a poor man of the first.

Diogenes lived cheerfully in his tub.[1] But Alexander found his world too small.[2] If we can affirm that Diogenes's untarnished poverty was his fortune, his wealth was great indeed.

TRANSLATED BY PETER H. LEE

---

[1]Diogenes: Greek philosopher of the fourth century B.C. who is said to have lived in a large earthenware tub in Athens.
[2]Alexander: Alexander the Great of Macedon (356–323 B.C.).

Yi Yangha

THE ROSE OF SHARON

Because of harsh weather, my hometown has few flowers, and no rose of Sharon to speak of. Although I have heard of it since my child-hood, it was only some ten years ago, when I began to live in Seoul, that I actually saw the rose of Sharon. Where did I see it for the first time? I think it was on the campus of Yŏnhŭi College. I still recall my disappointment at that first encounter. The purplish red blossom, withered and shrunk under the midday sun, its brilliance lost, recalled the *kisaeng*'s lips. I peered into the leaves to find beauty, but their tough and dark green color resembled that of a tree rather than a flower.

Not that I harbored any mysterious nostalgia for its name, the rose of Sharon, but I could not imagine that our national flower should be so common and mean. I was probably not alone in my frustration. England's sensual Red Tudor rose, France's elegant and neat golden fleur-de-lis, Germany's plump cornflower, Scotland's graceful thistle, Greece's sad-looking bear's breech, Japan's gorgeous and simple cherry blossom. Compared with these, our ancestors' choice, I thought then, was perhaps mistaken. The writer Yi T'aejun once enu-merated why the rose of Sharon could not be our national flower, and proposed instead the azalea—a familiar flower in Korea—in its place. But the one who expressed a feeling of disgust most aptly was my friend from Chŏlla province. He saw the flower many times as a boy without knowing its significance and learned about it only after he came to Seoul. "You mean the *mugang* tree?" he exclaimed. "The one we use as a hedge in my hometown?"

During ten years at Yŏnhŭi College I saw many roses of Sharon, however, and in the past four or five years I have lived in a house with several of its white-blossomed trees. So I have observed various aspects of the flower morning and evening, and my feeling for it has changed considerably.

Even today I'm not sure whether the rose of Sharon should be our national flower, but it is not a flower undeserving of such honor. Upon reflection, I feel that I have come to fathom the intent of my ancestors, and have discovered its special qualities. Indeed, it is too beautiful a flower to be ignored. After the cherry, apricot, and peach blossoms have fallen, the rose of Sharon has not even sprouted leaves. Because it begins to bud from the stump when the garden is full of green, it is unsightly to see its dried seeds still dangling on the branches. Only after the lilacs, yellow plums, and roses bloom do small leaves cover the whole tree from its trunk to the tips of its branches. Its flowers blossom one to two weeks after budding. In Seoul, it begins to blossom in early July, when summer vacation starts. After such a long wait, and after the glory of spring flowers is gone, a white blossom (for the true rose of Sharon should always be white) glimpsed through its leaves is unforgettable.

Our ancestors must have had this white blossom in mind. We have a saying, "white red heart," meaning a sincere heart. White is also the color of our traditional clothing, and the red in the flower's center is the red our ancestors loved to use in painting. One cannot view it without admiration. The blossom is shy, courteous, and humble, but not lacking in self-confidence.

Each blossom usually fades overnight, but a new one takes it place and blossoms continue to come out through August, September, and early October when a cool wind seeps through my cotton garments. If we count the number of flowers that bloom and fall in one season, it must be in the thousands and tens of thousands. The blossoms are at their peak in late August, and I can count several hundred on a tree as tall as I am. It must be for this reason that our ancestors, who considered it good fortune for brothers to be distinguished and sons and grandsons to continue through myriad generations, loved the rose of Sharon. Is it not a virtue for a flower to flourish and persist so?

They must also have loved its unpretentious and amiable quality. The rose of Sharon ignores the condition of the soil. Except for the winter, it grows whenever and wherever it is transplanted—on the borders of a field, along the hedges of a house, or in the garden of the guest quarters. Not that it was planted in all these places; it grows whenever a seed falls. Moreover, it is not sensitive to insects. It might get infested with aphids, or spiders might spread a web, but it does not wither because of them. One of the reasons why we have not generally appreciated this flower may be that it is not hard to tend. Because it is so approachable and untroublesome, even if no one cares for it, it does not die out. Man may leave it alone, but it will spread, grow, and flourish. Here again we can read our ancestors' wish for the prosperity of their children and the perpetuity of their nation.

In a sense—no, above all—the rose of Sharon is a flower of the hermit. I don't know why foreigners sometimes dubbed Korea the Hermit Kingdom, but if ours is in fact the land of the hermit, the rose of Sharon well symbolizes our country. In terms of gender, it is not feminine but neuter. It is neither enchanting nor fragrant. It suits the taste of our ancestors, who avoided the poppy as sensual.[1] I can imagine the appearance of one of our reclusive ancestors, garbed in hemp and cotton clothes, a bamboo-ribbed fan in hand, strolling through the garden of his grass-thatched hut. And I can think of no flower that better suits the scene than the rose of Sharon. It possesses the virtues that the recluse seeks and promotes. It is devoid of the vulgarity that he abhors, and devoid too of the worldly ambition, cruelty, fickleness, and arrogance that the virtuous spurn. Dignified, courteous, humble to the end, it is endowed with the appearance of the Confucian gentleman. I don't know which flower in the West represents humility, but above all other flowers the rose of Sharon seems to express it. Thus it eminently possesses the highest virtue, for humility is the most sublime state of mind we are capable of and the noble attribute of a man who wishes to rule our country. Thus the rose of Sharon expresses in some measure the character of the Korean people and corresponds with what we joyfully seek. It is fitting, therefore, that it should be our national flower. If we strive to learn and embody the virtue of this flower, we may one day become a great people.

TRANSLATED BY PETER H. LEE

---

[1]One sentence has been omitted at this point because of an unidentifiable allusion.

Yun Oyŏng

COOKED GLUTINOUS RICE

With a bundle of cooked glutinous rice, I left home at daybreak. I promised my friends I would go on a picnic with them today, so I had rice prepared for lunch.

When we took field trips in my grammar school days, other children would arrive, knapsacks bulging with cookies, fruits, and soft drinks. But not having even a knapsack, I used to carry cooked glutinous rice wrapped in a cloth. Mother would get up at dawn, make a charcoal fire, and cook rice, regretting all the while that she was unable to buy sweets for me. She did not have any money to set aside, so she used to save a bowlful of glutinous rice at the time of autumn sacrifices to tutelary spirits of the house. Knowing her anxious heart, I never coveted cookies and apples, but savored the rice cooked by my devoted mother. As I left home with a sense of confidence in the future, I would walk away bravely. Mother's gift of love became a source of encouragement and strength for me as a boy. Such is the origin of the cooked glutinous rice that I used to take every time I went on an excursion or hike.

Today I left home again with a bundle of cooked glutinous rice. As I came down from the veranda into the garden, I suddenly turned around and looked toward the kitchen. The image of Mother making a charcoal fire at dawn flashed through my mind, only to fade like mist. I had a bundle of cooked rice in my hand, but Mother was not there.

What did Mother receive from the son she raised with great hopes as she wrapped rice for him? Believing that her son would one day succeed in life, she eked out a scanty living with hope. But her son has known only life's bitter side.

In her last moments, Mother took hold of my hand with a faint quivering smile, her hope in her son unwavering. "I am leaving you before your success, but you must get on in life." I don't know what she meant by that, but to the end she tried to believe that her son would succeed. At that time, moved to tears, I responded vaguely.

After standing vacantly, seized with recollections, I looked at my watch. It was half past six. I had to be at the Pulgwang-dong terminal in an hour. The gray of the morning began to brighten, and a cool wind crept into me. As I was coming out of the gate, I glanced up at the sky and lowered my head. Here I was, gray-haired and fifty, having accomplished nothing in life, and leaving home with the same rice, the same frame of mind, as a boy of eleven. Mother, your once ambitious son, carrying cooked glutinous rice, grizzled hair blown in the wind, is brushing his tears away with the back of his hand.

TRANSLATED BY PETER H. LEE

P'i Ch'ŏndŭk

THE ESSAY

The essay is a celadon water-dropper.[1] It is an orchid, a crane, a chic and supple beauty. The essay is a level path by which beauty makes her way through the woods. The essay may even be a tree-lined boulevard, but it is one that passes through neat, out-of-the-way residential quarters.

The essay is not the genre of youth, but rather of one who has passed age thirty-six into the middle years. It is not a genre given to passionate or profound intellect, but rather a vehicle for the writer's most tentative reflections.

The essay provides a certain gusto, but without excitation. It suits the disposition of the peripatetic heart. Within its confines an essay contains the bouquet and resonance of life itself.

The essay is neither ecstatically resplendent nor strong in tone, nor is it colored either black or white. It is neither effete nor rustic, but is always filled with grace and an incomparable beauty. The hue of the essay is that of the dove or the pearl. If the essay were a length of silk, it would be of a subtly figured matte weave in a pattern to bring a smile to the reader's face.

While the essay is a leisurely genre, it is never idle. Though unshackled, it is never diffuse. Rather than dazzling, the essay is refined. Rather than mordant, it is refreshing.

The material of the essay is the experience of daily life, observations of nature, even new insights into human activity and social phenomena—all of these are appropriate. Whatever its topic, an essay is spun out in accord with the idiosyncrasies and the mood of the writer, much as a silkworm spins itself a cocoon. An essay requires no plot or climax; it is free to go wherever the writer wishes to lead it. Still, an essay resembles a kind of tea, in that a tea without bouquet will taste as insipid as tap water.

The essay is a soliloquy. The novelist or playwright must on occasion depict the experiences of a variety of characters: Shakespeare, for instance, created characters as different as Hamlet and Polonius. Yet,

---

[1]A vessel to hold water for the ink slab.

by way of contrast, essayists like Charles Lamb have always found it sufficient just to be themselves. The essay is the literary genre that reveals its author most candidly. Accordingly, an essay transmits a sense of intimacy—akin to that felt when reading a letter from a friend.

There is a celadon water-dropper in the museum of the Tŏksu Palace. This vessel is in the form of a lotus. The petals of the lotus are identically fashioned and form a uniform pattern, except for one single petal that differs ever so slightly from the rest. This exception in the midst of symmetry is not offensive to the eye, and is not an essay similar in this regard? To fashion an essay with one of its petals, as it were, slightly awry—this demands a certain breadth of mind.

Such breadth of mind is lacking in myself, and it is indeed sad that I therefore cannot write essays. At times I make efforts to broaden my mind. Yet once having done so, I find my very breadth of mind blameworthy, and I surrender even the last bit of myself to impatience and confusion.

SPRING

"Life is an empty wine cup, an uncarpeted staircase; April comes babbling like an idiot and strewing flowers," one poet wrote.

"April is the cruelest month," another poet wrote.[2]

These are men of extravagance. An ordinary man like myself waits for spring. When spring comes, just the act of discarding heavy, bulky clothing makes my body and mind feel lighter. My wrinkled face breaks into a smile in the warm sunshine; when I gaze up at the sky, I almost feel as though I could fly.

The coming of spring is like a return to my youth. When I listen to music or view a painting or sculpture, I have the impression of encountering, however fleetingly, my lost youth in the mist, and one of my joys as a literary man is to recall my youth through my readings. Yet it is spring above all that allows me to experience youth itself yet again.

To possess one's lost youth again, even for a moment, brings even greater joy than an encounter with a long-lost love. If the fondly

---

[2]Refers to "The Waste Land" by T. S. Eliot (1888–1965).

remembered love is a woman, she may have grown plump or scrawny. If he is a man, he may have begun to droop and sag like an old cardigan sweater; his face may have grown splotchy and red, and his eyes dull and lackluster.

Youth is always beautiful. Though our past loves may give us cause for disillusionment, everyone feels a lingering nostalgia for his lost youth.

It is said that if man gets older, he is delivered from the frustrations and samsara of youth, and he finds peace of mind. "Peace of mind," though, connotes a kind of apathy produced by inactivity. It is a phrase that offers scant consolation for a vegetating mind and dulled sensibilities. Even Plato said that he became a scarecrow in his old age. No wisdom is better than youth.

Some say that life begins at forty. This is really to say that life ends at forty. To cite only one example, ninety-three percent of the protagonists of the novels I have read are under forty. And man's years after forty are borrowed time. If one's span of life is forty years, then it is short. But on second thought, this is not so.

"With the butterfly showing the way, spring, ah spring, has come." Now, the butterfly that children sing of is surely not the same butterfly of last year. The swallows that fly south in winter are said to return each spring, but how many actually do?

The nightingale that Keats heard[3] is not the same bird that Ruth heard as she stood weeping "amid the alien corn" four thousand years ago. Because he was young, Keats used the splendid phrase "immortal bird" to characterize the nightingale. Yet human life is several times longer than that of a butterfly or a nightingale.

Spring, the season of dandelions and violets, of azaleas and goldenbells, of peach and apricot blossoms, of lilac and rose bushes that blossom continuously . . . It is no small blessing to sample the joys of this season even forty times, and for a man over forty the arrival of spring is a boon indeed.

Even a rusty old heart will throb with new vigor, and even one who can afford not a single purchase will still take pleasure in a shop window's lavish display. Thus, although I have left my youth behind, I feel no envy for that golden bird housed in its Byzantine palace.[4] Ah, spring is on its way; it draws closer every minute.

---

[3]Refers to "Ode to a Nightingale" by John Keats (1795–1821).
[4]Refers to "Sailing to Byzantium" by William Butler Yeats (1865–1939).

THE GOOD LIFE

First of all, I would have a good life if I could have fifty thousand *hwan* (at the current rate) to use as I please. I would want to admit this weary body into the Ch'ŏngnyangni Sanitorium. After lying down on a clean bed, I would like to take a bath about twice a day in clean, hot water. And I would buy my daughter, for her birthday, the velvet pants I was not able to buy her, and for my wife, a pound and a half of beehive woolen threads. For myself, I'd like to buy several tasteful trim neckties. The friends I did not have any money to invite before, and with whom I've become remiss in corresponding, I would want to invite to our house. My wife would be excited preparing the food. I would really love a life with fifty thousand, no, one hundred thousand *hwan* to use as I please. I would not sell my time and energy, and would leave aside about one-tenth of my work.

I want to have a life in which I could enjoy freedom and leisure. I like to walk on grass. I enjoy walking on wet sand. I like walking on asphalt in rubber-soled shoes. I like to feel someone's wife's otter fur scarf, which makes me feel sorry for my own wife.

I like beautiful faces. I like smiling faces even more. However, I even like smiling plain faces. I like Sŏyŏng's mother's smiling face gazing at her own child. I like it when the girls I know smile instead of greeting me. (And I love my daughter's smiling, new-toothed face.)

I like beautiful colors. When I gaze at the brilliant autumn leaves in every valley at the Grotto of Myriad Falls,[5] my step quickens. When I look back, it seems as though I were leaving even better autumn leaves behind, and I am at a loss for what to do. I like rapturous red, lavender, maroon, and green, like the colored paper our kindergarten teacher used to give us in the old days. I love the autumn sky of our country. I like the glow of pearl and the hue of the dove. I like the mahogany glow of old furniture. I like the salt and pepper hair of an aging scholar.

I like the morning skylark's voice, and the warbling of the nightingale makes me glad. The sound of a spring brook's bubbling brings happiness. I like the sound of wind blowing through reeds, and when I hear the sound of the waves, my heart still pounds. I like the sound of a piano which causes me to stop and tarry for awhile as I pass through a narrow alley.

---

[5] Grotto of Myriad Falls: a scenic spot in the Diamond Mountains.

I like youthful laughter. I like Sŏyŏng's whisper in my ear when there is no one else in the room. I like the smell of broiling meat from a back alley tavern on a rainy evening, of new Western books, and of woolen clothing. I like the fragrance of brewing coffee, of blossoming lilac, chrysanthemum, jonquils, and pine trees. I like the scent of the spring earth.

I like apples and walnuts, pine nuts and honey; I like to sip fragrant tea with friends. I like to put roasted chestnuts in my overcoat pocket and eat them as I walk along, and I like the ice cream cone I licked while walking along the Charles River on a winter day.

I like my house, a nine-p'yŏng structure on a lot of fifty p'yŏng.[6] I could not afford lumber, so it is a mud house, but I like it because it is mine. There is a space for flowering plants in the yard, and because nobody can tell me to move out I don't have to worry. My books will always be in their place, and if I live a long time in this house, there won't be any friends who can't visit because they cannot find the house.

On the morning of March 1—Independence Day—I feel the impulse to put on a silk hat and wear morning clothes. However, I know that I cannot do it. In the summer I like to put on farmer's clothes—hemp trousers and shirt—and put on straw sandals and walk on the mountain road.

I like shoes. I like embroidered shoes, black sneakers with my name on them, cleanly washed blue rubber shoes, sturdily made straw sandals encrusted with mud. I love all the small and beautiful things of which my life consists.

I like to look at a beautiful face without desire, and praise others' achievements without envy. I'd like to love many, hate none, and cherish a few people very deeply. I want to grow old gracefully. When I grow old and Sŏyŏng gets bigger, I'd like to walk down the snowy streets of Seoul with her.

TRANSLATED BY PETER H. LEE

---

[6]p'yŏng: an area measure of about 3.3 square meters.

Yi Ŏryŏng

THE MEANING OF STONE WALLS

Tagore[1] thought the culture of Western Europe was a culture of walls. He said that the culture of ancient Greece was built up in city walls, and that present culture also began in a cradle of lime and bricks. He regretted that walls engender a control mentality, and isolate people from each other. Because of the culture of walls, countries are divided from other countries, knowledge from knowledge, and people from nature. Whenever there are such walls, people inevitably wonder what is on the other side, and they invariably fight violently to find out.

But Tagore went on to say that Indian civilization is different from this, that it is not a culture of walls but a culture of the forest. This culture is surrounded by vast, natural life. It is clothed in nature and in contact continuously and intimately with various aspects of nature. So there is no isolation or division, no control and struggle; rather, it dwells as music—harmonious, penetrating, inclusive, and vast. The people of the forest culture are at one with the universe. They are not set in opposition to the earth or water, or to the sunlight, or to the fruits and flowers. They realize peace and empathy in harmony and unity. It is, so to speak, a culture of completeness.

When we hear Tagore's words, we think of our own stone walls. When Europeans from the "walled culture" first set foot on our soil, they were amazed by our rural stone walls. However poor or abject the thatched hut, there was always a wall around it. If there wasn't a stone wall, then there was an earth wall, and if there wasn't an earth wall, there was a woven reed wall screening the hut.

Our country is known for being mountainous. If we think of our fields, they are actually nothing more than borders connecting one mountain with another, and if we think of even our widest rivers and streams, they are nothing but valleys connecting the mountains with the sea. Wherever we go, our pervasive mountains divide us like walls. Where did we learn the custom of building more walls on our already confined land?

---

[1]Rabindranath Tagore (1861–1941): a Bengali poet who won the Nobel Prize for literature in 1913 for his collection Gitanjali (1910).

We can find the remains of walls in any rural area. Our towns have stone wall fortifications, our houses have stone walls, and again these walls in wealthy homes are further divided into walls with twelve gates.

But let's look for a moment at our walls. They do not seem to be the kind that Tagore discussed. They never serve as screens for solitude and division, nor for battle and control.

These stone walls of our country are neither high nor strong compared with those of Shanghai, which Lin Yutang called the third "Great Wall of Infinite Length."[2] China's walls are higher than houses. However high you may stand on tiptoe, you cannot see inside. They completely seclude and fortify, which means they block out the outside. All Chinese have their walls and live within them.

On the other hand, our stone walls are higher and bigger than those of the Japanese. Around the rural Japanese thatched house there is in many cases no wall, and even if there is a wall, it is of reeds through which the inside can be seen clearly. There is no difference between this and an open house. As in the case of Europe, except for castles, walls are not stressed at all in private houses.

Our stone walls are in a median position between the closed and open ones. If you look in from outside you can half see the interior. Over the earth wall you may see cockscomb and sunflowers and the upper body of a girl coming out of the open door. The walls of our country may be considered a kind of symbol for the "half-open" aesthetic, where the interior scenery is sometimes seen and sometimes unseen. And how beautiful that scene is: a landscape of red dragonflies sitting on a brushwood gate, green vines half-veiling white gourds hanging down over a stone wall! How decorative is this scene!

Do our walls protect us from thieves? No, a thief can jump over this kind of wall. As Yi Sang, the novelist, pointed out, a burglar would not feel like a burglar if he robbed a poor house with such a stone wall.

Moreover, does the wall protect us against animals? No, in one corner of the wall there is usually some ordinary hole so a weasel or stray cat can come and go freely. The wall is nothing but a boundary line. It does not divide "you" from "me" but is a means of alleviating emotional insecurity by drawing a boundary. Walls exist, but they never

---

[2]Lin Yutang (1895–1976): Chinese-American author of novels on Chinese life and translations from Chinese literature and philosophy, including *My Country and My People* (1935).

give an image of isolation or resentment toward others. This half-open nature of stone walls means unity in division, union in isolation, and openness in a closed state. In the boundary line of this hazy stone wall, so to speak, Korean culture has dimly grown—a stone wall culture, midway between the culture of fortified walls and the culture of the forest.

THE GOURD AND THE BEAUTY OF FORM

The gourd is one of a few objects with which Koreans have a special relationship. We plant a gourd beside a wall or by a back fence not for the practical reason of having the vines grow over them. In the poor life of the rural people the gourd is both a romantic luxury and an important asset. When the green vine grows around a dilapidated thatched hut, it never looks shabby. The gourd produces quite a different feeling from the wisteria of luxurious Western-style mansions.

The gourd's beautiful white flower blooms in the moonlight; it is also interesting to see the gourd growing day by day like the attractive full moon. Both the flower and the gourd possess simple elegance.

When the season is over, the gourd hardens. As it ripens, so do the expectations of the rural wives. The gourd is a gift from heaven which gives joy the year around. Small or large, it has various uses. The farmers pick one especially large and well ripened and make it into what they call a "lucky gourd." Auspicious characters—"long life," "luck," "health and peace," or "wealth and many sons"—are written on it and it is given to the daughter as a wedding gift.

We cannot count the uses of the gourd either as a toy or as an indispensable object in daily life. It is used as a measuring tool for rice, and as a mask in the masked dance plays. At the well it becomes a dipper; on the farm is becomes a bowl for rice or food.

In the popular Korean story about the two brothers, Hŭngbu and Nolbu,[3] the gourd plays an important role. It embodies the dream of the Korean miracle in which the poor but honest person finds happi-

---

[3]Hŭngbu and Nolbu: in the anonymous *Tale of Hŭngbu*, a classic tale about brotherly love, the good younger brother Hŭngbu was mistreated by his wicked elder brother Nolbu. One spring Hŭngbu nursed a wounded swallow, which rewarded him with a seed the following spring. The gourds that grew out of the seed yielded all that Hŭngbu and his family needed—and more—for their lives.

ness. The gourd is the Korean Messiah which brings joy to Hŭngbu but cold chills to Nolbu.

Moreover, we should focus on the fact that the gourd symbolizes the beautiful form the Korean loves.

We love an oval shape, like a gourd, which has slight irregularities and which is plain, rounded, and wide. The thin and elongated handle when hollowed out, the simple yet somewhat unbalanced and natural volume—nowhere does it look uneven or nervously angled. We can say that the archetype of Korean beauty might be founded on the shape of the gourd, demure and simple yet with a subtle diversity. Koreans don't like women's faces to be sharp and cubistic. They think that such faces are crafty, without virtue, and inauspicious. Hence their ideal face is round and natural, like the gourd which brings luck.

Pottery keeps to the original form of a gourd. The Grecian urn that so captivated Keats[4] is conical like a modern cocktail glass. But in Korean pottery the bottom is round and the neck at the top is slender, like a gourd set upside down. The contour of the shape is like an oblong gourd. The subtle shape of the gourd breathes primitive simplicity untouched by man. This is especially true of earthenware.

Not only pottery but the small bag, the button of a man's jacket, comma-shaped beads, the brazier, the grave, the head of Maitreya[5]— all resemble the shape of the gourd.

What on earth, then, is the beauty in the shape of the gourd? What is its special trait? Its humility, authenticity, and simplicity are born when things are reduced to their original shape. Its qualities derive not from the shape itself but from its closenss to the plane or line. It is the extremity reached when everything has been taken out, leaving nothing. It is the original nature of form which finally remains on the border of nothingness.

Originally, we developed not the beauty of three-dimensional things but a world of the plane or the line. Three-dimensional things can be broken. They change the nature of space into matter. Three-dimensionality does not allow room for space, or occasion for silence.

The form of Westerners is like a diamond, multifaceted and

---

[4]Refers to "Ode on a Grecian Urn" by John Keats.

[5]Maitreya: in Buddhism, the Friendly One, who receives confessions of sins and guides the departed after death. A bodhisattva of light and future, he lives in the Tuṣita Heaven waiting to come down to this world to succeed Śākyamuni.

pointed; but the form of the Korean, or for that matter every Asian, is like the gourd—plain, simple, and round. While the beauty of conquering space is the beauty of Western form, the Korean beauty of form is one of unifying and harmonizing with space. Our love for the round and abstract form of a gourd may be explained by the fact that we inherently aspire to be one with the nothingness of mother nature in order to efface ourselves. Westerners tend to turn a simple shape into a complex one, as when they cut a diamond; Koreans transform a complicated shape into a simple one, like a gourd.

Perhaps it is the image of the Korean, who, having been deprived to the utmost, has no heart left to feel suffering.

TRANSLATED BY DAVID I. STEINBERG

MODERN POETRY

IV

Kim Suyŏng was born in Seoul in 1927 and graduated in English literature from Yŏnsei University (1947). During the Korean War he was whisked away by the communists, captured by U.N. forces, and finally released from a POW camp in 1953. He then worked for a newspaper and lectured at several universities till he was fatally hit by a bus on 15 June 1968. An indefatigable champion of freedom, Kim understood modernism as the attitude the spirit assumes as it seeks to make sense of reality. Art is a pursuit of the impossible; hence it is disquieting. His poetry is a record of that struggle, and his gift for irony and commitment to the creative power of language often turn his frustrations and failures into terrifying revelations.

Kim Ch'unsu, born in 1922 in Ch'ungmu, South Kyŏngsang, studied in Seoul and Tokyo and since 1945 has been writing poetry and teaching at a university. Kim's search has been for ideas, for images beyond ideas, and then for the absurdity beyond ideas and language. Predominant throughout his search is a determination to get to the essence of our experience of self and the world. A strong sense of concrete existence, ineffable yet safe from the world's terrible forces, is our only defense against the brutalities of ideology and collective action.

Kim Namjo, born in Taegu on 26 September 1927, graduated in Korean literature from the College of Education, Seoul National University, in 1951. She has taught at Sungmyŏng Women's University since 1955 and currently serves as president of the Catholic Writers' Association. Married to a sculptor, she is the mother of four children. In her poetry Kim Namjo has been engaged in the affirmation of human nature. She expresses, in a fine balance of cadence and meaning, her boundless wish for peace, integrity, and freedom. The poem sequence "Candlelight" was published in 1980 in her ninth collection, *Going Together (Tonghaeng)*. "Like many of her works," writes David McCann, " 'Candlelight' gives expression to her passionate religious feeling. At the same time, in its characteristic blending of abstract, iconographic language with the personal statement of religious faith, the poems embody an accomplished poet's mature and lifelong intent both to instruct and to exemplify. For the reader who relishes the poem as an artifact, the poems are candles; in being *about* the candle's light, they are also about poems."

Ko Ŭn, born in 1933 in Kunsan, South Chŏlla, studied Chinese before his schooling. In 1952 he became a Buddhist monk, studied Zen, and led a wandering life. After he returned to the laity in 1962, his outspoken criticism of government policies and active participation in the free speech and youth movements earned him intermittent imprisonment. In May 1983 he married and settled down in Ansŏng, near Seoul. Since his literary debut in 1958, Ko Ŭn has published novels and essays, as well as *Collected Poems* in two volumes (1983). In a time of conflict and uncertainty, Ko Ŭn has tried to assimilate history into his own sensibility and has used his poetry as an instrument for reevaluating his Korean inheritance.

Shin Kyŏngnim was born in 1936 in Chungwŏn, South Ch'ungch'ŏng, and graduated in English literature from Tongguk University in 1960. Since his literary debut in 1955, his major theme has been the life of the farmer. Having suffered at first hand the pangs of social misery, and conscious of his roots, Shin views agrarian life with the penetrating eye of a modern man, taking as his own the frustration, anxiety, and despair of the farmer wrestling with the soil. His poems reveal an unobtrusive power to evoke an atmosphere and a mastery of the rhythms of the language, as in "Farmer's Dance."

Hwang Tonggyu, born in 1938 in Seoul, graduated in English literature from Seoul National University (1961). He then attended Edinburgh University (1966–1967) and took part in the International Writing Program at the University of Iowa (1970–1971). Currently he is a professor of English at Seoul National University. With a sense of irony, Hwang views history at a distance to determine the root of the Korean tragedy—a tragedy that has included the collapse of the old order, the subjugation of the nation, and finally its division. His later poems encompass such imagery as the barbed wire that besieges his consciousness and snowflakes that fall from the sky. The latter symbolize consciousness, purification, and the esemplastic power of the imagination. His conversational tone, disjunctive progression, rapid transitions, and reliance on symbols and a sequence of emotions for meaning all serve to arouse analogous emotions in the reader, as in "Snow Under Martial Law."

Chŏng Hyŏnjong, born in Seoul in 1939, graduated in philosophy from Yonsei University (1964). From October 1974 to March 1975 he took part in the International Writing Program at the University of Iowa. Currently he is teaching at Yŏnsei University. Chŏng has been concerned with exploring the relation between imagination and its diverse objects. His poetry shows an anguished perception of the groundlessness of human existence that emanates from the ordeal of the Korean War. He maintains a humorous distance from the human situation. One of his themes concerns the possibility of happiness in the dark occasions of life, as suggested by his image of a rainbow formed by waterdrops high in the air. His sense of happiness is a commitment to the ideal of freedom; in his engagement with life, he functions as a "festivalist of pain."

Hwang Chiu, born in 1952 in Haenam, South Chŏlla, made his literary debut in 1980. His first collection of poems, *Even the Birds Are Leaving the World* (1983), won a literary prize.

Kim Suyŏng

THE GAME ON THE MOON

A top spins.
Before my enormous eyes
That love to watch
The miraculous existence of children and grown-ups,
A child spins a top.
As the tidy child is beautiful,
So is the child who plays.
Sunk in thought, forgetful of the host,
I wish the child would spin it once again.
My life in the capital, harried and harassed,
My life more novel than a novel—

Let me dump such thoughts,
Mindful of my age that sits in repose,
Mindful of the weight my age accords me.
I watch the top spinning
Till it becomes black and stands still.
Every other house is better off, more at ease;
Theirs seems like another world.
A top spins.
      Spins.
Watch the string at the bottom,
Then a string between the fingers,
One throw on the *ondol* floor[1]
Makes the top spin, gray and soundless,
Like a game played on the moon
I've not seen for ages,
A top spins
And makes me cry.
In front of the host fatter than I,
Who sits beneath the jet plane poster,
I'm not the one to cry
But I need some revision of my fate, my mission,
I should not be so absentminded.
The top spins as if mocking me.
I can bring to mind
A propeller more easily than a top . . .
Like a sage of ages ago,
The top spins before me,
More good than evil.
When I think about it, the top is sad—
For the power that propels you and me to spin,
For some common cause, I must stifle my sobs.
Is that why the top spins?
A top spins.
      Spins.

---

[1]*ondol*: the Korean under-floor heating system.

WORDS

The root of a tree sank deeper toward winter.
Now my body is no longer mine,
Nor are my heartbeat, my cough, my chill,
Nor this house, my wife, my sons, my mother,
Today I work and worry again as before.
I do a day's work—earn money and quarrel—
But my life is a life already consigned,
My order an order of death,
The whole world changed into the value of death.

All distance shortens clownishly,
All questions vanish clownishly,
The world won't give a damn
About so many words I want to tell.

Because of these wordless words
I can't deal with my wife,
My sons and my friends,
So I keep my mouth sealed before this overwhelming difficulty,
Indulging in this terrible insincerity.

These wordless words,
Sky's color, water's color, chance's color, chance's words,
The death-piercing puny words,
The words for death, the words serving death,
The words that most abhor simple honesty,
These almighty words—
The words of winter and of spring,
Now my words are no longer mine.

HA, THERE IS NO SHADOW . . .

Our enemies are not dashing
nor as violent as Kirk Douglas or Richard Widmark.
They're not wild villains,
even are good to some extent.

Masquerading as democrats,
they call themselves
Good People,
Lawfully Elected;
white-collar workers,
they ride the tram or in a car,
enter a restaurant,
drink wine and gossip,
sympathize with a sincere face,
scramble and dash off,
write up their copy, keep books,
go to a movie;
they have charm.
In short, they're beside us.

Our battleline is invisible,
That's why our battle is so hard.
Ours is not Dunkirk, Normandy, Yŏnhŭi Hill,
it's not on the map.
It can be inside our house,
at our work site,
on our block—
but invisible.

Our is a scorched-earth strategy.
Unlike the bloody battle of Gun Hill,
it's not lively or spectacular.
But we're always fighting,
morning, day, night, at meal times,
as we walk the streets, talk,
run a business, build streets;
as we travel, cry and laugh,
eat our greens,
smell the fish in the market;
when our belly is full, when thirsty,
when we love, sleep, dream,
when we're awake, awake, awake . . .

when we teach, go home from work,
when we synchronize our watches with a siren,
when we polish our shoes,
our battle goes on.

Our battle fills heaven and earth.
A democratic battle must be fought democratically.
As there's no shadow in heaven,
there is no shadow in a democratic battle.
Ha, there is no shadow!
Ha, that's it!
That's right.
Ah, no doubt about it, of course—
uhm, uhm, what?
Ah, that's it, that's it, that's it.

BLUE SKY

Once a poet envied
The freedom of a lark,
Its rule of the blue sky.

One who has ever soared
For the sake of freedom
Knows
Why the lark sings
Why freedom reeks blood
Why a revolution is lonely

Why revolution
Has to be lonely.

GRASS

Grass lies down
Blown by the east wind
Driving rain.
It weeps at last,
Weeps louder at darkness,
Then lies down again.

Lying down
More quickly than the wind,
It weeps and rises
More quickly than wind.

Come clouds, grass lies down,
Even to its ankle and sole.
Lying down more slowly than the wind,
It rises before the wind,
Weeps later than the wind,
Laughs before the wind.
Cloudy—the root lies down.

TRANSLATED BY PETER H. LEE

Kim Ch'unsu

FLOWER

Before I called her by name,
she was nothing
but a gesture.

When I called her by name,
she came to me,
a flower by me.

As I called her by name,
I would have someone call me by name
as befits

this color, this fragrance.
I would go to him,
his flower by his voice.

We all yearn to become
an unforgettable meaning,
you to me, I to you.

HOMECOMING

Winds coax the forsythia to bloom
by the river and in the eyes,
mirroring the blue of the sky,
of the mountain rabbit chewing
the berries of pure mountain red.
Rabbit, rabbit, you saw boots stamping
on the faces of ancestral ghosts.
Winds coax the figs to ripen.
The fig is in the sixth month,
but the mind of youth is wilted.
The fire our mothers make is warm as ever
in the tradition-rich furnaces,[1]
but the mind of youth is wilted,
though still warm and pure.
Is it sad and drooping in the village
because our mothers still gather
pine needles for fuel,
not burning coal or petroleum
as modern city women do?
No, it is not that, not modern fuel
that is in the mind of youth.

---

[1]tradition-rich furnaces: anthracite coal is the main fuel used for heating in Seoul; some die of carbon monoxide poisoning, however, especially in the ill-ventilated houses of the poor.

Where there are no walls standing
and no innocence untarnished,
why should the flowers blush
as the girls did in the festivals?
Why should grass be sprouting
under a sky forever the same?

IN AUTUMN

We saw the blood of youth
spilled in the quickening month of April.
Now autumn comes and my poetry
will shed its feminine vanity
for the affliction of Rilke[2]
at the ancient castle of Duino.[3]
It is not fruit nor its sweetness
that is ripening to a fullness
but the darkness of the bullets
spilling the blood of youth in April.
It is the silence of darkness
that will ripen this autumn.

THE WINTER CHRYSANTHEMUM

Near the back gate to the compound
of the Eighth United States Army
with OFF LIMITS hung on the barbed wire,
children are sitting around,
warming their bodies at a brush fire.
Their shrunken puds shiver
like dark red boxthorn fruit.

---

[2]Rainer Maria Rilke (1875-1926): the great German poet whose works include *Sonnets to Orpheus, Duino Elegies,* and *The Notebooks of Malte Laurids Brigge.*

[3]Duino Castle: on the Dalmatian coast where, as the guest of Princess Marie von Thurn und Taxis-Hohenlohe, Rilke began to compose the poems of the cycle that came to be known as *Duino Elegies.*

For a lavish wedding
a pot of chrysanthemum sells
for three hundred *wŏn*.

THE CACTUS IN EARLY SPRING

With a breast and the lymph nodes removed
my wife lies unconscious.
I wonder, in her drugged sense
does she think she is being trundled down
the hallway to the operating room?
Time hovering over death
walks a hippopotamus
over my thin-ribbed chest.
Looking up, I see the cold budding
of a cactus beyond her white pillows.

TRANSLATED BY UCHANG KIM

Kim Namjo

CANDLELIGHT

I

Candle,
neither in one of my love songs
nor in the love itself that passes beyond
that song, climbing the folds of mountain ridges,
nor in the completeness of my life
shall you
who burns without ash
be surpassed.

2

Brightly, so bright
the one who passes my soul
passing my soul
one who makes me weep,
whose skirt's edge
even the wind does not stir.

3

All living things
watch in dread
this person, the one
burning in her own oil.
God Himself
for a moment pauses
in His work.
Utterly consumed,
in parting this world
you drive the nail
into a black coffin.

4

O Brightness
stronger than despair!
Magnetism
of existence that does not expire
even as it burns,
O love!

5

Candlelight,
with music
warming the hands until dusk

Ah, suddenly in the attire
of sunset
brimming,
you are the very one
whose figure stayed in my thoughts
three hundred years or more.

6

Bit of wax
touching flame becomes oil
turning clear becomes distilled water
again congealing
becomes oil, becomes wax
until its discarded
body turns again
to flame.

7

A lonely lad
of long ago
and a girl
grew up accustomed to their loneliness
serving in order
their long, lonely time
until they met
one later day.
We light
one candle in consecration.
Lord God the Creator,
grant us the blessing of age.

8

Not even once
to have known
a woman,
this fresh
inexperience,
wick
of chastity!

9

There is no one
who rode down in a gold bucket
the thousand, ten thousand
roads in the water.
At the bottom in cold, cold water
there is no one
who found the blind
and freezing woman
but you.

10

Just washed
rinsed clear, lighting
the candle, my soul
removes its clothing
and into the empty room
enters alone.

11

The candle knows
the wisdom that in loving
purifies sin.
And human destiny
joining sin and love,

blood and flesh,
the candle knows
the pity of it.

12

Winter trees,
candles grown life-size.
Fresh-blooded
phosphorescence
presses its kiss
on the flesh
of abstinence.

13

Having risen
into heaven
the candles become
stars
and become
stars
all night let fall
their rain of
light.

14

Look at me,
look at the woman
who is done with words of love.
Look
at the candle
so truly pitiful
that shrivels
away by its own hand.

15

As I cut
the tongues of flame
with the razor's blade
I cry out.
As the severed tongues
of flame turn again
to fire,
endlessly
my tears fall.

16

Not such a light
as illuminates the body,
nor yet the light
of the heart,
your spirit
would be the shadow and light
from an adjoining room.

17

Forgive
forgive me
Hear my entreaty,
far darker dream
ten fingers burnt
offering, kindling
the fire offering,
please accept
me.

18

For a thousand days, the one
I longed to see who for a thousand
days did not come, when the faint light
touches the paper of the door

the candlelight faint illumination
even for many more thousands
of days I
would open the door.

19

Offered to heaven
together with you
that heaven grant
together with you
—this
is my prayer.

20

Singing
a song of flame and light
making the kite of fire
and light
fly, the pure
the immortal
children.

21

Go to sleep, just
go to sleep
eyelid of pure gold,
sleepless through an entire life,
like love
exhausted,
ah, in death at last
closing its eye
—the candle's light.

22

You alone
not weeping
not able to sleep
out in the open alone
the candle drops all turned to flame,
after I die
my body
transparent will know how
to embrace you.

23

After all is done
you who rose
in smoke that could not express
whatever might have been said,
in the empty bowl that was given nothing,
you cast the shadow
of another life's
sun.

24

Soul of two
standing open, then
be like the candle's light:
learn
silence
and the burning.

25

The candles of the world
make a unified
religion
of long ago
and today:
turning to heaven
and burning,
return to heaven.

TRANSLATED BY DAVID R. MCCANN AND HYUN-JAE YEE SALLEE

Ko Ŭn

AT MY FATHER'S GRAVE

Father, south and north are not yet united.
  During the Japanese days
  You peddled salt about the country.
  But no matter how hard I try
  I cannot recall your Yalu and Tuman rivers—
  Only blood clots in my eyes.
  You saw the willows of Hoeryŏng along the Tuman
  And the Yalu's ruddy sunset waters,
  Glinting the bayonets of border guards.
  Roaming the villages south and north,
  You peddled white salt by the pint,
  Humming a tune from the northwest
  Or Miryang Arirang from the flowering south.
  Memory of your youth leaving no trace,
  You died—salt sprinkled on this land.
  Father, when our country is one again,
  Come back as a salt peddler,
  With resounding "Salt, Salt,"
  So that I can hear your resonance.

LAMENT ON GLOSSES

Wŏnhyo,[1]
    It would have been enough
    To read *Awakening Mahayana Faith*
    And then write your own work.
    But why write a commentary,
    Nodding, bowing intently,
    Like a servant to the strong text?
    Men with meager talent,
    Men who strut and brag,
    They're merely setting down notes,
    Marginalia—piddling badges and medals.
    Well, then, in your disgusting state,
    Why do you keep on adding notes
    As women powder their pretty faces?
    These days we can't even cry like earthworms;
    Yet we should be uttering words that will ignite a fire.
    What's your intention, learned doctors,
    To capitalize on a game of glosses,
    Squanderers of spring nights?

AT MY DEATHBED

I won't go to the Pure Land across a billion leagues,
Love, but will remain in my country after death.
My body will become dirt, water, and wind,
A gentle breeze over this land.
No, I'll burst from the region between this life and the next,
Linger and get drunk on our strong brew.
An heir of wanderers through the aeons,
I'll bid apricot trees blossom everywhere,
I'll roam along the parched Yesŏng River,

---

[1]Great Master Wŏnhyo (617–686): one of the most original thinkers of Korea, the author of a commentary on the *Treatise on Awakening Mahayana Faith*, which offers a theoretical system to resolve the controversy between the Mādhyamika and Yogācāra schools. It is one of the three great commentaries on the text.

Along the wretched riverbank in Nonsan,
Above the distant Floating Emerald Tower,
And teach a lesson to an earth life,
Devious and crooked, unable to stand firm.
I'll sing when the birds sing,
To be the song of my country;
I'll be the darkness at death of night
That arouses sighs, laughter, and stars.
I was born to roam the depths of my land,
Not to enjoy a life of bliss.
As agony becomes numberless sorrows,
Myriad moonbeams shine upon myriad waters.
Not to the Western Paradise will I go
But will be darkness at month's end.
When water freezes and the wind howls,
I'll be water running beneath ice and
The wind wailing atop the T'aebaek range.
Love, how could I forsake this land?
—Our soil, grass, pines on the yellow ridge
That have died and grown young again.
I'll be soaking rain that feeds
The grass, trampled but drunk from rage.
Love, I won't go. How could I,
Why should I go to the dissolute Pure Land?
There's no death: my country is my death.
Love, I won't go to the Pure Land.

TRANSLATED BY PETER H. LEE

Shin Kyŏngnim

FLOWER SHADOW

Where a whiskey bottle and dried squid
were left, on the farm co-op's porch,
the shadow of apricot blossoms.

The wind tugging
at the edge of our clothes
is still cold.
Hunting through newspapers
to find
  PLANT DRY FIELDS

    or

One Percent Less on Farm Taxes

if only our grins
like flowers
    grew bright.

Apricot petal
falling into a whiskey glass.
The co-op's cart
rolling to market.

FARMER'S DANCE

Gong sounded,
curtain lowered.
Makeshift stage, lights
strung from a paulownia.
The viewers have left
an empty playing field.

Faces stained with powder,
we drink, jammed into the wine shop
by the school.
Suffocating, exhausted,
lamentable life.

The cymbal in the lead
we start for the marketplace,
boys shouting, clinging to us
while young girls cling, giggling,
to the wall of an oil dealer's shop.

The full moon shines as one fellow
bellows like a bandit, another
sneers like Sŏrim the outlaw.
But what use is this commotion,
kicking the heels, crushed
into a hole in the mountains?

Better left to women, this farming
that won't even pay
for fertilizer.

Past the cow dealers, turning
by the slaughterhouse
the spell comes on, and I
lift one foot and blow the brass horn,
shaking my head, twisting my shoulders.

TRANSLATED BY DAVID R. MCCANN

Hwang Tonggyu

FOUR TWILIGHTS

I

Glad omen.
The Chunghŭng monastery[1] is burnt down,
The Taehwa Palace[2] is in ruins.
I balanced a boulder on the cliff
And, looking up day and night,
Trained my eyes.
I can see it.
In June a continuous rain,
In December came long snow.
It's easiest to take life easy;
So easy
I had nights of insomnia.
Glad omen.

2

Irrelevance,
Alternating seasons,
Winds over the spring hills,
The clanking of bells in late autumn.
Inconvenienced,
My ancestors
Fled to the island of Kanghwa.[3]
When winter covered the hills with snow,
Shivering in the cold, I saw sunbeams
In the mouse holes on palace walls.

---

[1]Chunghŭng monastery; a temple to the south of Mount Samgak in Seoul, which crumbled in 1915 leaving only the foundation.

[2]Taehwa Palace: a temporary royal palace built in 1129 near Taedonggun in South P'yŏngan. Only the ruins remain.

[3]island of Kanghwa: a mountainous island on the west coast off Seoul, a place of refuge for the royal court during the Yi dynasty.

As I grew older, I made friends
In the dark alleys.
Irrelevance.

3

The wine brewed from yam
Was not sweet on my tongue.
When I grew thin, I had my clothes taken in
And went out, unperturbed, to see a woman
To tell her a long story.
Nothing was easier than deliverance—
Every night I cast off my desire, my skin,
Every morning I found myself
Where I had been the night before.
Every night a dream of shipwreck
Shook me awake at midnight. I drank
Young wine and went back to sleep.
Every morning I remembered the blinding sunlight.

4

Fear assaults me when I walk by the deserted shore.
The girls at South Bank swear
That I'm not yet an old man.
But I'm afraid I may want to die.
My debts being small, my death
Won't make anybody sad.
Hands in pockets,
I watch the drunken sailors scuffle
Under blossoming clouds. I sit
On a deserted boat and smoke.
I'm afraid of the sea at dusk,
Though I know nothing about hell.
Darkness seeps into me before swallowing the sea.

NOTES OF A KING

FIRST LEAF

The king is but the shade for his subjects.
When you, my lords, raise me
As I kneel below the throne,
And lead me through the back garden
Full of peonies,
I will not look at
The morning or evening papers
Or the telescopes
But will roam among the lonely flowers.

The king should have the grace to depart,
Like the chief of a tribe and his sons
Who burn themselves in a lean year,
Who shout without a cry,
He should learn how to leave,
No cough, no ills, no thatched huts.

SECOND LEAF

I have forgotten at what leaf of the winds,
But it was at the death of sunset
I smoothed away some sand on an unknown beach
And knelt down with trembling knees.
I saw the minute islands disappear
Netted by the curved horizon.
Who will remember
My endless kneeling in solitude
Throughout this short evening?
Who will remember
The lights carefully put out
In this small land?
From north to south

The candles nurse the dark in small barracks.
Out there the sea barks slowly without a moon,
With the long waves of our longing.
The wind blows from four quarters.

The wind blows.
The islands are slowly sinking
Beyond our memory.
And this land!
Who will remember
These days of no light
Without even "we" to guard us in our tribulations?
Who will remember
The non-ruins where the non-castle was torn down,
The lightless night with its back to infinity?

No unhappiness, no life.
Surely there will be a time
When someone will remember them,
The wishes suspended over our twists and turns?
In the dark sky burning clouds
Fall here and there.
Darkness comes to every corner.
Kneeling, I want to fall
Like a lump of clay during the thaw
And float along the east sea, the south sea, the west sea,
And be caught somewhere,
My body changed into their ecstasy.[4]
The wind blows.

---

[4]changed into their ecstasy: expresses his affection for a small, blocked, and divided country. The protagonist is a king who, floating like "a lump of clay," changes into his people's ecstasy.

SNOW FALLS IN THE SOUTH

Pongjun[5] is weeping, illiterate, illiterate,
Utterly illiterate.
If only he knew how to read the classics,
If only he knew how to cry softly!
Greater kings[6] behind the king,
And now the kings' whip!
Under the winter fog
Horse and foot cross the border again
Without horse warrants,[7]
The earth cracks like the ribs of a fan,
Guns bawl like lusty children.
If he'd known he would end up
Rubbing his cheeks with cold snow,
He would have gone to Mount Kyeryong[8]
To till a field,
Till with a sturdy Chinese or Japanese plow.
Snow is falling on the stone bridge
We cross unthinking,
And on the gloomy thatched huts
Where our fathers suffer from a hidden disease.
Listen, snow is falling, unfeeling,
From the leaden sky,
Illiterate, illiterate.

---

[5]Chŏn Pongjun (1845–1895): a Tonghak (Eastern Learning) leader of a peasant rebellion of 1894 in Kobu county in North Chŏlla. The government troops were helpless against the uprising, and subsequently the forces of China and Japan were brought in, which resulted in the Sino-Japanese War.

[6]Greater kings: the rulers of China and Japan who intervened to quell the Tonghak rebellion in 1894.

[7]horse warrants: *map'ae*, a round copper badge about ten centimeters in diameter. On one side is a picture of one to ten horses; on the other side is the name of the issuing office and the date with a seal. Used by officials to levy horses in the provinces, horse warrants were also used by the Secret Royal Inspector as his identification.

[8]Mount Kyeryong: in South Ch'ungch'ŏng, 828 meters high, regarded in folk belief as the site of the capital for a millennium.

SNOW UNDER MARTIAL LAW

Ah, those are sick words.
My soles shiver.
I'm determined to become a simple man!
When dry winds,
Daylong,
Chase the snow here and there,
In the evening
Every snowflake is muddy—
With sun-shaped sun suddenly down,
My dream shattered,
Prostrate on the ground,
I wipe away my eyes, nose, and mouth.
Terrifying even to myself,
Am I turning into
Muddy snow
Driven about and trampled again?

THE ROOT OF LOVE

I

My hometown is
where you walked alone
your hometown is
where I was beaten, spellbound.

Our hometown sleeps
our beaters sleep too
winter has come
old ships are beached.

Taking off hometown and face
we're left only with dance
the sea swells suddenly
ships peel away rust, dripping with sweat.[9]

2

Now love is nothing
love, in that incredibly cloudy day
evening with snow burying the streets
streets blocked by cars, darkly,
bending the joints by the imprisoned taxi
clutching the jumping mighty engine
wheels at your side
running with long strides
sidestepping left and right
love, lift your arms
let's bring out our drawers
suck at the abandoned veins
pierce the dark clouds
and float into the air—
the suppressed dance starts—
Now love is nothing.

3

We're lovely children
we're lovely
lovely children

ah lovely
we're open

the trees standing neatly by the window
they too are busy—
after groping under the earth

---

[9]Two lovers are compared to "ships peeling away rust" in section 1. The next section describes the ecstatic state in which the lovers find themselves.

they hold their breath for a moment
and touch each other's roots.
Ah lovely

We're lovely children
lovely.

4

Bending its back
a stone edges the snow
and bites a stone.
The bitten stone
laughs brightly.
A wind stops, unwavering.
The moon hangs vast.

Even the forgotten stars gather and glitter—
Now, love is nothing.

TRANSLATED BY PETER H. LEE

Chŏng Hyŏnjong

THE ABYSS OF SOUND

I. SOUND LONGS FOR THE EAR

I peel the skin of sound:
it doesn't take too long.
Sound knows the ear, love-deepened,
and steals the ear to shape it for itself
as an ear attached to sound.
Sound listens to sound's voice,

shaking my whole body, now an ear.
Death coils in the heart of sound;
sound longs for sound's ear.

2. A BRIGHT-TEMPERED MAN

Why is my temper so bright?
Do you see how the sun walks
until day gathers its tail, sun-colored,
and hides in the night? Oh, me—
how bright-tempered, dizzily bright.

To choke the throat of high noon,
I walk to the sea of meals,
I walk to the sea of soup,
carefully taking daily bread
and nothing else. But even then
daily pleasure tempts me, nailing down
my wings, with the hammer of feet,
the hammer of laughter and tears.
O, bright, bright-tempered me,
dizzily bright.
It is possible to go up and down
the steps of the clear air of noon,
but all sound is lonely, as you well know.
Say that the blue eye of the sad wind
watches the sound of the wind,
which I hold in my hands, not knowing
what to do with what I hold.

3. THE HOLE OF SOUND

The form of a man goes away,
leaving a body-shaped hole;
the form of a woman goes away
leaving a body-shaped hole
in the air cut by her body.
The air keeps these holes.
My senses are closed to the world.
The hole tempts me where sound made it

in the air—form fixed by sound,
the lonely mode of its being.
One walks down the steps,
the darker the better for memory.
Sound and its hold are sharper-edged
in the dark; they hurt more
than the sound of the air
unstained by this darkness.
(Where are they, the sound-owners,
wrapped in love and tears?)

4. SOUNDLESS

I see a heap of stillness,
lying blood-smeared;
this stillness was once light,
stillness, comrade of sound.
I see a heap of stillness,
blood-smeared.
Word bites the tail of soundless,
soundless the tail of word,
each waiting to strike
like mortal enemies.

TO THE ACTORS

Throw away acting;
nothing is for keeps.
Throw away speech.
Have you thrown away?
Throw away when you've thrown away.
Throw it away when it is yours.
Throw away yourself.
Throw away applause.

Laugh the laughter being thrown away;
express the expression being thrown away.
Let sorrow belong to sorrow,

let action belong to action,
let speech belong to speech,
let each belong to each.
Then peace may be with you
even if sorrow stays,
even if death gives back
action and speech . . .
then, and yet,
then, and yet . . .

POETRY, IDLE POETRY

What can you love with poetry?
What can you mourn with poetry?
What can you get and what can you lose?
What can you set up, what can you pull down?
If you cannot love death with death,
It you cannot love life with life,
If you cannot grieve with grief,
If you cannot love poetry with poetry,
what then can you love with poetry?

No one sees the snow that falls at night;
no one walks on it, no footsteps.
It is: silent, clear,
beautiful of itself.

THE FESTIVAL OF PAIN, I

A LETTER

The seasons change. If you know the occasions of life,
I love you. Occasions? What big occasions! I love you.
When I see you, the world colors my senses. Color is the
void, the void color.[1] Life hangs between color and the void.
We say, it is color, and we say, it is void; but it is the reality
of things in this world. Just to think of it, I choke on
the thought. When I see you, I become colors, I become void.
The letters we write are the brotherhood of our feelings, our
secret channels. Thus I write a letter to you.

A ball of fire burns in the air, looking like a man thinking;
a ball of tears burns in the air, looking like citizens.
Tears wet the fire, and the ball of fire burns. The bonfire of flames
and tears shoots up in the air and becomes the shape of the people
of this country: a ball of blood burning in the black night sky.
"An age passes and an age comes," sings a chorus, circling
around the deep silence of night.

I do not want to write in chained words. Chained words tell
of things in chains. I want to write my letter in words
that cannot be chained. For ever and ever. I am a festivalist—
the festivalist of pain, which is, of all festivals, the most
brilliant. A chorus sings, "We are happy." I love you, you who
know the occasions of life. Peace and happiness to you.

THE FESTIVAL OF PAIN, II

Blinking, shining stars,
Look at the chorus of burning cigarettes
in the constellation of Sagittarius!

---

[1]color is the void, the void color: all existence is dependent on causation—all things are relative.
Color refers to the phenomenal world, often taken to mean sexuality, and void refers to the
Buddhist idea that all things of the phenomenal world are illusions.

Hear in the dark night of slogans
the long music of our passwords!
I give the sky wholly to the birds
and fly downwards to the earth.
    Pleasure binds the bodies;
    pain binds the souls.[2]

We wanted to pluck the roots of time;
it is we, instead, that are plucked.
Sorrow of things, beauty of things!
Wine flows, shining adjective of the spirit.
The song in our eyes harks back to home.
    Pleasure binds the bodies;
    pain binds the souls.

What keeps us in life? The power
of the miscellanies of the mind!
The blue sky of folk songs weeps today,
clear and blue. Care falls over the stars
and beggars us, cowed, wandering souls.
    Pleasure binds the bodies;
    pain binds the souls.

The shadow is heavier than the body;
we walk, therefore, hanging our heads
and sing of the things of man,
adding salt to blood, sugar to tears,
To love man is the loneliest thing of all.
    Pleasure binds the bodies;
    pain binds the souls.

TRANSLATED BY UCHANG KIM

---

[2]Pleasure binds the bodies . . .: the refrain from Miguel de Unamuno's "Love, Pain, Compassion, Personality" (1913): "For to love means to pity, and though their bodies are united by pleasure, their souls are united by pain." See *The Tragic Sense of Life in Men and Nations*, translated by Anthony Kerrigan, Bollingen Series 85:4 (Princeton: Princeton University Press, 1972), p. 149.

Hwang Chiu

EVEN THE BIRDS ARE LEAVING THE WORLD

Before the film begins
We all stand up for our national anthem.
On Ŭlsuk Island
In the "Splendid Land of Three Thousand *Ri*,"[1]
A flock of white birds
Leaving the field of reeds
Fly in one, two, three files,
Honking, giggling
Carrying their own world,
Separating their world from ours,
To some place beyond this world.
I wish we could fly off too,
Giggling, crackling,
Forming a file,
Carrying our world
To some place beyond this world.
But with "Preserve forever the integrity of Korea to Koreans"
We sit down,
Sinking into our seats.

---

[1]"Splendid Land of Three Thousand *Ri*": an epithet for Korea.

DAILY INSPECTION OF THE SCENE OF THE CRIME

Yesterday I came back with stakes driven into my ears.
Today I set barbed wire over my eyes and held it down with bandages.
Tomorrow I will shovel dirt in my mouth
And plug it with a cotton ball.
Day after day,
Night after night,
I bury a part of myself
To destroy the proofs of my living
To obtain my own survival.

TRANSLATED BY PETER H. LEE

MODERN FICTION

V

Yun Hŭnggil

Yun Hŭnggil was born in 1942 in Chŏngŭp, North Chŏlla, the second of six children of an employee in an industrial guild. The Korean War broke out when he was a second grader. After service in the air force (1961–1964), he taught in a grammar school and in 1966 began his apprenticeship as a writer. Since his literary debut in 1968, Yun has proved to be a major writer of short stories and novels.

One group of Yun's stories is narrated by children in the first person singular, sometimes from memory, as in "A Rainy Spell" (1973), widely considered his masterpiece. In another group Yun portrays people trampled by a dehumanizing society, fate, history, or authority and records their satiric indictment of injustice. His work is marked by a disciplined observation of gesture and expression and an artistic distance achieved by means of irony. Especially noteworthy is his inquiry into the world of indigenous shamanism and the Korean ethos.

"The Beating" (1975) concerns a crime committed unwittingly by oppressed and enervated people. While trying to dodge the police who have come for another reason, an unidentified youth—perhaps a student activist in the antigovernment demonstration—leaps from a tearoom to the street below. Like life in a closed and stagnant society, there is no kernel of truth here but only rumor—and excessive curiosity brings about death. Whether the cook's death was caused by Miss Hyŏn's romantic infatuation and irresponsible game or by Kim Sich'ŏl's befuddled act, men of passive nature have a propensity for evil that injures others.

THE BEATING

These days, we often find that people show more courtesy toward a container than its contents. Thus I feel it is necessary to explain the building in question. In short, the workers and the regular customers who come here have value only as appurtenances, no matter what their social standing, age, or sex. Those in a position to know this building at all know this well.

This building of ours is located in an ambiguous and awkward spot, neither at the center nor on the outskirts of the city. The building was so dilapidated that the city government, on the grounds that the building ruined the appearance of the street, had issued three repair orders with a time limit, but with the full, nauseatingly full, knowledge that a building with that much wear and tear would have a long history.

The building had indeed weathered a long span of time admirably. It had gone through unusual trials of all sorts amidst all sorts of hostile people in all conditions of life. Moreover, it had also had to fight with the power of nature that had begun to eat into its very foundations. Yet there was no end to the building's sorry lot: it was involved in a lawsuit.

When the repair order was ignored, and the time limit set by the city had passed, the city officials asserted their authority by issuing an evacuation order. The disgruntled owner of the building took the matter to court.

The order was quite lawful. The explanation for issuing the order would have been ninety-nine times more convincing, however, if it had stated that the collapse of a house would result in the loss of human life.

Directly across the street from the building stood a fire station. It was so close to the building that you could even see the young fireman in the lookout, whiling away the long summer afternoon by scratching his thighs in a carefree way. As though to measure themselves against the fire station lookout, newer buildings had risen one after another around the older one, with an alley between them leading to an agricultural equipment factory. This factory was a pitifully primitive affair in which sprayers and the like were manufactured by hammering iron plates this way or that by sheer brute strength. This factor was joined to a two-story frame house, the first floor of which housed a cheap inn. There used to be a popular Japanese eatery next to the inn, but the new inner wing of a hospital stands there now.

Most people who passed by the gate of this wing would find their attention attracted by something that made them feel uneasy, and they would involuntarily look back. Soon they would discover what had caused them to look back—the second floor of the two-story frame house with its shabby walls and windows and the cheap downstairs inn shakily propping it up. The meanness of it all was so glaring that even a blind man could sense it. Anyone who had two good eyes could even locate the sign and read it.

Old as it was, it was still a building. Like other buildings, it had walls. Originally the walls had been lime-plastered. Patterns of raised waves had been created by letting kneaded lime flow down the surface long enough to dry and then applying pink paint to the lime to show it off to best advantage. Time, however, had played havoc with the walls. The plaster and the coat of paint had come off in such democratic disorder that they reminded you of the slatternly face of an abandoned woman who had gotten out of bed late in the morning with her face devoid of makeup. Of the four walls, the one facing the street would attract the most attention because it had one small window with four panes. Each pane bore a letter in gold leaf: *san, ho, ta,* or *bang.* Arranged in that order, the letters spelled out the name of the Sanho Teahouse. This was the most refined part of the building.

This window either performed its original duty as a window or served as a signboard when opened. Usually it remained shut, but when somebody happened to open the right side or the left, those passing below would see the letters arranged to read either *san* and *ta* or *ho* and *bang.* Though this was the only means with which the house advertised its existence, no citizen had ever mistaken it for anything else.

Now that you have viewed the building from without, try to see what it is like inside. When you enter, it would be better to go straight ahead with quick steps, not turning to the right, because the toilet on the right is used by people from the teahouse and the downstairs inn alike and, irrespective of sex, would spoil your fun from the very onset whether its door was open or not. The stairs would come into view soon after the toilet. Exactly twenty-seven wooden steps going straight up at a steep angle with no landings. This stupidity in the design of the structure dictates that if you were accompanying a woman you would be able to show off your gallantry by helping her up the stairs with no need to lay plans in advance. The higher you climbed, the louder the worn-out steps would creak, until finally you would be seized with the fear that might be experienced by a seriously ill patient being wheeled into an operating room wondering if he will return alive to the bright world outside.

At the head of the stairs you would unexpectedly encounter your other self. He would have been there in advance to welcome you as you came up the steps short of breath. He would look larger or even fatter than you, or grotesquely uglier, because some parts of his face would be distorted. You would not have to bother yourself with him, however, because he would be nothing but the playful product of a full-length mirror hanging on the wall. Then there would be the letters inscribed on the upper and lower parts of the mirror. Those inscribed on the upper part would read "Congratulations on Your Growth," while those on the lower part would say "All the Members of the Seventh Full Moon Viewing Association of Yŏngsaeng Girls' High School."

The mirror, its originally uneven surface looking all the worse because the silver coating on its back had peeled off in places, was of the sort that befitted the general atmosphere of the place and the customers; it did not stare at them as they came up out of breath, treading on the creaky steps, and it did not remind them how they really looked.

Now you would be fully prepared to enter. A pull on the doorknob beside the mirror would be enough to make you a member of the Sanho family. Upon entering, you would find yourself in such darkness as you might experience in a cave. Then you would see two neat rows of teeth, like so many porcelain chips, smiling whitely. This smile would draw you into the depth of darkness without hesitation.

That day, too, things were as they used to be. Madam Son, the proprietress of the teahouse, greeted Kim Sich'ŏl, a primary school teacher from the country, with her usual white smile.

During the usual exchange of greetings with the proprietress at the counter, the darkness that had stood like a barrier before Kim Sich'ŏl gradually receded to the chairs in the hall, which were arranged in rows. One row after another, the chairs in turn began to occupy space as the darkness receded.

The second chair from the right, from which Kim Sich'ŏl could see the fire station lookout any time he opened the nearby window, was not occupied, just as he expected. Or, to be more precise, it was so arranged by the proprietress as not to be occupied.

Kim Sich'ŏl flopped down in his chair.

"Well, you went to work with a letter of resignation still in your pocket today, didn't you?" the proprietress asked as she sat down opposite Kim. A woman who still had some years to go until fifty, with the fleshiness that one often sees in a woman her age, the proprietress gave the impression of having grown old gracefully. For that reason, she had earned herself the nickname Bodhisattva Maitreya.[1]

"You know that well enough, don't you?" Kim Sich'ŏl answered bluntly.

Kim's chair was an old-fashioned wooden one with a low seat and two high armrests. Whenever he sat in it, he was forced to assume an arrogant posture unbecoming to a primary school teacher from the country.

"There aren't any good possibilities?" Son asked.

"Lots of possibilities. I'm just a primary school teacher. I can give up any time. It's not because there aren't any possibilities, but because I'm thick-headed. You know that, don't you?"

"You've been patient long enough. Now be patient a little longer. They say they're going to raise teachers' salaries. Then you'll be in a better position."

"Does the salary matter that much? What matters is social status. They usually grade a primary school teacher when they consider him as a prospective son-in-law or bridegroom."

"Take it easy. What you need first is rest. Go to your room and get some sleep," the woman said as she left. She knew just when to leave, Kim thought. Her voice rang pleasantly in his ears, as crisp as if he were eating a slice of ripe pear.

Kim Sich'ŏl slept some time and awoke to find the agricultural machinery factory below had begun its evening shift. They were busy beating away at iron plates, making a great clatter. Along with this came the sound of Madam Son's voice.

"Everybody thinks so at first, but soon you'll think nothing of it. People get used to regular sounds." The proprietress was addressing a couple of stray customers who had dropped in knowing nothing about the establishment. Their complaints, however, continued.

"What kind of teahouse is this? Look at the lights and decor. They're utterly hopeless."

---

[1]Bodhisattva Maitreya: The future Buddha who resides in the Tuṣita Heaven. See n. 5, p. 270.

"Didn't I tell you so? How about the music? A product of the nineteenth century—that's what this place is."

Such denunciations were a blow to the proprietress, who thought of herself as a humble fixture of the Sanho Teahouse. Nevertheless, she began to remonstrate with the young couple in a serene tone of voice while maintaining a broad, saintly smile. "Light accompanies shade. Of course, the former is better than the latter. But light alone won't do, because it only makes us tired and dried out. It's normal for shade to follow light, particularly in a city. It is in this sense that the Sanho Teahouse serves as a shade, the only shade left in our city today. Those afflicted by the burning sun of life drag their tired feet here seeking rest. Formalities or appearances have nothing to do with this place. Nobody finds fault with those who do things a little out of the ordinary. Formal clothes are unnecessary. Work clothes are better for you to roll in a weedy field."

This was a belief she held firmly, a weapon with which she had defended the Sanho for half her life. Her conviction had caused great problems for her. But her belief enabled her to maintain the Sanho as it stood on this day.

Madam Son never thought of her teahouse as a business. Rather, it was a social project for the seedy failures who sought shade in which to rest, like chickens seeking the shelter of a hen's wing. She was content with the thought that she was that hen.

"You want coffee?" Kim Sich'ŏl heard Miss Hyŏn, the waitress, ask the couple in a quarrelsome voice. She had a habit of glancing downward with her chin up when she talked. Several times the proprietress had told Miss Hyŏn to rid herself of the habit, but to no avail. She seemed disinclined to mend her ways, which were born of her disrespect for the customers.

"What do you want?" the woman asked the man.

"Coffee," the man answered.

"One coffee and one tomato juice," the woman said tersely.

Miss Hyŏn turned and went swinging her hips down the length of the aisle.

"You ordered tomato juice?" The proprietress asked with a look of surprise.

"Yes. Anything wrong?"

"Of course not. Tomato juice? Yes, it's good for a woman's looks. And . . ."

Then Madam Son went on in a persuasive tone. "But of all the things you could drink, coffee's the best. Don't you agree? Moreover, what we serve customers with confidence is coffee." Her praise of coffee went on and on. Her tone hinted that any woman who ordered juice could not be up-to-date.

The order arrived: two cups of coffee. The young couple looked dazed. Miss Hyŏn thrust her lips out into an "I-told-you-so" sneer and went back, filling the passage with her broad hips.

The coffee served at the Sanho was fake. Neither black nor red, the stuff gave off an unpleasantly sweet odor and tasted like dishwater. A single mouthful of it would make one nauseous. The long-haired cook made the coffee. He made it with such great confidence that if anybody complained about the quality of his product in his presence, he would talk back—any cook with the ability to make coffee that pleased everybody's taste would not be rotting away at a third-class teahouse. If a person wants real coffee, he should go to a tourist hotel coffee shop, the cook would say. Moreover, when there were not many customers around, he would come out to join the drinkers of his product and talk with them or even ask them for cigarettes.

Besides the cook, Madam Son was quite worried about Miss Hyŏn. Her name was fictitious. Maybe her temper was too. She placed too much confidence in her looks. The gap between the customers' objective appraisal of her looks and her own evaluation was considerable, but because she refused to accept the former, one could hardly expect her to change her ways. The cook would say, "She has a democratically formed face," which meant that Miss Hyŏn's eyes, ears, mouth, and nose had taken their respective places as they pleased. Miss Hyŏn measured her popularity by the number of cups of coffee she managed to "snatch" from the customers in a day. To augment her sales, Miss Hyŏn, avoiding Madam Son's eyes, would approach those who looked like easy prey and tease them into buying her cups of coffee. Joy alternated with sorrow, and sorrow with joy, according to the number of cups she had "snatched" from the customers in this way. Yesterday might be a good day, a day worth living, because she had sold as many as ten extra cups. Today, with only five cups, might be a bad day, maybe bad enough to kill herself, she would think.

In her younger days, Miss Hyŏn dreamed of becoming a singer, not the teahouse waitress she was now. Even now that dream possessed her day and night, and she despised those other silly waitresses who, in hopes of becoming a proprietress, would readily go after rich old men. On the dark-colored ceiling Miss Hyŏn would project the image of herself onstage, the limelight bathing her from head to foot, singing a sweet song that melted every heart in the packed audience. She also dreamed that just after she had become a leading singer, she would encounter a poor self-supporting student whom she would help devotedly. With her help, the student would graduate from college. But the moment would come when he would betray her in grand style; upon becoming a judge, a prosecutor, or some such thing, he would leave her. Things had to go that way, so that at the grand finale of her farewell recital she could die onstage by taking poison. As an encore she would give the "Eulogy of Death" that had been popularized by Yun Simdŏk, the famous woman singer who killed herself because of an unrequited love affair. Such was the plot of Miss Hyŏn's story.

The hour had grown quite late. Kim Sich'ŏl looked around at the other people in the room. All of them were regular customers, each occupying the seat he was used to taking, each killing time in a loose, boneless posture.

The man sitting nearest the counter was Mr. Ch'ae, a former chief of a newspaper branch office. He had retired a few years ago because of an incident involving money, or an affair with a woman. A widower in early middle age, he found his pleasure in life by criticizing young newspapermen who lacked the ambitious spirit of their elders. But those who knew Mr. Ch'ae well said that he had inordinate designs on Madam Son. Perhaps because of this, he invariably sat at the counter. There he would cup his chin in his hands and steal glances at the proprietress.

Sitting in the corner, facing Kim Sich'ŏl, was Mr. Ch'oe, an aging undergraduate. He had been attending school for nine years, including three years of military service. His circumstances were such that he had had to cut one school year into two halves, one for earning money for tuition and the other for actually studying. Now on leave of absence, he was working to earn his tuition. When he came to the Sanho, he would fumble around in one pocket or another for a cigarette butt and because of his wretched condition would be neglected by none other than Miss Hyŏn, whom he liked best. These were the two people with whom Kim Sich'ŏl had any measure of intimacy, though it did not go beyond an occasional exchange of glances in passing. Kim Sich'ŏl knew all about the other customers, however, because Miss Hyŏn had given him personal information about them that she had gathered like a sparrow as she made her rounds. All told, the customers were either out of active service or found the times against them, and they had no idea what the pleasures of life were.

The clatter of iron plates being beaten in the agricultural machinery factory stopped before Kim Sich'ŏl was aware. Now his ear caught the voices of men fighting. In a few minutes, as the fight began to heat up, the voices grew so loud that Kim pulled up the curtain, which was as thick as the entrance to a darkroom, and opened the window. From a bright lamp hanging from the eaves of a low U-shaped slate roof, light fell over the messy courtyard of the factory, where empty drums and iron bars were scattered. Two men, bare from the waist up, were fighting desperately; one was chasing the other, the sweat from their naked muscles reflecting the bright light. In his hand the man doing the chasing held a hammer as big as a wooden pillow, while the one being chased was empty-handed. Bickering and cursing they ran, one after the other, between the drums and around the pillars of the building. Arms folded, a few fellow workers watched them and chuckled.

Driven at last into a corner, the emtpy-handed man turned around and took a step toward his pursuer. "All right," he cried as he thrust his head forward. "Go ahead and hit me! Hit me if you dare!" The man with the hammer held up his weapon and glared fiercely.

Seeing this happen before his eyes, Kim Sich'ŏl felt tension overwhelm him for the first time in many days.

"Don't you know I've already chosen death before poverty? All right. Quick, go ahead and hit me. That way I'll get my wish," the empty-handed man challenged his pursuer.

The man with the hammer went through the motions of bringing his weapon down on the other's head. Kim Sich'ŏl imagined the empty-handed man's brain being smashed under the force of the blow, and he anticipated that moment. But the man with the hammer hesitated to follow through. He threw the hammer away and began to cry.

A man who looked like the factory manager appeared and began to give the two fighting men a piece of his mind in a clear, crisp voice. "You swine. You fight every day, eating expensive rice, because you have no intention of doing anything worthwhile. You rascals. You're all pitiful men leading a tough life. Yet you don't help each other but go crazy like this and beat one another. You rascals."

Kim Sich'ŏl closed the window and pulled down the curtain. He felt the tension of a few moments before still within him. Now, he thought, it was time to go to his boarding house where cold rice would be waiting for him. He would never come back to this teahouse, he thought.

It was a day like any other. Nothing was new. Kim Sich'ŏl's letter of resignation was still in his pocket. Madam Son's white teeth and smile were the same as ever.

Kim Sich'ŏl sat down and ordered coffee. He knew the quality of the coffee in this place, but no matter what he ordered, they served coffee—he knew that too. He never had to wonder what to order.

The coffee arrived. Miss Hyŏn brought it and set it down on the table with a smile on her lips. She had never smiled as she did now.

"You'll be surprised," she said.

"I'm already surprised. You mean you won first place in an amateur singing contest?" Except for something like that, nothing surprising could have happened, he thought.

Miss Hyŏn prepared to answer, but at this moment Madam Son cut in by calling out "Miss Hyŏn!" As she spoke, the proprietress fixed Miss Hyŏn with the stare of a dormitory supervisor.

"You'll soon know," Miss Hyŏn whispered hurriedly and turned back, a mischievous look in her eyes. Kim Sich'ŏl was surprised again. Something had happened, he thought. Something great.

He knew at once what that "something" was when he took a sip of the coffee. It did not have the taste of dishwater but that of really good coffee. Kim Sich'ŏl came close to spitting out the entire mouthful.

Seeing Kim's surprise, Madam Son approached him.

"You like the coffee?"

"What is all this?"

"We have a new cook. I found a good cook and let Yi, the old one, go." Kim Sich'ŏl turned toward the kitchen and saw an arm, as thin and white as a woman's, flit across the crescent-shaped opening.

The Sanho Teahouse began to change after the new cook arrived. The music changed first. Light, rhythmic popular songs replaced the plaintive "slow-slow-quick" songs that Miss Hyŏn liked to sing. Next came the curtains. The thick, dark-green wool curtains gave way to cool, light ones of hemp. The lighting fixtures increased in number so that the room became vivid and bright. Picture frames, seat covers, and so forth—all changed. Of all the changes, however, the most shocking was the proprietress's attitude toward life.

"Even in adversity, we should not retreat. We should at least find a way to amuse ourselves, even in a limited sphere. If the outside is too bright and glaring, we should adapt to it by cultivating our inner strength. If we refuse to make that bit of effort, we will fall behind for good."

Miss Hyŏn dropped a hint that all these changes had come about under instructions from the kitchen. All the customers tilted their heads in wonder, less at the unexpected change of environment than at the identity of the cook, who had accomplished in a few days the impossible task of altering the twenty-year-old atmosphere of the place.

Days stretched into weeks and weeks into months, but the cook never appeared in the hall, nor was he seen going to the washroom. Only his arms, thin and white as a woman's, could be seen occasionally through the opening, and these served only to whet the customers' curiosity.

Moreover, Madam Son and Miss Hyŏn seemed unusually unanimous in denying any knowledge of the cook. They flatly refused to reveal even his name, age, or place of birth. Indeed, they even saw to it that nobody peeped into the kitchen. Therefore the customers could only exchange simple guesses among themselves: because nobody heard him say anything, he might be dumb; or he might have a burn on his face that he did not want anyone to see.

But on one of these days when he had begun to find the world almost interesting enough to make him forget about resigning, Kim Sich'ŏl heard a strange rumor.

It was Mr. Ch'oe, the perpetual student, who brought it up.

Ch'oe came to Kim and asked, "Have you heard the rumor, Mr. Kim?"

"Well. Somebody said yesterday that the cook attended a first-rate university in Seoul."

"Is that all you know?"

"Yes."

"You are still in the dark."

"Am I?"

"The cook is a fugitive, they say."

"What?"

"Shhh! Don't raise your voice. He is a known criminal, one of those most wanted by the police. He has hidden himself here, they say."

"Who told you that?"

"Nobody knows the source. Remember Mr. Kim, the Erosion Control official? He said he heard it from somebody. It's the rumor itself that's important, not its source, don't you agree?"

Mr. Ch'oe was all excited, as though he himself were the very fugitive wanted by the police and was ready to flee at the slightest touch.

Not only Mr. Ch'oe, but all the rest of the customers were at a peak of excitement. They sat in groups and whispered to one another, stealing glances at the kitchen. Business at the Sanho began to drop off, too.

Seeing that the customers were behaving strangely, the proprietress glared at them in anger, pulling a long face.

Miss Hyŏn remained seated behind the counter, as nerveless as a centipede moistened with spit. The Sanho Teahouse had never seen its customers so full of life as they were now.

Later, Mr. Ch'ae joined Kim Sich'ŏl and Mr. Ch'oe in their discussion of the rumor. Before penetrating into the pith of the rumor, they began by gnawing at its rind, as a silkworm does with a mulberry leaf.

"What sort of crime could he have committed?" Kim Sich'ŏl took the lead.

"He must have been in disgrace," Ch'ae responded with confidence. "He was sent to prison on a false charge of murdering his wife. He broke out of prison to catch the real culprit himself, I'm sure."

"Damn you! That's the television story about Richard Kimball, isn't it?" Ch'oe scolded. Ch'ae laughed awkwardly.

"He is a murderer, I guess," the old undergraduate insisted.

"You said it!" Ch'ae again cut in and went on, "He couldn't forgive the criminal acts of a person as mean as an insect, a person who exploited good people. So he killed the old pawnbroker woman with an axe."

"That's another story I've heard many times," Ch'oe said.

"You've heard it? Then I think I'd better not go any further," Ch'ae laughed.

"You two are too conventional in your thinking. I'm disappointed with both of you," Kim Sich'ŏl commented.

"What is your unconventional way of thinking then, Mr. Kim?"

"I see the cook from a different angle. I have inferred his crime in a symbolic manner, not in a concrete, black-or-white way. In short, he is hiding in this teahouse having committed a crime that is at once real and unreal."

"What are you talking about? He's being falsely accused—he is unjustly stigmatized, you mean?"

"Not exactly. What I mean is that he certainly made a mistake. His mistake was that he was born extraordinary or superior. To be born superior to others means you have superior abilities or, in a sense, a superior conscience," Kim Sich'ŏl explained.

"How absurd! How could such a conscience or ability be a crime?"

"It could be. Because a man with superior abilities or a superior conscience drowns those around him. Those who are ordinary, or those snobs who always have something on their conscience, will find it impossible to keep up with him, even if they wear track shoes. Then they'll regard that quality in him as a deadly weapon that will eventually harm them. Can you, Mr. Ch'oe, allow a man with such a deadly weapon to ride in the same boat as you?"

"I like concrete things. A rapist, a notorious criminal, a communist, a thought criminal—they deserve the death penalty or life imprisonment. This way of classifying crimes makes it easier for me to understand them than your theory that a man is a criminal because he's superior to others. To be frank, I don't like your theory. I'd rather stand proudly on the side of convention."

Ch'oe and Kim Sich'ŏl spent most of the evening this way, each claiming that he had made the most accurate guess, until the proprietress announced that she would close up earlier than usual.

The two men had to halt their discussion, but before they left they agreed that the crux of the problem was the nature and extent of the cook's crime. Although they still had no precise clue about the crime, there would be no point in pursuing the matter as long as the cook was a felon that society could not tolerate under any law, written or unwritten. Anyway, he had to be a felon, for only a felon could be so conspicuous even in hiding that eyewitnesses could enjoy a vivid sense of having been at the actual scene. It mattered little whether the cook had brandished an axe or his conscience.

Back in his room at the boarding house, Kim Sich'ŏl had no appetite. The excitement he had experienced at the Sanho Teahouse made his heart pound. He decided to put an end to his imaginings by giving them a rational conclusion. He forgot his hunger and began to think deliriously. As the night advanced, Kim again realized that he knew nothing about the cook. He might be nondescript, of doubtful origins, or he might not be a university student, despite the rumor.

But part of Kim Sich'ŏl went for the rumor. Perhaps he wanted to believe the rumor because he sensed in it the hidden circumstances of the case. For one thing, there was the cook's mysterious power. He had at his beck and call Madam Son and Miss Hyŏn, who protected him from being noticed with as much passion as they might protect their ancestral tablets. Though there were some gaps in his theory,

Kim wanted to believe that the cook was a university student and an identified suspect wanted by the police.

As the night wore on, the image of the cook began to appear before Kim Sich'ŏl's eyes. It began to turn into many different-sized forms, like so many roasted silkworm cakes. Around midnight it unexpectedly turned into Atom, the space boy in children's cartoons. Like Atom in the cartoons, the cook was a superman, Kim Sich'ŏl thought. Having run out of his fuel, Atrontium or whatever, the cook had been forced down and was staying temporarily at places like the Sanho Teahouse under the guise of a cook, gathering his strength for the day he would ascend into the sky again. Then he would resume the fight with the evildoers and defeat them. The cook's victory would be Kim's own, because the cook was Kim's agent and would do for Kim what Kim himself had failed to do. Through the cook Kim would be saved. If the cook failed, Kim would fail too. Then he would not be able to get away from the Sanho. He would be tethered to it forever. Kim Sich'ŏl was a coward who could not even steal a piece of taffy from a roadside stall or cheat in an examination. A weakling who lacked the guts to send in his letter of resignation to the primary school that employed him, though he had long since been utterly disillusioned with the teaching profession.

The overexcited Kim Sich'ŏl spent a sleepless night.

The next day, an unimaginable atmosphere pervaded the Sanho Teahouse. A few regular customers including Ch'oe and Ch'ae were there, all gloomily silent. Madam Son was nowhere to be seen. Only Miss Hyŏn went about the room swinging her hips as she had done before the new cook arrived. Today she had returned to her old ways and her unrestrained former self.

After the cook's arrival, she had turned up at the teahouse a changed girl, docile and obedient to customers. Even her walk had changed, and her way of laughing too; she had begun walking gracefully and covered her face with her hands when she laughed. She had often blushed and acted bashful. All told, she had begun to grow ladylike for the first time in her life. Moreover, she had appeared full of happiness every day, and the happiness had seemed to come from an inexhaustible fountain of wealth and joy. She had seemed unable to contain herself and impatient to find an excuse for expressing her happiness.

Now she was no better than before. During the heaviest business hours, she thought nothing of drinking and flirting with the customers as she threaded her way through the narrow aisles between the chairs. She began to come to the tables and sit beside customers uninvited. Sometimes she would even ask a customer to buy her a cup of whiskey and tea. "A man should not be a miser. Just a cup of whiskey and tea, and I won't ask for more. What do you say? Shall I write up the order?" she would say.

Now she came to Kim Sich'ŏl and made her request. As soon as he nodded his consent, she hurried to the kitchen and, ignoring all precedent and protocol, made the tea herself and began to sip it. The cook did not appear in the kitchen, nor was his arm visible.

The cook was supposed to move to another place the following morning, Mr. Ch'oe, the aging student, came to inform Kim Sich'ŏl. "Let's have a drink somewhere," he suggested then. Utterly disappointed by the news, Kim felt weightless for a moment. He felt betrayed by the cook. After absorbing the initial impact of the news, the speechless Kim followed Mr. Ch'oe out.

In the tavern the two men exchanged cups in silence. When the wine began to show its effect, Mr. Ch'oe reluctantly began to speak. "That guy shouldn't go on running away from one place to another. He can't go far in a small country like this, can he? He's sure to be caught again. He should settle things right here, no matter what the consequences. It may be more heroic and honorable of him to be caught and have his say now rather than live on in humiliation. He has an obligation not to disappoint those who value him, hasn't he?"

Kim Sich'ŏl regretted having spent a sleepless night composing a happy picture of himself humbly seeking the superpower of the Atom Boy. How silly and vain a dream it was—like that of a cripple who dreams of forcing himself to stand! Kim Sich'ŏl let go a suppressed laugh. He kept on drinking and did not reply.

"For his own sake it's better for somebody to tell the authorities about him" Mr. Ch'oe said as he left.

After Ch'oe was gone, Kim Sich'ŏl trudged toward his boarding house alone, his eyes heavy from drink.

Before long a telephone booth came into view. Without thinking he went into it and stood before the phone. Then, as though following a prearranged procedure, he turned the dial calmly. One, one, then two.

A couple of rings could be heard, and then came the moment when the weapon of civilization broke down the barrier of distance.

"Yes. This is one, one, two." The thick voice of a man rang out as though it would strike him in the face. Overwhelmed by the voice, Kim Sich'ŏl looked down for a few seconds at the receiver in his hand.

"Hello. Hello." Like a living thing, the receiver gave out cries.

Deceiving himself with a contrived calm, Kim Sich'ŏl hung up the receiver and quickly stepped out of the booth. Outside a confused and unpleasant aftertaste seized him. He was not sure whether he had said anything on the telephone or not.

It happened that night or, to be more precise, during the space of time between the incident of the telephone and dawn of the following day. A little before midnight, a small group of citizens had the good fortune to happen upon the scene of a grotesque accident. It began with a local telephone request program called "Garden of Songs at Night." Although it was broadcast chiefly for youngsters, a handful of citizens who were either chronically poor sleepers or had insomnia for some reason turned on their radio and happened to hear the following dialogue.

"I'd like to request 'Eulogy of Death,' sung by Yun Simdŏk."

" 'Eulogy of Death'—let me see. Just mentioning the title fills your announcer's heart with a strange emotion. Is there anyone to whom you'd like to dedicate this song?"

"No. I just want to enjoy it all by myself."

"I see. Would you tell me your name and address, please?"

"My name is Semi. That is all I want to say."

"Then I'll play 'Eulogy of Death' for you. Any special reason for requesting this particular song, Miss Semi?"

Up to that point, the dialogue went as usual. Then it happened. In a tone that was rather agitated, yet indecent, the girl began to pour out words that would shock the listening audience: "I have just cut my artery with a knife. I feel so good—I can't tell you how good. I've been disappointed in love. I loved a poor, self-supporting student. I loved him so much that I helped him with his tuition, living expenses, and so forth. I loved him as devotedly as I could, but he betrayed me. He left me as soon as he graduated from college and rose to a high position. Thank you for the song. I am enjoying it. Semi is dying quietly, thinking of your song as a funeral march for her last journey."

"Hello. Please, wait, Miss Semi. Listen to me."

Under the circumstances the announcer, overflowing with compassion, had to use every conceivable means to prolong the dialogue with the girl while one of his colleagues contacted the police.

Once notified, the police took measures to locate the caller, enlisting the help of the telegraph officer and telephone company. It took more than two hours for them to succeed, however. During the whole time, the announcer had to sweat through the tortuous business of conducting a live broadcast with the most unusual dialogue in the entire history of broadcasting.

Spectators crowded around the old wooden structure housing the teahouse. Ropes marked out a square zone on the road in front. Within the ropes lay a bloodstained straw sack, looking as though somebody had tossed it there in the most casual manner possible. There were bloodstains now dried black in the sun. Shards of glass were scattered about on the road, reflecting the light of the sun. Even though the corpse had been carried away some time ago, the circles and arrows marked on the road in white chalk remained to indicate exactly where it had lain.

Kim Sich'ŏl, the primary school teacher, elbowed his way into the teahouse. The landlady of the downstairs inn was there, alone, in the broad, empty room, tearing down the curtains. She greeted him with an abstracted look. They had known each other for a long time. She said she had been summoned to the police station as a witness and had returned just before Kim arrived.

She continued: "At first I was so terrified that I almost fainted. I heard a terrible crash outside and rushed out. There he was lying all covered with blood. To make matters worse, he had jumped out, hugging the window frame and all. Since he jumped headfirst, he must have intended to kill himself, not to run away, I'm sure." Then, making clucking sounds with her tongue, she resumed her work on the curtains.

"Why are you tearing down the curtains?" Kim Sich'ŏl asked.

"Madam Son asked me to when I left the station. We were there together. She wanted to tear down the curtains and decorative lights, and she asked me to hire someone to do it. She said something like, 'After all, a city needs shade.'"

"How about Miss Hyŏn? What happened to her afterward?"

"You know what that bitch is doing, don't you? She's acting nonchalant and carefree, as though nothing had happened. What do you think she did when the policeman rushed in here? Cut through her artery? No. They say she was pouring herself cups of wine while she talked on the phone with the announcer. Because of her damned acting, an innocent soul was lost for nothing."

"Not necessarily because of Hyŏn. Who knows that somebody didn't tip off the police?"

The landlady raised her head in disbelief. "You don't mean that," she said as she looked Kim up and down with suspicious eyes. Her face seemed to turn white at this unexpected blow.

Kim Sich'ŏl turned back and descended the old, creaking steps. He remembered his letter of resignation still in his inner pocket. He took out the letter and tore it to pieces over the railing as he went down the stairs.

For a few days after the incident Kim Sich'ŏl, the primary school teacher from the country, scrutinized the social pages of the newspaper, but he could find no mention of the cook's leap to his death, not even in a one-column article.

TRANSLATED BY CH'OE HAECH'UN

Cho Sehŭi

Born in Kap'yŏng in Kyŏnggi in 1942, Cho Sehŭi graduated from Sŏrabŏl and Kyŏnghŭi universities. After his literary debut in 1965, he maintained a ten-year silence until he emerged again in 1975 with a group of stories that dealt with the urban proletariat and working class during the industrialization of Korea in the 1960s and 1970s. "A Dwarf Launches a Little Ball" (*Nanjangi ka ssoa ollin chagŭn kong)* was first published in the Winter 1976 issue of the magazine *Munhak kwa chisŏng* (Literature and Intellect). In this story Cho analyzes the realities of labor and the falsehoods of society, as the dislocated and downtrodden workers oscillate between their anguish and fantasies of flight. As Cho's characters do not forget their origins, the past keeps overtaking the present. Different perspectives on the same experience, meaning accumulated through the juxtaposition of fragments from the past and present, shifting viewpoints—these are major elements of Cho's narrative mode. Trapped in their past, Kim Puri and his children struggle to extricate themselves, sometimes by depraved means, from their barren confines. The story ends with anger at the society that caused their dislocation and alienation—anger that was also a predominant reaction against the government of the time.

A DWARF LAUNCHES A LITTLE BALL

I

People called father a dwarf. They were right. Father was a dwarf. Unfortunately people were right only about that. They weren't right about anything else. I always felt I could wager everything the five of us—father, mother, Yŏngho, Yŏnghŭi, and I—had on the fact that people were wrong. When I refer to "everything," that includes the lives of the five of us. Those who dwell in heaven have no occasion to concern themselves with hell. But since the five of us lived in hell, we dreamed of heaven: not a day passed without thoughts of heaven. Each and every day was an ordeal. Our life was like a war. Everyday we lost a battle. Nevertheless mother stood up well under everything. But the incident that morning seemed especially trying for her.

"The precinct chief brought this," I said.

Mother was eating breakfast, sitting on the edge of the wooden floor.

"What's that?"

"It's an order of condemnation."

"It finally came!" said mother. "So it means the house must be torn down. This is one of the things we must face!"

Mother stopped eating. I looked down at her meal. Barley rice with black bean paste, a couple of withered peppers and potatoes in soy sauce.

I slowly read the order for mother:

Paradise District
Residence: 444, 1- 197x. 9.10
Recipient: Kim Puri
      46-1839 Happiness Precinct, Paradise
      District, Seoul
Subject: Urban Renewal Program and An Order of Condemnation of Hilltop Buildings. Pursuant to the interim authority for urban renewal the house under your name has been found to be located within Happiness Precinct 3, which is zoned for reconstruction as provided in the Urban Renewal Act, Section 15, and Building Code, Paragraphs 5 and 42; therefore you are ordered to raze said building by September 30th, 197x. In the event you fail to act yourself by the aforementioned date, the law provides that we shall proceed to demolish the structure and recoup the expense from you.
Demolition Site: 46-1839 Happiness Precinct,
      Paradise District, Seoul
__Structure__Ground Area__Lot
               __End
Chief of Paradise Precinct

Sitting on the edge of the wooden floor, mother didn't say a word. The shadow of the high smokestack of the brick factory covered the cement wall as well as the narrow yard. The neighbors came out shouting into the alley. The precinct chief pushed his way through the crowd and walked toward the levee. Mother entered the kitchen with her unfinished meal. She sat with her knee drawn to her chest. With one hand she struck first the kitchen floor and then her chest. I went to the precinct office. The Happiness Precinct residents were swarming about and loudly expressing their opinions. There were only a couple of people listening, but several dozen people were noisily talking simultaneously. It was a useless gesture. It was not a problem that could be solved by shouting.

I read the notice posted on the bulletin board outside. Written on it were the procedures for obtaining an apartment and also the amount of moving allowance in case one gave up and decided to move elsewhere. The area surrounding the precinct office was like a marketplace. The residents and apartment brokers all mingled together and moved about in groups. There I met father, mother, my brother and my sister. Father was sitting in front of a seal-engraver's shop. Yŏngho went to the bulletin board which I had just left. Yŏnghŭi stood by a black sedan that was parked at the entrance of the alley. Having gone out very early in the morning in search of work, Yŏnghŭi returned upon hearing of the issuance of the order of condemnation. Who could possibly work on such a day? I went over to father and lifted his tool satchel to my shoulder. Yŏngho approached and took the satchel from my shoulder and carried it himself. As I let him have it, I saw Yŏnghŭi walking in our direction. Her face was flushed. Several brokers converged on us and sought to buy our apartment rights. Father was reading a book. This was the first time we saw father reading a book. Because the book was covered we couldn't tell what kind he was reading. Yŏnghŭi bent down and pulled him up by the hand. Father looked at us with a blank face and stood up, brushing off his pants. "There goes a dwarf," said those who had never seen him before.

Mother was prying the nails from the aluminum name plate which hung on the gate post. I took the knife and worked on the other side. Yŏngho seemed to be disturbed by what mother and I were doing. But we could hardly expect anything pleasant to happen to us. Mother knew all along that unless she kept the aluminum name plate with the house number on it things could later become difficult.

Mother looked speechlessly at the name plate in her palm. This time Yŏnghŭi pulled mother by the hand.

"If you were not out of work, I wouldn't worry so much," said mother. "In a mere twenty days there's no way we can solve this. Now we must take care of things one at a time."

"Are you going to sell the apartment rights?" asked Yŏnghŭi.

"Why would we sell?" Yŏngho exclaimed.

"There must be money for the apartment."

"We won't get an apartment either."

"Then what shall we do?"

"We will simply stay here. This is our house."

Yŏngho bounded up the stone steps and put father's satchel underneath the wooden floor.

"There were people saying such things only a month ago," said father. He had just finished reading the order of condemnation given to him by mother. "Since the city has already built the apartment, there's nothing to be done."

"It wasn't built with us in mind," said Yŏngho.

"Don't we have to have a lot of money?" Yŏnghŭi was standing by the pansies in the front yard. "We can't leave. No place to go. Right, big brother?"

"I won't just stand by and let some bastard come and tear down our house," said Yŏngho.

"Cut it out," I said. "The law is on their side. Like father said, talk is of no use now." Yŏnghŭi, who was still standing in the yard by the pansies, turned her head. She was crying. From childhood Yŏnghŭi was quick to cry. Then I said, "Don't cry, Yŏnghŭi."

"I can't help it."

"Cry quietly, then."

"All right."

But Yŏnghŭi continued crying aloud in the yard. I covered her mouth with my hand. Yŏnghŭi smelt of grass. From the alley of the residential area across the stream there came the aroma of roasting meat. Although I knew it was the smell of roasting meat, I used to ask mother, "Mommy, what's this smell?"

Mother kept walking without a word.

"Mommy, what's this smell?"

Mother held my hand. Mother said as she hastened her gait, "It's the smell of roasting meat. Later we too will have some."

"Later when?"

"Now let's go quickly," said mother. "If you study hard, you can live in a fine house and eat roast beef every day."

"It's a lie," I said, pulling my hand away. "Father is a bad man."

Mother stopped and stiffened.

"What have you just said?"

"Father is a bad man."

"You'll get a spanking for that. Father is a good person."

"I wish I had real pants with pockets."

"Let's go quick."

"Mommy, why don't you put pockets on my clothes? It's because you don't have money or things to eat to put in my pocket, isn't it?"

"Remember, if you talk about father that way I'll spank you."

"Father is not even a scoundrel. A scoundrel at least has lots of money."

"Father is a good person."

"I know," said I. "I've heard that a million times. But I don't believe it anymore."

"Mommy, he doesn't listen to you," said Yŏnghŭi, standing in front of the kitchen door. "He snuck out again to smell the roasting beef. I didn't go."

Mother was silent. I gave Yŏnghŭi a fierce look. Yŏnghŭi said again, "Mommy, he's trying to beat me because I said he snuck out to smell the beef."

Yŏnghŭi could hardly stop crying. I took my hand from her mouth. It was wrong of me to take Yŏnghŭi into the field. I regretted having given her a beating. Yŏnghŭi's cute face was wet with tears. We were wearing pocketless clothes.

Father laid the order of condemnation on the edge of the floor and began reading. It wasn't as if we expected anything special from father. Father had always worked hard enough. Suffered enough, too. It wasn't father alone who suffered. Father's father, father's grandfather, that grandfather's father, that father's grandfathers—and so on back from generation to generation. Perhaps father's ancestors could have suffered even more. Once at work I set the type on a strange sort of business record. I had to work attentively in order to typeset this content:

> Woman-servant Kim Idŏk engendered man-servant Kŭmdong, born in the year of the Tiger; Man-servant Kŭmdong and his good wife engendered man-servant Kŭmi, born in the year of the Rabbit; Man-servant Kŭmdong and his good wife engendered man-servant Tŏksu, born in the year of the Serpent; Man-servant Kŭmdong and his good wife engendered man-servant Chonse, born in the year of the Sheep; Man-servant Kŭmdong and his good wife engendered man-servant Yŏngsŏk, born in the year of the Cock; Man-servant Kim Kŭmi and his good wife engendered man-servant Ch'ŏlsu, born in the year of the Dog; Man-servant Kim Kŭmi and his good wife engendered man-servant Kŭmsan, born in the year of the Rat.

At the time I didn't realize what it was. After finishing that plate, as I was working on the next, I realized what it had been. It was a part of some serf trading records. For ten days I set the type of this same book. During all that time I didn't say a word to father. I didn't exchange a word with mother either. Mother's mother, mother's grandmother, that grandmother's mother, that mother's grandmothers—I knew the kind of work they, as the lowest, must have done. Mother has not risen above that. Even today there's no peace, and the drudgery is incessant. Our ancestors from birth submitted to toil. They were property to be bequeathed and given as the masters liked. One day mother said to me, "Because you happen to have been born my son, your life is full of suffering. It's not because of your father."

She said this only to me, her eldest son. Mother was passing on to me what her mother had told her. For a thousand years our ancestors left this message to their children. But I knew that father too was born of serfs.

Serfdom was abolished three generations ago. At the time my great-grandparents were not aware of it. Much later, when they learned about the emancipation, their reaction was, "Please do not throw us out." Grandfather was different. He tried to break out of the traditional customs. His old master gave him a house and some land. But it was no use. Grandfather was less ignorant than his father. Up until great-grandfather's generation one could benefit from ancestors' experience, but in grandfather's time that experience provided no help. Grandfather had neither education nor experience. He lost his house and the land.

"Was grandfather also a dwarf?" Yŏngho once asked.

I gave him a cuff on the head. Later when he was older he said, "Why do you hush it up as if it were something past? Nothing has changed. It's funny, isn't it?"

I remained silent.

Yŏnghŭi took out her handkerchief and wiped her eyes. Father kept reading his book. Mother was talking with Myŏnghŭi's mother who lived in the next house.

"How much did you get?"

"I got a hundred seventy thousand *wŏn.*"

Then how much more did you get than the city said they would pay as a moving allowance?"

"Twenty thousand *wŏn* more. You can't move into an apartment either, right?"

"With what money?"

"If you buy an apartment, it's five hundred eighty thousand, and if you rent it's three hundred thousand. Besides, either way you pay fifteen thousand a month."

"So is everyone selling their apartment rights?"

"You should hurry too."

Mother stood there with a pained face. Myŏnghŭi's mother urged mother:

"We are ready to leave anytime, if you can let us have the money you owe. As for the house, a few strokes of an ax will do."

Yŏnghŭi's eyes began to water. She was still the same. Girls were always crying. When I approached Yŏnghŭi, she pointed at the ledge where pots and urns were stored. Scrawled in the cement ledge was "Myŏnghŭi loves my big brother." It was doodling left from when the house was built. Yŏnghŭi smiled. For us that was the happiest time. Mother and father brought some stones from the ditch. With the stones they built steps and they cemented the wall. We were too young to do such difficult things. Still there were lots of things for us to do. For several days we skipped school. Every day was fun. Each day several groups of new faces showed up in the neighborhood. During that time the children in their dirty clothes didn't even cry. Dogs retreated without barking when their masters cast threatening looks their way. The whole neighborhood fell silent. Suddenly it became surprisingly peaceful. I was ashamed of the smell of our neighborhood. They greeted father with a bow to the waist. When father shook hands with them he stood on his toes. To us it didn't matter what posture father had to assume. In our eyes our dwarf father was a giant.

"You saw, didn't you?" I asked.

Yŏngho nodded.

"I saw too," Yŏnghŭi said.

The man who had greeted father with a deep bow promised that a bridge would be built over the ditch, the street paved, and the buildings legitimized. As the grown-ups applauded we children happily joined in. The next man said that the previous speaker who had promised to build a bridge over the ditch and pave the street should be made a district chief, but that he himself would do such and such work of national importance if he was elected. The grown-ups once more applauded. We did too. Even after I was grown I often thought of that day. The impression of those two men remained strongly in my memory. I despised them. They were liars. They made extravagant plans. But plans were not what we needed. Many people had previously concocted such plans. Nevertheless, nothing changed. Even if they had accomplished something it probably wouldn't have benefited us. What we really needed was a person who understood and shared our suffering.

"There's no one else like her!" said mother.

"Who do you mean?" asked Yŏngho.

"I mean Myŏnghŭi's mother. How generous she is. If she hadn't loaned us a hundred fifty thousand *wŏn*, we couldn't have refunded our tenant's deposit."

"Yŏnghŭi's mother," Myŏnghŭi's mother called through the fence. "Please don't feel bad about it."

"Of course not," said mother. "I'll give you the money no matter what, so please don't worry."

"That money wasn't just any money."

"I understand. The thought of Myŏnghŭi still breaks my heart."

I felt the same.

"Myŏnghŭi," shouted Yŏnghŭi. "Come over to our house."

"You like the new house, don't you?"

"Yeah."

"I won't come over to your house to play until you erase what you wrote on the ledge."

"I can't erase it."

"Why not?"

"I can't erase it since the cement is set."

"Then I won't come."

Yŏnghŭi seemed very disappointed. Yet I met Myŏnghŭi. Back then there was a forest on the right levee. If we sat there we could see the lights of the printing factory through the trees. The workers at the factory worked at night too.

"I'll let you if you promise," said Myŏnghŭi.

"Promise what?" I asked.

"That you won't work at that factory."

"You think I'm crazy? I'll never work at such a place."

"Really? You promise?"

"Right. I promise."

"You may touch then."

She let me touch her breasts. They were quite small.

"You're the first," said Myŏnghǔi. "No one but you has ever touched my breasts."

I placed my left arm around her shoulder and touched her breasts with my right hand. Her roundish breasts were warm.

"You shouldn't tell anyone," whispered Myŏnghǔi.

I felt her breath under my ear.

"I won't say a word."

"Not even to your brother or sister."

"I won't."

"As long as you keep the secret and the promise you made, then I'll let you do as you like."

"Really?"

"Yes."

"Is it all right if I touch elsewhere?"

But whenever we met Myŏnghǔi looked downcast. Sometimes she would just sit silent and still.

"What's the matter?"

I was worried.

"Aren't you well?"

"Yes."

"Then what's the matter?"

"I don't like the food at home."

"Why not?"

"I'm fed up."

"Then you'll die."

"I want to die."

"Myŏnghǔi, I won't work at such a factory. I'll study hard and will work at a big company. I promise."

"I'm hungry," said little Myŏnghǔi, smiling.

"What do you want to eat?" I asked.

Myŏnghǔi held my hand. She counted on my fingers, "Cider, grapes, noodles, bread, apples, eggs, meat, rice, and seaweed." Myŏnghǔi didn't count my tenth finger. At that time Myŏnghǔi might not have needed anything more.

Myŏnghǔi, as she grew up, first worked in a tearoom, then as a bus guide, and then as a golf caddy. One day she came looking very pale. It was her last visit. Later mother told me that each time Myŏnghǔi came she was bigger. Myŏnghǔi died at the suicide prevention center.

"No! Mother! No!" Myŏnghǔi screamed in the grips of the poison.

The grown-up Myŏnghŭi must have been wandering through her childhood memories during her last moments. There was a hundred nineteen thousand *wŏn* in her savings account.

"It's a hundred fifteen thousand *wŏn*," said Myŏnghŭi's mother. "Let the tenants out first."

Mother took the money. Couldn't say a word.

"Who would rent a room if they knew the house was to be condemned?"

"Exactly."

"If the tenants want to move out, let them go before they start slandering you."

"This is no ordinary money!"

"Sister Myŏnghŭi loved my big brother," said Yŏnghŭi. "You knew it too, didn't you?"

"Enough."

Yŏnghŭi played the guitar. I saw the moon over the brick factory smokestack. My radio was broken. For several days I couldn't listen to my high school correspondence course lectures.

I couldn't keep my promise to Myŏnghŭi. I quit school at the beginning of my third year of middle school. I could no longer attend. Father and mother hoped that I could continue studying, but they had no money to help me. If you looked closely father seemed older than others of the same age. This was known only to us. Father's height was one hundred seventeen centimeters, and his weight was thirty-two kilograms. Because of the predisposition associated with father's disfigurement, people weren't aware of father's advancing age. Father felt resigned and fell into depression as he realized the twilight of his life was upon him. His aching teeth kept him awake many nights. His eyes were growing dim and his hair thinner. His attention span and his powers of judgment diminished along with his will. In the entire course of his life father had had five different jobs. He was a trader of bonds, a knife sharpener, a high window washer, a pump installer, and a plumber. Father, who only had experience at these jobs, suddenly decided he wanted to do something different. It was with a circus. Father brought home a hunchback one day and they talked for a long while. The hunchback said that father could be his assistant at first. They talked about what their act would be on the stage. Then mother protested. We joined in. Father retreated helplessly. The hunchback sat and blankly watched us. He left with tears in his eyes. As he walked away he looked very lonely. Father's dream was shattered. With his heavy satchel on his shoulder father went out in search of work. It was that evening.

"Children!" called mother. "Father's voice has become strange."

"What's the matter?" I asked.

Father was silent.

"Go to a pharmacy."

Mother stepped down on to the dirt floor.

"Buy some alum," said father.

It wasn't like father's voice. It sounded as if his tongue was very short and curled inward. Mother brought some medicine called Hibitan Troches.

"They don't get alum anymore but they say this is better medicine. Suck on this pill."

Father quietly took the pill and put it in his mouth. After that night father didn't talk much. He only said that his tongue kept curling inward. When he slept he bit his tongue between his teeth.

"Father is too tired," said mother. "Understand? Don't depend on your father now. You must work in father's place."

Mother cried. Mother went to the printing factory and did paper-folding. She folded printed matter with rubber thimbles on. I was afraid. I started working as an assistant in the factory management section. I later learned that nothing could be gained without sweat. Myŏnghŭi didn't allow me to meet her. She was very cold to me. Both Yŏngho and Yŏnghŭi quit school within several months. We felt at ease. Nobody was hurting us. We received invisible protection. Just as aborigines in South Africa were protected within their reservations, we too received the protection fitting for an alien group. I realized that we could not take a single step beyond the confines of our zone.

After I had been an assistant distributing type—blank spaces and punctuation—I advanced to work as a typesetter. Yŏngho worked at the printing office. I didn't like the fact that Yŏngho and I worked at the same factory. He felt the same. So Yŏngho took a job as an errand boy at an iron foundry. He also worked at a furniture factory. I went there and found him at work. When I saw little Yŏngho standing in the sawdust-filled air, I told him to quit. The noise at the printing factory was abominable but at least there was no dirty sawdust. We worked very hard. Our biceps thickened at the factory. Yŏnghŭi worked at a bakery located in the corner of the supermarket on the main street. We were grateful that Yŏnghŭi's workplace was at least clean. Yŏnghŭi worked in a sky blue bakery uniform. Yŏngho and I saw her working through the window. She was pretty. People wouldn't believe that she was the daughter of a dwarf. We used to think that no matter what happened we would have to study. Without studying we knew we couldn't escape from our place. The world was sharply split into those who had studied and those who had not. Society was primitive to a shocking extent. It worked in a way totally contrary to what school had led us to expect. I read all the books I could get hold of. After I became a typesetter I developed a habit of pausing to read the manuscripts which I worked from. If I thought the material would be valuable for my brother and sister, I made several extra copies of the galley proofs for them. Both Yŏngho and Yŏnghŭi listened attentively to my advice. They eagerly read the galley proofs I brought home. All this extra time and effort were well used. I passed a high school entrance qualification examination and started correspondence courses.

Late one autumn evening that year father took me in a small boat toward the levee. Father rowed without a word.

"Come back," said Yŏnghŭi from the yard. "That boat is dangerous."

But father kept rowing toward the center of the levee. In the water I could see a faint reflection of Yŏnghŭi waving her hands. The starlight made the water by the levee sparkle. Water trickled into the boat. We had stolen some boards from the church which was being built on the hill. Yŏngho and I used to get up in the middle of the night to go out to steal boards. Yŏnghŭi had crawled under the barbed wire fence and stolen some boards before she went to sleep. The church was all right, but our boat leaked. Yŏnghŭi worried about father. I knew how to swim. Father stopped rowing near the middle of the levee. The water inside the boat was up to our ankles. I took off my shoe and used it to bail the water out. Father snatched it from me. He was smiling.

"Look, Yŏngsu," said father. "Do you remember the hunchback who came yesterday?"

"When?"

"Yesterday."

I took off the other shoe and bailed the water with it. Again father grabbed my hand.

"I don't know," I said.

"It's useless to pretend that you don't know. I know everything."

"What do you mean you know?"

It hadn't been yesterday but three and a half years ago. That was the first time I saw the hunchback. But father said:

"I used to work with him. We rode on a huge wheel."

"What are you talking about, father? When did you do this?"

"You're the eldest son. Since you don't believe it neither will your brother and sister."

"Even mother knows nothing of this."

"Look here," said father. "At least you should know. Your mother is not well. The hunchback who came yesterday will return. Don't stop me. Other work is too hard for me now. Do you think I can connect water pipes and fit pumps forever? I can no longer climb down ropes from high buildings."

"You don't have to work. We can do the working."

"Who told you to work?" said father. "You only need to go to school. That's your job."

"All right, father," I said. "Now give me the shoe."

Father gazed at me as he gave me back the shoe. I bailed the water.

"Yesterday the hunchback came with the thought of helping me. He'll come again tomorrow. I don't understand why you said you saw him for the first time. He and I worked together. Don't you dare try to stop me."

"When did you say that he came?"

"Yesterday."

"Give me the oar."

Father gave me the oar which he had been holding upright. I couldn't speak. Father wouldn't believe it if I told him that I saw the hunchback for the first time. He wouldn't believe it if I told him that it wasn't yesterday but three and a half years ago. I rowed carefully. The boat sank before we reached the bank. I made my way through the reeds with father in my arms. We brought father soaked and trembling to mother. No one in the world could take better care of father than mother.

"Father is ill," I said.

"Shut up!" said mother. "When will you understand? Father is tired."

Father spent that winter inside his room. I dragged the boat out and lashed it to a post. When the weather got colder I brought it inside the courtyard. That night the water froze over.

At night Myŏnghŭi's mother came again.

"Yŏnghŭi's mother," said Myŏnghŭi's mother. "Wait a little and see. The price of the apartment rights is going up. What in the morning brought a hundred seventy thousand *wŏn* jumped to a hundred eighty-five thousand *wŏn*. I wish we had waited instead of selling ours immediately."

"Oh, my!"

"A whole fifteen thousand *wŏn!*"

Mother wrapped in paper the aluminum name plate she had removed early in the day. She put it in the wardrobe together with the order of condemnation.

"Yŏnghŭi," called mother. "Where is your father?"

"I don't know."

"Do you know, Yŏngho?"

"He went out a while ago without a word."

"Yŏnghŭi, where's your big brother?"

"He's inside."

"Where could your father have gone?" Mother's voice was anxious. "Children, go find your father."

I was reading the book that father left. It was a book called *The World After Ten Thousand Years.* Yŏnghŭi sat all day long by the pansies and played the guitar with a broken string. The guitar had been bought at "The Lost Market." Yŏnghŭi went with me to buy a radio for my high school correspondence course. There was a decent radio. Yŏnghŭi picked up a dust-covered guitar and plucked it. She played the guitar with her head slightly tilted. Her profile, almost half-covered by her long hair, was quite pretty. The sound of the guitar as she played went well with her. I couldn't buy the radio that I had picked out. While finding a cheaper one, I pointed to the guitar in Yŏnghŭi's hands. The radio no longer worked, and her guitar had a broken string. Yŏnghŭi played her broken-stringed guitar. I couldn't figure out what was on father's mind. Father borrowed the book from a young man living in the residential area across the sewer ditch. His name was Chisŏp. He lived in a bright, clean three-story house. He was the tutor for the family. Somehow he and father understood each other well. I heard him talking. He said that now there was nothing we could expect from life on this earth.

"Why not?" asked father.

"People are possessed by loveless desires. Therefore no one sheds a tear for another. An earth where only such people live is a dead place," said Chisŏp.

"Indeed!"

"Haven't you ever worked in your life?"

"We, never worked? I have. Very hard. Our entire family worked hard."

"Have you done anything wrong then? Haven't you ever broken the law?"

"Never."

"Then you must not have prayed. You never prayed devotedly."

"I did pray."

"Then what is this? Isn't something clearly wrong? Don't you think it's unfair? Now we must leave this dead land."

"Leave? Where to?"

"To the moon!"

"Children!"

Mother's anxious voice rose. I closed the book and ran outside. Yŏngho and Yŏnghŭi looked in absurd places. I went out to the levee and looked up straight into the sky. The tall brick factory smokestack slid into my vision. On the very top of the smokestack stood father. The moon was about one step away from him. He held the lightning rod and lifted one foot. In that stance father launched a paper airplane.

II

I was lying on the grass along the levee. My entire body was damp with dew. Each slight movement made the dew clinging to the reeds fall on my body. I spent all night lying on the grass along the levee. I couldn't see a thing. The darkness gradually started to retreat. The pain of having missed the last night at "Our House" rose in my throat. The neighborhood was still in deep sleep. But I didn't have to wait any longer. The rumor that aliens in a flying saucer had taken Yŏnghŭi away was ludicrous. I didn't believe the rumor from the beginning.

"Children!" said mother. "What's going to happen if you just sit here like this?"

"What can we do, she's not to be found?" I said.

I met a drunkard in the vacant lot where a barber shop used to stand.

"It's useless to search for her."

"Have you really seen her?"

"Sure, I saw her."

His speech was slurred. He constantly hiccuped.

"You're the only person who says he's seen Yŏnghŭi. So please tell us more."

"Your father knows."

"Father doesn't know."

"That couldn't be. The flying saucer came in response to your father's signal."

It wasn't necessary to listen to him anymore. Even so I remained standing there.

"It was an enormous flying saucer. The monsters that appeared underneath the saucer scooped up Yŏnghŭi instantly. Later I found out it had been a flying saucer." The drunkard kept hiccuping.

"Please be serious," said I.

"Then you go and see for yourself," said the drunkard. "See where you can find your sister. She's not anywhere around here. My thirst woke me up. No one else would have been awakened at that hour. As soon as they took Yŏnghŭi aboard they flew away. They had huge heads and spindly legs."

"Good-bye," I said.

"I'm not leaving yet," said the drunkard. "After I drink these up, I'll go."

He pointed at six windows and two doors stacked on the foundation. He had been drinking on the money from the sale of the pump head, two urns, and the tile he took yesterday from the roof. More than two-thirds of our neighborhood had already razed their houses and moved away. I pulled myself up from the grass. The starlight in the sky above the levee was no longer bright. The day was beginning to dawn. The sound of children crying could be heard. I loosened my shoelaces, retied them, and hopped about. My elder brother came through the gate and walked up the levee road. His shoulders were slumped.

"Gather your strength, brother," I said.

"Strength is of no help here," said brother.

"Then what is? Courage?"

Instead of having lunch brother came to see me. We crouched behind the machine shop and talked.

"We can't express ourselves very well, but this is a kind of battle," said brother. He spoke with refinement. "We must fight even for the bare minimum of just treatment. When right and wrong collide, it always comes down to a fight. Decide for yourself which is our side."

"I know."

Brother skipped lunch. Lunch time was limited to thirty minutes. Although we worked at the same factory we never met on the job. All the workers worked all day in isolation. The company officials checked and kept the records of the quantity and quality of our production. They told us to finish eating in ten minutes and to spend the remaining twenty of our lunch kicking a ball around. We workers would go out into the small yard and kick that ball to death. Our play was not well tuned, and we only succeeded in sweating profusely. As it was, there was no respite. The factory decided our wants for us. We worked until night amidst murky air and deafening noise. Of course we weren't dying right then and there. But the combination of the sordid working conditions, the amount of sweat we shed and the paltriness of pay grated on our nerves. As a result those among us who were young had their growth stunted. The company's interests were always contrary to ours. The president of the company frequently spoke of depression. He and his men used "depression" to make the many shapes of exploitation they forced upon us. The rest of the time he would speak of the great wealth we all would realize if we worked hard enough. The kind of hope he was talking about had no meaning for us. Instead of such hope we would have preferred a little tasty dried radish on the factory lunch table. No change was made. It only became worse. Instead of two promotions per year, which used to be the custom, now we got only one. Overtime pay for night work was cut. They laid off some workers. The work load for the rest was increased and hours were lengthened. On paydays especially, we had to watch our tongues. We couldn't really trust the other workers. Those who complained about the unjust treatment were quietly fired. On the other hand the sales of the factory grew. They installed rotary presses, automatic folding machines, and offset presses. The president said that the company was facing a crisis. He said that if we lost the race with competitors he would have to close the doors. That was what we feared most. The president and his men knew this.

Even the thought of it was terrifying. If the big factory closed down, the workers would have no place to go. The number of employees that small factories could absorb was limited. I might find myself without work. Even if I found new work it would be a strange place. In a small factory, the workplace could be worse and the pay even less than here, with no opportunity for raises. The thought was horrific. The majority of the workers entered the factory while young and spent several of the most critical years of growth there. Except for the narrow skills learned at the factory, they had no means of making a living. Our knowledge of life was constrained by our factory duties. No one wanted to lose the foundation that had been molded by sweat. The company didn't like for us to think. The workers only had to work. The majority of the workers accepted the fact that no changes would occur. No one was there to enlighten them. Even the older among us lacked that ability. They saw that reality worked out to be the opposite of what they felt to be right. There was too much we didn't know. This was fortunate for the president. In his family they used a machine to cut the grass in the yard. In his garden the well-manicured trees grew tall in the radiant sun. Their trees were cared for by a tree surgeon from "The Tree Hospital." Once I walked past the tree hospital. A sign said, "Are your trees in good health?" Written underneath in small letters, it said, "Pest Infestation Diagnosis, Blight Diagnosis, Pruning and Other Surgery, and Preventive Treatment." A young worker walking with me said, "There are no trees in our house, but I am not in good health." We had a good laugh. I don't know what was so funny about it. At that time this young worker had been having nosebleeds nearly every day.

Brother took off his shirt and put it on my back. When we reached the grass, his pants were dampened by the dew.

"The drunkard was the only one who said he saw Yŏnghŭi," said I reluctantly. "Here is where the flying saucer supposedly landed."

"So what have you found out during the night?"

"Does it seem to you that I believe what the drunkard said?"

"No."

"There is no place left to search."

"Enough. Let's go."

"Why do you suppose Yŏnghŭi left the house?"

"Because of the two of you," said mother. "She left the house because you're only hanging around and not working. No money. No house. It's all your fault. Why were you two kicked out while the others remained there to work?"

"Didn't she always tell us where she was off to? I've no idea why she ran away."

"She probably couldn't stand it any more," said brother.

Brother looked pained. He always thought more deeply than I. He was knowledgeable. He read more books after he quit school. If only father weren't a dwarf, brother would have become a scholar. Whenever he had spare time he read. I used to bring him reading materials just off the presses. Even if it was quite difficult he would persevere in his reading. When he got paid he would sometimes go to a used bookstore and buy things to read. Books made everything available to him. Often I detected suffering in his expression. He used to write down in his notebook words beyond my understanding. In his notebook could be found things such as this: "What is violence? Bullets, nightsticks, and fists are not the only forms of violence. It is also violence when people ignore the fact that infants are starving in one corner of our city. A nation with no expression of dissent is a nation in ruins. Who would dare keep order through violence? Axel Oxenstierna,[1] a prime minister of seventeenth-century Sweden, said to his son, 'Son, do you realize how unwisely the world is ruled?' Since his time the situation has not much improved. When rulers lead lives of luxury, they tend to forget human suffering. Accordingly when they used the word 'sacrifice,' it smells of hypocrisy. I think that in the past exploitation and barbarism were at least uncontrived. Those 'educated' people who read Hamlet and shed tears over Mozart's music perhaps have lost the capability to weep over the desperate suffering of their neighbors? Centuries and generations have passed us by without effect. In our isolation from the world we had nothing to contribute or teach them. To human understanding we added nothing . . . and we received nothing but deceptive superficialities and useless accessories. To rule is to provide work for the people, to enable them to appreciate their own heritage, and to make their life meaningful lest they wander empty and aimless in the wasteland about them."

I couldn't understand brother. While I was reading his notebook he wore the look of a suffering man. It was indeed a face dignified by suffering. I stifled a laugh. Brother must have laughed at my ignorance and stupidity.

"What on earth are you going to do with this?" I asked.

"Yŏngho," said father. "You ought to read like your brother."

"It's not that I'm going to do something with this," said brother. "I learn about myself through books."

"I see, now," I said later. "You're an idealist."

Having said this, I felt very good. I wanted him to know that I was on his level. I wanted him to know that unlike others of my age I was

---

[1]Axel Oxenstierna (1583–1654): chancellor of Sweden who drafted the Parliamentary Law of 1617 and under whose leadership Sweden emerged as a great power in Europe.

able to use sophisticated words. I looked into the face of a suffering idealist. My expectation wasn't realized. Brother was angry. At the time I couldn't understand why he was angry. To myself I admitted my ignorance. We were the sons of a dwarf. With drooping shoulders brother rose from the grass and left. I picked up a pebble and threw it toward the levee. Noiselessly bubbles floated to the surface. In the front yard I threw pebbles for a while.

"Yŏngho," said mother. "Stop throwing rocks and go to the precinct office and take a look."

"I don't have to go find out. About an hour ago it was two hundred twenty thousand *wŏn*. Do you think it could have gone up since?

"Go and see anyway. Offer it for two hundred fifty thousand *wŏn*."

Again I picked up some pebbles and tossed them toward the levee. People were gathered in front of the precinct office. Several sedans were parked there as well. People of only two sorts were there: those who sought to sell apartment rights and those who wanted to buy. The sellers anxiously tried to size up the brokers. The sellers' faces all showed signs of malnutrition. The odor of tears lingered there, I could smell it with my heart. Someone grasped my arm. It was Yŏnghŭi. She shook her sun-reddened face. She had been to Chamsil. Two hundred twenty thousand *wŏn* was also the cost estimated by the real estate broker near the site of the new apartment. It seemed as if it wasn't necessary to wait any longer.

"Brother, tell mother we could sell now," said Yŏnghŭi.

"What if the price suddenly drops?"

"Sell it to me, please," said some woman. "I'm not a broker. I want it for myself. Is transfer of title possible?"

"Of course, it is," I said. "We have our name plate."

"What does the name plate look like?"

"It's a small aluminum plate. On it is engraved the unauthorized building number."

"What then is an unnumbered plate? It was cheaper."

"A house without a name plate is called an unnumbered plate. Several years ago when there was a city inspection of all unauthorized buildings, either the house was overlooked or mistakenly classified as private property and thus omitted from the records of unauthorized buildings."

The woman stood perspiring. As she mopped her sweat with a handkerchief, she pointed at the bulletin board. There hung a proper form for transfer of title to an unauthorized building. Underneath was listed the necessary supporting documents. The woman read: "1 request form, 1 copy of the seller's certified seal, 1 copy of conveyance, 1 copy of title warranty."

"You only need to fill out a single conveyance," I said.

"You need to backdate the form as if the purchase had been made a couple of months before the order of condemnation was issued."

"Would that really be safe, then?"

"It'll be changed into your name all right. When you move into an apartment, it'll be in your name."

"Isn't that illegal?" she mopped her sweat as she stiffly stood there.

"Go inside the precinct office and ask at the building section desk," I said. "Go and argue with them and see how they handle such illegal matters."

"Two hundred twenty thousand wŏn is expensive. Would you go ten thousand wŏn lower?"

"Ma'am," I said, "if you were to build a new house comparable to our condemned house, it would cost you one million three hundred thousand wŏn. My father has been working all his life for that house. Now we are in a position to exchange all that for two hundred twenty thousand wŏn. If we pay a hundred fifty thousand wŏn as a refund to our tenant we are left with only seventy thousand wŏn."

"Anyway, you won't sell it for less than two hundred twenty thousand wŏn, will you?"

I didn't respond. She turned away. Yŏnghŭi rapped me on the back with her little fist. After a while she rapped again. She was in blue jeans. On her even blue jeans were becoming. I turned and walked away without looking at her face.

"Wait, don't sell," said a man from a sedan.

"I'll buy it."

"How much?"

"For how much will you sell it?"

"Two hundred twenty thousand wŏn."

"All right. I'll come this evening. If there are other people wanting to sell in your neighborhood, tell them to wait and not sell cheap."

"Wait a little longer," said father, "there are people who speak the truth and are buried. You are like them."

We were standing on the cement bridge over the sewer ditch. Father sat with his legs through the rails and drank. We had to wait until he finished drinking. At the other end of the bridge the knocked-out drunkard was snoring. Father could hold not more than one-fourth as much drink as him. That night father had drunk half of what the drunkard had. The night was deep and the neighbors had all turned out their lights and gone to sleep. Only two houses were awake. They were the drunkard's house and ours. I was afraid that the drinking would kill father. Even brother couldn't get the bottle away from father. I thought of the day when father would close his eyes for the last time. Death is the end of everything. The minister at the church on the hill thought differently. He spoke of human dignity, suffering, and redemption. I couldn't understand him when he said that after death humans begin another life. Father had no dignity and no redemption would have been possible for him. There was only suffering. I had seen the serf transaction record which brother had set the type for. Surely father was not the only one suffering. Father and mother hoped that their children would lead an entirely different life. But we had already lost our first battle. I also thought of the day when I would close my eyes for the last time. I would have been less than father. Father, father's father, father's grandfather, that grandfather's father, were men shaped by their time. I felt that my body was smaller than father's. I will probably close my eyes as a clown.

No one had work for us. People blocked us from entering the factory. The president and his men looked at us through the window of the conference room. They robbed us of our jobs.

"So, let's talk it over," said father, "you mean that the two of you were there alone? Those fellow workers of yours who at the beginning stopped work and were going to join in the negotiations betrayed you and left the two of you alone, is that the story?"

"Drink no more, please, father," said I.

"Well done." Father tilted the bottle and drank. "You did right, and so did the others."

"We'll go home first."

"All right, go ahead. Go and send your mother."

"It's not necessary."

It was mother. She almost stumbled over the drunkard's body.

"Good work!" said mother, "two of you can't take care of your father."

"Wait." Father threw the empty bottle under the bridge. "Our children did a fine job today. They met the president and had a talk. If a company is to prosper, a few heads must roll, they said. They asked the president not to give orders to the workers that he himself wouldn't want to receive. Would your mother understand this? Hm?"

"Father, that wasn't it," said I, "we couldn't meet any one. The story leaked out and we were simply fired."

"It's all the same!" shouted father. "if you had met the president, you would have told him such things, wouldn't you? Isn't that right? Answer me."

"Yes," I answered in a small voice.

"You heard? Mother, did you hear?"

"There's nothing to worry about," said mother. "Our children are now first-rate journeymen. Whatever factory they go to, they can make money."

"Nonsense!"

"Nonsense? How is it nonsense? A change of workplace isn't bad."

"It doesn't work that way. This factory has already passed the word to others. They're all the same. There's not a factory that will hire our children. You must realize what kind of work our children have done today."

"Stop it. You're making a fuss as if these children have committed some treason."

"What?"

"Let's go."

With longish steps brother crossed the cement bridge. At the other side he lifted the unconscious drunkard and put him on his shoulders. His steps were wavering but he didn't fall. For the last few days brother hadn't been eating right. He hadn't had enough sleep either.

His tongue was inflamed and he lost his appetite. Even at night he couldn't sleep because he was so alert. Now all this was catching up with him. Brother laid the drunkard down on the wooden floor of his house. His young daughter came out rubbing her eyes and led him to his bed. We emerged from the alley and deeply inhaled the night air. We could see mother carrying father on her back. As he turned around, brother held his head with his hands.

The workers came out as usual into the small yard to kick the ball. They wouldn't turn their heads our way. At the end of twenty minutes, soaked with sweat, they flooded back into the workplace.

"What can we do?" brother muttered to himself.

"In the evening your story better be the same," said the man in the sedan.

"I won't say another word if you'll pay two hundred fifty thousand wŏn," I said.

That night this man in the sedan bought all of our neighbor's apartment rights. He paid two hundred fifty thousand wŏn and bought them all. That evening Yŏnghŭi again played the guitar in front of the pansies. Yŏnghŭi picked two pansies and put one on her guitar and the other in her hair. Without stirring she kept playing the guitar. The man offered father a cigarette.

"It's two hundred fifty thousand *wŏn*, isn't it?" asked mother.

The man's older assistant opened a black briefcase and showed them the money. He was sitting on the wooden floor and filling out the conveyance. Mother went into the other room and brought out an envelope containing the other documents and the seal. Father wrote down "Kim Puri" in the space for the seller's name on the conveyance and pressed the seal. The older man couldn't make out father's name. He couldn't have understood the painful hope that father's name signified. One at a time mother relinquished these valued items which she had been saving: the name plate slightly scratched by the kitchen knife; the order of condemnation that had led her to put down her breakfast spoon and beat her breast three times; two copies of the certified seal, which mother had had to obtain for the first time in her life in order to sell the house for this trifling price; a title transfer application which she had already signed; two copies of the household identity record on which the names and ages of our poor family members were inscribed in order. Yŏnghŭi, who was sitting in front of the pansies, hung her head. The man handed over the money. Mother moved away and sat down, shaking her head. Father took the money. He held it for exactly three seconds and gave it to mother. Mother took it with both hands.

Next morning, Myŏnghŭi's mother had her house torn down. Mother paid her the hundred fifty thousand *wŏn*. The two of them held each other's hands and couldn't speak. A pickup truck drove up the narrow alley and onto it was loaded Myŏnghŭi's mother's belongings. Myŏnghŭi's mother lifted the hem of her skirt and wiped the tears from her face.

"Oh, this compassion is a mystery to me!" said Myŏnghŭi's mother, "it makes parting so trying."

The exchange brought tears to our eyes. The pickup truck passed our house. Father lifted his right arm partway up and let it drop. In his left hand he held a book. Chisŏp's book was soiled by father's hands. Father and Chisŏp seemed to us to be like people traveling in outer space. The two of them made the circuit to the moon several times a day.

"Life is too hard," father had said. "So I've decided to go to the moon and work at an astronomical observatory. My job will be to maintain the telescope lenses. Since there's no dust on the moon it's not necessary to clean the lenses. Nevertheless a lense-keeper is needed."

"Father, do you believe it's actually possible," I asked.

"What have you learned so far?" said father. "Three centuries have passed since Newton discovered his laws. You learned it, too, didn't you? You must have learned it in grammar school. And now you talk like a man who never heard of the basic laws of the universe."

"By the way, who's going to take you to the moon?"

"Chisŏp wrote to the Johnson Space Center in Houston, America. Mr. Ross, a supervisor at the center, will answer. The year after next, we'll go to the moon with the space program specialists."

"Return the book to him, please," I said. "Also don't pay attention to what he says. He's crazy."

"Look at this picture in the book. This is Francis Bacon,[2] and that's Robert Goddard.[3] Their contemporaries called them crazy. Do you know what these crazy people have accomplished?"

"I don't know."

"You've received a sorry education in school."

"Anyway, return that book, please."

"Do you expect me to live on this planet, working hard until I die haggard and spent? You expect me to draw my last breath while thrashing about in the grips of unceasing toil, don't you?"

"Think as you like."

"Why don't you try to learn something from Chisŏp?"

"What on earth can we learn from him?"

"I've got something to show you before we hear from Mr. Ross. I'll talk to Chisŏp, and then you'll see how I will launch an iron ball."

"Nowhere?"

"No."

"If you haven't found her, what have you been doing all night?"

I picked up another pebble and threw it toward the levee. Mother was too tired to say another word. Brother gently pushed mother's back and they entered the house. The morning was quiet. Nearly a

---

[2]Francis Bacon (1561–1626): English philosopher and essayist, the author of the hitherto incomplete *The Great Instauration*, consisting of four parts, including *The Advancement of Learning* (1605), and the author of *New Atlantis* (1627), which describes a utopian community depending for its progress on collective scientific research.

[3]Robert Goddard (1882–1945): American physicist, the first to build and launch a liquid-fueled rocket.

hundred houses had been razed and only a few remained standing. We would have left a day earlier if only Yŏnghŭi hadn't run off. That was the only reason we didn't meet the condemnation deadline. The last several days of our lives in Happiness Precinct were like a nightmare. We searched high and low for Yŏnghŭi. Nobody had seen her. She had left the house without a bag. All she took with her was a broken-stringed guitar and two pansies. I picked up a slightly bigger pebble and threw it. Once again I couldn't detect any sound. The wavelets swept through the reeds. Chisŏp was walking up straight through the vacant lot where the barber shop used to be. He held in his hand some beef. Father came out to the front of the house and led him inside by the hand. Father gave the meat to mother in the kitchen. The inside of the kitchen was filled with smoke. Brother was on his knees at the hearth starting the fire. Wiping the tears from his eyes he got up to stoke the fire with wood. Mother came outside to dry her eyes. For several days we had been splitting and burning the wood from Myŏnghŭi's house. Brother split the main room beams from Myŏnghŭi's house, pushed them into the hearth, and came out of the kitchen. He smelt of smoke. Father let loose a shallow cough. Father and Chisŏp didn't say a word. Chisŏp read to father from the book he had lent him. Father said that Chisŏp had been in jail. According to father he had been innocent. He was sitting on the edge of the floor, reading. Brother and I stood by the cement wall and looked out. Since the houses had been demolished, the precinct office was now visible from where we stood. Beyond could be seen the bright and clean residential area. There was a supermarket on the right side of the thoroughfare. One could see the bakery where Yŏnghŭi used to work. She looked so pretty when brother and I saw her through the bakery window. No one would have believed that she was the daughter of a dwarf. We never did find her.

In the kitchen there was an aroma of beef soup. Beef was being broiled as well. Mother cleaned the meal table with a dishcloth. People were thronging before the precinct office. They held sledgehammers. They were coming across the vacant area toward our house. I locked the gate. Mother set the table. Brother brought the table and placed it on the floor. Brother was worrying about me. It was useless to worry. I wouldn't have stirred even if they had struck me over the head with their sledgehammers. Father was the first to pick up the spoon. Chisŏp, sitting next to father, picked up the spoon. Mother, seated on the edge of the floor, drank her soup. Brother and I mixed rice with our soup. A knock was heard at the gate. We continued our meal. We wondered where Yŏnghŭi might have been and what kind of meal she might be having. Here at this table was present all the hours of bondage from our ancestors' generations to ours. If it was penetrated with the blade of a knife, from it would flow blood and tears with the sound of meek laughter and shallow coughing. The people outside were now surrounding the house. They crushed the cement wall. Only holes could be seen at first and then the wall crumbled. Dust rose. Mother turned to face us. Quietly we continued our meal. Father took some broiled beef and put it in our rice bowls. Those outside watched us through the cement dust. They didn't come inside. They stood waiting for us to finish. Mother went into the kitchen and brought some rice water. Father and Chisŏp drank it. Mother picked up the meal tray after we finished drinking. I went down to open the locked gate. Mother went outside with the meal tray. Brother followed carrying on his shoulder a bundle in which he had packed a blanket and some clothes. The men with sledgehammers on the other side of the crushed wall silently watched us. One by one we brought out our belongings that mother had bundled up. Mother went into the kitchen and brought out the strainer, kitchen knife, and cutting board. Father came out last. He carried his tool satchel on his shoulder. In front of the men with sledgehammers stood a man holding a piece of paper and ballpoint pen. He looked at father. Father raised his hand, pointed at the house, and turned to go. The men started demolishing the house. They went at it all at once. Mother sat with her back turned and only listened to the sound of the house crumbling. When they smashed the north wall, the roof caved in. Dust rose as the roof fell. The men who stepped back then started in on the walls that were left standing. It was easily finished. They dropped their hammers and wiped off the sweat. The man filled in something on the paper. Chisŏp gave father the book he had been holding. He walked toward the man.

"What have you done just now?" Chisŏp asked. Only after several seconds did he understand Chisŏp's words. He said, "You were supposed to have demolished it by the thirtieth, weren't you? The deadline is past. We just did our job according to the law. No need to talk any further."

The man was about to turn away. Chisŏp hastily said:

"Do you realize what kind of work you have just ordered? For simplicity's sake let us say it was five hundred years, although it could have been more than a thousand years. You've just demolished a house that took five hundred years to build. Not five years but five hundred years."

"What the hell is that five hundred years?" asked the man.

"You don't know?" asked Chisŏp in response.

"Enough, out of my way."

"You set the trap. If not you, then your superiors. Didn't you know more than a hundred households had centered their lives here? Didn't you set a trap here? Go and tell them that I struck you."

Since the man was not expecting to be hit, he didn't have a chance even to turn his head. Chisŏp's fist struck him flush in the face. The man doubled up, covering his face with his hands. Blood streamed down through his fingers. Chisŏp hit the doubled-up man again. The man fell forward onto his face. There had been no time for us to intervene. The same was true for the men with the sledgehammers. They then attacked Chisŏp. Several men all at once beat, butted, and stomped Chisŏp. It was time for brother and I to help. But father pulled us by the arms.

"Stay out of it," father said. "Let someone who knows them be the one to talk to them."

Brother and I watched while being held by father. The man got up and Chisŏp was lying on the ground as if dead. The men pulled Chisŏp to his feet. Suddenly mother cried, trembling. Chisŏp's face was soaked with blood. Blood streamed down his face. They dragged Chisŏp away. They left across the vacant lots as they had come. We could see them as they passed the precinct office and headed toward the thoroughfare. Father turned around and gave brother the book he was holding. Father walked toward them. His little shadow was close behind. I couldn't take it anymore. Sleep was beckoning. I pulled out a broken gate and lay down there on my face. Feeling the sun on my back, gradually sleep enveloped me. Except for my family and Chisŏp, the world was strange. No, that's not so. Father and Chisŏp were somewhat strange, too. I dreamed in the sunlight. Yŏnghŭi was throwing two pansies into the waste water from the factory.

III

The cuckoo clock in the living room struck four. It was the first time I passed such a long night. How long my seventeen years have been compared to one night. And yet my seventeen years are like nothing compared to the long period of our ancestors' existence which my big brother once computed. This long stretch of time is the same. Father once said that he would go to the moon and work in an observatory. On the moon one can see the Coma constellation clearly.[4] According to Chisŏp's book, that constellation is located five billion light-years away from the moon.

My seventeen years cannot be compared with the five billion years it takes light to reach that constellation. Even a thousand years would amount to a few grains of sand on the shores of time. Five billion years is like an eternity to me. There is no way for me to feel eternity. If eternity is somehow related to death, then I might be able to understand a little something about eternity through death.

Whenever I think of death a certain scene appears to me. It is a desert horizon. At twilight, there is wind mixed with sand. At the end of the horizon line I stand, naked, my legs are slightly apart and I pull my arms inward. My head is halfway forward and my breasts are covered with my hair. If I close my eyes and count to ten, I disappear. Only the windy, gray horizon remains. This is death as I know it. Such death cannot but be related to eternity. Our life is gray. Only after I left my house could I see it from outside. The house and the people in it, shrouded in gray, appeared to me to be reduced in size. My family members were eating and talking forehead to forehead. I couldn't make out what they were saying as their voices were small.

Mother, who was reduced even smaller than father's actual figure, paused on her way to the kitchen and looked up into the sky. Even the sky is gray. I didn't run away from home hoping to liberate myself. Leaving the house couldn't make me free. From outside I was able to have a better look at my family.

It was horrible. Like my two older brothers, I had quit school. Just prior to that I read the following in one of my supplementary primers: "Water, water, everywhere, Nor any drop to drink."[5] An old mariner who had lost his ship was drifting out at sea. In the midst of water he was dying of thirst. I thought of the old mariner as from outside I observed my reduced house and family, shrouded in gray. I felt like the old mariner.

---

[4]Coma constellation: Coma Berenices, a constellation in the northern sky near Boötes and Leo containing the Coma cluster of galaxies.

[5]Refers to "The Rime of the Ancient Mariner" by Samuel Taylor Coleridge (1772–1834), lines 121–122.

I got up from bed. The bed shook but I didn't concern myself with it. He was sleeping soundly. Just in case I opened the lid of the bottle one more time, placed the handkerchief over it, and shook the bottle. I pressed lightly over his nose and mouth with the handkerchief and counted silently to ten. I recalled how it started.

He was standing next to me while the old man was filling out the conveyance. He still stood beside me when father signed his name and pressed his seal. Ever since I went to the precinct office on the day the order of condemnation was issued, he watched me. He left my side when mother brought out the items which she had been zealously saving.

As he turned around he lightly touched my breast with his right hand. Mother was holding the money with both hands. No one saw me leaving the house. I restrained myself from crying. I slipped through the alley along the levee and made my way to the precinct office. Where people had clustered during the day there were now none.

His sedan was parked in front of the bulletin board. I stood by the sedan and waited for him. Surrounded by his men, he came down talking loudly. He stopped abruptly upon seeing me. The old man handed him his black briefcase. He sent his men away and walked toward me.

"Have you been waiting for me?" he asked.

I nodded.

"Why?"

"Is ours there too?" I asked, pointing at the black briefcase.

"It probably would be."

"I've come for it."

"What are you going to do?"

I didn't know what to say.

"What will you do? I've got to go."

"That's our house," I barely managed to say. He looked down at me.

"Not anymore," he said. "I paid for it."

He took out his key and opened the car door. He put the black briefcase in the car and got inside. I banged the window with the palm of my hand. He opened the opposite door. Only as I got into his car did I realize that I had brought my guitar with me. He took the guitar and placed it in the back seat. He turned around in front of the precinct office. I half lay down on the seat to hide myself.

"Sit up straight," he said.

The car had already left Happiness Precinct and was on its way out of Paradise District. He looked at my face while driving. When the car stopped at a red light, he took the pansy from my hair and smelt it. He stuck the little flower in his left pocket.

"My house is in Yŏngdong," he said. "I'll drop you off in a while, you go back to your house."

"No," I said. "There's no house to return to."

"What will you do then? You mean to steal this briefcase?"

"I'm thinking about it."

"All right," said he. "I'll give you work to do. You'll have to obey me well. Otherwise I'll kick you out. The fact is I've had my eye on you because you are pretty. But you must remember that you can't say no to me under any circumstances. Then I'm willing to pay you more than any of my employees. Think it over and make up your mind."

For me there was nothing to think over. Big brother said that it took a thousand years to build our house. I didn't understand what he meant. Of course it had been, in a way, exaggerated. But it wasn't false. When I was seventeen, mother made an effort to teach me what the traditional duties of a woman were with respect to her family and home. Chastity was one of the values she repeatedly emphasized. Mother took the position that it was unforgivable for me even to think about a man in the dark.

She would have hanged herself if only she had known the sort of life I led after leaving the house. He was kind to me. First he had dresses made for me, quite a number at one time. I had to make myself pretty for him. His apartment was in Yŏngdong. So was his office. In his office I clipped newspaper articles concerning housing for his scrapbook. Every day I did the same work. When there were no articles on housing, I passed the time reading other items in the newspaper. His own advertisement was also in the paper every day. "Chamsil is everyone's concern. Anybody wanting to consult about a Chamsil apartment, please call immediately. Ŭna is your faithful Real Estate Company." There was also an ad for sale of residential lots. "A rapid development area, adjacent to Sinch'onho bridge, Chamsil district, and Kangnam 1st Street. Take advantage of this opportunity to buy a moderately priced dream house—Ŭna Housing."

He was a terribly determined person. At twenty-nine, there was nothing he couldn't do. The apartment rights he had bought from our neighborhood were for him only a relatively small number. He bought virtually all the rights in the entire redevelopment area. He also had quite a lot of land in the Yŏngdong area.

His family was rich. He told even me that this business of his was merely a small-scale exercise. He was a man who was destined to join his father's company and do big things. When he came in at night, he used to call home. At the other end of the line his father was sitting. He almost sat at attention as he talked to his father on the phone. After the call he meticulously checked the ledger kept by his employees. He sold the apartment rights purchased in our neighborhood for four hundred fifty thousand *wŏn*. He wouldn't take less.

It was beyond my imagination. I had thought he would only have made ten or twenty thousand *wŏn* profit on them. While he sat working in the living room, the maid put the evening meal on the table and waited for him to sit down.

It was a maid his mother had sent. He gave the maid extra money. It was an arrangement to prevent the family from hearing about me. She had moved out since I came. As promised in the beginning I never said no to him. No one could say no to him. I was living with someone from an entirely different world. Even from birth we were different. Mother told me that my first cry sounded like a shriek. My first breath might have been as hot as hell-fire. While still in mother's womb, I was insufficiently nourished. His birth was different.

My first breath was as if acid dripped into a wound while his was comfortable and sweet. Our development was different as well. He had plenty to choose from. My two brothers and I had never had anything except what was given to us. Mother dressed us in pocketless clothes. He grew stronger as time went by, while on the contrary we became weaker. He wanted me. He wanted and wanted me again. Every night I slept in the nude. Every night I dreamt. In my dream my brothers found work at another factory. In a day father made several trips to the moon. Half asleep I used to hear mother's voice.

"Yŏnghŭi, what are you doing now after leaving us?"

Then I answered, "Our apartment rights are in his safe. They are on the very bottom of the stack. They haven't been sold yet. Before they are sold, I'm going to bring them home. I found out the combination to his safe."

"Who asked you to do such a thing? Get up now and put your clothes on."

"No, mother."

"We've decided to go to Sŏngnam. Hurry and get up."

"No."

"One of your great-grandmother's sisters was found, a naked corpse, in an irrigation ditch. You know why? Because she shared the bed of the landlord. His wife beat her to death."

"Mother, I'm different."

"Same."

"Different."

"Same."

"Different!"

"You'll ruin yourself because of it. For a young girl, you like it."

"That's right. I like it."

"Damn you!"

It was the middle of the night when I opened my eyes at the close of the bitter struggle. He was sleeping deeply and was not about to wake up. My body smelt of his semen. He liked me. He liked young me. He liked me completely. Therefore I didn't suffer from moral guilt.

I took our apartment rights from his safe. In his safe were also money, a pistol, and a knife. I took out some money and the knife. I pictured father crouching underneath the telescope on the moon. Father might already have seen the Coma constellation five billion light-years distant. Five billion years is to me an eternity. Of eternity I have not much to say. Even a single night was too long for me. I took the handkerchief from his face and closed the medicine bottle. I was very thankful for the medicine. The first night it had anesthetized my agonized body and allowed me to sleep. So I couldn't see his face. I opened the briefcase and checked the contents. Everything was in order. I dressed myself.

I felt dizzy. I opened the door and went out to the living room. I didn't look at him. There was nothing else I needed to take. My old clothes, the shoes with worn heels, and the broken-stringed guitar which my big brother had bought for me were no longer in this house. I took a deep breath and opened the gate. Once outside I pushed the gate back. The gate locked itself as it shut.

It was long before daybreak. In front of the apartment, I waited a little and caught a taxi. The taxi's headlights were burning as it raced through the empty Yŏngdong streets. I closed my eyes from dizziness. I stopped the driver as we crossed the Third Han River Bridge. When I stepped out of the taxi, the cool air cleared my head. As I held the rail I looked down the flowing river which reflected the dim morning

light. The driver got out too and leaned on the rail. Smoking a cigarette in that stance he looked at me. The day began to brighten. During the winter father had spent convalescing, mother went out to
work. Now I caught sight of the morning colors that mother saw
every morning when she left for work. A sharp metallic sound could
be heard from the pebble-dredging boats. The taxi I was in drove
through Namsan tunnel and sped across downtown. Sinners were still
sleeping. These streets were merciless. I got off in Paradise District. I
passed my time walking the streets and alleys in Paradise District. At
last I entered a tea room and drank some tea. While drinking tea, I
took out the conveyance which had father's seal upon it and tore it
up. When we were young this whole area had been vegetable fields. I
finished my tea and walked along the streets that had once been
paved over the fields. There was no need to wander about anymore. I
walked straight toward the Happiness Precinct office. The precinct
office was already crowded. The construction desk clerk glanced at
me as I went to stand at the end of the line. He interrupted his work
and glared at me piercingly.

"Isn't that the dwarf's daughter?"

The office workers' whispering sound was audible even to me. I
stood rigidly and waited for my turn. Sounds of seals being stamped,
name plates being dropped, and laughter could be heard. I took out
our name plate. I could feel with the tip of my fingers the scratch
mother had made with the kitchen knife. It was my turn.

"What's up?" asked the construction desk clerk. "You know your
family has moved, don't you?"

"Yes," I said, "I came because I need a demolition confirmation."

"What do you need it for?"

He made an expression as if he couldn't understand.

"Didn't you sell your apartment rights? You already sold them off,
and now what do you need such a thing for?"

"The man in the sedan bought them," said the man sitting next to
the clerk.

For several seconds, I stood still.

"Which side are you on?" I said. "We are the ones who ought to get
into an apartment."

"I suppose you're right."

The clerk looked at the man beside him. They just shrugged their
shoulders.

"Do you have the documents?"

"What documents? She's the proper party to make this application. All she needs is the order of comdemnation and the name plate. If you have them, we have nothing to say."

I presented the order of condemnation and the name plate. The two men took them and compared them with the records. One of the men threw the name plate into a large container. Inside there were many plates. With a light metallic sound, our name plate came to rest on top of them. The construction desk clerk handed me the forms. I filled them out.

My hands trembled as I filled in father's name, date of birth, and the date of construction of the unauthorized building. I couldn't write well. I told myself it was because I had become weak. As big brother said, I was prone to cry from childhood. My tears obscured my vision so I stopped writing for a second and then went on. I pushed the building demolition confirmation form in front of the construction desk clerk.

"I don't know the date of demolition," I said.

As he looked me in the eyes, he said,

"Where were you?"

I didn't say. He filled in October 1, 197x.

"You don't know where you family's gone, do you?"

"No."

"Haven't you heard about it?"

I grabbed the edge of the desk where I stood because I felt the strength in my legs failing. The man beside the clerk gave him a nudge. The clerk pressed small seal next to the space where it said "Above Facts Confirmed" and passed the form back to the chief sitting in the interior of the office. I felt my forehead as I stepped out of the line. A light fever stirred inside me. From inside the chief gestured to me. He pressed his seal above "Precinct Chief, Happiness Precinct 1." Before he handed it over to me he took me to the window. He pointed at the area beyond the thoroughfare where a vineyard once was.

"It's the third from the top," he said. "Go and see the woman living there. She's Yun Sinae. She's an old acquaintance of your father. She used to come here several times a day looking for you."

"I've seen her before," I said, "I have to drop by the district office and then the housing corporation. I'll go and see her after I'm through."

"She'll tell you about everything," he said. "She's kind."

Number	458 Existing Unauthorized Building Demolition Confirmation					Effective date
						Immediate
Applicant	Name	Kim Puri	I.D.#	123456-123456	Birthdate	3-11-1929
	Address	46-1839, Happiness Precinct, Paradise District, Seoul				
	Perm. Add.	276 Happiness St., Happiness Township, Paradise County, Kyŏnggi Province				
	Location of Demolition Building	Same as present address				
	Status	Owner of house (o) Lessee ( )				
	Date of Demolition	————— ———, 197x	Date of Construction of Unauthorized Building		5-8-1968	
Purpose	Apartment Acquisition					
	Please Confirm the Above Facts. October 7, 197x Applicant: Kim Puri					
	Above Facts Confirmed. October 7, 197x Precinct Chief, Happiness Precinct 1					

"Thank you."

I came outside after saying good-bye. The clerks had been watching me while I talked with the chief. They wanted to tell me something. I couldn't stay another minute. I went to the thoroughfare and got a taxi. When we passed the supermarket, I saw the bakery. Other young people were doing the work I used to do. If I looked back then I could have seen my old neighborhood in a single glance. I resisted. I didn't dare look back. The business at the district office was easily done. I went to the building construction desk, gave them the demolition confirmation, and applied for apartment rights. As I was coming down the steps of the district office, I felt extremely dizzy. It seemed as if I had been living away from my family for several years.

He made me even weaker; since leaving home I hadn't had a comfortable night of sleep. Not only in mother's womb but also after birth I had been undernourished. Since I left home I had sat before an abundant table with him. The nourishment from it was never accumulated. It wasn't just because of the mental oppression I suffered. He offered me delicious food but only to take back the energy I had gained from it. The fact that I hadn't slept a wink the night before was also catching up with me. I only wanted to lie down some place. I would finish this business as fast as I could and go see Sinae. She would send me back to be with my family.

I retraced the streets I had traveled at dawn. I passed through the

Namsan tunnel and crossed the Third Han River Bridge. I saw his apartment standing alone in the field. I opened the briefcase and felt for his knife inside. On the top of the ivory grip was a small bead-sized metal button. I knew that if I pushed it the blade would spring out. I stopped the car at the entrance of the housing corporation. A lot of people were moving toward the main gate. Hastily I made my way inside. Even if you didn't walk, the crowd would have carried you along. I swept toward the center of the courtyard. The brilliance of the white building was almost blinding. It seemed like a holiday. Here and there were sun-shades. I stood in the line for application forms. The clerk asked to see the receipt I had obtained at City Hall. He handed me an application form. As I left I read over the lease contract. Among the conditions were that "only the prospective tenant may enter into the lease, that the lease may not be assigned to a third person, and that the lease rights may not be used as security for any bond." It was a moot provision. I filled in father's name, address, and identification number on the application form which contained that provision. Again my hands trembled. My legs felt sapped of strength and I wanted to sit down. I moved to the next line after I completed the application. I was the only person in the line who was from the redevelopment area. The clerk sitting at the desk at the head of the line was asking everybody, "You bought this, didn't you?" even though he knew the answer was yes.

To this inquiry, people were hesitant as if they didn't know how to answer.

"You bought this, didn't you?" the clerk asked me as well.

"Yes, I did!" thus I would have answered him if I hadn't been ill. He was unkind and abrasive. I was sick. I said nothing. The clerk stapled the application form, the receipt from City Hall and the copy of the family records. He vigorously pressed the receipt stamp to it. As I turned around with the receipt I sought to hide myself. I went to the far side of the line and carefully looked over the front. That man was standing in front of his sedan. There he stood in the best of health. I hid my weakened body and waited for him to leave. If I had had to face him I would have killed him. Most likely he had never confronted himself with death. He knows nothing of the suffering that is the lot of humans. Nor does he know about desperation. Perhaps he never heard the sound of empty bowls being scraped, the sound of teeth chattering from bitter cold, nor seen the way arms, legs, and knees shiver uncontrollably in deep winter. He never even sensed the groans that I stifled as I received him naked whenever he wanted me. He was on the side of those who branded their fellow men with red-hot irons. I opened the briefcase and felt for the knife. I saw him waving. A man came out of the building. The two men exchanged greetings, shooks hands, and got into the car. The people parted to make way for his sedan as he drove out from the Housing Corporation yard. My eyes clouded over again with tears. There was nothing he hadn't possessed.

I followed the others to the Business Department. Inside, lines were formed once again. Feeling my forehead with my hand, I waited my turn.

"Are you unwell?" asked the clerk when it was my turn.

"I'm all right." Having said this, I gave him the documents in my hand.

The clerk had the documents approved, assigned me a number, and told me to pay at the accounting desk. A woman brought me some water. I drank it. The people at the accounting desk asked me nothing. After counting the money, they gave me a stamped receipt.

"It's over and done now!" I said.

People looked at me. Would they have known? I left the Housing Corporation building. I made it to Sinae's apartment without collapsing on the street. I looked back toward my neighborhood as I rang her bell. Our house, the neighborhood's houses, and all of them were gone. The levee was gone, likewise the brick factory smokestack and even the hill was no longer there. There was no sign that the dwarf, the dwarf's wife, the dwarf's two sons, and the dwarf's daughter had ever dwelt there. Only a wide-open lot was to be seen there. Sinae came out, and loudly calling for her daughter, quickly offered her arms in support. I couldn't even say hello.

Sinae had once helped my injured father in the same way. She and her daughter helped me into the room and put me to bed. The daughter brought me a wet towel and Sinae loosened my clothes. With the wet towel she dabbed my face, hands, and feet and covered me with a warm comforter.

"Thank you," I said.

I barely opened my eyes.

"Now, don't try to speak," said she, "I'll bring a doctor. Let's not talk about anything today."

"I'm all right," I said.

My eyes closed under their own weight.

"I simply hadn't had any sleep. I'm sleepy, that's all."

"Go to sleep, then. Sleep well."

"I brought back what they took from us."

"Good!"

"I completed the procedure."

"Good."

"You know where my family has gone, don't you?"

"Sure, I do."

"I met the head of the precinct," said I, half asleep. "He said you would tell me about everything."

"He didn't say anything else?"

"Has there been anything else?"

"Go to sleep. We'll talk when you awake."

"I don't think I can sleep until I hear."

Again I opened my eyes. Her daughter went out of the room. Soon I heard the door open. She was on her way to the hospital for a doctor. Sinae said,

"Do you know how frantically your family searched for you after you ran away? You can see from this window where your mother stood on the site of your house. At that time not only were you missing but also your father was nowhere to be found. They had to move to Sŏngnam, but your father had disappeared. What's the use of dragging the story out? Your father passed away. They found out when they demolished the brick factory smokestack. The demolition crew found your father who had fallen into the smokestack."

I couldn't get up. I lay still with my eyes closed. Like an injured bug, I was lying on my side. I couldn't breathe. I beat my chest with my hands. In front of the remnants of the house stood father. Father was short. Mother came around the corner, carrying injured father on her back. Blood was dripping from his body. I called for my brother in a loud voice. They came out. We stood in the yard and looked up at the sky. A black iron ball flew across the sky directly over our heads. Father stood, his arm uplifted, on top of the brick factory smokestack. Mother placed the meal table on the edge of the wooden floor. I heard the doctor coming in. Sinae held my hands *A a a e e e h . . .* Such a cry slowly rose from my throat.

"Don't cry, Yŏnghŭi," big brother had said. "For Christ's sake, don't cry. Somebody might hear."

I couldn't stop crying.

"Big brother, don't you ever get angry?"

"Stop, I said."
"Kill any scoundrel who calls father a dwarf."
"Right, I'll kill them."
"Without fail, kill them."
"Right, without fail."
"Without fail."

TRANSLATED BY CHUN KYUNGJA

Yi Mungu

Yi Mungu was born in 1941 in Poryŏng, South Ch'ungch'ŏng. Since his literary debut in 1966, he has published short stories, novels, children's stories, and essays. Yi is known for his satiric or sympathetic portrayal of the realities of agrarian life. The Korean farmer's predicament began in the early part of the century and intensified after the Korean War—bringing dislocation, poverty, and family tragedy. The incalculable effects of modernization include the dissolution of family and community, the corruption of moral sensibility, and the disintegration of traditional human relationships. Exploited by local officials, ineffectual government policies, and consumerism, the farmer cannot withstand the brutal impact of the industrialized world.

Thus it is the losses, rather than the gains, that modernization has brought to the farm that concern Yi Mungu. Based on twenty years of life in his native village, the following story is one of eight that constitute the *Essays on Kwanch'on* (1977). Realistic portrayal of the physical and social setting, the use of dialect, the symbolic use of objects, long sentences describing a character's state of mind—these are the hallmarks of Yi's narrative.

THE BALLAD OF KALMŎRI

There are small-town railway stations that express trains never know —country railroad stations that one could not imagine a reason for ever visiting again if one happened to stop by for some unwelcome business on one leg of an infrequent official trip.[1]

In front of the station, in "The Square" no larger than an ordinary front yard of an ordinary house, little urchins who no doubt had rarely seen any water and whose feet were black as crows would jump rope or play marbles noisily. An old villager who could never tell the time except by the passing local trains would stare longingly at the distant hills, sitting on the handle of his shovel, anticipating the bowl of rice wine he would have before going home. Beside that old man one could usually find a couple of old women selling salted persim-

---

[1]Kalmŏri (or Kwanch'on): the author's native village in Taech'ŏn, South Ch'ungch'ŏng province.

mon or steamed sweet potatoes displayed on a board across a wicker basket and a porter reclining on his tilted A-frame carrier dozing through his leisure hours. The landscape would be complete when a young man, who had been released several days ago from military service, came along with a sleek dog conspicuously different from the other fluffies of the countryside canine family and bicycled around a dozen times, obviously hoping to catch the attention of a few blossoming young girls tittering by the crowded doors of the waiting room, wayward, flirting girls who would probably take off to Seoul sooner or later to seek an unknown future. Over there the pile of coal had been abandoned for so long that it had hardened into a mass and no ordinary breeze could stir up any dust. A withered rose of Sharon that had not grown in ten years stood awkwardly alone in the middle of the platform, flanked by a couple of twisted and gnarled spindle trees. Several sacks of fertilizer formed a small heap on the floor of the warehouse that had little left to it but the roof, a warehouse that looked friendly and proper because its posts carried no slogans except the usual fire prevention warning.

The gloomy station building looked like an empty warehouse discarded after long use and surrounded by several deposits of spent coal, a place that reminded one of a forge where the smith had stowed away his bellows and tools after a morning's work, or a rice shop where the shopkeeper had gathered up the strewn grains when market day was over. But all these aspects had disappeared from the entrance to Kwanch'on village half a generation ago.

In one and a half decades a lot of things had been modernized as the town grew. This modernization was not prompted to develop the traditional virtues as at Kyŏngju or Sudŏk monastery stations,[2] nor to create a holiday atmosphere as at Namwŏn station,[3] where one would be bombarded with songs of Ch'unhyang as soon as the train arrived. This place simply had gone through a metamorphosis of concrete. The outdoor waiting "room" on the wide paved square, the blaring public address system, the bus terminal opposite the taxi pool, the pay

---

[2]Kyŏngju: ancient capital of Silla (57 B.C.–A.D. 935). Sudŏk monastery: in Yesan, South Ch'ungch'ŏng, built by Dharma Master Chimyŏng in 599. Its main hall, built in 1308, has been designated a national treasure.

[3]Namwŏn: a town at the southeastern tip of North Chŏlla. It is the putative birthplace of Ch'unhyang (Spring Fragrance), the virtuous heroine in the *Tale of Ch'unhyang*, the most famous romance of traditional Korea.

latrine, the shoeshine stall next to it, and the unbecoming clock tower built by the Rotary Club. The station had grown to a complex consisting of a six-story hotel furnished with a barbershop in the basement, a public bath, a coffee shop, and a teahouse; around it there were also five other separate teahouses, twelve houses, and nine inns all crammed in side by side.

But whatever gaudy, modern components had been thrown in, the station did not look right. There was something incongruous. It was only that the natives had been pushed out by the outsiders who had proceeded to entrench themselves, but the whole thing seemed somehow incomplete and barren even to my native eyes.

The street in front of the station was as crowded as ever on the day I was there. The street was packed, bustling, and dirty that day with people who were waiting to leave, or people who were waiting for someone to leave, or who were waiting for someone to arrive, or who came to see what happened to someone that had come to the station to wait for someone's arrival, or people who were just there for no particular reason.

That day I was one of those waiting to leave. I was just passing time waiting for the three o'clock train in the afternoon, having missed the first one because there were no seats available, although I had come early. Many local trains stopped here, but there were only two "ordinary expresses." I suddenly noticed something familiar to me, however, for my bored eyes caught sight of Shin Yongmo in the square, which was as busy as a market.

Although I myself had changed much, I recognized him at a glance, for his face still carried much of the look of childhood. A softness hovered about his eyes and cheeks and he had youthful skin although his face had been tanned and weathered for a long time as befits the son of a family who had buried ancestors on their own land that they had farmed for generations. I imagined his personality had something to do with his unchanged looks. I knew him better than anybody because we had grown up together from runny-nosed childhood to early manhood. He was the kind of person who seemed never to grow old. Nothing made him hasten for work that everybody else considered breathlessly urgent. Even if people hysterically urged him to hurry up, he was always as relaxed as a chanting monk, taking all the time in the world, eternally tarrying over every detail before finally getting ready to start thinking about the matter.

Though Yongmo's personality could be described as magnanimous and even-tempered, it could not be mistaken for discreet fortitude, and in that sense it was not necessarily any better than undependable impertinence. He took his time with everything—not because a thorough mastery of the situation led him to try to avoid mistakes nor because he was a perfectionist willing to pay any price in order to do a thing properly; he simply dallied because he did not know what was happening and therefore was never able to cope.

His parents could afford his education but gave up when he finished junior high school; they sent him to school for a diploma so they could save their own face, but they probably realized later it was nothing but a waste of money on a lost cause. Born dull-witted, he was interested in nothing and indifferent to everything, so that they had to explain ten or twenty times—and even then to no avail—what other boys could understand at a single hearing. He would forget whatever was said to him the moment he turned around. As he was slow and dull and incompetent, many nicknames trailed after him, and there was one nickname he himself did not understand—Chang Pusik. It was, of course, a coined Chinese expression meaning "Never Know," but he never knew what it meant.

When I came across him for the first time in more than ten years it was the nickname Chang Pusik that came to my mind before his real name did. I almost made the mistake but managed to remember his proper name, thus avoiding a potentially embarrassing situation at our first encounter as grown-ups.

In chestnut corduroy trousers whose color was as dark as his own complexion, and an old faded turquoise shirt with long sleeves, his appearance was so outlandish and boorish that nobody could imitate it if he tried. He recognized my voice and hurried over to me and took hold of my sleeve. He slapped me on the back saying, "We should have a quick drink or something for the occasion, but it's too early for that. I've got to meet somebody at the tearoom over there, so why don't you come along with me?"

There was no reason for me to refuse the invitation and I was somewhat curious as to what on earth might have changed his inanimate and sluggish character that he should be in such a hurry, his face distorted by despair, so I decided to go with him and see what extraordinary situation might be bedevilling him. He pushed me into a tearoom called the Station Square. It was very dark inside but the tearoom was so small that you could see everything with one glance. It seemed the person Yongmo was supposed to meet was not there yet.

As I took a corner seat, he took the chair opposite me and muttered plaintively, "Strange that we ran into each other like this, on today of all days. Why don't you ever drop by our village?"

Instead of explaining my failure to visit his village, I asked him why he was in a rush.

He lit a cigarette and said in a gravelly voice, "When things start to go wrong they really go wrong, and all sorts of troubles get you. Oh, hell."

When the waitress, who had come to take our order and was frightened by his heavily creased forehead, hesitated for a while before putting down the barley tea and turning to leave, he looked angrily at her and hollered, "Hey you, Madam No—we aren't here just to have a couple of free barley teas and go. Don't you think you should bring us something we have to pay for?"

The waitress turned back with a simper and said, "I'm not the madam of the house."

"That's why you're Madam No."

"Should I serve you coffee?"

"You don't need to *serve* anything, just bring us something to drink. Don't you have anything sweet to drink? You know that's the way we rustics like it. Why are you smiling like that? You're a wench who'd wet your panties while watching a donkey's belly . . ." Yongmo gulped the barley tea and put a new cigarette in his mouth. "Seoul is a civilized city, but this out-of-the-way place is simply choking me to death. Whether we eat as well here as those in the city is not really the problem. It is simply this *place* that drives me crazy."

"Why don't you tell me what's bothering you?" I asked him again.

He glanced over at the door as if to start talking when the door opened and a middle-aged man in a leather windbreaker outfit entered, his glasses glinting.

"He came after all. That's my wife's uncle. You wait here for a while. It won't take long."

Yongmo hastened after the Windbreaker. They sat facing each other at a brighter table by the window, several tables away from me. Seen from this distance, Yongmo seemed extremely anxious, as if driven by something, somehow restless and exhausted. His expression and manners, tangled and tortured by something he could not handle himself, were far different from those of Chang Pusik of the old days. He looked as if he had been worn down to the core. He was trying to explain his problem to his wife's uncle, but the latter would not pay any attention. The older man just sat there, reclining comfortably and audaciously lifting his chin high, exposing the unbuckled belt under his windbreaker.

"Look here, Miss Chŏng, haven't there been calls for me? Didn't anybody come to see me?" the Windbreaker asked. The waitress said there were no messages for him. "Wait a minute. Wasn't there any message from the public information office? You mean there was no telephone call from President Kang of Taeil Enterprise? That's strange. Listen—maybe there *was* a telephone call, but somebody else answered it. Strange indeed. Look here, bring me a pack of Kŏbuksŏn."[4]

Even after this torrent of big talk, the Leather Windbreaker did not pay attention to what Yongmo was saying. I surmised that the talk and attitude of the Leather Windbreaker were simply a form of bragging. He looked across whenever the door opened, glanced back whenever the telephone rang at the counter, playfully pinched the waitress's buttocks or thighs whenever she passed by. This was the typical behavior of a small-town big shot. Bending with each wind, seeking opportunities to squeeze out a profit either from the government or individuals, such characters abided by the code of "honor among thieves," helping one another so they could share their easy gains unnoticed. Like others of his ilk, the Windbreaker was the type to scoff at his inferiors while barking like a smart dog for those he considered his betters. Therefore I presumed that Yongmo's supplication would never be answered, whatever the favor he was asking for.

Nevertheless, Yongmo sputtered on and on, craning his neck and pleading. When the door opened and closed once more, the Windbreaker turned and called, "Miss Chŏng, listen, call the deputy magistrate's office and see if he's there. If he's in, tell him I'm here."

The girl at the cash register made the telephone call and said, "Mr. Ch'oe is in his office."

"Good. Tell him to wait just a while. I'm leaving now." Rising, he looked down at Yongmo and said in a voice loud enough to be heard at my table, "Anyway, there's no other way but to pay the fine and forget about it all." He left in a hurry.

Yongmo came heavy-shouldered to my table and flopped down, muttering, "I used to wonder why they said it didn't pay to cut the

---

[4]Kŏbuksŏn (literally "Turtle Ship," referring to the ironclad warship invented by Admiral Yi Sunsin during the Japanese invasion of 1592–1598) is a brand of Korean cigarettes.

weeds and trim the grave of your wife's uncle, but now I understand what that saying means." He gulped down my barley tea. "Sure, everybody's a stranger when you're in need. If he were in trouble, he'd come to me and squeal like a sow in heat, but what happens when I need help? He's full of excuses, you know . . ."

Unable to repress his exasperation, he fidgeted, cracking the knuckles of his fingers.

"What's eating you?"

He was so restless that I didn't expect him to tell me what was bothering him, but neither did I want him to think I was sulking because he wouldn't talk to me.

"I did something silly and now I face trial. That's what's bothering me so much. Damn!" Yongmo spat.

I was surprised and asked him about the trial.

"What a joke, what nonsense . . . but sometimes these things happen."

"Did you quarrel with somebody? Or is somebody not repaying a debt to you? All right, what is it? I don't believe you're the sort of person who'd get involved with somebody else's wife."

I had to keep pressing him because he just kept shaking his head, grinning stupidly. When I was done with the questions, he resumed his former expression.

"People like us, you know, who are pushed around all the time without raising a word of complaint, have no choice but to do everything we're told. If they tell me to go to prison, I go to prison. If they tell me to pay a fine, I pay a fine. . . . You know what I mean," Yongmo said in a heavy voice, his eyes downcast and his expression resigned.

"There's no problem if you win the trial. Do you have reason to believe you're going to lose?"

He was not irritated a bit by my desultory and ignorant remark; he was slow and casual as ever in his reply. "Unlike Seoul, things turn out differently here. In a countryside trial, you either become a hero by winning or go bankrupt by losing, but this time it goes neither way. It'll simply make a fool out of me. The whole thing is driving me crazy. It has completely worn me out. I barely even have the strength to walk around."

"All right, it's a human rights matter?"

"Human rights are for civilized people. Some insignificant creature like me who lives in an unknown corner of the world doesn't hope for anything more than to be left alone. I won't bother anybody in the whole wide world, so just let me live my own life, that's all I want."

Yongmo probably felt awkward about going on; he kept silent for a while. I waited patiently until he volunteered to speak. First of all, I wanted to know the heart of the matter, so that I might give him some advice, if it was something within the range of my knowledge and experience from several years of attending court trials. It took quite a while for Yongmo to open his mouth again:

"Won't you come to the court for my trial this afternoon? This is the first time I've ever stood trial, you know . . ."

"I have a ticket for the three o'clock train."

"You've got enough time, then. The court opens at thirteen hundred hours. They say thirteen hundred hours, but it means one o'clock in the afternoon, right? What the hell do they mean by thirteen hundred hours? They can say one o'clock sharp or something, can't they?"

"I haven't attended the court here, but I've heard what it's like."

Since Yongmo did not know as much about the procedures of the local court as I did, I told him what I had heard. I hoped to give him some orientation so that, embarrassed and intimidated by the proceedings, he would not incriminate himself.

These were some of the things I knew about the court:

The assizes were held once a week for one hour from one o'clock in the afternoon on Wednesdays. The judge from the district court stationed at a nearby village would come by the noon local train, hold the trials, and go back by the three o'clock ordinary express. Civil or criminal cases were handled together through summary judgments. One of the peculiarities of this touring court was that there was no prosecutor or attorney present. The reason was not because there were no prosecutors, but because the cases were not so serious or important as to require their legal opinions. The variety of the cases, however, ranging from violence, misfeasance, embezzlement, larceny, and rape to adultery, matched that of big cities, although there were none relating to robbery, murder, or violation of curfew. The cases most often dealt with in this court were adultery and monetary transactions. This I had learned from a Mr. Nam who had worked here as a court reporter for thirty years.

When I finished this explanation, he said, "But people aren't treated like decent human beings in this damned place. My case, for instance, shows that those who are supposed to know law are the very ones who mock it. Just imagine, I don't know what on earth I did wrong, but who is ever going to listen to me? If you really don't know anything about anything, that's fine. But those who know something, they know all the tricks because they also know their ways out." He slammed the table with his clenched fist in exasperation. The metal ashtray, wrinkled as a walnut shell, jumped, spraying cigarette ash, but he was too irritated to notice it.

"They say when things start going wrong, even a fish'll bite your cock. This whole matter is really getting to me."

I could understand why he was so upset when he told me the trouble he was in. After simmering down, Yongmo explained his situation clearly enough for me to comprehend the whole picture.

Yongmo's family left Kwanch'on when the silt moor in front of the village was transformed into rice paddies. The waterway connecting the reservoir and the reclaimed land split his house in the middle. They would not have left if it had just been a matter of removing the house, but it was virtually impossible to maintain their livelihood when what little farming land and rice paddies they had next to the house were also cut off and flooded. They just had to accept what was offered them as compensation for the lost land and leave. The nominal compensation would not have helped them much even if they had received it in one payment, but it was paid in bits and pieces over a period of a year.

Yongmo's father, whose unyielding and dogged thrift was well known among the neighboring villages, did not waste a single penny of that piecemeal payment. But he had to move back to a remote hamlet surrounded by the sky and the woods to procure with that money as much farming land as he had lost. The compensation had been far less than the actual market value. That was why Yongmo had moved to Slow Village, where neither electricity nor even trucks had reached. There he had buried his parents, and there he still lived.

Slow Village was and always had been a community as large as a puppy's forehead, consisting of fifteen thatched hovels scattered at the foot of a hill. So remote and isolated was the village that nobody of any significance ever showed up there and, Yongmo said with a snicker, life was bearable because no petty officials ever annoyed them. Individual huts were cut off from one another by the sharp curves and corners of the road, so that much of the area was untrod by human beings all year round. So the woods were populated by many creatures like badgers, raccoon dogs, weasels, and lynx as well as birds such as eagles, hawks, and owls. And wild pigeons and pheasants were so numerous that you grew exhausted just looking at them. The crops would be seriously damaged if they left all those creatures unchecked. The villagers used to suffer damage from sparrows and field rats, but ever since wildlife preservation was ordered here too, the biggest nuisance was the pheasant.

But nobody seemed to care about the damage done by these birds. A couple of casually installed traps or snares would not have helped much, and everybody was too busy with their own work to bother sitting down and thinking about this problem.

It was last market day that Yongmo unwittingly got himself into trouble. That was four days ago, in the morning. Like everybody else in Slow Village, Yongmo came to the market every market day and spent the whole day even if he had no business to conduct there. However busy they might be, the villagers always found excuses to go to the market, such as sharpening the hoe blade or fastening the sickle slit. When no such petty excuse was available, they simply said they had to find out the current market price for crops or poultry. Some of them gave no reason, but just slung on the empty A-frame carrier and went.

Yongmo went to the market that day because the weather was at last warming up enough to begin melting the frozen earth even in the shade. Nothing would have gone wrong if he had listened to his wife's advice. When he was putting on his shoes, his wife, who was putting beans in a jar to grow sprouts, had said in the gloom of the room:

"What are you going to the market for when you haven't bought a bowl of pickled shrimp all winter? Why don't you repair the rake handle instead or split that half-rotten stump? We don't have even a handful of tinder to boil the fodder."

"But I've got to see somebody who works in town."

He told a lie so that he could go to the market. Since he hoped to get back in time to do some chores, Yongmo walked so fast that his legs hurt. He had barely reached the top of Tall Hill, where he could overlook the mill built by Han Namsong, a Vietnam veteran, when he saw a boy going down the hill ahead of him, carrying a red pheasant as big as himself under his arm. Even at this distance, he could tell that the boy had just caught the pheasant because its tail feather was straight. Yongmo thought he might try to catch one, too, and enjoy a delicious roasted pheasant, but forgot all about it after a few paces.

Down the hill was a shallow stream and a shoal where the flowing water did not freeze all winter. He could cross it without taking his shoes off because there was a loose bridge made of several decaying alder boughs. Yongmo crossed first the shoddy bridge, then the rice paddy dikes blackened by fire that children had set to burn the dry winter grass, and reached the open road. At last he felt he was somewhere near a human community. He heard the sputtering of the motor at Han's mill, the noisy twittering of sparrows clustering on the sagging branches of the poplar next to the mill, and the muttering of the vendors hurrying on their way to market in twos and threes.

Cho Sunman, who had come from Slow Village to sell hulled rice, and O Sugil of Mound Village, who probably wanted to sell several bags of rice, were in front of the mill, laughing and chatting with the boy Yongmo had seen earlier. O Sugil greeted Yongmo first.

"Where're you going?"

"I was bored and wanted to see if anything's happening out here," Yongmo said, approaching them.

Cho Sunman composed himself and asked, "Heading for the market?"

"What business would I have at the market in the morning? Just thought I might fill my lighter . . ."

The boy bowed to him and Yongmo recognized Sŏngmun, the son of Ko Haksŏng in Upper Village. The boy had the pheasant under his arm.

"Where did you get it? Caught the bird yourself?" Yongmo asked.

"The boy just wanted to try his luck with the snare and found the bird strangled to death in the noose this morning," O explained for the child.

"Then where're you taking it? Shouldn't you be roasting it for your ailing father?" Yongmo said reproachfully.

O said apprehensively, "Haksŏng isn't well yet? What's wrong with him? He's been sick for almost a month."

And O, stroking the pheasant, pleaded for the boy, "He's too poor to afford any medicine. Did your father ask you to sell it for tobacco money?"

"I don't know if he's recovering or getting worse because I haven't visited him often . . .," Yongmo said and asked Sŏngmun, "Did your father tell you to sell it?"

The boy said yes.

"How much can he get for the bird?" Cho asked.

"Who knows?" O tilted his head as if lost in thought.

"I won't sell it for a penny less than three thousand *wŏn*," Sŏngmun bluffed.

"Well, it's a good bird but I wonder if anybody would pay that much to eat it . . .," Yongmo muttered vaguely. When he left for the market again, Sŏngmun tagged along after him.

It was just before they entered the town that Yongmo took the pheasant from the boy's hand. He thought the child was too young to strike a good deal and wanted to help him get as much money as possible for the bird.

Clasping the pheasant by its shoulder joints, he strutted into the market. He decided to sell it to anybody interested and willing to pay properly so that he could send the boy home quickly. He went directly to the poultry shop area. As usual there were all sorts of piglets, goats, chickens, ducks, puppies that had been forcibly weaned, and kittens as small as mice. Yongmo went there first not because he expected somebody might want the pheasant but because he always dropped in there first whenever he went to the market. It seems he was more interested in the fluttering or squirming creatures on the ground than the pheasant he was holding.

After making the rounds in the poultry shop area, he was about to enter the cattle market.

"Is it for sale?" somebody spoke up beside him.

Yongmo turned around with a start to see a middle-aged man in an ordinary chestnut-colored windbreaker and dark blue trousers. He looked somewhat familiar so Yongmo guessed this man must be running a shop or an eatery somewhere in the market. Deciding it would be better to bargain with someone he knew even slightly than with a total stranger, Yongmo said in an amiable voice, as he showed the pheasant to the man, "Sure, it's caught this morning and is still fat and nice. Feel its weight yourself. Quite heavy, eh?"

Studying the pheasant this way and that, the man murmured, "I wonder if you caught it with poison . . ."

Yongmo said promptly, "Caught by snare. You can't use poison these days. It's dangerous to eat a poisoned bird, you know."

The man nodded and said, as he pushed Yongmo's back, "Let's go over there."

Stepping out to the road in a flurry, Yongmo looked back at the poultry shops and faltered. Noticing that everyone was staring at him fixedly, he had an odd feeling that something was wrong. He still did not realize, however, that the something was happening to himself; he simply thought he had found a good customer. As he came out onto the road, he looked back, for he vaguely felt he had lost Sŏngmun.

Surely he had found the perfect buyer, Yongmo thought as he looked around for the boy, but the child was bright enough to sense the danger and had run away. The man nudged Yongmo and said, "What are you up to? You should be grateful that I'm trying to save your face."

Now suddenly realizing who the man was, Yongmo felt the whole world sinking under his feet. But he said tentatively, "What is this? Don't push. . . . I've got nothing to do with this. This pheasant belongs to somebody else."

"Let's go and talk about it."

"You got it wrong. Why are you doing this to me without listening to what I've got to say?"

"I think you're too decent a person to tell a lie. I've been watching you the whole time."

"Oh, no, you're making a big mistake. I got nothing to do with that pheasant. A schoolboy from our village caught it, and I was just trying to sell it for him."

"It's nothing serious, you know, so let's go and have a talk. Come with me."

"Why are you taking an innocent person away?"

"Do you think I'm bothering an innocent person because I've got nothing better to do? Look, do you want every bone in your body broken to pieces and scattered in this marketplace? Aren't you old enough to understand what I am saying, you bastard? Don't ever try to argue with me. You should know it's wrong to catch something you're told not to. Are you trying to con me with some story about a child? You son of a bitch . . ."

Yongmo barely managed to hold himself straight as the man slapped him with both hands alternately in a flash. He realized it would not help him a bit to deny anything now. People gathered around them several deep. Noticing a few familiar faces among the onlookers, Yongmo hung his head. He decided it would be better to plead his case privately, where nobody was around.

He followed the man submissively. It had been wrong of him not to think of the consequences. Instead, he had simply admired the boy for catching the bird, and had tried to sell it to provide tobacco money for the child's father. And he should have guessed that detectives would be planted in the poultry shops and cattle market where pickpockets were rampant on market days. But it was no use regretting things now.

The other detectives called the man Officer Ch'oe. He was in plain clothes because it was Sunday and he was off duty. He had been summoned to the poultry shop area not to round up pickpockets but because of an urgent request by the cattle dealers guild which was complaining that a lot of local people were selling dead chickens, causing disease to spread from the poultry shops to the whole market. Yongmo found this out when he overheard the policemen talking among themselves.

Yongmo was taken to the police box between the agricultural cooperative building and the branch office of a bank in front of the railroad station. Probably because the market was open today, there were two uninformed policemen in the office, even though it was Sunday.

The office, with its tiny stove, was colder than the outside, and Yongmo felt his elbows grow cold as his knees began to shake. He sat down opposite Officer Ch'oe and put his resident certificate and reservist card on the desk between them as he was told to.

After confirming his domicile of record, present address, name in full, date of birth, residence registration number, and occupation, the police officer asked, "When did you catch it?"

Caught off guard, Yongmo replied in spite of himself, "Must have been around nine in the morning because it was right after breakfast."

"Did you catch it with a trap? What kind of trap was it?"

"You see, that is . . ."

"Just answer my questions. You couldn't have used a rattrap, so what kind of trap was it?"

"You see, you got it all wrong."

"What did I get wrong? How many traps do you have? You are a professional poacher equipped with proper tools. Now how many have you caught so far?"

"Sir," he said, "you've got it all wrong."

"You'd better behave yourself when I'm trying to be nice to you. It'll work better this way. You don't have to complicate things. Everybody knows that wild birds and animals are protected by law. . . . Schoolchildren are placing bird nests in the woods while you're poaching pheasants and whatnot. You'll have a rather hard time if you don't confess. You won't be going home for quite a while. You'll be imprisoned for at least six months."

"The whole thing is just crazy, sir. You saw what happened with your own eyes. A little boy was following me. You saw him. That child is the son of Ko Haksŏng, who lives in our village, and he's the one who caught the bird. I simply . . ."

"That boy is your son."

"Listen, he is . . ."

"You don't realize what you have done, do you? I don't believe it, I just don't believe it. How can you incriminate your own son? You're simply impossible. . . . Bastard, you stand up. I said stand up."

Next moment he was punched and thrown down, the back of his head hitting the wall. The heel of the officer's shoe kicked his thigh, stamped on his abdomen, ground into his side, trampled his buttocks, and then moved up to the shoulder. This was the first time in the more than ten years since Nonsan boot camp that he had been treated like this.

The other officers chimed in:

"How can a human being blame his own crime on his young child? That guy needs a lesson."

When Yongmo managed to raise himself, straighten the chair, and sit down, Officer Ch'oe softened his expression and said, "Mr. Shin Yongmo, let's handle this matter in a way easier for both of us. Do you understand what I mean? Whether you're guilty or not, whether you should be punished or not—those things the judge will decide according to the law. I am responsible for investigation and nothing else. There's no need to beg me for leniency, because I can't help you there. Nor is it wise of you to try to deceive me so brazenly. You can't fool me, you know. You don't really think you can, do you? I have a wife and children, too, so I fully understand you have your own reasons and maybe I can sympathize with you. That is, if you behave yourself, I can show you some favor accordingly. You understand that? You know why? I'm a human being too, you see. That is, I am not qualified to decide if you're innocent or guilty. Neither can I decide to punish you or not. But I may be able to reduce the charge to a lighter one and perhaps even lessen the sentence. That's what I mean. Do you understand what I mean, Mr. Shin Yongmo?"

"Sure, I understand," Yongmo replied, hardly aware of what his rash answer meant. Once the written deposition was made, it was too late to try and insist on what was true or deny what was not.

Besides, Officer Ch'oe casually remarked while writing the statement:

"Mr. Shin Yongmo, it's truly regrettable that we came to know each other under these unsavory circumstances. But this is not the last day of our lives, so we can consider it an occasion to begin our friendship. I hit you a while ago despite myself because I was so upset. But I didn't do it out of hatred for you. It's just that I have a terrible temper. But we come across all sorts of situations in our lives, don't we? Please don't hold a grudge against me. Just tell yourself you've had an uplifting experience. This kind of case is subject to severe punishment, as you should know from reading newspapers, listening to the radio, or watching television newscasts. So you should be properly arrested and booked. But I have decided to believe that this was your first offense, and out of special consideration I'll send this case to the summary court. Ask yourself. How much do you suppose you'd like sleeping in jail in this freezing weather? You've been very fortunate, and you should thank your lucky stars that you met a nice person like me."

It sounded like things were going in his favor, so Yongmo could do nothing but parrot thank you to the police officer, who asked him to read the deposition and seal it with his thumb impression. Yongmo meekly followed Officer Ch'oe's instructions.

"Suspect Shin Yongmo resides at the above-mentioned abode, earning his livelihood by agriculture on a confined space of terrain. Seeking methods to protect his crops in connection with damage committed by pheasant to said crops, the suspect attempted to capture the above-mentioned pheasants by utilizing contraptions, which he installed in a corner of the suspect-owned barley garden. This resulted in the capture of one head of pheasant at approximately 0900 hours on the third day of this month, and the suspect, who had been in pain of monetary need, schemed to sell the illegally acquired above-mentioned article in this town on the occasion of the market day, thus purposefully violating the law concerning preservation of wild animals. . . ."

What Yongmo read went on something like that. Officer Ch'oe told him to go home when it was almost suppertime and reminded him to be present at the summary court at thirteen hundred hours sharp Wednesday. As soon as he was released, Yongmo went to see every acquaintance in town. Despite such offical slogans as "elimination of social absurdities" or "renovation of administrative operations," he believed oiling with a little money would smooth things. He wanted to avoid appearing in court even if the oiling would cost more than the fine, for he knew there was still a possibility that he could be arrested in court immediately after the trial. But none of the few persons he went to see would lend him any money, even though it was market day. They did not say so outright, but it was obvious that they did not want to give a penny to someone who might never be able to pay it back. If they could not lend the money, he pleaded, please go talk to Officer Ch'oe and persuade him to drop the case, but nobody would listen to him. He had hoped the police officer would reconsider sending the case to the assize if someone he knew would plead Yongmo's case hard enough. But people showed not the least concern for what they considered none of their business. His father's cousin, who had the same surname as Yongmo and had for the past three years been running an eatery that sold dog's meat soup in summer and "hangover broth" in winter, shook his head claiming that he was being harassed enough as it was. He feared that any involvement in such a questionable matter might force him to close his shop. Another cousin, by a maternal aunt, owned an automobile parts shop and showed much the same attitude. It seemed they did not want to squander the authorities' favor on such a trivial problem, since such favors could be saved for a much more important matter in the future. His wife's uncle—he of the windbreaker, who headed the local circulation office for a newspaper—was no exception. He had promised to talk to the officer and let Yongmo know the outcome of the interview. But when they met at the Station Square teahouse, on the day of the trial, he simply told Yongmo to take it easy.

"Since it's already been transferred to the assize, you'd better behave yourself before the judge and don't talk any nonsense, understand? The officer and I are of the same family name, and we must remain on good terms. If anything goes wrong, it means trouble for both of us, so there's no other way but to pay the fine and forget all about it."

The man in the windbreaker and glinting glasses left without even paying for his tea, giving as an excuse a meeting with the deputy magistrate. Exasperated, Yongmo mimicked his speech mannerisms. Apparently he had resolved to trust his luck—not because his wife's uncle told him to, but because it seemed best for his own future. Perhaps he was afraid of possible retaliation if he denied the contents of the deposition. It was Yongmo's belief that life was hard if you were on bad terms with anybody in a confined community like this.

When Yongmo finished his story, I hoped he would have courage enough to reveal the truth hidden in the shadows of a lie born of intimidation. But that was too much to expect from him. Still I wanted to advise him because I myself was the kind of person who did not have enough courage to speak out freely, and I sympathized with him very deeply.

I told him truth is always the most sublime thing in the world, but it can occasionally, in certain situations, suffer temporarily from the outrages of lies. Therefore, those who know the truth may pretend to succumb to a lie occasionally when they cannot help it, I said, but that is nothing but a real truth. The one who knows the truth might sometimes pretend otherwise because that is necessary to preserve the evidence intact until the truth is revealed. The human conscience is the most perfect form of evidence by which the truth is manifested when justice is working as it should. And the belief of this final triumph of truth should be the basis of life, I reasoned. In Yongmo's case, however, not to deny the involuntary false statement in court would signify abandonment of life itself. And besides Sŏngmun and his father, there were two more witnesses, Cho Sunman and O Sugil, who had been at the mill and could also testify for Yongmo. But Yongmo was not the caliber of person who would demand a proper legal procedure, nor did he have enough courage to reverse the false statement.

Yongmo wanted to give me a treat and took me to the unmarked eatery next to the Station Square tearoom to buy me beef soup with rice and a drink.

The court was located at one corner of the registry office, the two-story brick structure newly built on the site of a former oil depot a little distance out to the street from the square. The court seemed unrealistic, even funny. It was hard to believe that law was solemnly executed in such a shabby room, that decisions were rendered on property and human rights, the winner or loser of a legal battle, the rise and fall of a family, the union or separation of man and wife, the gain or loss of fortunes, and all other human affairs happy and sad. I still had strong impressions from various small and large courts I had frequented for many years as my friends or senior members of the literary community had been involved in certain cases that I hesitate to elaborate here. Now, once again, I was aware of the shame deep in my heart for having given up, under all sorts of incongruous pretexts, even casual visits to such trials.

When Yongmo and I entered the court, there were a score of seedy characters who seemed to have been selected for their slovenly looks.

Although they were sitting side by side, it was apparent that they were in different situations from one another—defendant, plaintiff, witness, attendant, and the like. Two were elderly men in traditional clothes, the others were middle-aged, except for one who caught my eye—a youth with disheveled hair who looked like an ironworker. The court was rather small. Six three-seater benches, such as one would find at a grammar school, were arranged in two rows, and the seats were already filled with people. At one glance the differences from other courts were recognizable. There were no seats for the prosecutor, attorney, or clerk, nor was there a witness stand, and all the fixtures and furnishings were smaller and simpler.

Sitting modestly with their hats and coats off, the citizens gazed at the glowing kerosene stove, as big as an electric fan that stood beside the judge's seat, or at the judge's tall chair with its red velvet back. The judicial policeman who was present to supervise the court proceedings was sitting on the front bench by the door as meekly as the accused. Yongmo and I took the seats in the last row. Somebody up front asked, "What time is it now?" and somebody else replied, "It's almost time." Just then the court clerk entered and put a bunch of papers on the judge's table. Finally they all stood up at the call of "Court rise" and sat down again after the young judge, who looked not a year older than twenty-five, took his seat.

Immediately the judge took the paper on top of the pile and called out the persons involved in the first case, "Mr. Pang Sangho, Mr. Kang Yongch'un."

A man in his sixties who cut his grizzly hair up high leaving not much more than the strands on his forehead, and a man in his forties wearing a chestnut-colored windbreaker and leather boots, stepped out toward the judge.

"Mr. Kang Yongch'un, is it true that you borrowed fifty thousand *wŏn* six months ago from Mr. Pang Sangho to be paid back within the period of a month and that you have yet to pay either principal or interest?" the judge asked the man in the windbreaker.

"That's not true, sir. I begged him to wait a while until things get better for me. But he wouldn't listen to me. He just kept dunning me, so I told him to take my coal, which was all I had, instead. I never said I wouldn't pay him back, your honor."

"What about this accusation that you mobilized hoodlums to scare away the workers that Mr. Pang Sangho sent to take the coal?" the judge asked again.

Kang, who seemed to be a subcontract worker at a coal mine, replied, "Nothing of the sort ever happened. That's a slander fabricated by that old man. A human being is an animal with feelings, you see, Old Pang, and I really don't like it the way you're always getting on my nerves."

Then Pang bowed deeply and said, "Didn't you see him threaten me just now, your honor? When the workers returned without the coal I asked them what happened and they said a dozen youngsters who looked like hoodlums climbed to the top of the coal pile and glared at the workers as if they were looking for trouble. The workers did not want any trouble and returned empty-handed, because they thought it didn't make any sense to be beaten up for a truckload of coal. You see, the workers are paid for the actual work they've done, so they would not have returned with the empty truck without a good reason."

"Hey, you! Old man! Tell it straight. What on earth have you got against me? Surely a human being is an animal with feelings. How do you suppose the miners felt when total strangers suddenly showed up to take away the coal they had spent their lives digging up? What do you mean 'hoodlums'? Did they carry a label saying 'hoodlum' on their foreheads or something? Don't you know what kind of age we're living in? How dare you try to slander the nation by suggesting that hoodlums still exist in our society? Besides, it often happens that people aren't able to pay the interest for a couple of months. Don't you know that most of the tycoons in this country have gone through that kind of hardship once or twice in their past? Sometimes they don't even pay their debts to the government for years. And how can you bring a suit for that small amount of money when we know each other like friends? Indeed, you make me laugh!"

"So by not paying back the debt you're practicing to become a tycoon in the future? Or did you just, in fact, neglect it?" the judge said and was about to go on when Kang interjected.

"You're not likely to try too hard to pay back those who use all sorts of mean methods to collect the debt. A human being is an animal with feelings, you know. . . . I wouldn't be so mad if he behaved himself from the beginning, but if he duns me like this, all right, you can take all the coal you want. Old Pang, perhaps you believe law is everything. That's fine, and I want to see what you can do about it after all. Now I've been dragged here and gone through all this humiliation, you know."

"You watch your words," the judge stormed at him with a stern expression. "Do you want to be arrested for contempt of court? Apologize."

"Yes, your honor, I apologize to every person of the whole nation. Forgive me," Kang parroted, apparently not fully understanding what the fashionable political remark really meant. He bowed.

"You are impossible. The defendant should pay back the principal and the interest to the complainant not later than 5 P.M. of the fifteenth day of this month. The interest should cover six months. And the defendant will be responsible also to pay eight hundred and twenty wŏn, which is the cost on the part of the plaintiff for this suit." The judge gave the verdict and put the records aside.

I could not help laughing. It was Kang's repeating "an animal with feelings" to no avail and his self-righteous speech that finally trapped him. This was funny enough. But what made me laugh even more was the fact that those who had been enjoying their luck lately kept chorusing "owing to every person of the whole nation" whenever they were on television or radio, while the expression "bowing deeply in gratitude to the nation" was at the tip of every public tongue—and now even the defendant at an assize was following this linguistic fad.

"Mr. Chang Kuksŏn," the judge called the defendant of the next case.

Answering the call was the youth with disheveled hair. He was dressed in a pink sweater and blue jeans slimy with oil and grime. He looked like an auto mechanic or an ironworker, and most probably was a minor. Not only were his clothes smeared with greasy oil, but his hands and face looked as if he had not washed them for some time. His eyes were puffy, perhaps because he had spent a night in jail.

According to the report, he was an employee of an iron foundry in a corner of town. He had been sent to this summary court because he refused to have his hair cut when he left the workshop to buy a pack of cigarettes for his ironmaster and was caught by a policeman for growing his hair too long. In Seoul his hair would have been short enough to go unnoticed even during Long Hair Regulation Week, but it seemed there was still some discrepancy between urban and rural standards.

The judge said, "You do know why you are here, don't you?" Chang replied gruffly, his voice catching in the throat, "It didn't happen that way, sir, your honor. I simply said that the man should not touch my hair because he has no barber's license and that I didn't want my hair cut like that on the street, and then the man suddenly began to swear and call me all sorts of names."

The judge was trying not to smile, but the audience in the room was as stiff and expressionless as ever. "This report says you derided the judicial policeman and interfered in the execution of his duty. Now will you explain what really happened in your own opinion?"

"You see, honest to God, he jeered at me, 'If you're such a smart aleck, why did you become an ironworker instead of a judge or prosecutor?' So I retorted, 'If you're such a big man, what on earth are *you* doing here' And that's all."

The judge glanced through the records and said, "And you said something before that—you said regulating the length of hair by law is going against history—and what does that mean?"

"You see, honest to God, he ridiculed me, 'If you're that smart, you probably know that in Korea's five-thousand-year history, it was more than one hundred years ago that the decree to cut hair short was proclaimed, eh?' So, honestly, I said to him, 'If you're so smart yourself, you must know that in Korea's five-thousand-year history, people in our nation had the longest hair in the world for four thousand and nine hundred years.' Then the officer said 'I'll leave you alone if you twine your hair in a topknot and wear a horsehair hat, or have a long ponytail like those superstitious folks on Mount Kyeryong.' So I said, 'Why don't you cut their hair? Honestly, is there a law that says theirs isn't long hair?' And the officer said, 'They grow their hair long because of their religious conviction.' So I said, 'I can't have my hair cut either because I've got my own convictions, too.' "

"Can you tell me what those convictions are? What kind of convictions are they?" said the judge, his face grown red from suppressed laughter.

Chang hesitated a moment. Then, scratching the back of his head, he said, "That is, you see, sir, your honor. I thought it was necessary for aesthetic reasons . . ."

"Aesthetic reasons?" said the judge, reaching for Chang. "Aesthetic reasons are fine reasons. Come over here. Come closer—"

As Chang approached him a few steps, the judge pinched Chang's left ear, turned his head this way and that to take a look at the nape and back of the head, put aside the report, and gave his verdict: "To satisfy your aesthetic convictions, why don't you scrape out the grease from the nape of your neck and behind your ears? You don't deserve to discuss aesthetic anything, I believe." Then he said to the policeman sitting by the entrance, "Take this man and have his hair cut and have him bathed before sending him home."

Next it was Yongmo's turn. Yongmo answered to the call and, before leaving his seat, whispered to me, "I've been thinking and I think it's no good to bring up any trouble, so I'll just say I did it and let it go." He smelled badly of the alcohol he had had with lunch.

The judge glanced through the deposition and said, "Why did you do such a thing? I believe you certainly are civilized enough to know that all of us should do our best to preserve nature not only by protecting wild birds and animals but also by not destroying the woods or removing fallen leaves." The judge spoke in a kindly tone which made him look that much more dignified.

Yongmo simply bowed again and again, crestfallen, not saying anything.

"The pheasant is not a natural monument. But when they say we should protect sparrows, for instance, there must be valid reasons. What good would it be to protect something when someone else is just as earnestly busy trying to destroy it?"

The repeated accusation by the judge loosened Yongmo's tongue. Contrary to my expectation, his voice was neither timid nor overpowering. "You're right, of course. But listen, we have to reconsider if pheasants are indeed worth protecting right now. It's all right to protect something that's worth protecting, but what isn't worth protecting isn't worth protecting. People think only sparrows are damaging crops, but as for the pheasants, you know, they do more damage to farmers. I'm telling you this for your future reference." Yongmo said this vigorously as if there was nothing for him to fear. And his attitude did not seem to have been much affected by alcohol. I decided to interpret it as a grasp of rejuvenation by someone who has been living repressed all his life even though he has done nothing wrong.

The judge tilted his head, narrowed his eyes, looked down at Yongmo, and said, "So, you mean its' all right to catch pheasants? You simply eliminated vermin?"

"They say the handle of the ax you are wielding dictates the size of the branch you'll cut for a new ax handle. But I didn't exactly mean it, your honor."

"What do you mean you didn't mean it? We're trying to protect wildlife since they are on the verge of extinction because of people who think the way you do."

"I want to say something to you, your honor. I'm not afraid of the punishment. Yes, sir, I'm willing to accept the punishment I deserve. But, you know, I also want some protection from the law. I don't know if its' all right to talk about these things . . ."

"You're saying them now and that proves it's all right."

"Of course, your honor. Here is a court where, unlike the outside world, many things are protected. And as animals have their own importance, I too have my own importance. I am a wild animal—a wild human being too, you know. If you count human beings a bit more important than ordinary animals, sir, I don't think you should be doing this to me."

Watching Yongmo, I was suddenly reminded of what somebody had told me once—that water flows smoothly, but in cold winter, it freezes and breaks.

The judge put aside the deposition and gave his verdict. "Since the defendant shows no sign of remorse, attending the court of law in a drunken state and raving incoherently, no extenuating circumstances will be in consideration for judging this case. This kind of person should be punished severely as an example for everyone else. He will be fined twenty thousand *wŏn.*"

TRANSLATED BY AHN JUNGHYO

O Chŏnghŭi

O Chŏnghŭi was born in Seoul in 1947 and graduated from Sŏrabŏl College of Fine Arts with a degree in creative writing. She has published several volumes of stories since her literary debut in 1968 and has captured two major awards: the Yi Sang Prize in 1979 for "Evening Game" and the Tongin Prize in 1982 for "The Bronze Mirror." One of the most talented of contemporary Korean authors, O uses flashbacks, stream-of-consciousness technique, and a variety of narrative viewpoints to good effect. Her vocabulary is rich, her word selection deliberate and suggestive. Her best stories, such as "Evening Game," "The Bronze Mirror," and "Words of Farewell," are powerful, sensitive, carefully crafted portrayals of family relationships strained by unspoken emotions and unseen external forces.

"The Bronze Mirror" (1982) examines a couple on the threshold of old age, the husband facing physical debility and the wife tormented by memories of their dead son, a casualty of the April 1960 student revolution. The anxieties of the couple are personified in the audacious kindergarten girl who lives next door. The impact of the story is enhanced by the stark third-person narrative, which takes the husband's point of view, and by the assignment of a name to only one character—the dead son.

BRUCE AND JU-CHAN FULTON

THE BRONZE MIRROR

After watching his wife pour flour into a large wooden basin the man stepped outside for his midday stroll. He had just started out when he saw the girl next door coming down the sloping alley on a bicycle. Her face drew tense as she clutched the brake lever yet entrusted herself to the increasing speed. Her calves stood taut below her tight cotton shorts.

He was walking right at her, but he couldn't tell whether the girl was looking at him as she pushed the oversize pedals, sitting erect instead of trying to lessen the wind resistance. Her hair, blown by the headwind, and her forehead, not yet colored by the sun, registered briefly in his mind and then disappeared more quickly than the smile playing on his aging face.

The alley was empty, perhaps because of the unseasonable heat, and for this reason he felt thoroughly unfamiliar with this unvarying leg of his stroll. As his eyes pursued the girl's back, the image of her speeding through this alley of linked gray walls and low roofs was sucked into the blur of the bicycle wheels like grass conjoining after the wind has made a swath through it.

It was strangely quiet. Now and then he passed an open gate in the wall, but all he could see were bare gardens and limp bamboo blinds hung for privacy by the people inside. It was not yet time for the children to be returning from school.

Twice the girl sounded the bicycle's long, shrill bell, even though the alley was clear. She might suddenly have noticed the dead silence around her, or perhaps she had tired of pedaling incessantly down the empty way.

No doubt the girl had sneaked out of kindergarten. She disliked going there, and every morning he heard her crying on the other side of the wall. But in the end she would open the gate in the wall, cross his yard, and be off. On rainy days, wearing a yellow slicker that came down to her ankles, she lingered in his yard, picking out puddles to splash in. On her way home from kindergarten she would rent a bicycle from the bicycle shop or play house in a corner of his yard. His wife didn't like her coming and going as she pleased because she trampled the grass and plucked flowers from their stems. Something disappeared whenever she came by, his wife would tell him. For this reason she would always scrutinize the area where the girl had been playing.

The girl's mother worked at a beauty parlor on the second floor of a three-story building facing the main street. The structure also housed a drugstore, a butcher shop, and a billiard hall. The neighbors said that the girl's father, who had gone to work in the Middle East after her birth, had extended his assignment there.

Although the girl's mother rarely came through the side gate to visit, the man saw her frequently. When it was warm enough for people to open their windows, the clicking of clippers from the beauty parlor sometimes carried to the road when the traffic noise simmered down. Occasionally he saw her close the windows with a scowl to block out the cacophony. And late in the evening he would encounter her trotting along with some groceries. Still wearing the plastic apron she used when giving permanents, she reeked of chemicals and hair. On her biweekly day off she would squat in front of the drain in her yard and clear her throat. "I tell you," he had heard her say some time ago from the other side of the wall, "the hair gets into everything —even my throat. That's why I try to keep my mouth shut when I'm working, even though the customers say I'm not very sociable."

The man's slow pace brought him to the playground at the corner of the neighborhood. He saw the girl leaning against her bicycle. Other children, moving like crabs, were playing in a sandbox under the glare of the cloudless sky.

"Hey, you guys, have you seen my kaleidoscope? Who stole it?" the girl asked.

"We don't know," the other children sniffled.

Although the girl knew it would be in vain, she furiously dug through the piles of sand she had scoured the previous evening and destroyed the caves and sand castles the other children had fashioned. Then she got back on the bicycle saying, "Whoever stole it better put it back by the time I come around again. If you don't, I'm going to get you. I know who stole my kaleidoscope."

As the man departed one step at a time, pecking about with his cane as if it were a feeler, his stomach began moving feebly. The silence was enough to suffocate him, and the white sunlight enough to give him the shivers. In reaction to his stomach's movements, his innards, hanging in clusters large and small, began to squirm. Only now did these aging, feebly drooping organs reluctantly remind themselves of their function and more or less regain their vitality. When the weather got hotter he would probably have to abandon this half-hour walk he had prescribed for himself to stimulate his appetite for lunch.

Gradually becoming short of breath, he stopped and wiped the sweat from his forehead while gazing attentively at the curtains hanging thick and still in the open windows of the houses next to the alley. The route he took was always the same, and he would stare at the monotonous path through this neighborhood of low, small houses shaped exactly alike—a scene sufficient to arouse dread—and at everything else that appeared on his retina. But he didn't intend to observe or remember, was not even conscious of looking.

At any rate, his strolls would have to be suspended when the days got hotter. His shrunken, hardened internal organs would not endure hot weather, so he would spend the summer sitting in an armchair in the shade and letting scenes he had simply watched flash across his mind.

Though he had walked as slowly as possible for the thirty minutes, the back of his shirt was damp with perspiration as he neared his house. He was satisfied. Exercise that made him sweat profusely was excessive at his age, he believed, and so he made it a rule to exercise only to the point of breaking a sweat.

His efforts to maintain his regimen were important and worthwhile, he thought. Though it seemed he was force-feeding himself on the passing days, he enjoyed obeying the rules and rhythms that controlled his body and life, as if he had no idea that one day everything would stop in an instant.

He found that his wife had finished making enough dough for noodles for twelve. The expected visitors, however, had sent word that they would not be coming for home worship after all. Instead they were going directly to the mortuary at the general hospital because a church friend had just passed away after a long illness. As his wife told him this, she briefly gave him a blank look, still sticking her hands into the white dough filling the broad-mouthed basin.

The dough, much more than the two of them could hope to consume as noodles, was rising as if it would overflow the rim of the basin. A roller, a cutting board lightly floured to make noodle chopping easier, a wicker tray with colored garnishes, and other implements were spread about the veranda.

In preparation for the guests, his wife had begun cleaning the yard and scurrying back and forth between the kitchen and the veranda early that morning. After breakfast, he recalled, he had steeped himself in the vague tranquillity of his wife's busy footsteps, the muted chopping in the kitchen, and the smell of hot cooking oil. Was he anticipating the warmth of living in harmony with such vitality, even though he didn't believe it refreshed him anymore? Or was he simply becoming sentimental about everyday life?

Perhaps his wife's disappointment at the cancellation of the visit was not nearly as great as he had suspected. He couldn't believe, now that he thought about it, that her faith had suddenly become that profound.

Was it last month that his wife had taken pity on those two women who were making their way around the neighborhood, knocking on doors and proselytizing to everyone? She had asked them in for a short rest, which had turned into a four-hour lecture on church doctrine.

"Death is unconsciousness. Death is not even worth the life of a dog, it is said. Hell is death itself; the word means imprisonment in the earth. . . ." The lecture was clearly audible where he lay in his room.

"I just thought they might want to sit down for a moment. . . ."

Although his wife had spoken apologetically to him after the women left, the following Sunday she went to their meeting place. There they had decided to make their first official visit to her home today.

Life imprisoned in the earth, glimmers of life crying out, imprisoned in the earth.

It must have been twenty years ago that Yŏngno was buried. Twenty years imprisoned in the earth—the same amount of time he had spent among the living.

After his wife left to prepare lunch for him, he remained for some time on the veranda looking at the garden. His eyes, following the path his wife's eyes had taken, came to rest where his wife had been looking. The roses, hyacinths, dahlias, and other summer flowers were at their peak. Their petals were wide open in the midday sun, exposing the darker, deeper inner parts. Bees and butterflies inflamed with desire inserted their slender tubes deep in the pistils and stamens in search of nectar. Yearning to bloom more and more, the flowers darkened and began a slow trembling that he could scarcely discern. But now he realized that this was not the scene his wife had viewed. As he watched the trees in the garden, lowering his head as if pretending to listen to the cries imprisoned in the earth, their luxuriant foliage dropped leaf by leaf, the desiccated branches turned to fibers and burned blue like phosphorus, and presently the places where the branches stretched out so proudly became empty space adrift with callous death.

The bicycle passed the front gate, its bell piercing the empty space. If only he could call out and beckon her, this girl who flew by like an arrow: "Hey kid, come in and wash up." Riding like that all day long under the hot sun would make the blood vessels in her brain swell up, he thought. If only he could impress on the girl's mind for the rest of her life the memory, sharp as a cutting gleam of light, of the simple kindness of this old man.

His wife appeared with the meal tray. She had prepared his usual lunch of homemade noodles and a glass of liquor.

The noodles, though liberally decorated with the appropriate color of garnish, were completely bland. Without a word he looked across at his wife, who, seemingly unaware that the food lacked the slightest touch of salt, had lowered her head and was nimbly looping her own noodles about her chopsticks.

Was it because of his dentures? he wondered. But he had been wearing them for some time now. And besides, he had been eating these homemade noodles regularly ever since it had become a burden to eat hard food. He couldn't find fault with the way his wife had boiled the noodles. But how could she have forgotten to add the soy sauce? After all, she made noodles every day. As she sat there expressionless, eating the noodles, he resented and detested her almost as much as he hated his internal organs for neglecting their role.

"Get me some soy sauce," he said, suppressing his anger.

Sluggishly she got to her feet and returned with a small bowl of the condiment.

Since his teeth had been pulled and he had started using the dentures, he had lost most of the pleasure of chewing and savoring but had become very particular about the flavor of food. This, however, he refused to acknowledge.

Those dentures!

He had spent his working life as a petty official at City Hall. His assignment was almost always the same—drafting clean copies of instructions from superiors or decisions reached by his department. He enjoyed these scribal duties, and never copied incorrectly or used abbreviated forms of the Chinese characters. Although he realized that once his drafts had been approved and typed up they were immediately thrown in the wastebasket, he was proud of his clear, precise penmanship. Whenever his department heads saw his well-ordered drafts they exclaimed as one, "What fine handwriting!"

Then one day his teeth had begun to loosen. When his gums became swollen and blue and the roots of his teeth were exposed, he realized he would have to have all the teeth pulled and dentures fitted. He was much more angry than frustrated at this betrayal. From then on, symptoms of debility appeared in all his internal organs, including his stomach. His doctor told him these were common post-retirement symptoms. Because of the lethargy that follows an abrupt cessation of work, the body loses its tone and balance. Retirement disease, the doctor had called it.

The doctor's comment that this could happen to anyone didn't console him in the least. After all, he'd never had to apologize to his superiors for anything, but now they'd put him out to pasture at retirement age, just like the people who had merely coasted along dawdling away the hours. He had docilely accepted the decades spent in that gloomy, stuffy old office, but he just could not get used to the dentures. He couldn't help resisting these cold, hard, strange objects that irritated his soft gums.

Losing interest in his lunch, he smeared some toothpaste on a small cloth and polished the silver ornament on the handle of his cane. The simple, gentle movements of his hands seemed designed to soothe the walking stick, and when he saw the silver regain its milky sheen, his anger toward the noodles, his wife, and the dentures gradually faded. After standing the polished cane next to the shoe cabinet, he sat on the veranda and stared in boredom at the garden.

He wondered if he had been dozing momentarily. He hadn't heard the gate open, but there in a recess of the garden a young man was using an iron hook to remove the lid from the concrete housing of the water meter. His wife was squatting with her back toward him, observing the movements of the young man's hands. Above her white hair and bent, bony waist, the noontide stillness, ebbing hardly at all, flowed heavily like quicksilver.

"Well how about that—will you look at that cricket, ma'am," the young man said, recoiling as the cricket sprang into the sunlight and the open air. "Winter's long gone, so why don't you roll up all this stuff and burn it? That way you won't have any more bugs."

The young man was referring to the chaff and straw spread over the water meter the previous winter to prevent it from freezing. The man himself had seen cases of insects hatching amid the insulation after winter had set in, then nesting and growing along the dark, moist interior of the housing.

The man watched his wife nod silently in response. Her hair was snowy white. When his had started to grizzle prematurely, hers was already gray. Turning around after seeing Yŏngno into his grave, he had suddenly discovered that his wife, still patting down some of the thin turf placed on the mound of red soil, had become white-haired.

"My boy was growing just like green bamboo," his wife would say now and then to the peddler women she let into the house, "and when he died, my hair turned all white." Then she would explain to him that prematurely gray hair ran in her family. "Honey, you look good with your hair dyed," she would tell him, knowing he was particular about the way his hair was barbered and dyed. "Just like a young man."

From the time gray first appeared in his hair, he had never been lazy about dyeing it. And now, with the white, shiny dentures added to the black, well-groomed hair, he looked much younger. Often he would gaze at himself in the mirror as if looking at Yŏngno turned forty.

His wife looked idly at the water meter, then asked the young man as he was about to leave, "How about cooling off a bit before you go?"

"Okay. Could I have some water?"

The young man took out a handkerchief and mopped the sweat from his forehead and neck. He sat down on the edge of the veranda, and before long the woman appeared with a porcelain bowl of sweetened water blended with powdered roasted grain.

The man didn't like the way his wife trotted out from the kitchen continuously stirring the beverage as if afraid the young man would leave. Clicking his tongue, he muttered to himself, "Don't do that. He's just a common young fellow who does nothing but go around inspecting water meters. You can see his type anywhere."

The young man emptied the bowl in a breath. The man didn't fail to catch his wife's flustered look as her eyes greedily explored the young man's sturdy neck and ripe-red chest revealed by his casually unbuttoned shirt.

"That was good. Thank you, ma'am." The young man wiped the moisture trickling from his mouth and licked his lips.

"The way he drinks isn't decent either," the man impotently muttered again. "Like I say, I can tell people's qualities by the way they eat and drink."

Remembering that the water pipe had been left uncovered, the young man crossed the yard and replaced the concrete lid. As a rule, the man recalled, water meter inspectors left without doing this. They merely lifted the lid reluctantly with their iron hook, as if despising their job, and after reading the numbers on the meter they disappeared. His wife would usually be left with the laborious chore of replacing the cover.

"Say, young fellow, would you do me a favor?" his wife called out as the young man was about to leave through the front gate. Without waiting for an answer she went into the shed and came out embracing a heavy toolbox, which she set down with a thump.

The young man stared rather impertinently at the woman and the toolbox as if to say, "You cagey old lady, it looks like you'll get a generous reward for that bowl of refreshment."

"This clothesline is too high for me," she drawled, ignoring his expression. "Could you tie it a little lower? It's so difficult to hang the laundry. Only us old folks live here, and there's no one to help out."

"But if I lower it, the clothes'll drag on the ground—unless you're going to make it into a jump rope for the kids." The young man stared into the toolbox, arms folded. "Besides, all these nails are rusty. I can do it, if you've got your heart set on it, but I think it's a waste of time. Do you really think it'll do the job if we tie it lower?" Finally he rummaged through the toolbox and picked out a blacksmith's hammer and some of the cleaner nails.

It was not surprising that all the nails had rusted. Like all the tools the man had procured for himself—the blacksmith's hammer, a claw hammer, a small saw, a plane, and such—they had been virtually forgotten through long disuse.

"So, can you get a snack now and then while you're making your rounds?" his wife asked the young man.

"Yeah." The answer came indistinctly through the nails the young man held in his mouth. He quickly hammered in two nails, and now the line tightly spanned the yard at the desired lower height.

The line looked too low to the man. Surely his wife would complain of brushing against it and go to the bother of taking it down that very afternoon or the next morning.

"How can I repay you for your trouble?" his wife asked. "If you're not that busy, how about a bite to eat? I can boil up some noodles in a jiffy." She glanced at the dough filling the basin, which she had left in a corner of the veranda. Perhaps because of the warm weather and not just the yeast, the dough looked like a crazy, bloated thing.

"I've got several other houses to go to."

"It must be difficult walking around all day. Don't your legs get sore?"

"I just wish people would tie up their dogs," the young man sullenly blurted. He spat. "My pants are always getting ripped. All I have to do is look at a dog and it starts nipping at my heels."

The man watched his wife grudgingly follow the young man out, but heard no sound of the gate being latched. The house became quiet again. The shadows of the trees in the garden were a little longer, and now the man could sense only the flow of sunlight and time. No more did he hear the scuffing of his wife's shoes. Instead there was the slack, dreary clatter of bicycle wheels. He wondered if the girl, exhausted by the heat, having long forgotten about her kaleidoscope, her face expressing her unbearable boredom, was languidly walking her bicycle past the street corner that his wife would be absentmindedly watching, her hand against the gatepost.

He went into his room and sat down at the desk. It had long been his habit to sit there with a blank expression, rubbing faint ink stains, scars hollowed by knives, and scratch marks. He was comfortable in the chair, and much closer to the scenes and sounds beyond the wall, the desk being next to the window.

He had bought the desk when Yŏngno was in middle school. Although he rarely used it for reading and writing, the desk had remained there because of its handy drawers, occupying considerable space in the unheated part of the floor.

He spread out the foil liner from an empty cigarette pack, folded it into a flower shape, and spat into it. Then he opened the drawers, which were filled with water and electric bill receipts in addition to his reading glasses and whatnot. He took out a pair of nail clippers and began trimming his fingernails attentively.

He heard his wife gingerly pacing about the veranda. Trimming his fingernails and opening the drawers shouldn't have to be a secret, he told himself, yet he cringed and kept still whenever she passed by the room. She had said she was old enough to have turned into a spirit who could see and hear everything that happened in the house, even if she was sitting quietly in a corner, but how could she know he was brushing away his dandruff, trimming his fingernails, and opening and closing the drawers like children who sit unwillingly at their desks, hating to do homework? And so he strained for any indication of someone outside the room, thinking that even a trivial hand movement was a terrible plot if unknown to her.

Assuring himself that her steps had faded away, he took out the girl's kaleidoscope, which he had stored deep in one of the drawers. It was made of stout pasteboard rolled up and glued into a cylinder, and its surface was alive with crayon colors.

He put the kaleidoscope to his eye and turned it round and round. Tiny pieces of colored paper gathered and dispersed as light was refracted by the mirror in the tube, forming various flower shapes. These flowers struck him as neither florid nor original. They were merely imitations whose single and double layers were formed by the convergence and diffusion of the bits of paper. He recalled having heard that the people of antiquity had studied the principles and logic of the universe by turning a kaleidoscope.

Wasn't it a few days ago during his stroll before lunch that he emerged from the neighborhood alleyway onto the main street to find a pattern of light spinning around him wherever he went? He frowned while trying to deflect its rude touch on his shoulders, legs, and chest, terrified that his face would suddenly shrink when the glittering white light came to rest on it. It seemed to dance and jump like someone's soul between the street and the people in it. Closing his eyes to the strong rays, he shouted, "Who's that playing with the mirror?" A bright voice flew to him: "Hello, grandfather." The girl was sitting on the stairs to the beauty parlor, a sharp piece of mirror in her hand. "Now what are you going to do if you cut yourself?" Unfazed, the girl replied, "They said I could ask somebody in a glass shop to cut this into a circle. Tomorrow we're going to make kaleidoscopes in kindergarten. I heard it's a magic box where we can see everything." While saying this the girl ran across the street. "You can see everything?" he responded to her back. Of course, he hadn't asked out of genuine curiosity but was merely paraphrasing what she had said. Then yesterday he saw the kaleidoscope next to her school bag on a bench at the playground. As usual, he knew, she had rushed from kindergarten to the bicycle shop after flinging the satchel down, too impatient to go home first. What could she see through this magic box? He picked up the kaleidoscope, craving to see through the girl's eyes all that she had seen. Concealing it inside his shirt, he watched intently all afternoon as the girl vainly dug through the piles of sand to find the lost toy. "Somebody stole my kaleidoscope. Teacher told me to hand it in for an exhibition." In tears the girl looked under the bench where her satchel and kaleidoscope had been, where she had already looked time and again.

"We can see everything," he murmured, mimicking the girl. He turned the kaleidoscope quickly. The faster it turned, the greater the variety of patterns formed by the interaction of the mirror, glass, and bits of paper. Now the scene resembled bacteria dividing and multiplying at an inconceivable speed. Was it because of the vivid sense of color created by the paper? he wondered.

The liquor he had taken with lunch made his eyelids heavy and his body listless. He could never resist the temptation to sleep caused by this aid for his digestion, though he knew a nap would make him wake up at night and pace the silent yard as if in a nightmare.

He returned the kaleidoscope to the drawer and started for the bathroom.

His wife was sitting on the edge of the veranda rolling a handful of dough between her palms.

"What are you making?"

"Oh, I'm just playing."

Smiling sheepishly, she demolished the shape she had been form-ing. A human, a dog, a horse, and other clumsily modeled figures the size of a finger sat beside her.

He entered the bathroom and locked the door in order to remove his dentures.

The dentist had told him to try to wear the dentures until he was unaware of them, but he couldn't fall asleep unless he took them out and soaked them in a bowl of clean water, kept within his reach. But even then he couldn't rid himself of the fear that in the short weight-less state just before sleep there were only the dentures hanging heav-ily by his side, and that one day they alone would wake up and chat-ter of their own accord until finally his body vanished, leaving those cold, hard, lifeless things glaring cruelly in the void that had once been his life. And when he was talking he would sometimes become silent, convinced that it was not him speaking, but the dentures chat-tering and rattling.

He took out the dentures and his blackish, flaccid gums were revealed in the mirror. Unable to resist the obduracy of the dentures, the soft gums had been squashed down and finally had shrunk. With-out the dentures his mouth was no more than an empty, smelly, insig-nificant hollow. After making sure the door was locked, he started carefully brushing the dentures with the same hidden, bitter pleasure and shame as when he grasped his withered genitals in search of a consolation that was sure to be ephemeral and unavailing. With the bits of red pepper and the other remnants of his lunch cleared away, the dentures shone fresh and clean. Their pink gumlike base looked healthy, like freshly sliced meat. Breathing heavily from his efforts, he looked at the dentures. White with foam from the toothpaste, they seemed to be laughing. Then he looked in the mirror. His black hair, like that of a young man, contrasted with his collapsed mouth, the shrunken furrow between his upper lip and nose, and his cruelly sunken cheeks, making him appear younger indeed.

He returned to his room and lay down, his head on a box pillow and beside him the dentures soaking in a glass of water. Falling asleep was always like walking down a dim, endless corridor. Haven't I already turned into a spirit, walking along the passage inside a tomb? he wondered.

His wife's outline was clearly visible through the open door. Half asleep, he watched languidly as her hands rolled some dough into the shape of a body with ears and horns and a tail and legs. It was a queer shape that he had never seen before. Standing it in line with the other figures at the sunny edge of the veranda, she began muttering to herself: "Grandfather suffered from nightmares till he died, and he had these splitting headaches. He didn't know whether the headaches came from the nightmares or the other way around. We asked a shaman to perform an exorcism and a blind man to chant a Buddhist scripture, but the terrible headaches didn't go away. . . ." By now he had heard the story of her grandfather, a well-known master carpenter, several times. "He'd wake up screaming from an awful dream—sometimes at dawn, sometimes in the middle of the night—and then roam the house like a madman because of the headaches. Grandmother used to say he had built too many houses where graves used to be. . . ." In a hazy corner of the corridor he sees ahead of him a screaming old man with an arched back and a white headband. "That's why Grandfather carved strange animals with his pocket knife. They looked like elephants or bears; whatever they were, they sure looked strange. Tapirs, I think he called them, and he said they ate nightmares. . . ." His wife continued to form shapes from the dough in the basin. "Grandfather left them at his bedside next to the spittoon. The stuff he coughed up into the spittoon was like the nightmares the tapirs had eaten all night long and thrown up at dawn. Grandfather's dying wish was to have the tapirs put in his coffin. I guess he was afraid of being harassed by bad dreams even after he died. I wonder if the dead have dreams. It was very strange to me, a young girl at the time, but now I can understand why Grandfather did that. Didn't people in the old days make mud figurines of their belongings and even their servants, and ask to be buried with them? . . ." His wife's grandfather was sleeping comfortably now at the end of the long, faint corridor of time, the tapirs at his side.

As if hypnotized by his wife's slow, low-pitched chanting, he walked on through time, which was part buried in oblivion and part risen dimly before him. It was just like film applied unevenly with sensitizer: part of it clearly defined, almost luminous; part of it obscured, too dark. But he was not all that impatient to remember. Recalling only the things he wants to recall is the insignificant privilege of an old man. But what was this place where he hesitated to stop? An exhibition room in a museum he had once visited?

It was the room where clay figures, bronze mirrors, and other burial artifacts were displayed. When he saw the mirrors, cleansed of tarnish after thousands of years in the earth, he felt he had died long ago. All alone, he couldn't hear even his footsteps on the thick carpet. That was the reason, he told himself, for the mysterious, fleeting sentiment he experienced on his way out the long, dampish corridor.

What he had just buried, he thought as he turned away from Yŏngno's grave, was not a hurriedly decaying corpse that couldn't endure the riotous vigor of spring, but a piece of a mirror.

"Grandmother, what are you making?"

The short shadow in the front yard and the seemingly deliberate lisp told him it was the girl next door. He looked at the girl, struggling to extricate himself from his shallow sleep. She had changed into a white lace dress and was tightly embracing a doll. In her free hand she carried a plastic basket with things for playing house. He wondered if she had tired of riding the bicycle.

"Back from kingergarten?" his wife coldly asked as she continued to shape the queer-looking animals. She always watched the girl with suspicion. His old wife distrusted everything.

"I didn't go today. It's Saturday."

"That's a pretty dress you're wearing."

"My mom bought it for me." Again the girl made a point of lisping.

He continued to look at the girl, trying hard to think she was pretty. But he failed, as usual. Her pale eyes turning gold as they absorbed the sun's rays and her face sharp as an ax blade were not pretty at all. She always looked a little lonely when she crossed the yard holding the basket of playthings as if they were her household goods, or when she rode the swing in her yard, the doll under her arm. Even when the girl wasn't playing on the swing, it swayed by itself with a creak.

Was it last summer that he had looked over the wall all those times and seen the girl? After stripping herself naked in the sunny yard she would plop herself into a large wooden tub of water and tumble and splash about. Almost in agony as he hid next to the rosebushes creeping up the wall, he would hear her short and sudden laugh and observe her thin, light brown hair trailing down the back of her neck like corn floss, her belly swollen like that of a pregnant woman, her little pink genitals.

"Grandmother, what are you making?" the girl asked again, the lace of her dress fluttering as she swayed back and forth. Denied, rejected, and unloved, she had learned early to play the coquette.

Turning gracefully and spreading wide the bottom of her dress like the petals of a flower, she squatted. "They look strange, grandmother." Still squatting, she moved so close that her forehead was almost touching his wife.

"They're called tapirs. They're animals that eat bad dreams."

"Do you have bad dreams too? I always have scary dreams." The girl picked a rose moss that had bloomed and crushed it between her fingers.

"Why do you pick those flowers?"

Pretending not to hear the scolding, the girl continued to speak in a clinging tone: "I was flying just like a bird, but then I wondered what would happen if I wasn't a bird and I fell. Right away I was falling upside-down. It was so scary."

"It's because you're getting taller. Not going to the bathroom before you go to bed can also make you have bad dreams."

The girl plucked a dahlia and crushed it under her foot.

"I told you not to do that!" his wife shouted.

The girl stared spitefully at her.

"How many times do I have to tell you to make you understand? Good children don't break off flowers."

Even while his wife was spitting out these words in a much lower and firmer voice in order to cool her anger, the girl snapped off a hydrangea and an Indian lilac.

"You really don't listen. What a bad girl. I guess you need to be taught a lesson." Her arm raised, his wife glared at the girl. But then she dropped it feebly, for the girl, her face ridden with fear, had cuddled up to her as if to be embraced.

"Sometimes my quilt puffs up real thick and covers me all over so I can't even breathe. No matter how hard I cry, my mom can't hear me." The trembling words were like an appeal.

"You weren't dreaming. You were having a nightmare. Here, take one of these and put it right next to you when you go to bed. Then you'll be all right."

"Thanks, grandmother." The girl accepted the precious tapir, cautiously enclosing it tightly in her palm as if it were a souvenir from a temple or a seedling that would die if the roots were exposed.

"Oh, now your dress has gotten dirty."

As if crossing stepping stones, the girl was carefully walking away with her doll, basket, and tapir. She looked back, and seeing the large stain where the hem of her dress had swept against the ground, she burst into tears. "Mom'll spank me if I get my new dress dirty. She told me absolutely not to wear it till my birthday party at the kindergarten."

"Come here, I'll brush it off. That's why you shouldn't squat down just anywhere," said his wife, surprised at the urgency and vividness of the girl's unexpected, tear-filled proclamation.

But the girl was full of resentment and fear. She flung aside the tapir and picked all the flowers she could grab.

"Damn girl! I'm going to break your wrist." His wife sprang up and chased the girl, who continued to wail as she fled. The sound of her crying retreated through the side gate, and his wife returned, panting, to her seat at the edge of the veranda. She began kneading the dough more roughly.

He heard a sound like the front gate creaking. Had someone come? Or perhaps the girl was riding the swing in her yard. But his wife showed no sign of having heard anything. It was not unusual for him to hear something she didn't and for her to see something he couldn't make out at all. Now and then he would hear the swing creaking in the middle of the night. When he told his wife this she would snort and turn on her side, saying, "Why would a little girl want to ride a swing at night? It's pitiful." Eventually, though, he would go out to the yard as if drawn by the end of a disturbing dream. Standing close to the wall, he would gaze with the silliness of one in love at the swaying of the empty swing ridden only by the wind.

Untiringly his wife kneaded the dough and formed more tapirs. What bad dream could be disrupting the old woman's sleep? The old don't sleep deeply, and they have many dreams, he told himself.

The yard had been infused with shade, and the shadows of the trees had lengthened considerably.

Looking at his wife's white hair, the crimson flowers over her head, the trees burning blue in his mind's eye, he heard, as if drugged by another light slumber, a shrill, rending song coming over the wall:

Cuckoo, cuckoo, spring has come.
Cuckoo, cuckoo, peach blossoms fall.

"Damn girl! I'm going to have to break your habits the hard way!" his wife gasped, still unable to soften her anger toward the girl.

Like rays of the sun, the girl's singing clung tenaciously to his eyelids, made heavy by his brief dozing.

"All she has to do is touch a stem and she breaks it," his wife muttered. Then, as if seeking agreement, she called out to him: "Are you sleeping?"

After struggling to open his eyes, he examined his wife.

"You'd better exercise during the day if you want to get to sleep at night," she said. "Instead of having a drink with lunch, how about going out for another walk after you eat?"

She may have been right. The glass of liquor he had drunk with lunch had not stirred his limp stomach.

Without waiting for an answer, his wife continued to speak. Her voice was full of an inordinate vitality. It was not so much that she wanted to express something clearly to him; rather, she was struggling to erase the sound of the incessant singing.

"It's so strange. These days I think a lot about people who have died. Everything that happened during their lives comes into my head just as if they were still alive. And yet I honestly can't remember the years *we've* spent together. No matter how I try, it's like a faint dream that I can't remember. Can you remember your forties and fifties? I can't for the life of me recall what you looked like back then. Somehow or other, I often think I've lived too long. Even the yardwork's getting to be too much. If I let it go just one day, the weeds come up like hungry ghosts—especially at a time of year like this."

The girl's singing became more shrill, and his wife paused. Then she continued in a much louder voice: "Let it go. That's what our boy said way back then. He used to ask what the point was of trying to differentiate between flowers and grass. They look better growing together, he said."

A smile rose on his face.

"What was it like when you were fifty? How about forty? Thirty? I just can't remember at all. Tell me."

Her questions were persistent and tantalizing, as if she were hypnotizing him. Afraid of an answer, she quickly continued. Her voice and the girl's singing were like the dissonance of musical instruments competing with each other.

"He was so wonderful when he was twenty, and I was proud of him. That was the year he went to college. I can remember it just as clearly as if it had happened yesterday. And those itchy feet of his."

He didn't want to listen to his wife anymore. Yŏngno was always telling them his feet were itchy. The boy had never recovered from the frostbite he had suffered while riding atop his father's rucksack on the way south during the war. He used to say he felt better when he slept with his feet in a sack of cold beans, even in winter.

"Can you remember the time he lost my shawl at the ballet? I think he was five then. It was made of real silk, something even the Japanese couldn't get all that often. After the performance I put it around his shoulders so I could go to the rest room. It probably fell off and the boy didn't realize it. He could be dumb like that. Everybody said that bishop's purple looked marvelous on me. I really can't see something like that coming my way again."

How much longer would his wife tell the story of that lost shawl?

Little by little her speech accelerated, as did the manipulations of her hands as she made the tapirs. As the basin was emptied of dough, the row of tapirs became too tight to admit any more.

"He'd just turned twenty. What do people know when they're that young? He thought he could turn the world around at an age when he should have been squeezing pimples. Can you believe it? The boy's dead, and here we are still living like this."

One spring day Yŏngno, fresh out of high school, had flown out of the house like a nighthawk, his schoolboy crewcut not quite grown out and sticking up indignantly in all directions.

An old man does not reflect on his conduct, he thought, because he does not expect a new life that requires it.

The girl's shrill singing gradually became louder:

Cuckoo, cuckoo, spring has come.

Cuckoo, cuckoo, peach blossoms fall.

"She really is a bad girl." Everting her lips, his wife suddenly started crying.

"Kids are all the same." Despite the discomfiture of having to speak with his hollow, dentureless mouth, he managed to eject the syllables.

"No, the dead ones are special," his wife sobbed, covering her face with her hands.

"Grandmother, what are you making?" The girl was standing in front of his wife. The signs of her own crying had vanished.

"Go away!" his wife said with a fierce wave of her hand.

"Grandmother, what's the matter? Why are you crying?"

"I told you never to come to this house again!"

"Grandmother, I'm going to make a kaleidoscope out of this mirror," the girl said triumphantly. "My mom gave it to me. Somebody stole the one I made in kindergarten." Without budging, she opened a compact to reveal a round mirror.

"Don't you lie. That's still new. There's no way your mom gave it to you. She's still at the beauty parlor, isn't she? If you get into your mom's cosmetics without a good reason, you'll get another spanking from her."

Glaring grimly at his wife, the girl ran to the sunny side of the yard. Then, turning the mirror this way and that, she flashed it in his wife's face.

Dazzled, his wife covered her face with one hand and motioned with the other. "Get out of here!"

But the girl merely smiled amiably.

"Put it away, I said! You damn little girl. I'm going to tell your mother."

"Then tell her! Squeal! Tell her everything!"

Bouncing around the yard like a ball, the girl continued to flash the mirror in his wife's face. Frightened, his wife climbed onto the veranda. The light from the mirror coursed by the line of animals drying white and firm and clung agilely to his wife's face, clearly exposing its layers of wrinkles like aluminum foil crumpled and then spread out.

"Child, now child, for heaven's sake go away. Don't do that," his wife pleaded tearfully.

The girl giggled, delighting in his wife's sudden fright. To escape the mirror, his wife tottered into the room where he was lying.

Now the light glittered constantly on his wife's small, tear-soaked face and on the rims of his eyes and the edges of his broken-down mouth. It seemed somehow a reflection from a mirror buried in the bottomless earth. The girl wouldn't put the mirror away until she found a more interesting game, perhaps not until the rays of the sun had completely died out, perhaps not until night when her tired mother returned. But what could be more fun for a child than driving the old into a feeble state of terror?

One corner of the yard was already submerged in shade, and the flowers had started to darken and close in the thick gloom spreading up from the ground. How long would it last, that unseen flow of flower-blooming space into the silent abyss?

He wondered what he could say to soothe his wife, who was no longer attempting to conceal her crying. She needed some affectionate words. Feeling boyishly shy and a bit apprehensive, he opened his mouth, but his wife couldn't understand his stammering. Frustrated, she pressed her ear to his mouth and repeatedly questioned him: "What was that? What did you say? Did you ask if somebody came?"

He lay there, his hair black as coal and his broken-down mouth open halfway, incapable of further speech.

The reflection from the mirror flitted from the ceiling to the walls and came to rest on the glass of water in which the soaking dentures glittered bright and lucid. It seemed that they alone were trying to say something in the silence dark and calm against the light from outside.

TRANSLATED BY BRUCE AND JU-CHAN FULTON

Ch'oe Inhun

Most of Ch'oe Inhun's works are colored by the division of Korea and the shock of being wrenched away from his birthplace. Driven by a nostalgia for his home, one character probes the nightmare of Korean history in search of his cultural patterns. Realizing the uselessness of bookish knowledge, another escapes to the world of imagination and dream. A third laments the misapplication of Western ideology and the anguish of a people who are geopolitical pawns. A fourth finds both Koreas wanting and sails to a neutral country. Convinced that a revolution is futile in postwar Korea he seeks salvation in love, which turns out to be another illusion. These agonized journeys of the mind reflect the dispossession and dislocation Ch'oe experienced in his flight from the north.

Born in 1936 in Hoeryŏng, North Hamgyŏng, Ch'oe Inhun, together with his family, evacuated the north in 1950 during the Korean War. After leaving Seoul National University Law School without taking a degree (1957) and military service (1958–1964), he devoted himself to writing. He prefers the dramatization of ideas and man's inner sanctum to chronological realism; his characters are faceless abstractions—sometimes only a voice. That is probably the reason why the general public regards his sophisticated experiments with form and content as a display of narrative gamesmanship rather than a cry of aesthetic independence. In any case, Ch'oe is widely credited for his unremitting self-exploration and devotion to literature.

Upon returning to Korea in June 1976 after three years at Iowa, Ch'oe turned to drama with *Away, Away, Long Time Ago* (1976).

Based on a legend in North P'yŏngan, the play begins with the sound of wind and the hooting of an owl and a broken dialogue between a pregnant young woman and her starving husband. When the baby boy is born, the husband presses it to death with a sack of millet because soldiers have surrounded the cottage in an attempt to destroy the legendary dragon horse and the baby. In the past people believed that the neighing of the dragon horse heralds the descent of a general —a great leader or redeemer—from heaven. After the baby's death, a dragon horse does appear in front of the wicker gate, and astride the animal the three ascend to heaven scattering flowers. Villagers entreat them as they leave, "Ask the highest of the heavenly gods not to send us any more redeemers." The horse's neighing may stand for the popular vision of life after death, the horse as a symbol of life itself. As the incarnation of the supernatural, the birth of the baby represents the creation of a new era. A stale and bigoted society, Ch'oe seems to be saying, must expel the artist who creates a new world with his imagination.

AWAY, AWAY, LONG TIME AGO

Characters

WIFE

HUSBAND

OLD WOMAN

NEIGHBORS 1, 2

SOLDIERS 1, 2, 3

KAETTONG'S MOTHER

BABY

VILLAGERS

Act I

A small thatched house. It is snowing. It is twilight. Dim lamp. The WIFE *is sewing in the room. She is expecting a baby. She looks fifteen or younger. Lifting the sewing material, she measures it by eye. There is no furniture except a table. A square area of the stage represents the floor of the room where she is sitting. There is a lamp and a stove in the room. She lifts the sewing material to her eye to measure it and then sits staring vacantly. She looks down at her stomach and caresses it softly.*

A sound.

She listens.

Wind blows.

She listens.

Wind blows.

She sews again.

She lifts the wick of the lamp with her needle.

An owl hoots.

She listens.

She feels the soup pan on the stove and rearranges the coals with a pair of tongs.

She sews again.

A sound.

She listens.

Wind blows.

She stands and walks across the floor, out of the room area, to approach a gate made of twigs. She peers into the distance.

Snow falls on her head.

Wind blows.

An owl hoots.

Pause.

She walks slowly back into the room, turning back at some sound.

Pause.

Again starts walking back to the room.

Lifts the wick of the lamp.

Picks up the sewing material and starts sewing again, stopping from time to time.

Caresses her stomach.

Smiles.

Wind blows.

Owl hoots.

Lifting her head, she listens.

Sound.

She stands up.

The HUSBAND *comes into the yard.*

He is carrying an A-frame on his back with two logs hanging from it.

Takes off the A-frame and stands it at the edge of the room.

The WIFE *helps him take off the A-frame.*

She brushes snow from his shoulders.

He shakes snow from his shoes.

She brushes his trousers.

[*Each move is performed slowly as if the thought had suddenly occurred to the actors. Each character speaks more slowly than usual, as if his or her thoughts were disconnected. The* HUSBAND *has a distant stutter. The conversations are not very clear but seem natural for the characters themselves. Pauses between conversations are much longer than normal. Although they say nothing of great consequence, they speak with much difficulty.*]

WIFE: The road must have been slippery.
HUSBAND: A little bit.
WIFE: [*Feeling the sack.*] You made it.
HUSBAND: I begged and begged. . . .[*Picks up the sack and puts it on the floor.*]
WIFE: [*Feeling the sack.*] Millet and bean . . .
HUSBAND: Yes . . .
WIFE: Please, come in quick. You must be awfully hungry. You had a small breakfast and haven't eaten anything else since. [*Moves the sack.*]

HUSBAND: Don't move it.

[*But the wife moves the sack anyway.*]

HUSBAND: [*Wildly.*] I told you not to move it. You should not lift anything heavy. [*Snatches the sack from her and moves it himself.*]
HUSBAND: Now it's all right.

[*They look at each other.*]

WIFE: Please, sit down here and warm yourself. [*She pushes the brazier aside and sets the stew pot aright.*]
HUSBAND: I don't mind.
WIFE: [*Setting the table.*] Please, come and sit here.
HUSBAND: Wait. You sit here.
WIFE: Dear, I haven't been outdoors as you have.

[*Getting angry, the* HUSBAND *forces his wife to sit down on the warmer side and continues setting the table.*]

WIFE: You must be hungry.

[HUSBAND *opens the sack and pours out a bowl of millet.*]

WIFE: Dear?

[HUSBAND *fastens the sack again.*]

WIFE: What are you doing?

[HUSBAND *stands up with the bowl.*]

WIFE: [*Getting up.*] What are you going to do with it?
HUSBAND: Please, just stay seated there. I'll make a bowl of millet. All through the winter you haven't had a bowl of rice. And now your time is growing close.
WIFE: Are you crazy? How can I eat the millet we need for seed?
HUSBAND: It's all right. I'm supposed to pay it back next fall with interest. Now is the time for you to take a bowl of millet. I'll cook it quick.
WIFE: No, I can't. Please give it to me.
HUSBAND: I said it's all right.
WIFE: No! Give it to me! Is eating millet supposed to make me give birth to a prime minister?
HUSBAND: Huh? I tell you, don't interfere.
WIFE: No, I can't eat it.

[*They struggle together. Finally, trying to snatch the bowl, the* WIFE *upturns it.*]

WIFE: Oh, no! What shall I do?

[*Crawling about, she starts picking up the grain.*]

WIFE: My goodness! You must be hungry. [*Pointing to the stove.*] The soup! It's burning! [*Putting the lid on the stove.*] Quick! Please help yourself.

[*Turning, the* HUSBAND *picks up the scattered grain with his wife. She pours the seed into the sack and pushes her husband to the warmer side of the room.*]

WIFE: Please.

HUSBAND: [*Silently sitting opposite each other with a poorly made dinner table between them, he stares at his wife, urging her to eat wild greens and gruel.*] All through the winter, wild greens and gruel . . . darling.

WIFE: No! Never. [*She stands in front of the sack to prevent her husband from taking it away. He is forced to eat the gruel. Both eat.*]

WIFE: [*Feeling the sack.*] You really made it.

HUSBAND: ———

WIFE: Dear, you are worrying about something.

HUSBAND: No, it's nothing.

WIFE: Nothing? Then there must be something else.

HUSBAND: I tell you it's nothing.

WIFE: Don't make me feel so upset.

HUSBAND: ———

WIFE: ———

HUSBAND: Well, they say the bandits came down to the other village.

WIFE: Bandits?

HUSBAND: They say that bandits set fire to the town hall and robbed the state granaries.

WIFE: Oh, no!

HUSBAND: There's a notice on the board telling who you should notify if any strangers like these bandits show up.

WIFE: Every year they appear . . .

HUSBAND: I saw one of their heads hanging in front of the town hall.

WIFE: Tut, tut—what's the difference between dying of hunger or being hanged?

HUSBAND: They rob to live but if they get themselves killed, what's the point?

WIFE: That's true.

HUSBAND: Darling!

WIFE: ———

HUSBAND: Can you guess who the one they hanged might be?

WIFE: ———?

HUSBAND: Can you?

WIFE: How—can—I guess?

HUSBAND: It's really queer. Remember the merchant who came through dragging that shabby mule and selling salt?

WIFE: . . . Yes.

HUSBAND: It was the salt merchant.

WIFE: What?

HUSBAND: Yes, it was him.

WIFE: Oh, no. You mean that one who was coughing?

HUSBAND: Yes, it's really queer.

WIFE: Good heavens! He was sitting at the edge of the room and panting so much.

HUSBAND: Yes, he was.

WIFE: How could he set fire to the town hall?

[*Noise from outside. The two hold their breath. The noise sounds like snow falling from a bough.*]

HUSBAND: [*In a low voice.*] It's nothing, right?

[*She listens, then goes near the door and tries to peep out.*]

WIFE: It must be nothing.

HUSBAND: Yes, it must be.

WIFE: [*Stirring the stove fire.*] We don't have anything for anyone to steal. [*Noticing the sack of grain, she stops talking.*]

HUSBAND: [*Quickly, as if speaking to someone outside.*] Yes, it's true. Mr. Bandit should go where there are things to be taken. Sure, it's true.

WIFE: You're right. We are lucky we don't have to worry.

HUSBAND: Sure, we are lucky.

[*Pause. Outside it's still snowing. The two are motionless. At last they relax and change their positions. A wolf howls. They listen.*]

WIFE: This snow—must be the last one.

HUSBAND: This year it has snowed so much. I hope we get a good harvest.

WIFE: I pray.

HUSBAND: There will be another mouth to feed—

WIFE: It won't eat much for a couple of years.

HUSBAND: People say that in a bad harvest year adults die of hunger and kids die from eating too much.

WIFE: They probably die of drinking too much water. That kind of thing must have happened in some luckier village. [*Caressing her stomach.*] Even after it's born, it will have a hungry life, poor thing!

HUSBAND: We have lived that way. Our offspring will be like us. Heaven willed it that way.

WIFE: Dear, I wish I didn't have to give birth to it.

HUSBAND: ———?

WIFE: The baby wouldn't have to suffer in this world. Yet you ask me to eat seed millet. What right have I to such luxury?

HUSBAND: Have you ever heard of anyone who didn't have to give birth, once she was pregnant?

WIFE: You are right.

HUSBAND: You know Tot'origol Village, don't you?

WIFE: Yes, I know.

HUSBAND: After planting this spring, I'm going to cultivate that part of the land.

WIFE: Cultivate it?

HUSBAND: Yes.

WIFE: How can we cultivate it?

HUSBAND: I studied it carefully last summer. Of course, it will be very tough, but . . .

WIFE: Yes—if we take pains. . . . It's a hill and stony . . .

HUSBAND: That's why that part of the land has been left.

WIFE: Yes, you're right.

HUSBAND: If we plant potatoes there, it will help our food problem a little bit.

WIFE: Even so, will we get to eat any of it?

HUSBAND: Even if we give some to the superiors, there will be some left for us.

WIFE: I will till the land with you after the baby is born.

HUSBAND: Then by next spring we can plant something there.

WIFE: If there isn't another bad harvest like last year.

HUSBAND: Well, I . . .

WIFE: ———?———

HUSBAND: The main thing is . . .

WIFE: The main thing?

HUSBAND: They say there are so many bandits.

WIFE: They can't rob us of anything.

HUSBAND: I don't mean that.

WIFE: ———?———

HUSBAND: It's not bandits that I'm afraid of . . .

[WIFE *nods*.]

HUSBAND: After a bad harvest year the bandits come down, and then there's a punitive expedition.

WIFE: Dear! [*Holds her husband by the arm.*]

HUSBAND: If I am forced to become a soldier . . .

WIFE: There are so many soldiers at the town hall . . .

HUSBAND: There are more of them than usual, but not enough to take care of all the bandits. Still, this year the soldiers from Seoul drove them out.

WIFE: Good heavens . . .

HUSBAND: ———

WIFE: So what are people saying?

HUSBAND: Bandits?

WIFE: Yes.

HUSBAND: Well, they seem to have fled over the border.

WIFE: Is that so?

HUSBAND: They say so.

WIFE: It should be so. From the time our baby is born, we should have a good harvest and there should be no bandits.

HUSBAND: It is the same story.

WIFE: You are right. I didn't realize it.

HUSBAND: Well, the baby is happy, and we don't have to worry. [*Caressing his wife's stomach.*]

WIFE: Dear . . . [*caressing her stomach*] . . . this baby must be lucky.

HUSBAND: How do you know?

WIFE: How couldn't I? Look at this. [*Caresses the grain sack.*] That honorable man lent us this again, didn't he?

HUSBAND: That's true. Mr. Kim from over the hill couldn't borrow and went back empty-handed.

WIFE: I was right. Our baby must be very lucky. [*Caresses the grain sack.*] Our baby brings this much.

HUSBAND: This much. [*He pushes the sack a little, without purpose.*]
WIFE: And you know . . .

[*A sound interrupts her. She listens attentively and the* HUSBAND *listens with her.*]

WIFE: It's snowing so much.

[HUSBAND *nods his head.*]

[WIFE *smiles and again touches the seed sack to neaten it.* HUSBAND *helps her whenever she moves.*]

HUSBAND: If it's a boy . . .
WIFE: He will help his dad . . .
HUSBAND: Working in the field.
WIFE: If it's a girl . . .
HUSBAND: She will help her mom with the housework.
WIFE: Dear?
HUSBAND: Yes?
WIFE: What will we do with the child when we both go to the field?
HUSBAND: We will take [*pause*] it with us.
WIFE: Oh, yes, we can take it with us.
HUSBAND: Sure.
WIFE: We'll lay it down in the shade.
HUSBAND: Yes, we will.
WIFE: It will see squirrels and hear birds singing.
HUSBAND: We'll bathe him in the stream.
WIFE: When clouds pass, it will smile at them.
HUSBAND: If only we have a good harvest.
WIFE: If only there are no bandits.
HUSBAND: I told you it is the same story.
WIFE: Oh, yes, so it is.
HUSBAND: ———

[*The two laugh.*]

HUSBAND: Darling, let's go to sleep.
WIFE: Oh, it's already time we went to bed.
HUSBAND: ———

[*The two laugh.* WIFE *puts the light out. From afar, a wolf's howl is heard.*]

Act II

Spring. Same scene as Act I. A BABY *cries.* WIFE, *coming out of the kitchen, enters with a* BABY *in her arms.*

WIFE: Oh, oh, our baby—hungry, eh? Here it is . . .[*She takes the* BABY *to her breast but it still cries.*] No milk comes? What shall I do? I don't eat anything, that's why there isn't any milk in my breast. [*Standing up, she tries to soothe the* BABY. *Then laying it down in the room, she comes out.* KAETTONG'S MOTHER *enters.*]

KAETTONG'S MOTHER: Is the baby growing up all right?

WIFE: Are you Kaettong's mother?

KAETTONG'S MOTHER: He must be sleeping.

WIFE: Yes, he went to sleep just now.

KAETTONG'S MOTHER: Is your breast good?

WIFE: Not so good.

KAETTONG'S MOTHER: You have to eat well. Anyone would feel hungry in spring, especially after giving birth to a child recently. Here, take this. [*She hands* WIFE *a wooden bowl.*]

WIFE: Oh, what is it?

KAETTONG'S MOTHER: Nothing special. Just acorn custard.

WIFE: But you have so many kids to feed at home.

KAETTONG'S MOTHER: It's impossible to satisfy them—I mean nine kids at home. I thought I'd better give it to you. You are the one who deserves it most.

WIFE: At this time of need?

KAETTONG'S MOTHER: Last summer, when I was sick in bed, who could have taken care of me so well as you? I have not forgotten your kindness.

WIFE: It was . . .

KAETTONG'S MOTHER: Please taste this. Here, I brought some soy sauce to have with it too. [*Takes out a pot.*]

WIFE: Oh, this is too much.

KAETTONG'S MOTHER: Go get a bowl. [WIFE *goes to the kitchen and brings back two bowls and two spoons.*]

KAETTONG'S MOTHER: Good. [*From a large scooped wooden bowl she pours acorn custard into the bowl and pushes it toward the* WIFE.]

WIFE: You take some too.

KAETTONG'S MOTHER: [*Shaking her head.*] I didn't come here to eat, did I? Please take it yourself. [WIFE *takes one spoonful.*]

KAETTONG'S MOTHER: How is it?

WIFE: It's pure honey, nothing else.

KAETTONG'S MOTHER: [*Feeling proud.*] I am good at making acorn custard, at least. [*Watches* WIFE *eat.*] Oh, your face is swollen. If your own mother could see you, she would feel very sorry for you.

[*Wiping tears with the fringe of her skirt,* WIFE *stops eating and cries a little.*]

KAETTONG'S MOTHER: Oh, no, damn my mouth! [*Slaps her mouth.*] I deserve to be treated that way by my husband. He says if my mouth and stomach [*pointing*] would just stay shut, his fate would be open. But now that I think of it, who is it that opens my stomach?

WIFE: [*Laughing.*] You have a lot of kids, but they will work when they grow up.

KAETTONG'S MOTHER: Work? Where is there any land to work on? Anyway, did you hear what happened?

WIFE: Yes . . .

KAETTONG'S MOTHER: Surely it's strange. It seems that anything can happen when it's hard for people to survive. Have you heard a spirited horse crying?

[WIFE *shakes her head.*]

KAETTONG'S MOTHER: I haven't heard it either. But Soedol's father over the hill is said to have heard it twice.

WIFE: Is that so?

KAETTONG'S MOTHER: Yes, it is.

WIFE: How does it cry?

KAETTONG'S MOTHER: How should I know? I've never heard it. I wanted to hear it but my husband didn't let me. After crawling all day long with a hoe in the field, he crawls all over me at night. After that, I'm as good as dead till morning. How can I hear anything during the night? But you know, they say when a redeemer is born, a spirited horse is born also.

WIFE: A redeemer?

KAETTONG'S MOTHER: [*Nodding.*] Yes, they say so.

WIFE: What does a redeemer look like?

KAETTONG'S MOTHER: My grandma told me that a redeemer has scales on his body and two wings under his arms.

WIFE: Oh, then our baby isn't one.

KAETTONG'S MOTHER: No, he wouldn't be. And a redeemer is said to be able to walk at birth.

WIFE: Our baby can't even turn his body yet. Ha, he isn't much of a redeemer, is he?

KAETTONG'S MOTHER: Of course not. If a redeemer is born, he, and his parents too, will be killed. Even the neighbors will be killed.

WIFE: Why should the neighbors be killed?

KAETTONG'S MOTHER: A long time ago a redeemer was born in some village. And they say they burnt down the whole village with all the people in it.

WIFE: Oh, how terrible. [Looking at the room.] Our innocent baby . . .

KAETTONG'S MOTHER: That mountain where the horse is said to be crying overlooks three other villages besides ours. The redeemer must be born in one of those villages.

WIFE: Oh, I hope so.

KAETTONG'S MOTHER: In that village the town hall ordered the arrest of every child that is a little bit unusual—from infants to ten-year-olds.

WIFE: Oh, no!

KAETTONG'S MOTHER: All the parents are afraid their kids might be strong, but our damned kids refuse to go to the mountain to fetch firewood. Even the younger ones won't move at all.

WIFE: Oh, they shouldn't act that way.

KAETTONG'S MOTHER: We're going to spoil all of them, aren't we? They all want to be corpses so they don't have to be redeemers.

WIFE: Besides newborn babies—you mean, even fairly grown-up kids—

KAETTONG'S MOTHER: There's no way of knowing how old the horse is, so we can't guess the age of its owner. Has anyone seen it? So they say that all the children who haven't married yet are being watched by the officials.

WIFE: [As if relieved.] I thought only the newborns were watched . . .

KAETTONG'S MOTHER: Oh, I must be going. May I look at the baby? Don't pick it up. I'll go peek. [She opens the door quietly and looks in at the BABY.] He is so handsome. Not like a redeemer.

WIFE: [Pleased.] Certainly not.

[HUSBAND enters hurriedly.]

HUSBAND: Darling?

KAETTONG'S MOTHER: Why are you panting so?

HUSBAND: Listen to me! Right now, the soldiers are going up into the mountains through Tot'origol.

KAETTONG'S MOTHER: Are they? What for?

HUSBAND: They say they are going to catch the horse.

KAETTONG'S MOTHER: Do they say it's in our village?

HUSBAND: It's the order from town hall, they say. The soldiers have to inspect their own villages.

KAETTONG'S MOTHER: I hope there is no redeemer and no horse in our village.

HUSBAND: The soldiers just tore up the mountain trying to catch the horse.

KAETTONG'S MOTHER: I don't think it can be caught that easily.

WIFE: Oh, you are sweating so much.

HUSBAND: I've been to the village myself.

WIFE: What for?

HUSBAND: They seem to have hunted all over the mountain for several days. I was tilling the field when the government officials came. I had to carry their rice and wine to Tot'origol.

KAETTONG'S MOTHER: Can't they carry their own things? If they hadn't come across you, they would have had to go without them.

HUSBAND: Oh, no. They had all their things carried from the start.

KAETTONG'S MOTHER: They must have. We farmers haven't sowed yet. When we are busiest . . . Anyway, the horse isn't supposed to cry for nothing. By the way, who did the carrying?

HUSBAND: It was . . . your husband.

KAETTONG'S MOTHER: Good heavens! He must have been caught while he was in their path. He plowed last night, too.

HUSBAND: You mean at night?

[WIFE *turns around timidly.*]

KAETTONG'S MOTHER: No, I don't mean that kind of field—oh, this damned mouth! [*Slaps her own mouth.*]

[*Singing from nearby.*]

> Our baby, good baby,
> Grows up without milk,
> He grows up crying.
> In a bad harvest year, he turns into a bandit.
> As a bandit he has no place to go

And at the top of the town hall's beam
He turns into a severed head.

[*Singing comes closer. Husky voice. The three listen to where the singing comes from.* HUSBAND *walks several paces. A grandma appears, white-haired and stooped, in ragged clothes, leaning on a staff. At her side, according to the old custom, hangs a bag. The bag is empty and flat.*]

HUSBAND: Where do you come from?

[OLD WOMAN *looks vacantly at the three.*]

KAETTONG'S MOTHER: She is a stranger.
OLD WOMAN: Water, please.

[WIFE *enters the kitchen. The* OLD WOMAN *sits down on the ground.*]

WIFE: Here it is.

[*The* OLD WOMAN *takes the bowl and drinks.*]

KAETTONG'S MOTHER: Where did you come from?
OLD WOMAN: From over there. [*Lifts her hand and points into the distance.*]
KAETTONG'S MOTHER: From there? You mean over the mountain?

[OLD WOMAN *nods her head.*]

KAETTONG'S MOTHER: Where are you going?

[OLD WOMAN *looks at her blankly.*]

KAETTONG'S MOTHER: Where are you going?
OLD WOMAN: To look for my son.
KAETTONG'S MOTHER: Son?
OLD WOMAN: Yes, my son.
KAETTONG'S MOTHER: Where is your son?
OLD WOMAN: In the town hall.
KAETTONG'S MOTHER: Town hall?

[OLD WOMAN *nods.*]

KAETTONG'S MOTHER: Where in the town hall?
OLD WOMAN: In a high place.
KAETTONG'S MOTHER: [*A little frightened.*] How come a person in such a high place leaves his mother on the street? Anyway, how high is your son?

OLD WOMAN: In a high place.

KAETTONG'S MOTHER: You don't mean he is the highest person in the town hall?

OLD WOMAN: The highest place.

KAETTONG'S MOTHER: Oh, no, you don't really mean he is the highest one there.

OLD WOMAN: In a high place.

KAETTONG'S MOTHER: What? What kind of position is that?

OLD WOMAN: At the top of the beam.

[*The three look at one another.*]

KAETTONG'S MOTHER: Then, is your son by any chance the bandit?

[OLD WOMAN *nods her head.*]

KAETTONG'S MOTHER: So it's your son, the bandit, whose head hangs on the top of the beam?

[OLD WOMAN *nods. The three retreat.*]

OLD WOMAN: I should hurry, even if it's only his head. Thanks for the water. [*With the help of her staff she gets up and walks in the opposite direction, singing*]:

> As a bandit he has no place to go.
> At the top of the beam
> Is a severed head.
>
> If a crow pecks at it,
> "Mummy, it hurts me," it cries.
>
> Oh, no, it's not my baby.

[*The three stand motionless listening to the* OLD WOMAN's *song.*]

KAETTONG'S MOTHER: So, where's my husband?

HUSBAND: He's still up the mountain.

KAETTONG'S MOTHER: With those government officials?

HUSBAND: Yes.

KAETTONG'S MOTHER: What do you mean? Did you come down alone?

HUSBAND: He remained there of his own accord.

KAETTONG'S MOTHER: Of his own accord? I don't follow you. Explain.

HUSBAND: The officials made it a point to catch every chicken in the coop and he said your brood hen was caught too.

KAETTONG'S MOTHER: Oh, no.

HUSBAND: So he seems to want to get it back if he can.

KAETTONG'S MOTHER: Good heavens! Our only brood hen. If they want to take fowl away, they should have caught males and females, even though they are not human beings. They shouldn't have taken our precious brood hen.

HUSBAND: [*To* WIFE.] Have they been here?

WIFE: No.

HUSBAND: I am afraid. Is our baby sleeping?

WIFE: No, he's awake.

HUSBAND: I am afraid. Is he sleeping?

WIFE: Yes, he is.

KAETTONG'S MOTHER: I'm leaving. I left the kids at home alone. It must be chaos by now. Oh, whether it's a redeemer or a horse, it's our enemy. . . . [*She disappears hurriedly.*]

[BABY's *crying is heard.* WIFE *brings it into the room, singing.*]

> Our baby, good baby,
> Grows up without milk,
> He grows up crying.
> In a bad harvest year, he turns into a bandit.

[*The same night.* HUSBAND *and* WIFE *sit opposite each other. The* BABY *is sleeping beside them at the back of the room. The two listen. Wind blows.*]

WIFE: Is it going to be caught?

HUSBAND: I don't know.

[*A wolf howls.*]

Act III

The same scene. WIFE *and* KAETTONG'S MOTHER *enter together. Both are carrying hoes.*

WIFE: I wonder if he's awake. [*To* KAETTONG'S MOTHER.] I'm through working in the field for now. [*She goes into the room and brings out the* BABY *in her arms and takes it to her breast.*]

KAETTONG'S MOTHER: [*Looking at the* BABY.] He's so good. . . . [*Sits down comfortably.*] There is never a time when there's no disaster.

I thought we were going to have a good harvest when it snowed so much. But that horse made all the menfolk go up the mountain looking for it. So when can we plow and sow the field? It's not only that. If they take everything away from us—from acorns to chickens, as they've done these past ten days—they'll kill us in the end, won't they?

WIFE: Your chicken?

KAETTONG'S MOTHER: Which chicken did you mean?

WIFE: I mean your cock.

KAETTONG'S MOTHER: Which cock?

WIFE: Do you have several?

KAETTONG'S MOTHER: I want to know which cock you mean—human cock or rooster cock?

WIFE: Oh, you . . .

KAETTONG'S MOTHER: Rooster cock was taken away three days ago. The human one is still on the mountain.

WIFE: My husband was here for a little while yesterday.

KAETTONG'S MOTHER: So what did he say? Did he say he was going to stay there till summer? Did he tell you he would give birth to a horse?

WIFE: He said he would probably come down today.

KAETTONG'S MOTHER: Is that so? Abandon everything?

WIFE: You might have heard they can't catch that horse.

KAETTONG'S MOTHER: So they say. When they follow the sound of its crying, it cries from the opposite direction. They say they feel as if they are spellbound. As if we villagers were to blame. These days the officials eat and drink all day and night, and if the horse cries at night they let our husbands go after it.

WIFE: Oh, what shall we do?

KAETTONG'S MOTHERS: And the big problem is that we can't sow on time.

WIFE: They might come down today.

KAETTONG'S MOTHER: Oh yes, so you said.

WIFE: Yes, I did.

KAETTONG'S MOTHER: So they have spent all that energy for nothing. The horse is beyond human power. It can't be caught by us.

WIFE: So it seems.

KAETTONG'S MOTHER: Sure. It came to carry a redeemer. It can't be caught by such a man as my husband. I must be the only horse he can catch easily.

[WIFE *gets up as if she hadn't heard. She takes her baby into the room and returns.*]

KAETTONG'S MOTHER: The baby is really good. I should work the field some more before the sun sets. Oh, my husband should come home soon, even though he tires me out at night. Since my kids won't move, I till the land, cut firewood, and cook all alone. If a redeemer is someone strong enough to carry the A-frame on his back with firewood and lift the garden hoe, then everybody must be one. But my damned kids refuse to move.

[*The two women start to go out with their tools.*]

WIFE: [*Pointing up the road.*] Look at that!
KAETTONG'S MOTHER: Oh, they're coming down.
WIFE: Yes, the officials . . . to the stream . . .
KAETTONG'S MOTHER: They are going towards town . . . no, why are they coming this way?
WIFE: Yes, they are.
KAETTONG'S MOTHER: Look at that.
WIFE: Yes?
KAETTONG'S MOTHER: They must be going to take a rest there.
WIFE: Yes, they must be.
KAETTONG'S MOTHER: I must be leaving. [*She leaves hurriedly.*]

[WIFE *looks back as she follows her out. A sound from the room.*]

WIFE: Oh, my God! [*She falls down in the yard, shaking wildly. She looks into the room. Through the open door the* BABY *doll can be seen walking around the room. He walks firmly, raising and lowering his arms.*]
WIFE: Oh, what shall I do, what shall I do? [*Still sitting, she crawls over and grabs the threshold.*] Oh, my baby! Oh, my baby!
BABY: [*Sounding like an echo from a microphone.*] I can't stand it any more!
WIFE: ———!
BABY: [*Like an echo.*] I can't bear it!
WIFE: No, baby, no.

[*The scene is lit by red light like blood. Then it fades. Like a deaf person, the* WIFE *gesticulates with her hands and feet. She straightens her body but can't get up. The* BABY *is walking steadily in the room.* WIFE *locks the door and listens as when she was waiting for her husband in the first act, but with a different feeling. Whenever a sound is heard, she listens and looks at the room to see if something is happening. She repeats this action. There is a sound.* WIFE *walks to the gate and looks far away.* HUSBAND *enters, exhausted, barely walking. He drops the basket and falls on the ground.*]

HUSBAND: Oh my!

WIFE: ———

HUSBAND: It was all in vain.

WIFE: ———

HUSBAND: The highest official is said to be more than angry.

WIFE: ———

HUSBAND: The lower officials are angry too.

WIFE: ———

HUSBAND: They say the highest official told them not to come back to town if they failed to catch it.

WIFE: ———

HUSBAND: So they're staying across the river, awake, and plan to search every village to find it. Oh . . .

WIFE: ———

[HUSBAND *stares at his wife for the first time and stops talking. She says nothing but looks at him.*]

HUSBAND: What . . .? What has happened?

[WIFE *remains silent. She looks at the discarded basket vacantly.*]

HUSBAND: Yes?

[WIFE *looks at him.*]

HUSBAND: What on earth's the matter?

[WIFE *shakes her head.* HUSBAND, *holding her by the arm, looks around but finds nothing.* WIFE *looks at the closed door. A sound comes from the room.*]

HUSBAND: [*Looking in that direction.*] Why? Why? [*He moves toward the door but the* WIFE *detains him.*]

WIFE: [*Loosening his arm.*] Dear!

HUSBAND: ———

WIFE: We are the ones.

HUSBAND: What? [*Sensing the problem, he stops walking.*] Is it true?

[WIFE *nods her head.* HUSBAND *stares hard in the direction of the room. A sound comes from the room. He looks at her.* WIFE *nods her head. The* BABY *rattles the doorknob.*]

HUSBAND: Oh, good heavens! [*He collapses on the ground.* WIFE *squats beside him. They look at each other, then turn their gaze toward the room.*]

HUSBAND: Darling! [*Stands up and moves closer to the room and looks back at her.* WIFE *walks toward the room and is about to open it, but stops. She peeks through a hole, then makes room for him. He looks in.*]

HUSBAND: Oh, no! [*He falls sidewise and in a sitting position inches his way back into the yard.* WIFE *still stands in front of the door.*]

HUSBAND: [*In a subdued voice.*] Darling, what should we do?

[WIFE *is motionless.* HUSBAND *beckons her.* WIFE *does not move. He beckons her again.* WIFE *comes out into the yard and squats beside her husband as before.*]

HUSBAND: What should we do?

[WIFE *is silent. The two are sitting opposite each other. Long pause. A sound. The two listen. Wind blows.*]

HUSBAND: It's just the wind.

[WIFE *stands up. She enters the kitchen and comes out with a basket of vegetable greens which she spreads in front of the room. She sits down, blocking the view of the door.* HUSBAND *watches her and finally nods his head feebly, as if he didn't quite understand her. He catches a glimpse of the door. The doorknob is shaken again.*]

WIFE: [*Slowly, in a common lullably tune.*]

> Our baby, good baby,
> Grows up without milk,
> In a bad harvest year, he turns into a bandit.
> As a bandit he has no place to go
> And at the top of the town hall's beam
> He turns into a severed head.
>
> If a crow pecks at it,
> "Mummy, it hurts me," it cries.
> Oh, I'm afraid it's not my baby.

[*The doorknob rattles again, then stops.* HUSBAND *looks at her and watches the door.* WIFE *stirs the greens aimlessly. The two listen.*]

HUSBAND: It's only wind.

[*Wind blows.* WIFE *continues to stir the greens.* HUSBAND *watches her hand.*]

[WIFE *gets up and enters the kitchen as her husband watches. She comes out again.* HUSBAND *follows her with his eyes until she sits down by the threshold. As* WIFE *begins to mix the greens again, he stops watching her and casts his glance in the direction of the gate. After a while, he turns back to watch his wife again. Lifting her head a little, she is on the verge of saying something, but stops.* HUSBAND *stands up and goes to the back of the yard. He returns with straw for making rope.* WIFE *looks at him. He suddenly stops braiding the rope, as if startled.* WIFE *stops stirring. There is a sound from outside. Pause.* HUSBAND *painfully moves nearer the gate. He listens. Sound. He turns around, breathing heavily, as his eyes meet his wife's eyes.*]

HUSBAND: It's only a squirrel.

[WIFE *lowers her head and stirs the greens again. He braids the rope, looking across at her.* WIFE *mixes the greens without looking at him. Birds sing. Suddenly they raise their heads and look at each other, watching the room as if they heard something. Again, she stirs the greens and he braids the rope. Pause. The room is quiet. All of a sudden it grows dark. The two look up at the sky.*]

HUSBAND: Cloud . . .

[*Slowly the stage brightens again. The doorknob rattles.* HUSBAND *springs to his feet and blocks his ears. He looks back at the door, confused, then takes his hands from his ears and looks at the gate, then at his wife.*]

WIFE: [*Singing slowly and sadly.*]

> Our baby, good baby,
> Grows up without milk,
> In a bad harvest year, he turns into a bandit.
> As a bandit he has no place to go
> And at the top of the town hall's beam
> He turns into a severed head.
>
> If a crow pecks at it,
> "Mummy, it hurts me," it cries.
> Oh, I'm afraid it's not my baby.

[*The rattling of the doorknob stops abruptly. Meanwhile the* HUSBAND *comes back from watching the gate.* WIFE *calmly mixes the greens.* HUS-

BAND *sits down and braids the rope as if knitting his inner fear. Twilight sets in. The sunset becomes more intense, turning red, red as blood. It turns to purple. It becomes dark all of a sudden. Pause. From afar a horse's cry is heard. The two are shocked and stiffen. First there is light only on the* HUS-BAND's *face, then light on the* WIFE's *face. The doorknob rattles.*]

BABY: [*Through a microphone, like an echo.*] Hungry!

[WIFE *stands up.* HUSBAND *stands up.* WIFE *goes into the room. Stage is completely dark. Dim light is turned on in the room.* WIFE *comes out. A circle of light falls on the* HUSBAND's *face. The two come into the middle of the yard and fall down. Pause. An owl hoots. The two listening faces are lighted. Sound. Light disappears from the faces. Stage is dark. Pause. Light comes on only on the* HUSBAND's *face.*]

HUSBAND: A bird is passing.

[*Light comes on the* WIFE's *face too. The fluttering sound of a bird moving from one tree to another is heard. An owl hoots. The light goes out. Pause. Stage dark. A wolf howls. At last pulsating as if it were the* HUSBAND's *breathing, light comes on, still only the faces. The two faces turn toward the room. They jump to their feet. The sound of the* BABY *rattling the doorknob is like thunder in the middle of the night. Light falls on the* HUSBAND's *face as he looks toward his wife.*]

WIFE: [*Slowly and sadly.*]

> Our baby, good baby,
> Grows up without milk,
> In a bad harvest year, he turns into a bandit.
> As a bandit he has no place to go
> And at the top of the town halls' beam
> He turns into a severed head.
>
> If a crow pecks at it,
> "Mummy, it hurts me," it cries.
> Oh, I'm afraid it's not my baby.

[*Pause. The rattling of the doorknob stops. Again the cry of a horse. The doorknob rattles even more violently in the middle of the night. This violent sound is like an echo.*]

BABY: [*Through the microphone.*] My horse!
HUSBAND: [*Jumping to his feet.*] Darling! [*He looks down at* WIFE.]

WIFE: [*As they look at each other.*] No! [*She hangs onto his leg.*]
BABY: [*Like an echo.*] My horse! [*The doorknob rattles.*]

[HUSBAND, *kicking his wife aside, approaches the door.* WIFE *grabs him by the leg again.* HUSBAND *kicks her with all his might.* WIFE *falls down.*]

[HUSBAND *opens the door and enters the room. Shadows appear behind the paper door. The big shadow lays the small shadow down. The shadow of a big sack obscures the shadow of the* BABY. HUSBAND *comes out.* WIFE *jumps to her feet.* HUSBAND *puts his arms around his wife and collapses.* WIFE *struggles but* HUSBAND *doesn't let go. Shadow appears behind the paper door—the shadow of the* BABY *struggling under the sack. Long pause. From the room, like an echo . . .*]

BABY: Mum!

[WIFE *gets up.* HUSBAND *kicks her as before.* HUSBAND *enters the room. The shadow of another sack on the* BABY. HUSBAND *comes out. As before,* WIFE *holds her husband in her arms and squats. From time to time she lifts her head and looks at the shadow on the paper door. At last the shadow doesn't move. A horse's sad cry sounds like an echo. The lamp in the room is put out. The moonlight gradually fades until the moon is completely shadowed by clouds. Wind blows. Darkness. Dim moonlight.* HUSBAND *goes out with something hanging on his A-frame. Wind blows across the yard.*]

Act IV

Dawn the next morning. A bird sings. The stage is empty. Singing is heard. . . .

> My baby, cold baby,
> He grows up with milk,
> In a bad harvest year, he turns into a bandit.

[*The singing voice grows nearer. It is a husky voice but distinctly singing.* OLD WOMAN *appears, dressed as before, only the bag at her side has become bigger. It bulges out like a gourd.* WIFE *comes out from the back yard and stares vacantly at the* OLD WOMAN.]

OLD WOMAN: I got it! [*Turning the bag so the bulge swings to the front.*] I got my son.

[WIFE *looks blankly at the rounded bag.*]

OLD WOMAN: [*Feeling the bag.*] I got my son.

[WIFE *goes back to the back yard.* OLD WOMAN *sits down on the ground. Feeling the bag, she sings a lullaby in a murmuring voice which is almost inaudible. Only one or two words can be heard as the tune rises.* WIFE *comes out. She moves like a body without spirit, like a doll.* WIFE *hands* OLD WOMAN *a bowl of water.*]

OLD WOMAN: Thanks. [*Drinks it.*] Thanks a lot. [*Puts down the bowl and turns the bag around toward her back.*] You are neither thirsty, hot nor cold, hungry nor a crybaby. You are such a nice son. [OLD WOMAN *gets up.* WIFE *just stares at the bag.*]

OLD WOMAN: Let's go, son! I'll bury you at the head of the field where I till, where it's sunny and birds sing. [*She walks on, patting the bag on her back with one hand.*] You are so light, lighter than when you were born.

[OLD WOMAN *disappears.* WIFE *stands a long time looking in the direction where* OLD WOMAN *disappeared. Birds sing sweetly. Enchanted by the singing of the birds and the sunny spring day, she stands listening, then goes inside, leaving the bowl of water in the yard. Pause.* HUSBAND *comes in with an A-frame on his back and a hoe in his hand. He puts down the A-frame without saying anything. Finally, feebly . . .*]

HUSBAND: Darling!

[HUSBAND *goes to the back of the yard and returns. Going out the gate, he looks here and there. After a while he comes back alone and falls down in the yard, his head down. As he happens to look back at the door of the room, it opens.* WIFE *has hanged herself from the beam.* HUSBAND *rushes in and cuts down the body.*]

HUSBAND: Darling!

[*He holds his wife and shakes her. Finally he falls down beside her with his head between his knees. Pause. He gets up, hangs the unfastened belt on the beam. A horse's cry is heard. From the direction of the gate comes the* BABY, *riding the horse. Both horse and* BABY *are dolls with abstract structure. As* BABY *comes into the yard, light shines on the* WIFE *in the room.*]

HUSBAND: [*Coming down the yard, falls again when he sees the horse and* BABY.] I just came back from burying you!

[BABY *shakes its head and hands him a wreath of azaleas.* HUSBAND *moves as if in a dream and takes it.*]

BABY: [*Through the microphone.*] Mummy, Mummy!

HUSBAND: [*Entering the room, puts the wreath on his wife's breast.*] Your baby brought you this. He came back alive.

BABY: [*Through the microphone.*] Dad, Mum! Hurry and get on.

HUSBAND: [*Putting* WIFE *on the horse.*] Now, go away quickly. People might come, since I told them you were dead.

[BABY *gesticulates.*]

WIFE: Hurry, hurry! The soldiers are coming.

HUSBAND: [*Wiping his tears with his sleeve.*] All right. [*He stubbornly refuses to mount the horse and finally goes out the gate leading the horse by the bridle.*]

[*Empty stage. Scene becomes light again. Numerous* VILLAGERS *and the* SOLDIERS *enter.*]

VILLAGER 1: Hey!

[*One* SOLDIER *grabs the doorknob violently.*]

SOLDIER 1: Where did they go?

SOLDIER 2: Are you sure?

VILLAGER 1: Yes, the baby got sick all of a sudden last night.

SOLDIER 3: I see.

VILLAGER 1: The baby's father told me he was coming back from the mountain where he buried the baby.

VILLAGER 2: Look at that!

PEOPLE: Oh, look!

[HUSBAND, WIFE, *and* BABY *go up into the sky on the horse.*]

PEOPLE: They are throwing flowers to us. . . . When you get there, please ask the highest of the heavenly gods not to send us any more redeemers.

[*When the* PEOPLE *quiet down, a voice is heard from heaven . . .*]

Our baby, good baby . . .

PEOPLE: [*Gesticulating as if they were chasing away birds.*] Go away, go away! Don't come back! Away, away!

FROM HEAVEN:

Grows up without milk . . .

PEOPLE: Away, away! Don't come back. Away, away!

[PEOPLE *dance, clapping their hands, moving their heads and shoulders as if dancing an exorcism.*]

FROM HEAVEN:

He grows up crying and in a bad harvest year . . .

PEOPLE: Away, away! Never come back. Away, away!

[*Heaven and earth get more and more excited. As heaven and earth give and take, the curtain slowly falls.*]

TRANSLATED BY PAK HŬIJIN

BIBLIOGRAPHY

Chung Chong-hwa, ed. *Meetings and Farewells: Modern Korean Stories*. St. Lucia: University of Queensland Press, 1980.

Fulton, Bruce, and Ju-chan Fulton, trans. *Words of Farewell: Stories by Korean Women Writers*. Seattle: Seal Press, 1989.

Hwang Sunwŏn. *Shadows of a Sound: Stories by Hwang Sun-won*. Edited by J. Martin Holman. San Francisco: Mercury House, 1990.

———. *The Stars and Other Korean Stories*. Translated by Edward W. Poitras. Hong Kong: Heinemann, 1980.

Kim Chong-un, trans. *Postwar Korean Short Stories: An Anthology*. Seoul: Seoul National University Press, 1983.

Korean National Commission for UNESCO, ed. *Modern Korean Short Stories*. 10 vols. Seoul: Sisa-youngosa Publishers, 1983.

Kuh, K. S., ed. *Koreanische Literatur: Ausgewählte Erzählungen*. 2 vols. Bonn: Bouvier, 1986.

Lee, Peter H., ed. *Flowers of Fire: Twentieth-Century Korean Stories*. Rev. ed. Honolulu: University of Hawaii Press, 1986.

———. *The Silence of Love: Twentieth-Century Korean Poetry*. Honolulu: University of Hawaii Press, 1980.

Leverrier, Roger, trans. *Liberté sous Clef*. Paris: Editions le leopard d'or, 1981.

Oh Yŏngsu. *The Good People: Korean Stories by Oh Yong-su*. Translated by Marshall R. Pihl. Hong Kong: Heinemann, 1985.

O'Rourke, Kevin, trans. *A Washed-out Dream*. Larchmont, N.Y.: Larchmont Publications, 1980.

Suh Jih-moon, trans. *The Rainy Spell and Other Korean Stories*. London, Onyx Press, 1983.

INDEX